Patrick O'Brian is the author of the acclaimed Aubrey-Maturin tales and the biographer of Joseph Banks and Picasso. He translated many works from French into English, among them the novels and memoirs of Simone de Beauvoir and the first volume of Jean Lacouture's biography of Charles de Gaulle. In 1995 he was the first recipient of the Heywood Hill Prize for a lifetime's contribution to literature. In the same year he was awarded the CBE. In 1997 he was awarded an honorary doctorate of letters by Trinity College, Dublin. He died on 2 January 2000 at the age of 85.

Visit www.AuthorTracker.co.uk
for exclusive information on your favourite
HarperCollins authors.

D1513871

The Works of Patrick O'Brian
*The Aubrey-Maturin Novels
in order of publication*

PATRICK O'BRIAN

Treason's Harbour

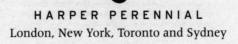

HARPER PERENNIAL
London, New York, Toronto and Sydney

Harper Perennial
An imprint of HarperCollins*Publishers*
77–85 Fulham Palace Road
Hammersmith,
London W6 8JB

www.harperperennial.co.uk

This edition published by Harper Perennial 2007
1

Previously published in paperback by HarperCollins 2003
(reprinted thirteen times)
and 1997 (reprinted six times),
and by Fontana 1984

First published in Great Britain by
William Collins Sons & Co. Ltd 1983

A catalogue record for this book
is available from the British Library

ISBN 978-0-00-789278-5

Set in Imprint by
Rowland Phototypesetting Ltd, Bury St Edmunds, Suffolk

Printed and bound in Great Britain by
Clays Ltd, St Ives plc

TREASON'S HARBOUR

MARIAE SACRUM

The sails of a square-rigged ship, hung out to dry in a calm.

 1 Flying jib
 2 Jib
 3 Fore topmast staysail
 4 Fore staysail
 5 Foresail, or course
 6 Fore topsail
 7 Fore topgallant
 8 Mainstaysail
 9 Main topmast staysail
10 Middle staysail
11 Main topgallant staysail

12 Mainsail, or course
13 Maintopsail
14 Main topgallant
15 Mizzen staysail
16 Mizzen topmast staysail
17 Mizzen topgallant staysail
18 Mizzen sail
19 Spanker
20 Mizzen topsail
21 Mizzen topgallant

'Smoothe runnes the Water, where the Brooke is deepe.
And in his simple shew he harbours Treason.'

2 HENRY VI

Chapter One

A gentle breeze from the north-east after a night of rain, and the washed sky over Malta had a particular quality in its light that sharpened the lines of the noble buildings, bringing out all the virtue of the stone; the air too was a delight to breathe, and the city of Valletta was as cheerful as though it were fortunate in love or as though it had suddenly heard good news.

This was more than usually remarkable in a group of naval officers sitting in the bowered court of Searle's hotel: to be sure, they looked out upon the arcaded Upper Baracca, filled with soldiers, sailors and civilians pacing slowly up and down in a sunlight so brilliant that it made even the black hoods the Maltese women wore look gay, while the officers' uniforms shone like splendid flowers – a cosmopolitan crowd, for although most of the colour was the scarlet and gold of the British army many of the nations engaged in the war against Napoleon were represented and the shell-pink of Kresimir's Croats, for example, made a charming contrast with the Neapolitan hussars' silver-laced blue. And then beyond and below the Baracca there was the vast sweep of the Grand Harbour, pure sapphire today, flecked with the sails of countless small craft plying between Valletta and the great fortified headlands on the other side, St Angelo and Isola, and the men-of-war, the troopships and the victuallers, a sight to please any sailor's heart.

Yet on the other hand all these gentlemen were captains without ships, a mumchance, melancholy class in general and even more so at this time, when the long, long war seemed to be working up to its climax, when competition was even stronger than before, and when distinction and worthwhile appointments, to say nothing of prize-money and promotion, depended on having a sea-going command. Some were absolutely shipless, either because their vessels had sunk under them, which was the case with Edward Long's archaic *Aeolus*, or because promotion had set them ashore, or because an unfortunate court-martial had done the same. Most however were only grass-widowers; their ships, battered by years of blockading Toulon in all weathers, had been sent in for repair. But the dockyards were overcrowded, the repairs were often serious and far-reaching and always very slow, and here the captains had to sit while the precious sea-time ran by, cursing the delay. Some of the richer men had sent for their wives, who were no doubt a great comfort to them, but most were condemned to glum celibacy or to what local solace they could find. Captain Aubrey was one of these, for although he had recently captured a neat little prize in the Ionian Seas it had not yet been condemned in the Admiralty court and in any case his affairs were horribly involved at home, with legal difficulties of every kind; besides, accommodation in Malta had grown shockingly expensive and now that he was older he no longer dared lay out large sums that he did not yet possess; he therefore lived as a bachelor, as modestly as a post-captain decently could, up three pair of stairs at Searle's, his only amusement being the opera. Indeed, he was perhaps the most unfortunate of those whose ships were in the repairers' hands, for he had contrived to send no less than two separate vessels into dock, so that he had a double set of slow devious stupid corrupt incompetent officials, tradesmen and artificers to deal with: the first was the *Worcester*, a worn-out seventy-four-gun ship of the line that had very nearly come apart in a long, fruitless chase of the French fleet in dirty weather, and the second was the *Surprise*, a small, sweet-sailing frigate, a temporary command in which he had been sent to the Ionian while the *Worcester* was repairing and in which he had engaged two Turkish ships, the *Torgud* and the *Kitabi*, in an extremely violent action that had left the *Torgud* sinking, the *Kitabi* a prisoner and the *Surprise* full of holes between wind and water. The *Worcester*, that ill-conceived, ill-built coffinship, would have been much better broken up and sold for firewood; but it was upon her worthless, profitable hull that the dockyard spent all its slow creeping care, while the *Surprise* lay in limbo for want of a few midship knees, the starboard knighthead and bumkin, and twenty square yards of copper sheathing, while her crew, her once excellent crew of picked seamen, grew idle, dissolute, debauched, drunken and unhealthy, while some of the very best hands and even petty-officers were stolen from him by unscrupulous superiors and even his perfect first lieutenant left the ship.

Captain Aubrey should have been the gloomiest of a glum gathering, but in fact he had been rattling away, talking loud, and even singing, with such good will that his particular friend, the *Surprise*'s surgeon Stephen Maturin, had withdrawn to a quieter arbour, taking with him their temporary shipmate Professor Graham, a moral philosopher on leave from his Scottish university, an authority on the Turkish language and Eastern affairs in general. Captain Aubrey's high spirits were caused partly by the beautiful day acting on a constitutionally cheerful nature, partly by the infectious merriment of his companions, but more, very much more, by the fact that at the farthest end of the table sat Thomas Pullings, until very recently his first lieutenant and now the most junior commander in the Navy, the very lowest of those entitled to be called captain, and that only by courtesy. The promotion had cost Mr Pullings some pints of blood and a surprisingly ugly wound – a glancing blow from a Turkish sabre had sliced off most of his forehead and nose – but he would willingly have suffered ten times the pain and disfigurement for the golden epaulettes that he kept glancing at with a secret smile, while his hand perpetually strayed to the one or to the other. It was a promotion that Jack Aubrey had worked for these many years, and one that he had almost despaired of achieving, for Pullings, though an eminent seaman, likeable and brave, had no advantages of person or birth: even on this occasion Aubrey had had no confidence that his dispatch would have the desired effect, since the Admiralty, always loth to promote, could take refuge in the excuse that the *Torgud*'s captain was a rebel and not the commander of a ship belonging to a hostile power. Yet the beautiful commission had come straight back, travelling in the *Calliope* and reaching Captain Pullings so short a time ago that he was still in his first amazed happiness, smiling, saying very little, answering at random, and suddenly laughing out loud with no apparent cause.

Dr Maturin too was fond of Thomas Pullings: like Captain Aubrey he had known him as midshipman, master's mate and lieutenant; he esteemed him highly and had sewn back his nose and forehead with even more than his usual care, sitting by his cot night after night during his days of fever. But Dr Maturin had been baulked of his John Dory. This was Friday; he had been promised a John Dory and he had looked forward to it; but on Tuesday, Wednesday and Thursday the gregale had blown with such force that no fishing-boats had put out, and since Searle, unused to Catholic officers (rare birds in the Navy, where every lieutenant, on receiving his first commission, was required to renounce the Pope), had not even laid in any salt stock-fish, Maturin was obliged to dine on vegetables cooked in the English manner, waterlogged, tasteless, depressing. He was not ordinarily a greedy man, nor very ill-natured, but this disappointment had come on top of a series of vexations and some very grave anxieties, and on the second day of his giving up tobacco.

'You might say that Duns Scotus stands in much the same relationship to Aquinas as Kant to Leibnitz,' said Graham, carrying on their earlier conversation.

'Sure, I have often heard the remark in Ballinasloe,' said Maturin. 'But I have no patience with Emmanuel Kant. Ever since I found him take such notice of that thief Rousseau, I have had no patience with him at all – for a philosopher to countenance that false ranting dog of a Swiss raparee shows either a criminal levity or a no less criminal gullibility. Gushing, carefully-calculated tears – false confidences, untrue confessions – enthusiasm – romantic vistas.' His hand moved of itself to his cigar-case and came away disappointed. 'How I hate enthusiasm and romantic vistas,' he said.

'Davy Hume was of your opinion,' said Graham. 'I mean with regard to Monsieur Rousseau. He found him to be little more than a crackit gaberlunzie.'

'But at least Rousseau did not make a noise,' said Maturin, looking angrily at his friends in the farther bower. 'Jean-Jacques Rousseau may have been an apostate, a cold-hearted prevaricating fornicator, but he did not behave like a Bashan bull when he was merry. Will you look how they call out to those young women now, for shame?'

The young women, who nightly capered on the stage or lent their voices to the chorus, and who often accompanied the younger officers on their boating picnics to Gozo or Comino or their expeditions to what meagre groves the island had to offer, did not seem outraged: they called back and laughed and waved, and one of them, coming up the steps, poised herself for a moment on the arm of Captain Pellew's chair, drank off his glass of wine, and told them they must all come to the opera on Saturday – she was to sing the part of the fifth gardener. At this Captain Aubrey made some amazingly witty remark: it was lost to Maturin, but the roar of laughter that followed must certainly have been heard in St Angelo.

'Jesus, Mary and Joseph,' said Maturin. 'In Ireland I have known many a numerous gathering rejoice at little more than a genteel murmur; and it is to be supposed that the same applies to Scotland.'

Graham could suppose no such thing, but he was benevolently inclined towards Maturin and he said no more than 'Heuch: ablins.'

'Some of my best friends are Englishmen,' continued Maturin. 'Yet even the most valuable have this same vicious inclination to make a confused bellowing when they are happy. It is harmless enough in their own country, where the diet deadens the sensibilities, but it travels badly: it is perceived as a superabundancy of arrogance, and is resented more than many worse crimes. The Spaniard is a vile colonist, murderous, rapacious, cruel; but he is not heard to laugh. His arrogance is of a common, universal kind, and his presence is not resented in the same way as the Englishman's. Take the case of this island alone: it is scarcely a decade since the Navy rescued the people from the horrible tyranny of the French and filled the place with wealth rather than carrying away the treasures of the churches by the shipload, but already there is a great and growing discontent and I believe the laughter has much to do with it. Though there is enough plain stupid arrogance to account for much of it, for all love. Will you look at this, now?'

Graham took the paper, held it at arm's length, and read 'The King's Civil Commissioner observes with regret that some weak and inconsiderate persons, deceived under specious pretexts, have suffered themselves to become the instruments of a few turbulent and factious individuals. They have been seduced to subscribe a paper purporting to be an application to the King for certain changes in the existing form of government of these islands.'

'There is Sir Hildebrand's style in all its shining perfection,' said Maturin. 'Ebenezer Graham, you have his ear: could you not advise him to forget his pomp, his righteous indignation, for a moment and reflect upon the immense importance of Maltese good will? Could you not persuade him to address them with common civility and in their own language, or at least in Italian? Could you not . . . what is it, child?' he said, breaking off to attend to a little boy who had slipped through the greenery and who was standing at his side, smiling shyly, waiting to say that his sister – fifteen years of age, no more, my lord – was kind to English gentlemen: her fees were astonishingly moderate, and full satisfaction was guaranteed.

It was not much of an interruption, but it broke Maturin's flow of speech, and when the boy had gone Graham observed, 'For your part, you have Captain Aubrey's ear. Could you not advise him to avoid Mr Holden's company, rather than hail him in that public manner?'

Mr Holden had been dismissed the service for using his

6

ship to protect some Greeks fleeing from a Turkish punitive expedition: he was now acting for a small, remote, ineffectual and premature Committee for Greek Independence, and since the English government had to keep on terms with the Sublime Porte he was a most unwelcome visitor to official Malta.

The advice, of course, was far too late. Holden was already sitting at his old shipmate's table, one hand holding a glass of wine, the other stretched out, pointing at a singularly magnificent diamond spray in Jack Aubrey's hat. 'What, what is that?' he cried.

'It is a chelengk,' said Jack with some complacency. 'Ain't I elegant?'

'Wind it up again. Wind it up for him,' said his friends, and the Captain set his hat, his best, gold-laced, number one full-dress scraper, on the table: the splendid bauble – two close-packed lines of small diamonds, each topped by a respectable stone and each four or five inches long – had a round, diamond-studded base; this he twisted anti-clockwise for several turns, and as he put on his hat again the chelengk sprang into motion, the round turning with a gentle whirr and the sprays quivering with a life of their own, so that Captain Aubrey sat in a small private coruscation, a confidential prismatic firework display, astonishingly brilliant in the sun.

'Where, where did he get it?' cried Holden, turning to the others, as though Captain Aubrey might not be addressed while the chelengk blazed and trembled.

Did Holden not know? – Why, from the Grand Signior, of course, the Sultan of Turkey – For taking the rebellious *Torgud* and her consort – Where had Holden been, not to have heard of the action between the *Surprise* and the *Torgud*, the neatest action this last age?

'I knew the *Torgud*, of course,' said Holden. 'She carried very heavy metal, and she was commanded by that murderous bloody-minded dog Mustapha Bey. Pray, Jack, how did you set about her?'

'Well, we were just opening the Corfu channel, do you

7

see, with a steady topgallant breeze at south-east,' said Jack. 'And the ships lay thus . . .'

In the quieter, more philosophic bower Dr Maturin, sitting with his legs crossed and his breeches unbuckled at the knee, felt a slight movement upon his calf, as of an insect or the like: instinctively he raised his hand, but years of natural philosophy – of a desire to know just what the creature was, and a wish to spare the honey-bee or the innocent resting moth – delayed the stroke. He had often paid for his knowledge in the past, and now he paid for it again: he had scarcely recognized the great twelve-spotted Maltese horse-fly before it thrust its proboscis deep into his flesh. He struck, crushed the brute, and sat watching the blood spread on his white silk stocking, his lips moving in silent rage.

Graham said, 'You were speaking of your freedom from tobacco: but should we not consider a determination not to smoke as an even greater deprivation of liberty? As an abolition of the right of present choice, which is freedom's very essence? Should not a wise man feel himself free to smoke tobacco or not to smoke tobacco, as the occasion requires? We are social animals; but by ill-timed austerities, that lead to moroseness, we may be led to forget our social duties, and so loosen the bonds of society.'

'I am sure that you mean kindly in speaking so,' said Maturin. 'Yet you must allow me to say that I wonder at it – I wonder that a man of your parts should believe in a simple, single cause for so complex an effect as a state of mind. Is it conceivable that mere absence of tobacco alone could make me testy? No, no: in psychology as in history we must look for multiple causality. I shall smoke a small cigar, or part of a small cigar, out of compliment to you; but you will see that the difference, if it exists at all, is very slight. Indeed, the springs of mood are wonderfully obscure, and sometimes I am astonished at what I find welling up from them – at the thoughts and attitudes that present themselves, fully formed, before the mental eye.'

It was quite true. The John Dory and the yearning for tobacco were not enough to account for Maturin's ill-temper, which in any case had lasted for some days, surprising him as he woke each morning. As he pondered it suddenly occurred to him that at least one of the many reasons was the fact that he was sexually starved and that recently his amorous propensities had been stirred. 'The bull, confined, grows vicious,' he observed to himself, drawing the grateful smoke deep into his lungs: but that was not a full explanation, by any means. He moved out into the sun, to the leeward side of the arbour, so that he should not fumigate Professor Graham; and there, blinking in the strong light, he turned the matter over in his mind.

His move brought him into sight from the Apothecary's Tower, a tall, severe building with an incongruous clock in its forehead. Its gaunt, unfurnished topmost room had not been occupied since the time of the Knights; the floor was coated with soft grey dust and bat-dung, and in the dim rafters high overhead the bats themselves could be heard moving about, while all the time the clock ticked away the seconds in a deep, resonating tone. It was a cheerless, inimical room, yet it provided watchers with a fine view of the Baracca, of Searle's hotel and of its courtyard, though not, obviously, of its covered bowers. 'There is one of them,' said the first watcher. 'He has just moved into the sun.'

'The naval surgeon, smoking a cigar?' asked the second.

'He *is* a naval surgeon, and a very clever one, they say; but he is also an intelligence-agent. His name is Maturin, Stephen Maturin: Irish father, Spanish mother – can pass for either; or for French. He has done a great deal of damage; he has been the direct cause of many of our people's death and he was aboard the *Ocean* when your cousin was poisoned.'

'I shall deal with him tonight.'

'You will do nothing of the kind,' said the first man sharply. His Italian had a strong southern accent, but he

9

was in fact a French agent, one of the most important French agents in the Mediterranean, and the Maltese with him bowed submissively. Lesueur was the Frenchman's name and he was not unlike a somewhat older version of the Dr Maturin whose face he was now examining so attentively with a pocket spy-glass – a slight man of under the middle height, sallow, stooping, bookish, with an habitually closed, reserved expression, a man who would rarely draw attention but who having drawn it would give the impression of more than usual self-possession and intelligence: and Lesueur also had the easy authority of one with great sums of money at his command. He was dressed as a fairly prosperous merchant. 'No, no, Giuseppe,' he said more kindly, 'I commend your zeal, and I know you are an excellent hand with a knife; but this is not Naples, nor even Rome. His abrupt, unexplained disappearance would make a great deal of noise – the implications would be obvious, and it is absolutely essential that our existence should not be suspected. In any event there is little to be learnt from a corpse, whereas the living Dr Maturin may supply us with a great deal of information. I have set Mrs Fielding on him, and you and Luigi will watch his other meetings with the greatest care.'

'Who is Mrs Fielding?'

'A lady who works for us: she reports directly to me or Carlos.' He might have added that Laura Fielding was a Neapolitan married to a lieutenant in the Royal Navy, a young man who had been captured by the French during a cutting-out expedition and who was now confined in the punishment-prison of Bitche for having escaped from Verdun; and as he had killed one of the gendarmes who were pursuing him it was likely that he would be condemned to death when his trial came on. But the trial was postponed again and again, and by an exceedingly roundabout route Mrs Fielding was told that it might be postponed indefinitely if she would cooperate with a person who was interested in the movements of shipping. The matter was put to her as having to do with international insurance – with great Venetian and Genoese firms whose French correspondents had the government's ear. The story might not have answered with anyone thoroughly accustomed to business, but the man who told it was a convincing speaker and he produced a perfectly authentic letter written by Mr Fielding to his wife not three weeks before, a letter in which he spoke of 'this exceptional opportunity to send his love and to tell his dearest Laura that the trial had been put off again – his confinement was now much less severe, and it seemed possible that the charges might not be pressed with the utmost rigour'.

Mrs Fielding was well placed for the gathering of intelligence: not only was she very widely received, but to eke out her minute income she gave Italian lessons to officers' wives and daughters and sometimes to officers themselves, and this brought her acquainted with a good many pieces of more or less confidential information, each in itself trifling enough, but each helping to build up a valuable picture of the situation. In spite of her poverty she also gave musical parties, offering her guests lemonade from the prolific tree in her own courtyard and one Naples biscuit apiece; and this added to her value from Lesueur's point of view, for she played the piano and a beautiful mandoline, sang quite well, and gathered all the more talented naval and military amateurs in a singularly relaxed and unguarded atmosphere. Yet he had not made anything like full use of her potentialities until now, preferring to let her get thoroughly used to the notion that her husband's welfare depended on her diligence. Lesueur might have told Giuseppe all this without any particular harm, but he was a man as close and reserved as his face, and he liked keeping information to himself – all information. Yet on the other hand Giuseppe, who had been away for a great while, had to have some knowledge of the present situation: he also had to be humoured to a certain degree. 'She teaches Italian,' said Lesueur grudgingly, and paused. 'You see the big man in the arbour on the far left?'

'The one-armed commander in a scratch-wig?'

'No. At the other end of the table.'

'The great fat yellow-haired post-captain with that sparkling thing in his hat?'

'Just so. He is very fond of the opera.'

'That red-faced ox of a man? You astonish me. I should have thought beer and skittles more his line. Look how he laughs. They must surely hear him in Ricasoli. He is probably drunk: the English are perpetually drunk – do not know decency.'

'Perhaps so. At all events he is very fond of the opera. In passing, let me caution you against letting your dislike cloud your judgement, and against underestimating your enemy: the red-faced ox is Captain Aubrey, and although he may not look very wise at present he is the man who negotiated with Sciahan Bey, destroyed Mustapha, and turned us out of Marga. No fool could have done any one of those things, let alone all three. But as I was about to say, being here for some time and being fond of the opera, he decided to have Italian lessons so that he might understand what was going on.' Giuseppe was about to make some remark on the simplicity of this notion, but seeing the look on Lesueur's face he closed his mouth. 'His first teacher was old Ambrogio, but as soon as Carlos heard of this he sent proper people to tell Ambrogio to fall sick and to recommend Mrs Fielding. Let us have no interruptions, I beg,' he said, holding up his hand as Giuseppe's mouth opened again. 'She is already twelve minutes overdue and I wish to say all that I have to say before she comes. The whole point is this: Aubrey and Maturin are close friends; they have always sailed together; and by bringing the woman into contact with Aubrey I bring her into contact with Maturin. She is young, good-looking, quite intelligent, and of good reputation – no known lovers at all. No lovers since her marriage, that is to say. In these circumstances I have little doubt of his becoming involved with her, and I look forward to some very valuable information indeed.'

As Lesueur said these words, Maturin turned in his seat and looked straight at the Apothecary's Tower: it was exactly as though his strange pale eyes pierced the slatted shutters to the men within and they both silently fell back a pace. 'A nasty looking crocodile,' said Giuseppe, in little more than a whisper.

Stephen Maturin's general uneasiness had been increased by the sense of being stared at, but this had scarcely reached the fully conscious level: his intelligence had not caught up with his instinct and although his eyes were correctly focused his mind was considering the tower as a possible haunt of bats. He knew that since the departure of the Knights its lower part had served as a merchant's warehouse, but the top was almost certainly unused: a more suitable place could hardly be imagined. Clusius had dealt with the island's flora at great length, and Pozzo di Borgo with the birds; but the Maltese bats had been most pitifully neglected.

Yet although Dr Maturin was devoted to bats, and to natural philosophy in general, it was only the surface of his mind that was concerned with them at present. The healing cigar had taken off some of his more peevish discontent, but he was still deeply disturbed. As Lesueur had said, he was an intelligence-agent as well as a naval surgeon, and on his return to Malta from the Ionian he had found the already worrying situation more worrying still. Not only was confidential information bandied about in the most reckless way, so that a Sicilian wine-merchant of his acquaintance could tell him, quite correctly, that the 73rd Regiment would leave Gibraltar next week, bound for Cerigo and Santa Maura, but far more important plans were being conveyed, at least in part, to Toulon and Paris.

There had been a most unfortunate vacation of power. In Valletta itself the popular naval governor, a man who had fought with the Maltese against the French, a man who liked the people, knew their leaders intimately well, and spoke their language had, against all reason, been replaced by a soldier, and a stupid arrogant booby of a soldier at that, who publicly referred to the Maltese as a pack of Popish natives who should be made to understand who was master. The French could not have asked for better: they already had intelligence networks in the island and now they reinforced them with money and men, recruiting the dissatisfied in surprising numbers.

But even more important was the interval between the death of Admiral Sir John Thornton and the appointment of a new Commander-in-Chief. Sir John had been a good chief of intelligence as well as an outstanding diplomat, strategist and seaman, yet by far the greater part of his improvised organization was unofficial, based upon personal contact, and it had fallen to pieces in the incompetent hands of his second-in-command and temporary successor, Rear-Admiral Harte: men of substance, often important officials in governments from one end of the Mediterranean to the other, would trust themselves to Sir John or his secretary, but they had nothing to say to an ill-tempered, indiscreet, ignorant stop-gap. Maturin himself, whose services in this respect were wholly voluntary, he being moved by nothing but an intense hatred of the Napoleonic tyranny, had declined to appear in any character other than that of a surgeon while Harte held the command.

This period was now at an end, however: Sir Francis Ives, the new and respectable Commander-in-Chief, was now with the main body of the fleet, blockading Toulon, where the French, with twenty-one line-of-battle ships and seven frigates, showed signs of great activity, while at the same time he was picking up all the complex threads of his command, tactical, strategic, and political, with their necessary complement of intelligence. At the same time the Admiralty was sending an official to deal with the situation in Malta, their acting Second Secretary, no less, Mr Edmund Wray. He had a reputation for brilliant parts, and he had certainly done very well at the Treasury under his cousin Lord Pelham: there was no doubt that he was an exceptionally able man. And Maturin had no doubt that quite apart from coping with the French he would need all his abilities to overcome the ill-will of the Army and the jealousy and obstruction of the other British intelligence organizations that had made their devious way into the island. There were mysterious gentlemen from various departments, darkening counsel, hampering one another, and causing confusion; and Stephen Maturin's only consolation when he contemplated the situation was that the French were probably worse. Despotic government tends to breed spies and informers, and there were traces of at least three different Paris ministries at work in Malta, each in ignorance of the others, with a man from a fourth keeping watch on them all. The obstensible purpose of Mr Wray's visit was to check corruption in the dockyard, and it appeared to Maturin that he would probably be more successful in this than in counter-espionage. Intelligence was a highly specialized concern, and as far as he knew this was Wray's first direct connection with the department. Corruption on the other hand was universal, open to all; and since Wray in his youth had kept a carriage and a considerable establishment on an official salary of a few hundred a year and no private means it was likely that he was tolerably well acquainted with the subject. Maturin had first met Wray some years ago, when Jack Aubrey was ashore, uncommonly rich in prize-money and the spoils of the Mauritius campaign: the meeting – a casual exchange of bows and how d'ye do, sirs – had taken place in a gambling club in Portsmouth, where Jack was playing with several acquaintances. The introduction amounted to nothing in itself and Maturin would never have remembered Wray but for the fact that some days later, when Maturin was in London, it seemed that Jack had accused Wray or his associates, in terms only just ambiguous enough for decency, of cheating at cards. Wray did not ask for the barbarous satisfaction usual in such cases. It is possible that he understood Jack's words to apply to some other player – Stephen had had no first-hand account of the affair – yet there had been signs of hostile influence inside the Admiralty for some time past: ships refused, good appointments going to men with a far less spectacular fighting-record, no promotion for Jack's subordinates, and at one time Stephen had suspected that Wray might be taking his revenge in this way. But on the other hand it might be the result of other causes; it might for example be the result of the ministers' dislike of General Aubrey, Jack's father, an everlasting member of parliament in the Radical interest and a sad trial to them all – an explanation supported by the fact that Wray's reputation had not suffered. Ordinarily a man who did not fight in such circumstances was put to the hiss of the world, but when Aubrey and Maturin, who had had to sail very shortly after the unpleasantness, came back from the Indies and beyond Stephen found that it was generally assumed that there had been either a meeting or an explanation, and that Wray was received everywhere: Stephen saw him several times in London. And if Wray had not suffered in reputation he could hardly feel lastingly revengeful. In any case his manner of life had changed entirely since those days: he had made a very good marriage, from a worldly point of view, and although Fanny Harte brought him little beauty and less affection (she was against the match from the start, being attached to William Babbington, of the Royal Navy), her fortune allowed him to lead the expensive life he liked, to lead it without recourse to expedients, and to look forward to a much greater degree of wealth when the Rear-Admiral died, since Harte had inherited an extraordinarily large sum from a money-lending relative in Lombard Street, and Fanny was his only child. Furthermore, after Jack Aubrey's brilliant and very publicly acknowledged little victory in the Ionian where among other things he had provided the Navy with an excellent base and had delighted the Grand Turk, a point of great diplomatic importance at this juncture, he was reasonably safe from the insidious marginal comment hinting at misconduct or the semi-official note bringing up the indiscretions of his youth.

'Here is the other one,' said Lesueur, as Graham came out of the green shade and sat by Stephen Maturin. 'There were confusing reports about him, and at one time he seemed to be part of a different organization altogether; but now it appears that he is only a linguist, employed to deal with Turkish and Arabic documents, and that he must soon go back to his university. You will have him watched, however, and his connections noted. Where that woman can be I cannot tell. She was supposed to be here twenty-three, no, twenty-four minutes ago, to give Aubrey his lesson. Now she will not have time before his meeting.'

A long pause, and Giuseppe, who had the corner shutter to peer through as well as that which gave the frontal view, said, 'There is a lady hurrying down the side-alley with a maid.'

'Has she a dog? A great enormous Illyrian mastiff?'

'No, sir, she has not.'

'Then it is not Mrs Fielding,' said Lesueur in a cross, positive voice. But he was mistaken, as he perceived the moment the lady and her black-cowled maid turned the corner and hurried into the court of Searle's hotel.

All the men at Aubrey's table sprang to their feet, for this was not an example of local solace, no fifth gardener: far from it. Indeed, when Captain Pelham fell flat on his face it would hardly have been an exaggerated testimony of his respect if it had been voluntary, instead of too much Marsala and an inconvenient chair-leg.

There was an amiable hubbub as Mrs Fielding tried to apologize to Captain Aubrey and at the same time to satisfy those officers who wished to know how she did, and what had happened to Ponto. This was the grim censorious puritanical unsmiling creature with a collar of steel spokes, the Illyrian mastiff, an animal the size of a moderate calf that always stalked by Laura Fielding's side, holding in its long stride to match her shorter step and protecting her from the least familiarity by its mere presence; or if that were not enough then by a thunderous growl. As far as it could be made out, Ponto had been left at home in disgrace for killing an ass; he was perfectly capable of doing so, but Mrs Fielding's English was sometimes a little wild and the calmness with which she spoke of the act made it seem that there was some mistake. 'Upon my word, gentlemen,' she went on, with scarcely a pause, 'you are all very fine today. White breeches! Silk stockings!'

Why, yes, they said. Had she not heard? *Calliope* had

brought Mr Wray of the Admiralty last night, and they were going to pay their respects at the Governor's in twenty minutes, square-rigged and with a vast expenditure of breeches-ball and hair-powder, confident that their collective beauty would strike him dumb with amazement.

It was pleasant to see how the captains, some of them true tartars aboard, most of them thoroughly accustomed to battle, and all of them capable of assuming great responsibility, played the fool before a pretty woman. 'There is a capital book to be written on the human mating display in all its ludicrous variety,' observed Dr Maturin. 'Not, however, that this is more than a faint shadowing-forth of the full ceremony. Here we have no strong rivalry, no burning eagerness among the men, no real hope' – this with a penetrating glance at his friend Aubrey – 'and in any event the lady is not at leisure.' Mrs Fielding was certainly not at leisure in Maturin's particular sense of the word, but it was pleasant too to see how well she took their open though respectful admiration, their kindly banter and their flights of wit – no missishness, no bridling, no simpering, but no bold over-confidence either: she hit just the right note of friendliness, and Maturin watched her with admiration. He had earlier noticed her ignoring of Pelham's drunkenness – she was used to men of war – and now he observed her instant recovery from the shock of seeing Pullings' face as Jack Aubrey led him out of the arbour's shade to be presented and the particularly kind way in which she wished him joy of his promotion and asked him to her house that evening – a very small party, just to hear the rehearsal of a quartet: he saw her childish delight when the chelengk was put through its paces and her frank greed when she had it in her hands and she was admiring the big stones at the top. He watched her with curiosity, and with something more than that. For one thing she reminded him strongly of his first love: she had the same build, rather small but as slim and straight as a rush, and the same striking dark red hair; and by a very singular coincidence she too had arranged it so that a touchingly elegant nape was to be seen, and an ear with a delicate curve. For another she had shown him particular attention.

Insects might still delude Maturin and pierce his skin, but at this late stage it was difficult for women to do so. He knew that no one could possibly admire him for his looks; he had no illusions about his social charms or his conversation; and although he felt that his best books, *Remarks on Pezophaps Solitarius* and *Modust Proposals for the Preservation of Health in the Navy*, were not without merit he did not believe that either would set any female bosom in a blaze. Even his wife had not been able to get through more than a few pages, in spite of her very real good will. His status in the Navy was modest – he was not even a commissioned officer – and he had neither patronage nor influence. Nor was he rich.

Mrs Fielding's amiability and her invitations were therefore prompted by something other than a notion (however remote) of gallantry or of profit: what it might be he could not tell unless indeed it had to do with intelligence. If that were so then clearly it was his duty to be all compliance. There was no other way in which he could sift the matter; no other way in which he could either surprise her connections or induce her to reveal them, or use her to convey false information. He might be completely mistaken – after a while an intelligence-agent tended to see spies everywhere, rather as certain lunatics saw references to themselves in every newspaper – but whether or no he intended to play his part in the hypothetical game. And he the more easily persuaded himself that this was the right course since he liked her company, liked her musical evenings, and was convinced that he could govern any untimely emotion that might rise in his heart. It was for Mrs Fielding that he had put on these white stockings (for neither his rank nor his inclination required his presence at the reception), and it was for Mrs Fielding that he now advanced, swept off his hat, made his most courtly leg and cried, 'A very good day to you, ma'am. I trust I find you well?'

'All the better for seeing you, sir,' said she, smiling and giving him her hand. 'Dear Doctor, cannot you persuade

Captain Aubrey to take his lesson? We only have to memorate the trapassato remoto.'

'Alas, he is a sailor; and you know the sailor's slavish devotion to clocks and bells.'

A shadow passed over Laura Fielding's face: her only disagreement with her husband had been on the subject of punctuality. With a slightly artificial cheerfulness she went on, 'Just the *regular* trapassato remoto – not ten minutes.'

'Look,' said Stephen, pointing to the clock in the Apothecary's Tower. They all turned, and once again the watchers involuntarily recoiled. 'Ten minutes is all these fine gentlemen have in which to pace stately to the Governor's; for they must not pelt up the cruel slope, creasing their careful neckcloths, losing their hair-powder, gasping in the heat, and arriving in a state of crimson dissolution. You had much better sit down with me and drink a glass of iced cow's milk in the shade; the goat I cannot recommend.'

'I dare not,' she said, as the captains took their leave, walking off in order of seniority, 'I should be late for Miss Lumley. Captain Aubrey,' she called, 'if by any chance I should be delayed for this evening's rehearsal, I beg you will step in and show Captain Pullings the lemon-tree – it has been watered today! Giovanna is going to Notabile directly, but the door will not be really shut.'

'I should be very happy to show Captain Pullings the lemon-tree,' said Jack, and at the word *captain* Pullings laughed aloud once more. 'It is the finest lemon-tree of my acquaintance. And pray, ma'am, will Ponto be going to Notabile too?'

'No. Last time he killed some goats and childs. But he knows the naval uniform. He will not say anything to you, unless perhaps you touch the lemons.'

'Your plan seems to answer, sir,' said Giuseppe, watching the officers and Graham start climbing the steps towards the palace and Stephen and Mrs Fielding sit down to a dish of iced cream flavoured with coffee – they had agreed that Miss Lumley was not a sea-officer and could not therefore have so morbidly acute a sense of measured time.

'I believe it may answer very well,' said Lesueur. 'In general I have found that the uglier the man, the greater his vanity.'

'Now, sir,' said Laura Fielding, licking her spoon, 'since you have been so very kind, and since I should like to send Giovanna off to Notabile, I shall ask you to be kinder still and walk with me as far as St Publius: there are always a great many blackguard soldiers hanging about the Porta Reale, and without my dog . . .'

Dr Maturin declared that he should be happy to act as vicar to so noble a creature, and indeed he looked unusually pleased and cheerful as they left the courtyard and as he handed her across the Piazza Regina, crowded with soldiers and two separate herds of goats; but by the time they were walking past the Auberge de Castile part of his mind had drifted away, back to the subject of mood and its origins. Another part was very much in the present, however, and his silence was in some degree deliberate; it did not last long, but as he had foreseen it disturbed Laura Fielding. She was under a constraint – a constraint that he perceived more and more clearly – and both her tone and her smile were somewhat artificial when she said, 'Do you like dogs?'

'Dogs, is it?' he said, giving her a sideways glance and smiling. 'Why now, if you were an ordinary commonplace everyday civilly-prating gentlewoman I should smirk and say "Lord, ma'am, I dote upon 'em," with as graceful a writhe of my person as I could manage. But since it is you I shall only observe that I understand your words as a request that I should say something: you might equally have asked did I like men, or women, or even cats, serpents, bats.'

'Not bats,' cried Mrs Fielding.

'Certainly bats,' said Dr Maturin. 'There is as much variety in them as in other creatures: I have known some very high-spirited, cheerful bats, others sullen, froward, dogged, morose. And of course the same applies to dogs – there is the whole gamut from false fawning yellow curs to the heroic Ponto.'

'Dear Ponto,' said Mrs Fielding. 'He is a great comfort

to me; but I wish he were a little wiser. My father had a Maremma dog, a bog-dog, that could multiply and divide.'

'Yet,' said Maturin, pursuing his own thought, 'there is a quality in dogs, I must confess, rarely to be seen elsewhere and that is affection: I do not mean the violent possessive protective love for their owner but rather that mild, steady attachment to their friends that we see quite often in the best sort of dog. And when you consider the rarity of plain disinterested affection among our own kind, once we are adult, alas – when you consider how immensely it enhances daily life and how it enriches a man's past and future, so that he can look back and forward with complacency – why, it is a pleasure to find it in brute creation.'

Affection was also to be found in commanders: it fairly beamed from Pullings as Jack Aubrey led him up to the Governor and his guest. Jack did not at all relish this meeting with Wray, but since he felt that he could not avoid it without meanness he was glad that etiquette required that he should present his former lieutenant: the necessary formality would take away some of the awkwardness. Not that there seemed a great deal of awkwardness ahead, he reflected, looking along the line. Wray looked much the same, a tall, good-looking, animated, gentlemanlike fellow wearing a black coat with a couple of foreign orders; he was perfectly well aware of Jack's approach – their eyes had met some time before – but he was laughing away with Sir Hildebrand and a red-faced civilian, apparently quite unmoved, as though he had not the least reason to look furtive, or even uneasy in his mind.

The line moved on. It was their turn. Jack made the presentation to the Governor, who replied with a slight inclination of his head, an indifferent look, and the word 'Happy'. Then he urged Pullings on a step and said, 'Sir, allow me to name Captain Pullings. Captain Pullings, Mr Secretary Wray.'

'I am delighted to see you, Captain Pullings,' said Wray, holding out his hand, 'and I congratulate you with all my heart on your share in the *Surprise*'s brilliant victory. As soon as I read Captain Aubrey's dispatch' – bowing to Jack – 'and his glowing account of your unparalleled exertions I said Mr Pullings must be promoted. There were gentlemen who objected that the *Torgud* was not in the Sultan's service at the moment of her capture – that the promotion would be irregular – that it would establish an undesirable precedent. But I insisted that we should attend to Captain Aubrey's recommendation, and I may tell you privately,' he added in a lower tone, smiling placidly at Jack as he did so, 'that I insisted all the more strongly, because at one time Captain Aubrey seemed to do me an injustice, and by promoting his lieutenant I could, as the sea-phrase goes, the better wipe his eye. Few things have given me greater pleasure than bringing out the commission, and I am only sorry that the victory should have cost you such a cruel wound.'

'Mr Wray: Colonel Manners of the Forty-Third,' said Sir Hildebrand, who felt that this had been going on far too long.

Jack and Pullings bowed and gave place to the Colonel: Jack heard the Governor say 'That was Aubrey, who took Marga,' and the soldier's almost instant keen reply 'Ah? It was held by the enemy, I recollect?' but his mind was deeply perturbed. Was it possible that he had misjudged Wray? Could any man have such boundless impudence to speak so if it were false? Wray could certainly have barred the promotion if he had wished; there was the perfect excuse of the *Torgud*'s being a rebel. Jack tried to recall the exact details of that far-away unhappy, angry evening in Portsmouth – just what was the sequence of events? – just how much had he drunk? – who were the other civilians at the table? – but he had been through a great deal of much more open violence since that time and he could no longer fix the grounds of his then certainty. Cheating there had been, and for large sums of money, of that he was still sure; but there had been several players at the table, not only Andrew Wray.

He became aware that Pullings had been talking about the Second Secretary in a tone approaching enthusiasm for some time – 'such magnanimity, magnanimity, you know what I mean, sir – benevolent eye – uncommon learned too, no sort of doubt about it – should certainly be First Secretary if not First Lord' – and that they were standing at a table covered with bottles, decanters and glasses.

'So here's to his health, sir, in admiral's flip,' cried Pullings, putting an ice-cold silver tankard into his hand.

'Admiral's flip, at this time of day?' said Jack, looking thoughtfully at Captain Pullings' round, happy face, with its livid wound now glowing purple – the face of one who had already swallowed a pint of marsala and who was in any case quite overcome with joy – the face of an ordinarily abstemious man who was now in no state to drink champagne mixed with brandy half and half. 'Would not a glass of pale ale do as well? Capital stuff, this East India pale ale.'

'Come, sir,' said Pullings reproachfully. 'It's not every day I wet the swab.'

'Very true,' said Jack, remembering the time he first put on a commander's epaulette – only one in those days – and his unbounded delight. 'Very true. To Mr Secretary's very good health, then. May he prosper in all his designs.'

The admiral's flip did for poor Pullings even sooner than might have been expected. They were separated by a tide of thirsty officers, many of whom wished Pullings joy of his promotion, and Jack had not been talking to his old friend Dundas for five minutes before he saw two of them leading, almost carrying, Pullings away. He followed and found that they had put him on a seat in a quiet corner of the garden, where he was very nearly asleep, pale, but smiling still. 'You are all right, Tom, are you not?' he asked.

'Oh yes, sir,' said Pullings from a great distance. 'It was only a little close in there. Like the hold of a slave-ship.' He added that he was thinking of Mrs Pullings, of Mrs Captain Pullings, and what she would say to an income of sixteen guineas a month. Sixteen beautiful guineas a lunar month!

'What she will say to your poor phiz is more to the point,' said Jack to himself, contemplating the now mute, insensible commander. A very ugly wound indeed: he had rarely seen an uglier. Yet Stephen Maturin assured him that the great gash would heal and that the eye was in no danger; and in medical matters he had never known Stephen go far wrong. A bell struck within his mind, a warning-bell for his appointment. He said, 'Mrs Fielding, pretty thing,' and returning to the palace he walked fast through the crowd to the fore-court and there called '*Surprise*'. The cry was at once taken up by the various seamen and Marines there present and within seconds his coxswain appeared, wiping his mouth – a rather splendid coxswain, for on these occasions any ship worth her copper liked her captain, his barge, and those that belonged to it, to do her credit, and Bonden had come out in a tall round hat with *Surprise* on it, a light-blue coat with a velvet collar, satin breeches and silver-buckled shoes, the whole (apart from the shoes, which had been taken from a dead renegado) the work of his own and his friends' needles. 'Bonden,' said Jack, 'Mr – Captain Pullings is taken a little poorly.'

'Paralytic, sir?' asked Bonden in a spirit of pure enquiry: no moral or even aesthetic question arose.

'Not as who should say paralytic,' said Jack: but this was at once understood as decent form, no more, and Bonden said that he would borrow a stretcher from the pile always ready in the guard-room when the Governor gave a party, rouse out a couple of strong, reliable bargemen for the fore-end, and cut round to the garden-gate, for to avoid scandal, sir, and letting the redcoats laugh.

'Make it so, Bonden, make it so: the garden-gate in five minutes,' said Jack. Ten minutes later he was half way down the ladder-like street that led to his hotel, walking beside the stretcher borne shoulder-high in front by two of the frigate's bargemen and at knee-level by the powerful cox-swain behind, so that it was tolerably straight: the com-mander himself was lashed in with the traditional seven turns, like a hammock. The scandal of a naval officer dis-guised in drink no longer seemed to affect any of the party now that the palace redcoats were out of sight, and Jack's only care was to preserve his hat. The houses on either side had covered, closed-in balconies, and every twenty yards or so, where the slope of the street brought the balcony conveniently low, a hand from behind the shutters would make a dart at his head, accompanied by a laugh, silvery or beery as the case might be, and an invitation to step within. Officers as imposing as post-captains were rarely treated so, at least in daylight, but this was the feast of St Simeon Stylites, and a great deal of licence was tolerated; in any case Jack's hat (which, out of love for Lord Nelson and a liking for the ways of his youth, he wore athwartships rather than fore and aft) had been snatched at in countless ports since before he needed to shave, and he was fairly good at preserving it.

He preserved it now, and reaching the court of the hotel he hailed his steward, who could be seen on the roof, staring in the wrong direction. 'The roof, there. Lend a fist, Killick: bear a hand, now.'

Killick came running down. 'There you are at last, sir,' he cried, clapping on to the stretcher in an absent-minded way, his eyes fixed on Jack's hat. 'Which I been looking out for you this last bleeding watch and more.' Killick was an unimproved foremast-hand, rougher than most, impervious to what civilizing influence the cabin might exert and deeply, obstinately ignorant, self-opinionated, and ill-informed. But he did know that 'a diamond the size of a pea was worth a king's ransom', and he did know that the chelengk was made of diamonds because he had privately written *Preserved Killick HMS Surprise none so Pretty* on a window-panel with it. The two topmost stones were certainly as big as the dried naval peas he had eaten all his life – the green kind he had never seen – and he was persuaded that the chelengk ranked with the crown jewels: or even higher, since not one of the crown jewels had clockwork in it. Ever since the present had arrived from Constantinople his life had been one long anxiety, particularly as they were now ashore, with thieves at every hand; he hid the object in a different place every night, usually wrapping its outer case in sailcloth and covering that with filthy rags, the whole nestling among concealed fish-hooks and rat-traps set to go off at a sneeze.

He and Bonden put Pullings tenderly to bed in a neat, seamanlike fashion, and Jack, looking at his watch, realized that if he were not to be late for Mrs Fielding's rehearsal he would have to step out; he also realized that he had not sent his violin round earlier in the day, a foolish oversight in a town where all officers wore uniform, and could not be seen carrying so much as a packet themselves, let alone a musical instrument. 'Bonden,' he said, 'jump to the Doctor's parlour, take my fiddle-case from the window-seat, and come along to Mrs Fielding's with me. I am going drectly.'

Bonden made no reply, only twisting his head to one side, looking dogged, and pretending to be busy with the string of Captain Pullings' nightcap; but Killick plucked Jack's hat from the bedside table with such force that the chelengk quivered again and said, 'Not in that scraper you ain't.' The diamonds were of course his first consideration, but there was also the hat itself, Captain Aubrey's best gold-laced hat, and Killick hated to see good uniforms worn to skin and bone, rack and ruin; or indeed worn at all. And although he was an open-handed creature himself (none more prodigal than Preserved Killick when ashore with a hat-full of prize-money) he disliked seeing Captain Aubrey's victuals or wine eaten or drunk by anyone but admirals or lords or very good friends; and he had been known to give junior officers and midshipmen the mixed leavings of yesterday's bottles. Now he came back with a little mean shrunken threadbare hat that had seen cruel hard service in the Channel. 'Oh well, damn the scraper,' said Jack, reflecting that the chelengk would be horribly out of place at the rehearsal. 'Bonden, what are you at?'

'I shall have to shift my togs first,' said Bonden, looking away.

'Which he means was he to carry a fiddle the redcoats might call out *Give us a tune, sailor*,' said Killick. 'You wouldn't like that, your honour, not with *Surprise* on the ribbon of his hat. No. What you would like is for me to call

27

a blackguard boy to carry it; and Bonden will go along and keep an eye on him, as in duty bound.'

It was all hellfire nonsense, began Captain Aubrey, and they were a couple of God-damned swabs; but then reflecting that they had followed him many a time on to the deck of an enemy man-of-war, when there was no question of carrying fiddle-cases or being laughed at, he said there was no time to be lost – they might do as they chose – but if that fiddle were not at Mrs Fielding's within five minutes of his own arrival, they might look out for another ship.

In fact the fiddle was there before him. Bonden's little barefoot boy knew every short cut and they were waiting at the big double doors giving on to the street when Jack came hurrying down through an adverse tide of black-cowled women, men of half a dozen nations, some scented, and goats. 'Well done,' he said, giving the boy a shilling. 'I shall be just in time. Bonden, you may cut along: I shall want my gig at six in the morning.' He took his fiddle and hurried down the long stone passage that pierced the building from front to back, leading to the little garden house where Laura Fielding lived; but when he reached the door that opened on to this inner court he found that his haste had been quite unnecessary – there was no answer to his knock. He waited a decent interval, then pushed the door; and as it opened he caught a great heady waft from her lemon-tree. It was an enormous tree, certainly as old as Valletta, if not older, and it had some flowers all the year round. Jack sat on the low surrounding wall, rather like a well-head, and gasped for a while; the bed had had its enormous quarterly watering that very day, and the damp earth gave out a grateful freshness.

He had quite recovered his good humour during his walk – it rarely deserted him for long – and now, opening his coat and taking off his hat, he contemplated the lemons in the gathering twilight with the utmost satisfaction, the cool air wafting about him. He had stopped puffing and he was about to take his fiddle out of its case when he took notice of a sound that had been vaguely present for some time but that now seemed to increase – a desperate unearthly wailing, fairly regular.

'It is scarcely human,' he said, cocking his ear and trying to think of possible origins – a windmill turning with no tallow on its shaft, a lathe of some kind, a man run melancholy-mad and shut up behind the wall on the left. 'Yet sound is the strangest thing for reverberation,' he reflected, standing up. Beyond the lemon-tree there stood the little house, and from its right-hand corner ran an elegant flight of arches, screening another courtyard at an angle to the first: he walked through, and at once the sound grew very much louder – it was coming from a broad, deep cistern sunk in the corner to receive rain-water from the roofs.

'God help us,' said Jack, running towards it with a vague but very horrible notion of the maniac's having flung himself in out of despair. And when he leant over the edge of the dark water some four or five feet below, the notion seemed to be confirmed – a dim hairy form was swimming there, straining up its huge lamentable head and uttering a hoarse wow wow wow of extraordinary volume. Another glance, however, showed him that it was Ponto.

The cistern had been more than half emptied to water the lemon-tree (buckets stood by it still): the wretched dog, impelled by some unknown inquisitiveness and betrayed by some unknown blunder, had fallen in. There was still enough water for him to be out of his depth but enough had been taken to make it impossible for him to reach the rim and heave himself out. He had been in the water a great while, and all round the walls there were the bloody marks of his paws where he had tried to scrabble up. He looked quite mad with terror and despair and at first he took no notice of Jack at all, howling on and on without a pause.

'If he is out of his wits he will have my hand off, maybe,' said Jack, having spoken to the dog with no effect. 'I must get hold of his collar: a damned long lean.' He took off his coat and sword and reached down, far down, but not far enough although he felt his breeches complain. He straightened, took off his waistcoat, loosened his neckcloth and the band of his breeches and leant over again, down into the dimness and the howling that filled the air. This time his hand just touched the water: he saw the dog surge across, called out, 'Hey there, Ponto, give us your scruff,' and poised his hand to seize the collar. To his vexation the animal merely swam heavily to the other side, where it tried to climb the hopeless wall with its flayed, clawless paws, howling steadily.

'Oh you God-damned fool,' he cried. 'You silly calf-headed bitch. Give us your scruff: bear a hand now, you infernal bugger.'

The familiar naval sounds, uttered very loud and echoing in the cistern, pierced through the dog's distress, bringing sense and comfort. He swam over: Jack's hand brushed the hairy head, whipped down to the collar, the damned awkward spiked collar, and took what grip it could. 'Hold fast,' he said, slipping his fingers farther under. 'Stand by.' He drew breath, and with his left hand gripping the cistern-rim and his right hooked under the collar, the two as far apart as they could be, he heaved. He had the dog half way out of the water – a very great weight with such a poor grip, but just possible – when the edge of the cistern gave way and he fell bodily in. Two thoughts flashed into his plunging mind: 'There go my breeches' and 'I must keep clear of his jaws', and then he was standing on the bottom of the cistern with the water up to his chest and the dog round his neck, its forelegs gripping him in an almost human embrace and its strangled breath in his ear. Strangled, but not demented: Ponto had clearly recovered what wits he possessed. Jack let go the collar, turned the dog about, grasped his middle, and crying 'Away aloft' thrust him up towards the rim. Ponto got his paws on to it, then his chin; Jack gave his rump one last powerful heave and he was gone: the mouth of the cistern overhead was empty, but for the pale sky and three stars.

Chapter Two

Malta was a gossiping place, and the news of Captain Aubrey's liaison with Mrs Fielding soon spread through Valletta and even beyond, to the outlying villas where the more settled service people lived. Many officers envied Jack his good fortune, but not unkindly, and he sometimes caught knowing, conniving smiles and veiled congratulatory expressions that could not make out, he being, in the natural course of events, one of the last to know what was said on these occasions. It would in any case have astonished him, since he had always regarded fellow-sailors' wives as sacred: unless, that is to say, they threw out clear signals to the contrary effect.

He therefore experienced only the inconveniences of the situation – a certain disapproval on the part of a few officers, some wry looks and pursed lips on the part of some naval wives who knew Mrs Aubrey, and the ludicrous persecution that had given rise to the whole tale.

He and Dr Maturin, followed by Killick, were walking along the Strada Reale in the brilliant sunshine when his face clouded and he cried, 'Stephen, pray step in here for a moment,' urging his friend into the nearest shop, one kept by Moses Maimonides, a dealer in Murano glass. But it was too late. Jack had barely time to reach the farthest corner before Ponto was upon him, roaring with delight. Ponto was a clumsy great brute at the best of times and now that he wore cloth boots to protect his injured paws he was clumsier still; he scattered two ranges of bottles as he came bounding in, and as he stood there with his fore-paws on Jack's shoulder, eagerly licking his face, his tail, waving from side to side, scattered chandeliers, sweetmeat jars, crystal bells.

It was a horrid scene, a scene repeated as often as three times a day on occasion, the only variety being the kind of shop, tavern, club or mess in which Jack took refuge, and it lasted long enough to do a great deal of damage. In decency Jack could not positively maim the dog, and nothing short of serious injury would answer, for Ponto was thick-witted as well as clumsy. Eventually Killick and Maimonides hauled him backwards into the street, and once there he proudly led Jack up to his mistress, giving an ungainly bound or two, and stepping high, reuniting them with an evident and very public approval that was observed and commented upon once again by a number of sea-officers, land-officers, civilians, and their wives.

'I do hope he has not been a nuisance,' said Mrs Fielding. 'He saw you a hundred yards away, and nothing would stop him, but he must wish you good-day again. He is so grateful. And so am I,' she added, with such an affectionate look that Jack wondered whether it were not perhaps one of these signals. He was the more inclined to think so since he had breakfasted on a pound or two of fresh sardines, which act as an aphrodisiac upon those of a sanguine complexion.

'Not at all, ma'am,' said he. 'I am very happy to see you both once more.' The voices of Killick and the glass-merchant behind him grew shriller and louder – on these occasions Killick paid for the breakage; but he paid not a Maltese grain, not a tenth of a penny too much, insisting upon seeing all the pieces and fitting them together, and then demanding wholesale rates – and he moved Mrs Fielding out of hearing. 'Very happy to see you both,' he repeated, 'but just at this moment may I beg you to hold him in? I am expected at the dockyard, and to tell you the truth I have not a minute to lose. The Doctor here will be delighted to lend you a hand, I am sure.'

Expected he was, and not only by the cynical shipwrights labouring at enormous cost upon the worthless *Worcester* and by those who were not working at all upon the *Surprise*, which stood, deserted and gunless, perilously shored-up in a pool of stinking mud, but also by what was left of his ship's company. He had started out from England in the *Worcester* with some six hundred men: on being temporarily transferred to the *Surprise* he picked two hundred of the best, and with these he had hoped to return to England to take one of the new heavy frigates out to the North American station as soon as this brief parenthesis in the Mediterranean was over. But the Mediterranean fleet was always short of seamen, while in this respect the admirals and senior captains were not so much short of scruples as totally devoid of them; and since the little battle-scarred frigate had gone into dock on her return from the Ionian her crew had dwindled sadly, hands being drafted away on one pretext or another with such naked greed that Jack had to fight hard to keep even his own bargemen and personal followers. The remaining Surprises were lodged in nasty wooden sheds, painted black; and these they made nastier still by instantly caulking all vents and filling the confined space with tobacco-smoke and the human fug they were used to between-decks. Since the ship was in the hands of the dockyard mateys they could devote much of their time to wasting their substance and destroying their health, and this they did in the company of a crowd of women who gathered at the gates, some of them seasoned old warhorses from the time of the Knights but many surprisingly young – squat, thick girls of a kind rarely seen anywhere but in the neighbourhood of naval or military barracks.

It was this thin crew, dissolute and frowzy, that was waiting for Jack when he had listened with what patience he could command to the lying excuses of those who should have been attending to the frigate and who were not doing so. The seamen were assembled as though for the usual inspection aboard, toeing lines chalked out to represent the seams of *Surprise*'s deck as accurately as possible, each division under its own officers and midshipmen. The frigate's Marines had been returned to their barracks as soon as she was docked, so there were no redcoats, no ritual shouting and stamping and presenting arms as Captain Aubrey approached: only William Mowett, her present first lieutenant, who stepped forward, took off his hat and said, in the rather quiet, conversational, unmilitary voice of one afflicted with a severe headache, 'All present and sober, sir, if you please.'

Sober perhaps, at least by naval standards, though some were swaying as they stood and most smelt strongly of the drink – sober perhaps, but unquestionably squalid, reflected Jack as he passed his shipmates in review: familiar faces, some of them known to him ever since his first command or even earlier, and nearly all looking more puffy, blotched, and generally unhealthy than ever before. In the Ionian the *Surprise* had taken a Frenchman with some chests of silver coin aboard, and rather than wait for the slow process of the prize-court Jack had ordered an immediate sharing-out. It was not strictly legal and it meant that he would be liable for the whole if the prize were not condemned; but it had a piratical directness that encouraged the crew far more than a larger sum in the remote, prudential future, as he knew with absolute certainty. Each man received the equivalent of a quarter's pay, laid down in Maria Theresa dollars on the capstan-head, and at the time this had caused a great deal of quiet satisfaction; but the sum had evidently not lasted – no sum would ever have outlasted the hands' appetite for fun ashore – and it was clear that some were already selling their clothes. Jack knew very well that if he were to give the order 'On end bags' it would be seen that instead of a well-found crew the *Surprise* had a pack of threadbare paupers with nothing but their holy shore-going rig (never worn at sea) and only just enough in the way of slops to protect them from the gentlest Mediterranean weather. He had done what he could to keep them occupied, but apart from small-arms exercise for all hands and chipping round-shot there was little they could be set to in the nautical line; and although cricket and expeditions to see the island where St Paul was wrecked, his ship being caught on a lee-shore with a nasty gregale blowing, did something, they could not really compete with the pleasures of the town. 'Deboshed, improvident fish,' he muttered, passing down the line with a stern and even righteous expression. And their officers were not much better, either: Mowett and Rowan, the other lieutenant, had both been to the Sappers' ball, and they had evidently competed in drinking deep by land, just as they competed in versemanship by sea; and both were suffering from the effects. Adams the purser and the two master's mates, Honey and Maitland, had been to the same party, and the same pall of liverish heaviness hung over them; while Gill, the master, looked ready to hang himself – this however was his usual expression. Indeed, the only cheerful, alert, creditable faces belonged to the frigate's remaining youngsters, Williamson and Calamy – useless little creatures, but gay and, when they thought of it, attentive to their duty. Pullings, though present, did not count. He no longer belonged to the *Surprise* and he was attending only as a visitor, an interested spectator; and in any event his face could not be described as wholly cheerful. In spite of the conscious glory of his epaulettes, an accurate observer could make out an underlying loss and anxiety, as though Captain Pullings, a commander without a ship and with little likelihood of a ship, were beginning to realize that a hopeful journey was better than the arrival, that nothing could come up to expectation, and that there was a great deal to be said for old ways, old friends, and one's old ship.

'Very well, Mr Mowett,' said Captain Aubrey when the inspection was over, and then to the general dismay, 'All hands will now proceed to Gozo in the boats.' And seeing Pullings looking somewhat disconsolate and lost, he added, 'Captain Pullings, sir, if you are at leisure you would infinitely oblige me by taking command of the launch.'

'This will claw some of the jam off their backs,' he reflected with satisfaction as the boats rounded St Elmo Point and the barge, launch, gig, the two cutters and even the jolly-boat settled down to a long pull against the current and right into the moderate north-west breeze without the least hope of hoisting a sail until they reached Gozo, thirteen unlucky miles away. And even then, thought the seamen, the skipper, in his present sodomitical state of mind, might make them pull right round Gozo, Comino, Cominetto, and the rest of bleeding Malta itself: the bargemen, with their captain looking straight at them as he sat there in the stern-sheets between his coxswain and a youngster, could scarcely express their opinion of his conduct by anything more than a reserved, stony look; nor could the rowers in the other boats really do justice to their sentiments, particularly those seated right aft. But the boats were crowded, the oars were relieved every half hour, and even in the boats commanded by Pullings and the two lieutenants the hands managed to say, or at least utter, a good deal about Captain Aubrey, all of it disrespectful; while in the cutters and the jolly-boat, under the young gentlemen, it was downright mutinous, and Mr Calamy's voice could be heard at intervals crying, 'Silence fore and aft – silence, there – I shall report every man in the boat,' his voice growing shriller at every repetition.

Yet in an hour or so much of the ill-humour was sweated out, and when they came into the smooth water under the lee of Comino they took a speronara in chase, pursuing it with cheers and a mad expenditure of useless energy right into Megiarro Bay and the port of Gozo; there they landed, gasping and exhausted, calling out traditional witticisms to the last boats to reach the shore; and when they heard that their captain had ordered them refreshments in the long vine-covered skittle-alley beside the beach they beamed on him with all their former kindness.

The officers walked up to Mocenigo's, where they found others of their kind, come out to enjoy the glorious day or to visit friends on the island; there were some redcoats too, but in general the services kept apart, the soldiers on the side towards the fort and the sailors occupying the terraces that commanded the sea, with the naval captains gathering on the highest. Jack led Pullings up the steps and introduced him to Ball and Hanmer, post-captains, and to Meares, who was only a commander. A brilliant play upon this name occurred to Jack, but he did not give it voice: not long before this, on learning that an officer's father was a Canon of

Windsor he had flashed out a remark to the effect that no one could be more welcome aboard a ship that prided herself upon her artillery-practice than the son of a gun, only to find the officer receive it coldly, with no more than a pinched, obligatory smile.

'We were talking about the confidential mission,' said Ball, when they had sat down again and drinks were ordered.

'What confidential mission?' asked Jack.

'Why, to the Red Sea, of course,' said Ball.

'Oh, that,' said Jack. For some time there had been talk of an operation to be carried out in those uncomfortable waters, partly to diminish the influence of the French, partly to please the Grand Turk, who was at least the nominal ruler of the Arabian shore as far as the Bab el Mandeb and of the Egyptian as far as the dominions of the Negus, and partly to satisfy those English merchants who suffered from the exactions and ill-usage of the Tallal ibn Yahya, who ruled over the small island of Mubara and part of the mainland coast and whose ancestors had levied a toll on all ships that passed within reach and that were neither strong enough to resist nor swift enough to outsail their cumbrous dhows. The practice stopped well short of real piracy, however, and the old sheikh was regarded as a minor local nuisance, no more; but his son, a much more forceful character, had welcomed Buonaparte's invasion of Egypt, and in Paris he was looked upon as a potentially valuable ally in the campaign that was to drive the English out of India and destroy their trade with the East. He had therefore been provided with some European vessels and with shipwrights who built him a small fleet of galleys; and although the Indian campaign now seemed tolerably remote Tallal was still used to embarrass the Turks whenever their policy became too favourable to England. His increasing influence made both the Sublime Porte and the East India Company most uneasy; furthermore in a recent fit of religious enthusiasm he had forcibly circumcised three English merchants, in retaliation for the forcible baptism of three of his ancestors – his family, the Beni Adi, had lived in Andalusia for seven hundred years, spending most of their time in Seville, where they were known and mentioned with guarded approval by Ibn Khaldun. Yet the merchants in question were not members of the Company but interlopers and three unlicensed foreskins scarcely merited a full-scale campaign: the general idea seemed to be that the Company would lend one of their country ships to the Turkish authorities in the Gulf of Suez, that the Royal Navy should man her, and that the English, in the character of technical advisers, should proceed to Mubara with a body of Turkish troops and a more suitable ruler of the same family and take the sheikh's galleys away from him. The whole thing was to be done quietly, so as not to offend the Arab rulers farther south and in the Persian gulf – no less than three of Tallal's wives were from those parts – and it was to be done suddenly, by surprise, so that there should be no resistance.

'Lowestoffe is to be the man,' said Ball, 'and quite right too: he is used to dealing with Turks and Arabs, he is on the spot, and he has no ship. But Lord, to think of him sweating over the desert, ha, ha, ha! They are to walk across to Suez: oh Lord!' He laughed again, and all the others grinned. Lord Lowestoffe was one of the best-liked men in the Navy, but he was short-legged and exceedingly fat – his red, round, jolly face perpetually shone – and the idea of his marching across a sandy waste under the African sun was irresistibly comic.

'I feel for him,' said Jack. 'He complained of the heat even when we were in the Baltic. He would be much happier on the North American station, where I hope to be very soon. Poor Lowestoffe: I have not seen him this great while.'

'He has been out of order,' said Hanmer. 'I do assure you he looked almost pale when he came to see me the other day, asking about the Red Sea, wanting to know about the winds, shoals, reefs and so on and writing it all down most conscientiously, wheezing like a bulldog, poor fellow.'

'Are you a Red Sea pilot, sir?' asked Pullings, speaking for the first time: he asked in all good faith, being interested in the subject, but his wound changed his civil smile into an offensively incredulous leer, and his nervous tone did little to contradict it.

'I do not suppose my knowledge of those parts can compete with yours, sir,' said Captain Hanmer. 'Far from it, no doubt. Yet I do have a certain superficial acquaintance with them, and I did have the honour of leading the squadron all the way from Perim right up to Suez itself when we were turning the French out of the place in the year one.' Hanmer was much given to strange romantic tales, but he happened to be keeping to the exact truth and this made him more sensitive to disbelief than usual.

'Oh sir,' cried Pullings, 'I have never been there at all – the Indian Ocean, no more – but I have always heard tell that the navigation is uncommon difficult, the tides and currents up at the north end uncommon deceptive, and the heat almost uncommon hot, as one might say; and I should very much like to know more.'

Hanmer looked more attentively at Pullings' face, saw the perfect candour beneath the wound, and said, 'Well, sir, the navigation *is* uncommon difficult, to be sure, especially if you come in, as we had to come in, through the devilish eastern channel round Perim, which is only two miles wide and nowhere more than sixteen fathom deep in the fairway, with never a buoy, never a buoy from one end to the other; but that is nothing to the excessive hellfire heat, the excessive hellfire *humid* heat – perpetual God-damned sun, no refreshment in the breeze, tar dripping from the rigging, pitch bubbling from the seams, hands running mad, washing never dry. Meares here,' – nodding towards his neighbour – 'very nearly went out of his wits, and was obliged to be dipped in the sea twice an hour: dipped in an iron basket, because of the sharks.' Hanmer gave Meares a thoughtful look, and reflecting that although he had been in a sad way he was still perfectly capable of detecting any deviation from the truth, continued his plain, factual account. Jack, listening with what attention he could spare from his tankard of iced lemonade heightened with marsala, heard of coral reefs running out as much as twenty miles on the east coast but keeping closer inshore in the northern waters, of the volcanic islands, the dangerous shoals in the latitude of Hodeida, the prevailing north and north-west winds in the hither regions, the sand-storms in the Gulf of Suez and the wind called the Egyptian. He was glad that Hanmer was not vapouring away about sea-serpents and phoenixes – in spite of years and years of practice Hanmer was still a most indifferent liar, and his want of skill was often embarrassing – but he was sorry to hear so much loose talk about what was meant to be kept quiet – Stephen had always preached a tomb-like discretion – and in any case he felt that Hanmer was going on far, far too long. He was now talking about the Red Sea sharks.

'Most sharks are gammon,' said Jack in one of the rare pauses. 'They look fierce and throw out their chests, but it is all my eye and Betty Martin, you know, all cry and no wool. I dived plump on to an enormous hammerhead off the Morocco coast – just south of the Timgad shoal, to be exact – and all he did was to ask my pardon and hurry away. Most sharks are gammon.'

'Not in the Red Sea they ain't,' said Hanmer. 'I had a ship's boy called Thwaites, a little stunted fellow from the Marine Society, and he was sitting in the lee mainchains, trying to keep cool by trailing his feet in the water: the ship heeled a strake or two with a puff of wind and a shark had his legs off at the knee before you could say knife.'

This struck a chord in the mind of Captain Ball, whose attention had wandered long ago. 'I am going to have such a fish for dinner,' he cried. 'They showed him to me when I arrived – a lupo. Very like a bass, but more so. Aubrey, you and Captain Pullings must share him; he is quite big enough for three.'

'You are very good, Ball, and indeed there is nothing like a lupo,' said Jack, 'but for my part I must hurry away. I am going to wait on Admiral Hartley, and it will be strange if he don't make me stay to dinner.'

Captain Hartley, as he was then, was not perhaps the most estimable of naval characters, but he had been kind to Jack as a midshipman, and he had particularly mentioned his name, with strong commendation, in his dispatch when the *Fortitude*'s boats cut out a Spanish corvette from under the guns of San Felipe. He had also been one of the examining captains on that dread Wednesday when Mr Midshipman Aubrey presented himself together with many others at Somerset House, furnished with a paper falsely certifying that he was nineteen years of age, and with others from his various captains stating with perfect truth that he had served the requisite six years at sea and that he could hand, reef and steer, work his tides and take double altitudes; and it was Captain Hartley who spoke up when Jack, already so flustered by a malignant hungry ill-tempered mathematical captain that he could hardly tell latitude from longitude, was brought up all standing by the sudden, unfair, and totally unexpected question 'How does it come about that Captain Douglas disrated you, turned you out of the midshipmen's berth and sent you forward to serve as a common foremast-hand when you was in *Resolution* at the Cape?' Jack was horribly puzzled to find an answer that should make him seem reasonably innocent while at the same time it did not reflect upon his then commanding officer; he called upon his intelligence (for his usual candour did not seem appropriate on this occasion) and upon all the subtlety he possessed, but he called in vain, and he was infinitely relieved to hear Captain Hartley say, 'Oh, it was only a question of a girl hidden in the cable-tier, nothing to do with his seamanship at all: Douglas told me when I took him on to my own quarterdeck. Now, Mr Aubrey, let us suppose you are in command of a transport: she is in ballast, light and crank, heading south under topgallantsails, the breeze due west, and a sudden squall lays her on her beam-ends. How do you deal with the situation without cutting away her masts?'

Mr Aubrey dealt with the situation by veering away a good scope of hawser, made fast to water-stops such as spars and hen-coops, from the lee quarter and then hauling upon it until the ship wore, with a last hearty heave by all hands to bring the wind on to what had been her lee quarter, when she must infallibly right herself and save her hawser too.

A little later he left the Navy Office with a beaming face and another certificate, a beautiful paper that said he had been found fit to serve as a lieutenant; and it was in this rank that he shipped with Captain Hartley during a commission in the West Indies, a commission cut short by the captain's elevation to flag-rank. Although Hartley was not a popular man in the service, being an odd combination of profligacy and avarice – the mistresses he sailed with were of the cheapest kind, and they were turned off in foreign ports with no great regard for their convenience, while his rare dinners were sad, shabby affairs – they got along quite well together, partly because they were used to one another, partly because they were both keenly interested in gunnery, and partly because Jack pulled Hartley out of the water when his gig overturned off St Kitts. Jack was a powerful swimmer and he had saved a surprising number of sailors: those few who had had time to realize how disagreeable it was to drown and how much the world they were leaving still had to offer were sometimes touchingly grateful: but most were so taken up with gasping and calling out and suffocating, sinking and rising, that they had no leisure for reflection; and those who, like Captain Hartley, were snatched directly from the sea would often maintain that they could have managed perfectly well by themselves – meaning, it is to be presumed, that they would suddenly have learnt how to swim or to walk upon the water. Yet however grudging their reactions might be, Jack nearly always retained a private fondness for those he had rescued, even the most bitterly ungrateful; and Hartley was by no means one of these.

Jack was thinking of him quite affectionately as he walked inland along the white, dusty road among the olive-trees: they had not met for many years, although Jack had quite often been able to carry barrels of wine and crates of books and furniture for him, dropping them at the nearest port, nor had Jack seen his house in Gozo; but he had a clear picture of the Admiral in his mind's eye, and he looked forward to their meeting. It was an unfrequented road: one ox-cart, one ass, one peasant in the last half hour. Unfrequented by men, that is to say; but in the olive-trees on either hand the cicadas kept up a metallic strident din, sometimes rising to such a pitch that conversation would have been difficult had he not been alone; and once he left the small fields and the groves, walking over stony, goat-grazing country, the highway was very much used by reptiles. Small dun lizards flickered in the scorched grass at the edge and big green ones as long as his forearm scuttled away at his approach, while occasional serpents brought him up all standing: he had an ignorant, superstitious horror of snakes. On a walk of this kind in the Mediterranean islands he usually saw tortoises, which he did not dislike at all – far from it – but they seemed rare on Gozo, and it was not until he had been going for some time that he heard a curious tock-tock-tock and he saw a small one running, positively running across the road, perched high on its legs; it was being pursued by a larger tortoise, who, catching it up, butted it three times in quick succession: it was the clap of the shells that produced the tock-tock-tock. 'Tyranny,' said Jack, meaning to intervene: but either the last blows had subdued the smaller tortoise – a female – or she felt that she had shown all the reluctance that was called for; in any case she stopped. The male covered her, and maintaining himself precariously on her domed back with his ancient folded leathery legs he raised his face to the sun, stretched up his neck, opened his mouth wide and uttered the strangest dying cry.

'Bless me,' said Jack, 'I had no notion . . . how I wish Stephen were here.' Unwilling to disturb them, he fetched a cast quite round the pair and walked on, trying to recall some lines of Shakespeare that had to do not exactly with tortoises but with wrens until he reached a wayside shrine dedicated to St Sebastian, the martyr's blood recently renewed with startling brilliance and profusion. Beyond the shrine there was a high stone wall, partly fallen, with an ornate wrought-iron gate, once gilded, leaning unhinged against the masonry. 'This must be it,' he said, calling his directions to mind.

'But perhaps I am mistaken,' he said some minutes later. The drive, the arid sort of park or rather enclosed scrubland on either side and the gaunt yellow house in sight ahead were unlike anything he could remotely connect with the Navy. He had seen the same kind of nonchalance in Ireland – the overgrown paths, the shutters hanging half off their hinges, the broken window-panes – but in Ireland it had usually been veiled by gentle rain, and softened by moss. Here the sun beat down from a cloudless wind-swept sky; there was nothing green apart from a few dusty holm-oaks, and the sawing of the countless cicadas made it all harsher still, harsher by far. 'That fellow will tell me,' he observed.

The gaunt yellow house was built around a court; an arched gateway led into it, and against the left-hand pillar leant a man, half-groom, half-peasant, picking his nose. 'Pray does Admiral Hartley live here?' asked Jack.

The man did not answer, but gave him a sly, knowing look and slipped inside the door. Jack heard him speaking to a woman: it was Italian, not Maltese, that they were talking, and he caught the words 'officer – pension – take care'. He was conscious of being looked at through a small window, and presently the woman came out, a hard-faced slattern in a dirty white dress. She had assumed a genteel expression, and in quite good English she said, 'Yes, this was the Admiral's palace – was the gentleman come on official business?' Jack explained that he was there as a friend, and he was surprised to see disbelief in her small, close-set eyes: she retained her smile however and asked him to walk in; she would tell the Admiral he was there. He was led up dim stairs and shown into a splendid room: splendid, that is to say, in its proportions, its pale green marble floor with white bands, its lofty carved plaster ceiling, and its chimney-piece, which enclosed a hearth larger than many of the cabins Lieutenant Aubrey had lived in; less so in its furniture, which amounted to a couple of upright chairs with leather seats and backs, looking lost in all that light-filled space, and a little round table. There seemed to be nothing else at all, but when Jack, having reached the middle window in a noble flight of seven, turned towards the fireplace he found himself looking straight at the likeness of his former captain at the age of thirty-five or forty, a brilliant portrait, wonderfully fresh and clear. He contemplated it, standing there with his hands behind his back; and the minutes dropped by in the silence. He did not know the artist: it was not Beechey, nor Lawrence, nor Abbott, nor any of the usual painters of the Navy; probably not an Englishman at all. But a very able fellow in any case: he had caught Hartley's strong, masterful, dominating air exactly, and his energy; but, reflected Jack after a long communing with the portrait, he had certainly not liked his sitter. There was a cold hardness in that painted face, and although the portrait was truthful enough in its way it took no account of Hartley's good nature – rarely expressed, to be sure, but real enough upon occasion. The picture was not unlike a statement made by an enemy: and Jack remembered how a brother-officer had said that even Hartley's undoubted courage had a grasping quality about it, that he attacked the enemy in a state of furious indignation and personal hatred, as though the other side were trying to do him out of some advantage – prize-money, praise, employment.

He was reflecting upon this and upon the true function of painting when the door opened and a very cruel caricature of the portrait walked in. Admiral Hartley was wearing an old yellow dressing-gown, its front stained with snuff, loose pantaloons, and down-at-heel shoes by way of slippers; the bones of his nose and jaw had grown and his face was much bigger; it had lost its fierce distinction, its authority, and of course its weather-beaten tan; it was ugly and even ludicrous; and its large clay-pale surface now expressed no more than a settled commonplace sour discontent. He looked at Jack with an inhuman absence of interest or pleasure and asked him why he had come. Jack said that being in Gozo he thought he would pay his respects to his former captain and ask whether he had any commands for Valletta. The

Admiral made no clear reply and they stood there with Jack's voice echoing in the empty room as he spoke of the weather for the last few days, the changes in Valletta, and his hopes of a breeze for tomorrow.

'Well, sit down for a minute,' said Admiral Hartley: and then, making an effort, he asked whether Aubrey had a ship at present. But without waiting for a reply he said, 'What's o'clock? It is time for my goat's milk. Always late, these buggers. It is essential that I should have my goat's milk regular,' and he looked eagerly at the door.

'I hope you keep well, sir, in this climate?' said Jack. 'It is reckoned very healthy, I believe.'

'There ain't no such thing as health when you're old,' said the Admiral. 'Health to what end?'

The milk came in, brought by a man-servant remarkably like the woman Jack had seen, apart from the blue-black stubble of a five-days beard. 'Where is the signora?' asked Hartley. 'Coming,' said the servant; and indeed she appeared in the doorway as he left, carrying a tray with a wine-bottle and some biscuits and a glass upon it: she had changed her dirty white dress for another, perceptibly cleaner and cut remarkably low. Jack saw Hartley's dead face come to life: yet in spite of his animation his first words were a protest – 'Aubrey don't want wine at this time of day.'

Before anything could be decided on this point a bawling broke out in the courtyard and the Admiral and the woman hurried over to look out. He fondled her bosom, but she brushed him off and began shouting through the window in a flawed metallic voice that must have carried a mile and a half. This went on for some time. Jack had not much more penetration than the next man yet it was perfectly evident to him that Hartley had fallen unlucky; but that mixed with his obvious lechery there was what might be called love or infatuation or at any rate a strong attachment.

'A splendid temperament,' said the Admiral when she had run out of the room to carry on the argument at close quarters. 'You can always tell a fine spirited girl by the jut of her bum.' There was a slight flush on his face and in a much more human tone he said, 'Pour yourself a glass of wine and then one for me – I'll hob and nob with you. They don't let me drink anything but milk, you know.' A pause in which he took snuff from a screw of paper, and he said, 'I go over to Valletta now and then to see about my half-pay; I was there not a fortnight ago and Brocas mentioned your name. Yes, yes: I remember perfectly well. He talked about you. It seems you still have not learnt to keep your breeches on. So much the better. Play the man while you still can, I always say. I wish I had not lost so many opportunities in the past; I could weep blood when I think of some of them – splendid women. Play the man while you can; you are a gelding long enough in your grave. And some of us are geldings before we get there,' he added, with something between a laugh and a sob.

As Jack walked back towards the sea the heat was greater, the glare of the white road more blinding, and the harsh clamour of the cicadas louder still. He had rarely been so sad. The black thoughts flooded in, one upon another: Admiral Hartley, of course; and the perpetual rushing passage of time; inevitable decay; the most unimaginable evil of impotence . . . Instinctively he jerked back as something shot past his face like a block hurtling from high aloft in action: it struck the stony ground just in front of his feet and burst apart – a tortoise, probably one of the amorous reptiles of a little while ago, since this was the very place. And looking up he saw the huge dark bird that had dropped it: the bird looked down at him, circling, circling as it stared. 'Good Lord above,' he said. 'Good Lord above . . .' And after a moment's consideration, 'How I wish Stephen had been here.'

Stephen Maturin was in fact sitting on a bench in the abbey church of St Simon's, listening to the monks singing vespers. He too was dinnerless, but in this case it was voluntary and prudential, a penance for lusting after Laura Fielding and (he hoped) a means of reducing his concupiscence: to begin with his pagan stomach had cried out against this

47

treatment, and indeed it had gone on grumbling until the end of the first antiphon. Yet for some time now Stephen had been in what might almost have been called a state of grace, stomach, break-back bench, carnal desire all forgotten, he being wafted along on the rise and fall of the ancient, intimately familiar plainchant.

During their stay in Valletta the French had been more than usually unkind to the monastery: not only had they taken away all its treasure and sold off its cloister but they had wantonly broken the armorial stained-glass windows (which had been replaced with cane matting) and had stripped the walls of the exceptionally fine marble, lapis lazuli and malachite that covered them. Yet this was not without its advantages. The acoustics were much improved, and as they stood there among the dim, bare stone or brick arches the choirmonks might have been chanting in a far older church, a church more suited to their singing than the florid Renaissance building the French had found. Their abbot was a very aged man; he had known the last three Grand Masters, he had seen the coming of the French and then of the English, and now his frail but true old voice drifted through the half-ruined aisles pure, impersonal, quite detached from worldly things; and his monks followed him, their song rising and falling like the swell of a gentle sea.

There were few people in the church and those few could hardly be seen except when they moved past the candles in the side-chapels, most of them being women, whose black, tent-like faldettas merged with the shadows; but when at the end of the service Stephen turned by the holy-water stoup near the door to pay his respects to the altar, he noticed a man sitting near one of the pillars, dabbing his eyes with his handkerchief. His face was lit by a shaft of light from a small high opening on to the secularized cloister, and as he turned Stephen recognized Andrew Wray.

The doorway was filled with very slowly moving, eagerly talking women, and Stephen was obliged to stand there. Wray's presence surprised him: the penal laws were not what they had been, but even so the acting Second Secretary of the Admiralty could not possibly be a Catholic; and although Stephen had caught sight of Wray at concerts in London from time to time it had never occurred to him that love of music rather than of fashionable company might have brought him. Yet the Secretary's emotion was genuine enough; even when he had composed himself and was walking towards the door his face was grave and deeply moved. The women heaved the leather curtain to one side, the door opened, letting them out and a beam of sunlight in. Wray took no notice of the holy water, nor of the altar – a further proof that he was no Papist. He glanced at Stephen. His expression changed to one of urbane civility and he said, 'Dr Maturin, is it not? How do you do, sir? My name is Wray. We met at Lady Jersey's, and I have the honour of being acquainted with Mrs Maturin. I saw her, indeed, a little before I sailed.'

They talked for a while, blinking in the brilliant sun and speaking of Diana – very well, when seen at the Opera in the Columptons' box – and of common acquaintances, and then Wray suggested a pot of chocolate in an elegant pastry-cook's on the other side of the square.

'I go to St Simon's as often as I can,' he said as they sat down at a green table in the arbour behind the shop. 'Do you take a delight in plainchant, sir?'

'I do indeed, sir,' said Stephen, 'provided it be devoid of sweetness or brilliancy or striving for effect, and exactly phrased – no grace-notes, no passing-notes, no showing away.'

'Exactly so,' cried Wray, 'and no new-fangled melismata either. Angelic simplicity – that is the heart of the matter. And these worthy monks have the secret of it.'

They talked about modes, agreeing that in general they preferred the Ambrosian to the plagal, and Wray said, 'I was at one of their Masses the other day, when they sang the Mixolydian *Agnus*; and I must confess that the old gentleman's *dona nobis pacem* moved me almost to tears.'

'Peace,' said Stephen. 'Shall we ever see it again, in our time?'

'I doubt it, with the Emperor in his present form.'

'It is true that I am just come from a church,' said Stephen, 'but even so I could wish to see that tyrant Buonaparte doubly damned to all eternity and back, the dog.'

Wray laughed and said, 'I remember a Frenchman who acknowledged all sorts of very grave faults in Buonaparte, including tyranny, as you so rightly say, and even worse a total ignorance of French grammar, usage and manners, but who nevertheless supported him with all his might. His argument was this: the arts alone distinguish men from the brutes and make life almost bearable – the arts flourish only in time of peace – universal rule is a prerequisite for universal peace – and here as I recall he quoted Gibbon on the happiness of living in the age of the Antonines, concluding that in effect the absolute Roman emperor, even Marcus Aurelius, was a tyrant, if only in posse, but that the *pax romana* was worth the potential exercise of this tyranny. As my Frenchman saw it, Napoleon was the only man or rather demi-god capable of imposing a universal empire, so on humanitarian and artistic grounds he fought in the Garde impériale.'

A host of very passionate objections rose in Stephen's bosom; but he had long since ceased opening himself to any but intimate friends and now he only smiled, saying 'Sure, it is a point of view.'

'But in any event,' said Wray, 'it is clearly our duty to hamstring the universal empire, if I may use the expression. For my own part' – lowering his voice and leaning over the table – 'I have a somewhat delicate task in hand at present, and I should be grateful for your advice – the Admiral said I might apply to you. As soon as he comes in there will be a general meeting, and perhaps you would be so good as to attend.'

Stephen said that he was entirely at Mr Wray's service: a number of clocks striking near at hand and far reminded him that he was already late for his appointment with Laura Fielding, and springing up he took his leave.

Wray watched Stephen hurry across the square and disappear down the busy street; then he returned to the church, quite empty at this hour, looked at the arrangement of the candles in the chapel dedicated to Saint Rocco and walked round to the south aisle, where a small door, usually locked but now only latched, let him into the secularized cloister. It was filled with barrels of one kind and another, and a passage in the far corner led to a warehouse, also filled with barrels: among them stood Lesueur with a pen and a book in his hand and an inkhorn in his buttonhole.

'You have been a very long time, Mr Wray,' he said. 'It is a wonder the candles had not gone out.'

'Yes. I was talking to a man I met in the church.'

'So I am told. And what did you have to say to Dr Maturin?'

'We were talking about plainchant. Why do you ask?'

'You know he is an agent?'

'Working for whom?'

'For you, of course. For the Admiralty.'

'I have heard of his being consulted: I know that reports have been submitted to him because of his knowledge of the political position in Catalonia, and that he has advised the Admiral's secretary on Spanish affairs. But as for his being an agent . . . no, I should certainly never think of him as an agent. His name does not appear in the list of orders for payment.'

'You do not know that he is the man who killed Dubreuil and Pontet-Canet in Boston and who almost wiped out Joliot's organization through false information planted in the ministry of war – the man who ruined our cooperation with the Americans?'

'Not I, by God,' cried Wray.

'Then it is clear that Sir Blaine has not been open with you. It may be his native cunning or it may be that someone, somewhere, has smelt a rat: you must look to your lines of communication, my friend.'

'I have the lists of payments almost by heart,' said Wray, 'and I can absolutely assert that Maturin's name is not on any of them.'

'I am sure you are right,' said Lesueur. 'He is an idealist, like you, and that is what makes him so dangerous. However, it is just as well that you did not know; you would never have been able to talk to him so naturally. If any rats have been smelt, and if he knows about it, he is likely to dismiss them. Have you spoken to him about your mission?'

'I made a general reference to it, and desired him to attend the meeting when the Commander-in-Chief arrives.'

'Very good. But you would be well advised to keep your distance: treat him as a political consultant, an expert witness, no more. Apart from the ordinary surveillance, I have an agent working on him. He certainly has a private network of informants, some of them in France, and the name of even one might lead us to the rest and so to Paris . . . But he is a difficult, coriaceous animal and if this agent does not succeed quite soon, success is improbable, and I shall have to ask you to find some plausible manner of putting him out of the way, without compromising my position here.'

'I see,' said Wray. He considered for a while and then observed, 'That can be arranged. If nothing else offers before, the Dey of Mascara will certainly deal with the situation. Indeed,' he added after a moment's reflection, 'I believe the Dey can be used to the greatest advantage. He can be used to kill two birds with one stone, as we say.'

Lesueur looked at him thoughtfully, and after a pause said, 'Pray count the barrels on your side of the pillar. I cannot see them all from here.'

'Twenty-eight,' said Wray.

'Thank you.' Lesueur noted it down in his book. 'I get seven francs fifty back on each, which is appreciable.'

While he multiplied these figures to his own satisfaction Wray was visibly formulating his next words. When they came they had the awkward lack of spontaneity of a prepared speech and something more of righteous indignation than the occasion warranted. 'You spoke of my being an idealist just now,' he said, 'and so I am. No sum could purchase my support: no sum did purchase my support. But I cannot live on ideals alone. Until my wife inherits I have only a very limited income, and while I am here I am forced to keep up my position. Sir Hildebrand and all those who can make a good thing out of the dockyard and the victualling play for very high stakes, and I am obliged to follow suit.'

'You drew a large addition to your usual . . . grant-in-aid before leaving London,' said Lesueur. 'You cannot expect the rue Villars to pay your gambling debts.'

'I certainly can when they are incurred for a reason of this kind,' said Wray.

'I will put it to my chief,' said Lesueur, 'but I can promise nothing. Yet surely,' he said with a burst of impatience, 'surely you can win these men's confidence without playing high? It seems to me very poor practice.'

'With these men it is essential,' said Wray doggedly.

Chapter Three

The sharper distress of Jack Aubrey's meeting with Admiral Hartley was softened by a sudden spate of mental and physical activity. The Admiralty court sat on the French vessel he had captured in the Ionian Sea and condemned it as lawful prize; and in spite of the proctors' swingeing fees this provided him with a comfortable sum of money – nothing like the fortune required to deal with his horribly complicated affairs at home, but quite enough to remit ten years' pay to Sophie, begging her not to stint, and to justify him in moving to rather more creditable quarters at Searle's. And, the proper channels having made themselves apparent at this juncture, to lay out the necessary bribes to get work started on the *Surprise*. But a deep sadness remained, not easily driven away by company or even by music; a sadness accompanied by a determination to live hearty while yet he could.

When Laura Fielding came to give him his Italian lesson in these more comfortable rooms, therefore, she found him in a startlingly enterprising mood, despite a heavy day at the dockyard and a great deal of concern about his frigate's knees. Since Jack Aubrey had never deliberately and with malice aforethought seduced any woman in his life, his was not a regular siege of her heart, with formal lines of approach, saps and covered ways; his only strategy (if anything so wholly instinctive and unpremeditated deserved such a name) was to smile very much, to be as agreeable as he could, and to move his chair closer and closer.

Very early in their recapitulation of the imperfect subjunctive of the irregular verb *stare* Mrs Fielding saw with alarm that her pupil's conduct was likely to grow even more irregular than her verb. She was aware of his motions rather before they were quite clear in his own mind, for she had been brought up in the free and easy atmosphere of the Neapolitan court, and she had been accustomed to gallantry from a very early age; ancient counsellors, beardless pages, and a large variety of gentlemen in between had attacked her virtue, and although she had repulsed the great majority it was a subject that interested her – she could detect the earliest symptoms of an amorous inclination, and upon the whole she found they did not differ very much, from man to man. But none of her former suitors had been so massive as this, none had had so bright and formidable an eye, and although some had sighed none had ever chuckled in this disturbing way. The poor lady, worried by her lack of progress with Dr Maturin and vexed by the rumours of her misconduct with Captain Aubrey, was in no mood for fooling: she very much regretted the absence of her maid, since Ponto, her usual guardian, was of no use whatsoever in these circumstances. He sat there, smiling at them and beating the ground with his tail every time Captain Aubrey moved his chair a little nearer.

They dismissed the imperfect subjunctive with perfect indifference on either side, and Jack, his imagination now somewhat heated, was speaking of the gossip that concerned them. In spite of her imperfect knowledge of English and his want of perfect coherence she caught the general drift of his remarks and before he could reach the point of expressing his earnest desire that these rumours should be given a solid foundation – his view that natural justice required such a course, since they had suffered innocently – she cut him short. 'Oh, Captain Aubrey,' cried she, 'I have a service to beg of you.'

Mrs Fielding had but to command, said Jack, smiling at her with great affection; he was at her orders entirely – very happy – delighted – could not be more so.

'Why then,' she said, 'you know I am a little talkative – the dear Doctor has often said so, desiring me to peep down – but alas I am not at all writative, at least not in English. English spelling! Corpo di Baccho, English spelling! Now if I give you a dictation and you write it down in good English, I can use the words when I write to my husband.'

'Very well,' said Jack, his smile fading.

It was just as he had feared: and he must have been quite mistaken about the signals. Mr Fielding was to understand that the excellent Captain Aubrey had saved Ponto from being drowned: Ponto now doted upon Captain Aubrey and ran up to him in the street. Wicked people therefore said that Captain Aubrey was Laura's lover. Should these rumours reach Mr Fielding he was to pay no attention. On the contrary. Captain Aubrey was an honourable man, who would scorn to insult a brother-officer's wife with dishonest proposals; indeed she had such confidence in his perfect rectitude that she could visit him without even the protection of a maid. Captain Aubrey knew very well that she would not ply the oar.

'Ply the oar, ma'am?' said Jack, looking up from his paper, his pen poised.

'Is it not right? I was so proud of it.'

'Oh yes,' said Jack. 'Only the word is spelt rather odd, you know,' and he wrote *she would not play the whore* very carefully, so that the letters could not be mistaken, smiling secretly as he did so, his frustration and disappointment entirely overcome by his sense of the ridiculous.

They parted on excellent terms, and she gave him a particularly friendly look as she said, 'You will not forget my party, will you? I have Count Muratori coming, with his lovely flute.'

'Nothing shall keep me away,' said Jack, 'short of the loss of both legs. And even then there is always a stretcher.'

'And you will remember it to the Doctor?' she said.

'He will remember it to himself, I am sure,' said Jack, holding the door open for her. 'And if he don't . . . but there he is,' he said, cocking his ear to the stairs. 'He often comes up more like a herd of mad sheep than a Christian, when he is in a hurry.'

Dr Maturin it was, and his face, ordinarily pale, grave, and withdrawn, shone pink with haste and happiness. 'Why, you are all wet,' they both cried; and indeed a little pool was fast gathering at his feet as he stood there before them. Jack was on the point of asking 'Did you fall in?', but he did not like to expose his friend, since the answer must necessarily be yes: Dr Maturin was wonderfully unhandy at sea, and very often, in clambering from boat to ship or even in stepping from a solid, stone-built quay into a motionless dghaisa, a local craft expressly designed for the safe, dry transport of landlubbers, he would contrive to miss his footing and plunge into the sea – so much so that his smallclothes and the skirts of his coat ordinary showed whitish tidemarks, where the salt had dried.

Laura Fielding had no such inhibitions however and her 'Did you fall in?' came out as naturally as the day.

'Your most devoted, ma'am,' said Stephen, absent-mindedly kissing her hand. 'Jack, give me joy. The *Dromedary* is come in!'

'What of it?' said Jack, who had seen the slab-sided transport beating up, tack upon tack, since early dawn.

'She has my diving-bell aboard!'

'What diving-bell?'

'My long-awaited Halley's diving-bell. I had almost lost hope of it, so I had. It has a window in the top! I am with child to plunge. You must come and see it at once – I have a dghaisa at the waterside.'

'Gentlemen, good day,' said Mrs Fielding, who was not accustomed to being slighted for a diving-bell.

They begged her pardon. They were extremely sorry: they had meant no disrespect, and Stephen handed her down the stairs with Jack and Ponto following solemnly. 'It is Halley's model, you know,' said Stephen as the long, lean dghaisa shoved off and began to skim across the Grand Harbour towards the *Dromedary*, urged by the promise of double fare. 'How briskly these worthy creatures do propel the bark, to be sure; and have you noticed that they stand up to do so, that they face the direction they are going, like the gondoliers of Venice? Surely this is a laudable practice that should be introduced into the Navy.'

Stephen often put forward ideas for the improvement of the service. In his time he had advocated the serving out of a modest allowance of soap, the cutting of the monstrous rum-ration, the provision of free, warm, serviceable uniform clothes for the lower deck, particularly for the ship's boys and new hands, and the abolition of such punishments as flogging round the fleet: these proposals had met with little more success than his present suggestion that in defiance of all tradition the Navy should look where it was going – Jack swept straight past it, saying eagerly, 'Halley? Comet Halley, the Astronomer Royal?'

'Just so.'

'I knew he commanded the *Paramour* pink, when he was working on the southern stars and the Atlantic chart,' said Jack, 'and I have an amazing respect for him, of course. Such an observer! Such a calculator! But I had no idea he was concerned with diving-bells.'

'Yes I told you of his paper, the *Art of Living Under Water*, in the Philosophical Transactions, and you commended my desire to walk upon the bottom of the sea. You said it would be a better way of finding lost anchors and cables than creeping for them with a grapnel.'

'I remember it perfectly. But you did not mention Dr Halley's name, and you spoke of some kind of a helmet with tubes, no more.'

'I certainly mentioned Dr Halley's name, so I did, and I treated the bell at some length; but you did not attend. You were playing cricket at the time: you were watching out, and I came and stood by you.'

'That was on another occasion, when we were playing the gentlemen of Hampshire: I had to desire Babbington to lead you away. I have never been able to make you understand how seriously we take the game in England. However, pray tell me again. What is the principle of the bell?'

'It is beautiful in its simplicity! Imagine a truncated cone, open at the bottom, furnished with a stout glass window at the top, and so weighted that on being lowered into the sea it sinks perpendicularly – a commodious bell whose occupant sits at his ease upon a bench diametrically placed a little above the lower rim, enjoying the light that shines upon him from the glass above, and revelling in the wonders of the deep. You will object that as the bell sinks, the air within becomes compressed and the water rises proportionably,' said Stephen, holding up his hand, 'and in ordinary circumstances this is profoundly true, so that at thirty-three feet the bell would be half full. But you are also to imagine a barrel, similarly weighted and provided with a hole at the bottom and another at the top. The top hole has a leathern hose fitted to it, an air-tight, water-tight leathern hose, well dressed with oil and beeswax, while the bottom hole is open, to let the sea in as the barrel sinks.'

'What is the good of that?'

'Why, do you not see? It replenishes the bell with air.'

'Not at all. The air has rushed out by way of your leathern hose.'

The remark struck Stephen dumb. He opened his mouth, then closed it; and for some minutes, as the slim boat ran fast through the ships and small craft in the Grand Harbour, with the noble mass of the Three Cities ahead and Valletta astern, the air itself blue from the high and brilliant sky, he puzzled over the problem. Then his face cleared; the delight came back, and he cried, 'Why, of course, of course: what a brute-beast I am! I had quite forgot to say that the leathern hose is kept below the lower bung-hole by an appended weight. It is kept down during the barrel's descent – that is of the essence – and the man inside the bell grasps it, pulls it in, and raises it. As soon as he has raised it above the surface of the water in the barrel, the confined air rushes into the bell with great force, refreshing him and repelling the sea in the lower part of the machine. He then gives a signal, and as the first barrel is hauled up, so another comes down. Dr Halley says – and these, Jack, are his very words – "an alternate succession furnished air so quick, and in so great plenty, that I have myself been one of five who have been together at the bottom, in nine or ten fathom water, for above an hour and a half at a time, without any ill effects."'

'Five people!' cried Jack. 'God love me, it must be a most enormous affair. Pray what are its dimensions?'

'Oh,' said Stephen, 'mine is only a modest bell, a small little bell indeed. I doubt you could get into it.'

'What does it weigh?'

'Sure, I forget the exact figure; but very little at all – only just enough to make it sink, and sink slowly at that. Will you look at that bird, almost directly ahead, at some thirty-five degrees of elevation? I believe it to be a hangi. They are said to be peculiar to this island.'

It was clear that the *Dromedary*'s people were already used to Dr Maturin: they lowered a quarter-ladder as soon as the dghaisa came alongside, and when he came labouring up it two powerful seamen took him by the arms and lifted him bodily over the rail. They also seemed quite attached to him, for in spite of their more urgent official tasks they had already cleared away his bell and its appurtenances, and the transport's master, accompanied by several of the crew, all smiling, led the visitors forward to see it. 'There she lays,' said the master, nodding at the main hatchway, 'all ready to be hoisted out. You will see, sir, that I have followed Dr Halley's instructions to the letter: there is the sprit, stayed to the masthead, and there are the braces, to carry her with-out-board and within, according; and Joe here has given the brass a rub, so she will not look paltry.'

She looked very far indeed from paltry. The broad brass ring surrounding the bell's glass top was over a yard across, and it gazed up at them like the eye of an enormous expectant cheerful simple-minded god: Jack returned its gaze with a sinking heart.

'It seems quite large, in that confined space,' said Stephen. 'But that is an optical illusion. When it is pulled up you will see that it is remarkably small.'

'Three foot six across the top, five foot across the bottom, eight foot deep,' said the master with great satisfaction. 'Holds nigh on sixty cubic foot, and weighs thirty-nine hundredweight odd pounds.'

Jack had meant to take his friend aside and tell him privately that it would not do; that the machine would be obliged to be set ashore or sent home; that Jack was tolerably fly, not having been born yesterday, and was not to be taken in by a fait accompli; but these very shocking figures so startled him that he cried 'God help us! Five foot across – eight foot high – close on two ton! How can you ever have supposed that room could be attempted to be made for such a monstrous thing on the deck of a frigate?' All around him the smiling faces turned grave and closed and he was aware of a strong current of moral disapproval: the Dromedaries were obviously on Stephen's side.

'To tell the truth,' said Stephen, 'I engaged for it when you had the *Worcester*.'

'But even in a seventy-four, where could it conceivably go?'

Stephen had thought that it might prove an acceptable ornament upon the poop, where it would be ready to be launched, or rather *roused*, over the side whenever the ship was not actively engaged.

'The poop, the poop . . .' began Jack; but this was no time for a description of the horrid effects of a wind-resistant two tons perched so far aft and so high above the centre of gravity, and he went on, 'But there is no question of a ship of the line: we are speaking of a frigate, and a small frigate at that; and perhaps I may be permitted to observe, that no frigate yet built has ever had a poop.'

'Why, that being so,' said Stephen, 'what do you say to the convenient little space between the foremast and the front rail?'

'Two tons right over her forefoot, pressing on her narrow entry? It would make an angel gripe: it would cut two knots off her rate of sailing on a bowline. Besides, there is the mainstay, you know, and the downhauls; and how should I ever win my anchors? No, no, Doctor, I am sorry to say it will never do. I regret it; but had you spoken of it earlier, I should have advised against it directly; I should have told you at once that it would never do in a man-of-war, except perhaps in a first-rate, that might just find room for it on the skids.'

'It is Dr Halley's model,' said Stephen in a low voice.

'But on the other hand,' said Jack with an unconvincing cheerfulness, 'think what a boon it would be to a shore establishment! Lost cables, hawsers, anchors . . . and I am sure the port-admiral would lend you a broad-bottomed scow from time to time, to look at the bottom with.'

'For my part I shall always acknowledge a great debt to Dr Halley, whenever I take the altitude of a star,' said the master of the *Dromedary*.

'All mariners must be grateful to Dr Halley,' said his mate; and this seemed to be the general opinion aboard.

'Well, sir,' said the master, turning to Stephen with a most compassionate air, 'what am I to do with your poor bell – with poor Dr Halley's bell? Set it ashore as it stands, or take it to pieces and strike it down into the hold until you have considered in your mind? One or the other I must do to clear my hatchway, and double-quick, do you see, for the lighters will be putting off the moment the Clerk of the Cheque reaches Admiralty Creek. There he is, just by *Edinburgh* over there, nattering with her skipper.'

'Pray take it to pieces, Captain, if that should not be too laborious,' said Stephen. 'I have *some* friends in Malta upon whose attachment I believe I can rely.'

'No trouble at all, sir. A dozen bolts, and Bob's your uncle, if you will excuse the expression.'

'If it takes to pieces,' said Jack, 'the case is altered. If it takes to pieces it may come aboard and travel below, being put together on suitable occasions – during dead calms, or in port, or when the ship is lying to. I shall send my barge at once.'

'It is an odd thing,' he reflected as their dghaisa skimmed towards the dockyard, 'but if I had been standing on my own quarterdeck they would never have presumed to prate about Dr Halley. I felt like Julian the Apostate in the midst of a bench of bishops – should have dismissed it out of hand aboard my own ship – authority very much a matter of place – meek in my father's house – most people are, I dare say.' Yet his own daughters were not outstandingly meek: he thought of their shrill bawling 'Oh Papa, Papa, do come on, Papa. We shall never get up the hill at this rate. Pray, Papa, do not be such a slug.' Early it would have been 'goddam slug', they having caught a free way of speaking from the seamen who formed part of the household, but since the last voyage or two Sophie had taken the matter in hand, and now girlish cries of 'infernal swab' or 'short-arsed cullion' were to be heard only in the remoter parts of Ashgrove wood.

'I wonder what Graham will give us,' said Stephen, speaking suddenly from the silence.

'Something good, I am sure,' said Jack, smiling. Professor Graham was known to be careful of his pennies, but those who called him parsimonious illiberal avaricious niggardly penurious near close or mean were mistaken, and when he gave a feast – in this case a farewell dinner to his former shipmates of the *Worcester* and the *Surprise* and to some friends and relations in the Highland regiments – he did so very handsomely indeed.

'It will be strange if you do not get a spotted dog. He particularly asked me to tell him your favourite dishes.'

'I shall look forward to that' – his voice rose effortlessly to an enormous volume as he called out 'Come athwart my hawse and I shall ride you down, you half-baked son of an Egyptian fart,' to a wool-gathering jolly-boat; and *art* echoed from either shore. 'But now I come to think of it,' he went on, 'I have a mind to pull over to the *Edinburgh* and borrow Dundas's launch. It is remarkably beamy, much more suitable than our barge and since he is lying in ten fathom water, much more suitable than *Surprise*'s fetid puddle, I make no doubt he will clap a tackle on to your bell and give you a dip: though it might be as well to let a ship's boy or a midshipman go down first to make sure it works.'

*   *   *

'Professor Graham, sir, a good evening to you,' said Dr Maturin, walking into his colleague's room. 'I am come from walking on the bottom of the sea.'

'Aye,' said Graham, looking up from his papers. 'So I understand. They were watching you from the Baracca with perspective glasses, bubbling away in your inverted cauldron: Colonel Veale laid two and a half to one you would never come up again.'

'I trust with all my heart he lost, the inhuman wretch.'

'Of course he did, since you are here,' said Graham impatiently. 'But you are being facetious again, no doubt. The bottom of the sea must have been a sad stinking muddy place, to judge from your shoes and stockings.'

'So it was too, a great stretch of yellowish-grey mud rippling away in that wonderfully strange light; but the annelids, my dear Graham, the annelids! Hundreds, nay thousands of annelids of at least six and thirty several kinds, some plumed and others plain. And wait until I tell you about my holothurians, my sea-slugs, my sea-cucumbers . . .'

'Cucumbers, aye,' said Graham, making a note; and at the first real pause he said, 'Just cast a wee glippet on this listie, and give me the benefit of your lights. I have settled the dinner pretty nearly to my satisfaction, but not the seating of my guests; as well as the sea-officers, with their own hierarchy, there are some Highland gentlemen coming, belonging to various clans, and I must take notice both of precedence within the clan and the precedence of the clans themselves, or there will be wigs on the green. Can you imagine a McWhirter giving place to any MacAlpine? For in an informal gathering of this kind mere army rank does not apply with us; though to be sure the officers of the Forty-Second are very unwilling to yield to those of any other Scotch regiment whatsoever.'

'You must number the chairs and let each man draw his number from a hat. You may pass this off with a graceful witty remark.'

'A graceful witty remark? Heuch. I wish it were all over.'

'Sure, you will like your dinner once you are well set to

it,' said Stephen, looking at the bill of fare. 'What are bashed neeps?'

'Neeps hackit with balmagowry. It is not so much the dinner that I wish to be over and done with . . . no. It is the whole of it. I shall be glad to get home, to the quiet of my study and my lectures. I shall miss your company, Maturin, but apart from that I shall be glad to leave: I do not like the smell of Malta. From the point of view of intelligence, you understand. There are too many people at work and too many of them are poor loose-tongued clacking bodies. There are schemes for the Barbary Coast that I do not like at all; and when you consider Mehemet Ali's real sentiments with regard to the Sublime Porte, this Red Sea business seems but a dubious undertaking. There are many things I do not like at all.' He paused, looking steadily at Maturin. 'Did you ever hear tell of a man named Lesueur, André Lesueur?' he asked.

Stephen considered. 'I connect the name with intelligence: with Thévenot's organization. But I know nothing about him and I have never seen him.'

'I saw him in Paris during the peace; one of our agents pointed him out. And I am almost certain I recognized him in the Strada Reale today, walking about as though he were at home, while you were in your boatie. I turned as discreetly as I could and tried to follow him, but the crowd was too thick.'

'What is he like?'

'A small pale man, narrow-shouldered, rather bowed, gloomy, black coat with cloth buttons, buff breeches: forty-five or thereabouts: the appearance of a man of business or a not inconsiderable merchant. Since you were not in the way and since I have my doubts about the discretion of the secretariat, I went straight to Mr Wray.'

'Ah? And what did he say?'

'He listened very attentively – he is a far more intelligent man than I had supposed – and he desired me to mention it to no one else. He is gathering all his threads to make a single, decisive coup de filet.'

'I wish he may succeed. I have the impression that the French are as well installed here in Malta as we were in Toulon in 1803: no movement of ships or troops or munitions but we knew within four and twenty hours.'

'I wish he may. But that will not do away with the rivalry between soldiers and sailors on the island, the divided counsels, the loose talk, and the perpetual coming and going of foreigners and discontented natives. Nor with the perhaps untimely zeal of the new Commander-in-Chief and his followers.'

'Maybe we shall know more of that, more of the whole situation, when he holds his conference. As no doubt you are aware, he has been signalled to the west of Gozo, and a change of wind might bring him in tomorrow or the next day.'

'I doubt it will tell us much. A meeting of this kind, with Sir Hildebrand and his soldiers present and with several of the members seeing one another for the first time, is not likely to produce anything but platitudes. Who is going to pour out his heart on confidential matters before strangers, whatever their credentials? I am very sure Mr Wray will confine himself to generalities; and I shall say nothing whatsoever. I should say nothing even if it were not for the presence of that long-eared looby Figgins Pocock.'

Stephen was aware that Mr Pocock, a distinguished orientalist who accompanied Admiral Sir Francis Ives as adviser on Turkish and Arabic affairs, had disagreed with Professor Graham over an edition of Abulfeda, that each had written pamphlets, attaining a rare degree of personal abuse, and that this might colour Graham's view of the Commander-in-Chief's eastern policies; but even so he felt inclined to agree when Graham said, 'The atmosphere in Valletta is most unhealthy: even if Mr Wray deals with the immediate situation, it is likely to remain most unhealthy, with divided authority at the top, ill will and rivalry at all levels, and fools in charge; and since as I understand it you are to remain a while, might you not do well to keep your distance, and mind your physic, your natural philosophy, and your bell?'

'I might indeed,' said Stephen, staring at his feet. 'But for the moment I must mind my shoes and stockings. I am bid to an elegant soirée, to Mrs Fielding's concert-party, and must go without further loss of time; yet I perceive that in drying they emit a most offensive smell. Do you think that by rubbing I might get them clean?'

'I doubt it,' said Graham, inspecting them more closely. 'There is an unctuous quality about the undried parts that precludes any such measure.'

'My coat I can shift, and even my shirt and stockings,' said Stephen. 'But these are my only good shoes.'

'You ought to have put on an old pair, if you wished to go a-diving,' said Professor Graham, who had not studied moral philosophy in vain. 'Or even half-boots. I should not be altogether unwilling to *lend* you a pair, although they have silver buckles; but they must necessarily be too big.'

'That is of no importance,' said Stephen. 'They can be stuffed with handkerchiefs, paper, lint. So long as the heels and toes press against a firm but yielding support the external dimensions of the shoe do not signify.'

'They were my grandsire's,' said Professor Graham, taking them from a cloth bag, 'and at that time it was usual for men to add a couple of inches to their stature by the means of cork heels.'

Stephen's 'cello, though bulky in its padded, sea-going sailcloth case, was not a heavy instrument, nor had he any shyness about carrying it through the public streets. It was not weight or embarrassment that made him pause and gasp and sit down on steps so often, but mere agony. His theory on the size of shoes was mistaken and it had proved to be so within a very short space of time, the evening being uncommonly warm, while his only clean, wearable stockings were made not of silk but of lamb's wool. His feet, already cramped by the unnatural heels, swelled in the course of the first two hundred yards, and began to chafe, blister, and grow raw even before he reached the crowded, cheerful Strada Vescovo. His staggering progress gave the impression that he was drunk, and a little group of whores and street boys kept him company, hoping eventually to profit from this state of affairs.

'Calor, rubor, dolor,' he said, sitting down again at a street corner under the gently-lit image of St Rocco. 'This cannot go on. Yet if I take off my shoes, I cannot carry them and the 'cello too: on the other hand any of these wicked boys might run off with them, and then what should I say to Graham? Again, I am unwilling to trust the instrument to their careless hands: the bag must be nursed in both arms, like a tender, ailing child. If only there were a good-humoured girl among these trumpery queans . . . but they seem a hard-faced set entirely. I am on the horns of a dilemma.' Yet even as he defined the horns, so they collapsed. A band of the *Surprise*'s liberty men, rounding St Rocco's corner, came plump upon him.

They made no bones at all about carrying his shoes, and one of them, a dark, sinister forecastle hand who had almost certainly been a pirate in his youth, said he would carry the big fiddle, and would like to see the sod that offered to laugh, or call for a tune.

The Surprises were not as who should say drunk, or even merry by naval standards, but they did stagger and trip over things and stop to laugh or argue from time to time, and when at last they left him at Laura Fielding's outer door it was late – so late that as he hobbled along the passage he heard Jack Aubrey's violin in the unseen courtyard, answered by a soft, complaining flute. 'The next time I shall leave my 'cello in the dear creature's house,' he said as he waited there outside the door for the music to come to an end: and then, cocking his ear to the flute's most distinctive voice, 'That must be a flauto d'amore: I have not heard one in a great while now.'

The movement closed with a conventional flourish. Stephen glided through the door, bent low in deprecation, and sat on a cool stone bench just inside the courtyard with his 'cello beside him. Laura Fielding, at the pianoforte, gave him a very welcoming smile, Captain Aubrey a stern look, and Count Muratori, now raising his flute to his lips again, a singularly vacant stare. Most of the other people were hidden from him by the lemon-tree.

The music was of no great importance but once he had slipped off his shoes it was pleasant sitting there with the sound weaving decorative patterns in the warm, gently stirring air: the lemon-tree was giving out its well-remembered scent – strong, but not excessive – and on the side farthest from the lanterns, the darkest corner of the court, there was a troop of fireflies. They too weaved decorative patterns and with a certain effort of the imagination, a little elimination of unnecessary notes and unnecessary flies, the two could be made to coincide.

Ponto came pacing across, smelt Stephen in an offensively censorious way, avoided his caress, and walked off again, flinging himself down among the fireflies with a disgusted sigh. Presently he began to lick his private parts with so strong a lushing sound that it quite overlaid a pianissimo passage for the flute and Stephen lost the thread of the argument, such as it was. His mind drifted away to fireflies he had known, to American fireflies and to an account a Boston entomologist had given him of their ways. According to this gentleman the different species emitted different signals to show their willingness for sexual congress: this was natural enough – indeed, a laudable practice – but what seemed less so was the fact that certain females of say species A, moved not by any amorous warmth but by mere voracity, would imitate the signals of species B, whose males, all unsuspecting, would descend, not to a glowing nuptial couch but to a dismal butcher's block.

The music ended, to a civil patter of applause. Mrs Fielding sprang up from her piano and met him as he advanced to make his excuses. 'Oh, oh,' she cried, glancing down at his stockinged feet. 'You have forgot your shoes.'

'Mrs Fielding, joy,' he said, 'I shall never forget them while I live, they have killed me so cruelly. But I thought we were old enough friends not to stand upon the strictest letter of etiquette.'

'Of course we are,' she said, squeezing his arm affectionately. 'I should certainly take off my shoes in your house, was they hurting. You know everybody? Count Muratori, Colonel O'Hara? Of course you do. Come and drink a glass of cold punch. Bring your shoes, and I will put them in my bedroom.' She led him into the house and there indeed Stephen saw that a punch-bowl had taken the place of the traditional pitchers of lemonade: nor did innovations end here, for the Naples biscuits had given way to anchovies and little daubs of fiery paste on bread. Furthermore, Mrs Fielding had spent some hours under the hands of a hair-dresser; and in front of a well-lit looking-glass she had done her best to improve her already very fine complexion. Stephen, his mind directed downwards to his feet and for-wards to the indifferently-rehearsed sonata that he was to play, was not distinctly aware of this, but he did notice that she had a scent upon her and that she was wearing a flame-coloured dress, remarkably low-cut. He disapproved of it. Many men were strongly moved by a pretty bosom, partly bare – Jack Aubrey had been bowled over many a time – and he thought it cruelly unfair in a woman to excite desires that she had no intention of satisfying. He dis-approved of the punch, too: it was far, far too strong. And when he bit into the red paste it made him gasp again. Beneath all the fire there was a taste not unfamiliar but unnamable within some minutes' recollection, and that was impossible, seeing that in common decency he was obliged to congratulate Mrs Fielding on her brew, assure her that the fiery things were ambrosia, eating another to prove it, and to exchange civilities with the other guests. And it seemed to him that the atmosphere of the party was not what it usually was, which saddened him: there was not the same easy gaiety, conceivably because Laura Fielding was trying too hard – she seemed to be on edge – and conceivably because at least some of the men were minding her person more than their music. But when Jack Aubrey came up to him and said, 'There you are, Stephen. There you are at last. How did your diving go?' his cheerfulness returned with the recollection of that glorious afternoon and he said,

'Upon my soul, Jack, it is the bell of the world! As soon as his launch brought it alongside the *Edinburgh*, Captain Dundas, that worthy, deserving man, called down did I choose to make a descent directly, because if so he was my man: he would be' – lowering his voice '– *damned* if he let me go down alone; and . . .'

'Dear Doctor, am I interrupting you?' asked Laura Fielding, handing him his score.

'Not at all, at all, ma'am,' said Stephen. 'I was only telling Captain Aubrey about my diving-bell, my new diving-bell.'

'Oh yes, yes! Your diving-bell,' she said. 'How I long to hear about it. Let us hurry through our music and you will tell me about it in peace. Pearls, mermaiden, sirens . . .'

Their piece was a Contarini 'cello sonata with no more than a figured bass and hitherto Laura Fielding had always played her part beautifully; harmony came to her as naturally as breathing, and the music flowed from her like water from a spring. But this time they had hardly travelled ten bars together before she produced a chord so false that Stephen winced, Jack, Muratori and Colonel O'Hara raised their eyebrows and pursed their lips, and an aged Commendatore said 'Tut, tut, tut,' quite loud.

After the first trip she concentrated hard – Stephen could see her pretty head bent over the keyboard, her grave, concentrated expression, her lower lip caught between her teeth – but studious application did not suit her style at all and she played indifferently until the end of the movement, sometimes throwing him off balance, sometimes sounding a most unfortunate note. 'I am so sorry,' she said. 'I will try to do better now.'

Alas for the word. The adagio called for subtle phrasing, and it called in vain: she cast him several apologetic looks until a particularly wild aberration made him pause, his bow in the air, when she laid her hands in her lap and said, 'Shall we go back to the beginning?' 'By all means,' said Stephen. But it was not a successful experiment: between them they slowly murdered poor Contarini, Maturin now playing as badly as his partner, and when his A string broke with a

71

solemn twang two thirds of the way through the adagio there was a general feeling of relief.

After this Colonel O'Hara played some modern pieces on the pianoforte with great fire and dash; but the evening never really recovered from the blow.

'Mrs Fielding is not in spirits,' observed Stephen, standing by the lemon-tree with Jack Aubrey. 'Not in real spirits, that is to say,' he added, since she could be seen talking and laughing at a great rate.

'No,' said Jack. 'She is grieving about her husband, no doubt. She mentioned him earlier in the day.' He was looking at her through the leaves with great good will and commiseration: he always esteemed women who refused him kindly, and Laura Fielding, though somewhat harassed, was unusually fine this evening in her flame-coloured dress.

'It is my belief she would welcome the sight of our backs,' said Stephen. 'As soon as it is decent, I shall make my adieus: perhaps indeed I may take up my shoes – Graham's shoes – even now, ask may I leave my 'cello, and slip away unseen.' His last words were covered by the laughter of a group of men the other side of the tree and by the approach of Captain Wagstaff, who hailed Jack in a rather loud, familiar voice, asking him 'if he had ate many of these fiery red things?' Stephen padded away into the house, where he found Mrs Fielding carefully filling glasses with punch from a kitchen jug. Her expression changed to one of the fondest welcome; she said, 'Be a tesoro and help me with the tray,' and then coming close she whispered in his ear, 'I am trying to get rid of them, but they will not go. Tell them it is a good-night hat. Cap, I mean.'

'I was just about to take my leave,' he said.

'Oh no,' she said, amused. '*You* are not to go now. Oh no, *you* are to stay. I must consult you. Have a glass of punch and eat one of the marzipane; I have kept them for you.'

'To tell you the truth, my dear, I believe I have eaten all I can for one day.'

'Just half, and I will eat it with you.'

They carried out the trays, he the larger one with the glasses and she another on which he recognized his old friends the Naples biscuits. As they made their round Mrs Fielding made pretty speeches, thanking her guests for having come and for having played so charmingly; yet still they would not go away, but stood there, laughing unusually loud and talking with an unusual freedom. If, earlier in the evening, she had behaved with a certain wantonness – perhaps artificial wantonness – she regretted it now; but present formality and reserve did not do away with the effect. Liberty tended to give way to licence; and Wagstaff, looking from Jack to Stephen, said, 'Upon my word, Doctor, you are in luck; there are men who would give a great deal for your place as butler.'

It was not until she had had a private word with the Commendatore that they began to make their farewells in small, slow groups; and even then Wagstaff stuck interminably in the open door, telling an anecdote that had just occurred to him, an anecdote whose obviously improper dénouement was obliged to be stifled by the companions who led him away at last, still laughing, down the long arched echoing corridor to the street, where an unseen watcher ticked them off on his list.

At last only Aubrey and Maturin were left, Jack lingering to help his friend limp home: he was unusually aware of the fact that he was a man and that Laura Fielding was a woman, but he still regarded her with great benevolence, as one of the angelic kind, until he heard her ask him to shut Ponto into the farther court – 'He hates to go, but he will do anything for you' – and then, as he passed through the outer door, to close it for fear of cats. The dear Doctor was not leaving yet; he was going to indulge her by staying for a while; and this she said with a smile at Stephen, a smile that Jack intercepted and that gave him a blow as sharp and sudden as a pistol-shot. For although he might mistake signals addressed to himself he could scarcely be mistaken about those flying for another man.

He concealed his feelings with a very fair show of

equanimity, returning his best thanks for a most enjoyable evening and hoping that he might have the honour of waiting upon Mrs Fielding again in the very near future; but there was no deceiving Ponto, who fixed nervous, placating eyes on Jack's face and who walked obediently off without a word, his ears drooping, to imprisonment in the cistern court, although he loathed sleeping anywhere but by his mistress's bed.

'For fear of cats, upon my word of honour,' said Jack, pulling the outer door to behind him. 'I should never have believed it of Stephen.'

Stephen himself was standing a little uncertainly among the many glasses and little plates scattered about the court-yard when Laura reappeared, equipped to deal with the disorder. 'I will just make a clean sweep,' she said. 'Go indoors, into my bedroom: I have put some fiamme and a pot of wine.'

'Where is Giovanna?' he asked.

'She does not stay here at night,' said Laura with a smile. 'I shall not be long.'

It was perfectly usual to receive in one's bedroom in France and in most countries that had adopted French manners, and Stephen had been in Mrs Fielding's bedroom before this – in bad weather her parties overflowed into it from her little sitting-room – but never had he seen it look so pleasant. In front of the sofa set cornerwise at the far end stood a low table of gleaming brass with a lamp upon it, a lamp that shed a pool of white light on the floor and a smaller round on the ceiling, while its translucent red shade filled the rest of the room with a rosy glow, particularly agreeable on the bare whitewashed walls. Beyond the sofa nothing could be seen very clearly – the curtained bed loomed vaguely on the left and there were some chairs with boxes on them scattered about – but as he sat down he did notice that a large and hideous picture of Mr Fielding had been removed. He remembered it well: the lieutenant (he was acting first of the *Phoenix* at the time) was shown in striped pantaloons and a round hat, holding a speaking-trumpet in one hand and the broken starboard forebrace in the other as he guided the ship over a reef in a West Indian hurricane; most of it had been painted by a shipmate and Jack asserted that there was not a rope out of the exact position you would expect in such a blow, but the face had been put in by a professional hand. It was a perfectly human face, energetic, sombre, humourless, and it made a shocking contrast with the wooden, theatrical figure. In a woman with so delicate a taste as Mrs Fielding, only a high degree of devotion could have given it house-room. The dish or plate next to the decanter of Marsala on the brass table gave a much more accurate notion of what she liked: a red-figured Greek pinax from Sicily. It was chipped and repaired, but its cheerful nymphs still danced beneath their tree with infinite grace, as they had done these two thousand years or more. 'Yet how does it come about that she put those two reds together?' he asked, looking from the nymphs to the rounds of fiery paste. 'A horrid clash, indeed.'

Then he contemplated his feet for a while, before returning to the paste and its probable ingredients, apart from red pepper. 'What an elusive thing smell can be at times,' he said. 'One may know it intimately well, yet be quite unable to place it.' Again he brought his nose close to the dish, narrowing his eyes as he sniffed, and instantly, to contradict his words, the scent gave up its name: cantharides, more commonly known as Spanish fly, a substance occurring in the wing-cases of a thin iridescent yellowish-green beetle with a powerful smell, familiar to every southern naturalist and used externally for blistering, as a counter-irritant, and sometimes internally, to arouse sexual desire, the most active ingredient of love-philtres.

'Spanish fly is it, poor dear?' he said. And then having considered the implications for a moment he said, 'In all likelihood she got it from Anigoni' – an apothecary notorious for the adulteration of his wares – 'but even so I dread to think of those men roaming Valletta like a herd of hungry bulls. I very distinctly perceive the effects in myself; and no doubt they will presently increase.'

Laura Fielding came in at last. It was not clearing away alone that had kept her, for now she had a blue sash on, making her slim waist look even slimmer, and she had rearranged her hair; but she was obviously nervous as she sat down next to Stephen, much more so than when there had been a courtyard full of guests. She said brightly, 'Why, you have drunk nothing: I will pour you a glass of wine while you finish these' – advancing the pinax with its red rounds.

'A glass of wine with all my heart,' said Stephen, 'but if I may I will eat one of those capital little marchpane cakes with it.'

'I can refuse you nothing,' she said, 'and will fetch them at once.'

'And while you are up, would you pass by the piece of chalk, now?' called Stephen after her – the piece of chalk with which Laura reminded herself of her day's appointments. He too was nervous: what little experience he had had of women in the course of his career had, upon the whole, been discouraging; he knew he must tread very carefully, yet he was by no means sure just how he should direct his steps.

'There,' she said, coming back. 'Marchpane and the piece of chalk.' She took the decanter and said, 'We shall have to share the glass; it is the only clean one left. Do you dislike drinking with me?'

'I do not,' he said, and they sat there without speaking for some minutes, nibbling cakes and silently passing the wine-glass to and fro: a friendly, companionable pause in spite of the tensions on either side. 'Listen,' he said at last, 'was it as a medical man that you wished to consult me?'

'Yes,' she said. 'That is to say no. I will tell you . . . but first let me say how sorry, oh so sorry, I am I played so badly.' In some detail she told him how the first blunder had led to others, how she had begun to have to think, and how fatal thought was to her fingers. 'Is there anything I can do to make you forgive me?' she asked, laying her hand upon his knee and blushing.

'Sure, my dear, I forgive you with all my heart.'

'Then you must give me a kiss.'

He gave her a kiss, a genuinely abstracted peck, for his mind was elsewhere: he knew very well that although he had fortified himself by regarding her as a patient he was near his limit; and what brought him nearer to unchastity was his hatred of behaving like a scrub, for the insult of his apparent indifference was growing more blatant every minute. Nevertheless he reached across and took the piece of chalk, saying, 'Will I tell you about my bell, so?'

'Oh yes!' she cried. 'I am longing to hear about your bell.'

'This, you must understand, is the bell seen sideways,' he said, drawing on the lamplit floor. 'Its height is eight feet; the window at the top is a yard across, as near as no matter; the width here, where the bench runs across, is a little better than four feet six; and the whole contains fifty-nine cubic feet of air!'

'Fifty-nine cubic feet?' said Laura Fielding: she had had a very long, very hard day, and a more attentive ear might have caught a note of despair under the bright, intelligent interest.

'Fifty-nine cubic feet to begin with, of course,' said Stephen, drawing two dwarfish figures on the bench and adding in parenthesis 'There sat the worthy Captain Dundas, and there sat I – elbow-room galore, as you see. But naturally as the bell sank, as it was *lowered away* a couple of fathoms, the water rose, compressing the air, so that we felt a certain pringling in our ears. When it reached the bench we raised our feet, thus' – setting his own on the sofa – 'and plucked the cord, the signal for the barrel.' He drew the barrel with its two bung-holes and its leather hose travelling down guide-lines to the lower edge of the bell, explaining that it was not quite to scale. 'Down it came, the good barrel, compressing its own air as it came, do you see? We seized the hose, and the moment we raised it above the surface – the surface of the water in the barrel, you understand – the compressed air rushed into the bell with inconceivable force and the water sank from the bench to the lower rim! And so the barrels came down one after another and so the dear bell sank, the light growing a little dim, but not too dim to read or write, oh no. We had lead slabs to write on with an iron stylus, which we sent up with a string; and to let out the vitiated air, so that it was always fresh, there was a little cock at the top. Will I draw you my little cock?'

Eventually he brought the bell to the bottom, and making a last effort she said, 'The bottom of the sea, Mother of God: and what did you find there?'

'Worms!' he cried. 'Such worms. Marine worms in great abundance . . . It was there that I made an inconsiderate step into the fetid mud of ages, yet it scarcely disturbed any but the nearest. These were of the plumed kind known as . . .'

At the beginning of his account of the Maltese annelids he noticed that her bosom was heaving. He knew very well that it was not heaving for him but he did not realize that grief was the cause until he reached the bizarre mating habits of Polychaeta rubra, when to his intense embarrassment and distress he saw tears coursing down her cheeks. His exposition faltered; their eyes met; she gave him a painfully artificial smile and then her chin trembled and she broke into passionate weeping at last.

He took her hand, saying meaningless comforting words: for an instant she was on the point of snatching it away but then she clung hard and between her sobs she said, 'Must I go down on my knees? How can you be so hard? Cannot I make you love me?'

He did not answer until she was calmer, and then said, 'Of course you cannot. How can you be so simple, my dear? Surely you must know that these things are reciprocal or they are nothing. It is not possible that you should be enamoured of my person. You may have kindly feelings for me – I hope so, indeed – but as for love or desire or anything of a stronger nature, sure there is not a breath of it in you.'

'Oh but there is, there is! And I will prove it.'

'Listen,' he said firmly, patting her knee with an authoritative hand, 'I am a medical man, and I know for a fact that you are quite unmoved.'

'How can you tell?' she cried, blushing violently.

'Never mind. It is a fact; and I can measure the degree of your indifference by the strength of my own desire. Believe me, believe me, I do most ardently wish to enjoy the last favours, to *possess* you, as people so absurdly say; but not on those terms.'

'Not at all?' she asked, and when he shook his head she wept even more bitterly; but still she clung to his hand as if it were her only anchor. She made no coherent reply when he said, 'It is clear that you wish me to do something of a particular nature. For a woman of your kind to propose such a sacrifice it must be unusually important and certainly most confidential. Will you tell me now what it is?'

All he could gather from her disconnected words was that she could not – she dared not – it was too dangerous – there was nothing to tell.

He was sitting in a somewhat cramped position in the corner of the sofa, with his stockinged foot tucked under him and Mrs Fielding pressed against his side, trembling convulsively from time to time. His crooked knee was cruelly uncomfortable and he longed to reach out for the glass of wine; but he felt that the crisis might well come in the next few minutes and he continued to wonder aloud what the nature of the service might be. His words about medical certificates, supplies, the release of impressed men and so on were meant to provide little more than a comforting thorough-bass or continuo: his mind was much more taken up with gauging his patient's state of mind and body, because quite apart from Jack's remark and the absence of the picture he was almost sure that he had the solution. Her sobbing stopped; she sniffed, breathing easier but by no means quite evenly. 'Would it be to do with your husband, my dear?' he asked.

'Oh yes,' she cried despairingly, and her tears ran fast again. Yes – they had him in prison – they would kill him if she did not succeed – she dared not tell them she had failed – they had been pressing her to move quickly – oh would not dear Dr Maturin be kind to her? – they would kill him otherwise.

'Nonsense,' said Stephen, standing up. 'They will do nothing of the kind. They have been deceiving you. Listen, have you any coffee in the kitchen?'

Over their pot of coffee and rather stale pieces of bread and olive oil the miserable story came out piece by piece: Charles Fielding's unfortunate position – his letters – her collecting of information (nothing wicked: only to do with marine insurance: but confidential) – the sudden much graver mission, on which her husband's life depended – they told her that Dr Maturin had connexions in France with whom he corresponded in code – it was all concerned with finance and perhaps smuggling – she was to win his confidence and obtain the addresses and the codes. Yes, she knew the name of the man who had brought her Charles's last letter: he was Paolo Moroni, a Venetian, and she had seen him from time to time in Valletta – she thought he was a merchant. But she neither knew the names nor the appearance of the other men who spoke to her. They changed: there were perhaps three or four of them. Sometimes she was sent for, and she could get into touch with them by leaving a paper with the time on it at a wine-merchant's house. She was always required to go to St Simon's, to the third confessional on the left, at a stated hour, there to give her information and to receive her letters if there were any; the man in the confessional did not pull back the little door like a priest but spoke through the lattice, so she never saw his face. There was one she did know, however, because she had seen him talking with Moroni, a man who spoke good but not quite perfect Italian with a strong Neapolitan accent. He was often in the confessional. Yes, she thought he knew that she knew him. Certainly she could describe him, but she never would while Charles was in their hands: it might be unlucky. She would never do anything that might do Charles any harm. She was worried about his letters, however; they had been strange these last weeks, as though he were unwell, or unhappy. What did Dr Maturin think? There was nothing private – they had to be sent unsealed – and she did not mind showing them.

Mr Fielding wrote a clear strong hand, and his style was equally straightforward; although his letters were necessarily discreet they gave a sense of powerful, direct, uncomplicated affection; Stephen had not read two before he felt a liking for him. But as Laura had said, the more recent were shorter, and in spite of the fact that they used many of the same phrases and expressions they seemed laboured. Could he be writing against his will, from dictation? Or is it not himself at all? wondered Stephen. If he has died, or if they have killed him, Laura Fielding's life will not be worth a Brummagem groat, once she knows it for a fact. No chief of intelligence could let her run about Malta, knowing what she knows, without he has a very strong hold over her; and a woman is so easy to kill without a hidden motive being suspected, since it can always be coupled with a rape. Aloud he said, 'Clearly, I do not know him as you know him, but a cold or a slight indisposition or a lowness of spirits could answer for all this and more.'

'I am so happy you think so,' she said. 'I am sure you are right: a cold, or a slight indisposition.'

'But attend to me now,' he said after a long pause. 'This Moroni and his friends have been led into the strangest mistake: I have nothing whatever to do with finance or smuggling or insurance by land or sea. I give you my sacred word of honour, I swear by the four Gospels and my hope of salvation that you might have searched my papers for ever without finding a smell of a code or an address in France.'

'Oh,' she said, and he knew that although his words were literally true, she had pierced through to their essential falsity and that she did not believe him.

'But, however,' he went on, 'I believe I know how this mistake has arisen. I have a friend whose occupation brings him into touch with confidential affairs; we have very often been seen together, and these men, or more probably their informants, have confounded us, taking the one for the other. Yet there is something so amiable about a lady's concern for her husband, and he a prisoner, that I am persuaded my friend will furnish us with what is needed to satisfy Moroni. I do not say that it will really be useful to Moroni, but that it will satisfy him in the matter of his own penetration and of your success. It will satisfy him that I am your lover. I will come here when you are alone; you will come to my rooms, perhaps wearing your maid's faldetta; and you will present the documents as the fruit of your labours.'

There was the light of dawn in the little courtyard as he took his leave, but his mind was so busy that he did not notice it; nor did he notice the change in the wind. 'If Wray is the man I think he is, all this may be unnecessary,' he reflected, walking along the dark corridor with Graham's shoes in his hand. 'But if not, or if this is a different, quite unconnected organization, how far can I go without compromising Laura Fielding?' A thousand delightful forms of very damaging false information to be conveyed through her had occurred to him even before he reached the outer door, and as he opened it the tired watcher on the other side of the street saw him smiling in the early light. 'Lucky, lecherous dog,' said the watcher, pulling his hat over his eyes: at the same moment the air shook with the first of the guns saluting the arrival of the Commander-in-Chief, and a thousand pigeons flew up into the pure pale-blue sky.

Chapter Four

Jack Aubrey was not of a vindictive nature and he had so nearly forgiven Stephen his good fortune by breakfast-time that when the people of the hotel told him Dr Maturin could not be roused although a messenger had come to summon him to the Commander-in-Chief's meeting he sprang to his feet and ran up the stairs to put him in mind of his duty. No answer to his knock or hail. 'La, the poor gentleman is dead,' cried the chambermaid. 'He has cut his throat, like number seventeen: I can't bear it: I shall run down. Oh, oh!'

'Give me your pass-key first,' said Jack; and walking through the door he called out, 'Rouse and bitt, out or down, show a leg there,' and when this brought no response he seized the sleeper and shook him hard. Stephen opened his red-rimmed eyes, struggled up through the fog of sleeping-pills and gave his friend a look of pure hatred: Jack had plucked him from a brilliantly vivid dream in which Mrs Fielding felt a flame of equal warmth with his own. He took the wax balls from his ears and said, 'What's o'clock?' in a thick, stupid voice.

'Half past three, and a freezing drizzly night,' said Jack, drawing the curtain, throwing back the shutters and letting in a blaze of sun. 'Come now, this will never do.'

'What's afoot, sir?' asked Bonden in the doorway. He and Killick had arrived in the kitchen as the chambermaid came down with her tale of blood flowing under the door, just like number seventeen all over again and the poor gentleman's head almost off of his body so desperate was the stroke, no doubt, and a mort of scrubbing to be done.

'The Doctor must be at the palace in seven minutes,

washed, shaved, and in his number one uniform,' said Captain Aubrey.

In an angry whine Stephen said that his presence was not necessary, that the meeting, such as it was, would go along perfectly well without him, and that the note from the flagship should be construed not as an order but as a mere invitation, to be accepted or not according to the . . . Jack walked out during these remarks, however, and as neither mercy nor reason was to be expected from Bonden or Killick Dr Maturin said no more until he was installed in a chair in the crowded council-room, very shortly before the arrival of the great man. His face was unusually pink from friction, his uniform and even his shoes were all they should be, and his wig was set rigidly square on his head; but his eyes were still bleary from want of sleep and he gave his neighbour Graham little more than an animal grunt by way of good day. This did not deter Graham for a moment: the words came fairly pouring from him as he hissed in Stephen's ear, 'Do you know what they have done to me? They have ruined my dinner. I must not go on the returning *Dromedary* on Thursday. No, sir. I must go aboard the *Sylph* today at half-past twelve precisely. Ruined, ruined, my dinner is quite ruined, and it is all the doing of that long-eared looby Figgins Pocock. There he sits, the illiterate, ill-deedy gowk, next to the Admiral's secretary. Have you ever seen such a foul fa'd face?'

Stephen had seen fouler fa'd faces by far, and quite often at that; in fact although Mr Pocock had an improbable amount of hair growing from his ears and nose and although his cheeks were a dusty, parched yellow, his looks compared rather well with Mr Graham's. Though far from beautiful, Pocock's was a strong, mature, intelligent face, much more so than that of the Admiral's secretary, a surprisingly young man for such an important appointment: not that Mr Yarrow looked at all stupid, but he gave the impression of being anxious, inexperienced, and harassed. He was now clutching a great sheaf of papers and leaning towards Mr Wray, listening to him with the utmost deference.

The Commander-in-Chief, Sir Francis Ives, came in and the meeting began. As Graham had predicted a great many words were uttered and very little was said; but for some time Stephen looked attentively at Sir Francis: he was a small, compact admiral, rather elderly, but trim and unbowed in his splendid uniform, and he had an immense air of energy and natural authority. Although he belonged to a well-known naval family and had served with great distinction he had not had a sea-going command for some years, and it was said that he intended to run the Mediterranean fleet with such effect that it would earn him a peerage at last: both his brothers were lords, and no effort would be too great to overhaul them. He gazed round on the assembled officers and advisers with his odd hooded eyes as the talk went on, weighing them up but giving nothing away, a man thoroughly used to committees. Mr Wray had the same ability to sit through long meaningless speeches without apparent emotion, but his father-in-law, Rear-Admiral Harte, an officer remarkable only for his wealth – his recently-inherited wealth – and his lack of seamanship, had not. The Rear-Admiral was glaring at Sir Hildebrand as the Governor went on and on, stating that although unauthorized persons might possibly have obtained information, none of the departments under his control could conceivably be held to blame; he had the utmost confidence in his officers, in his secretariat, and in all those concerned with the civil administration.

Having contemplated Sir Francis long enough to see that his wall of reserve was not likely to give way and that he would discuss serious matters only later, in a smaller council, Stephen lost interest in the proceedings and sat there with his head bowed, at times allowing himself to doze and at times sullenly eating pieces broken from the slice of toast that he had darted into his pocket when Bonden was not looking. At intervals he heard gentlemen declare that the war should be prosecuted with the utmost vigour, and that no efforts should be spared, while others were of the opinion that there should be no relaxation of discipline, and that the heartiest good-will and cooperation should prevail between the services. At one point he thought he heard the clever-looking soldier who fed Sir Hildebrand the figures and notes observe that he was opposed to tyranny and to the French domination of the world; but that might only have been a passing dream. In any event neither he nor Graham was directly called upon to express an opinion; they both ignored all opportunities for intervention; and Graham for one spent his time being doggedly, ostentatiously silent.

Stephen expected Wray, who had greeted him with a civil bow, to join him when the conference broke up and to enlarge upon the 'delicate affair' he had spoken of at their earlier meeting. 'I shall have to know much more of his mind and his discretion before I involve Laura Fielding however,' he reflected: for Laura had already put her head well into the noose, and although she would almost certainly be allowed to escape by turning King's evidence a heavy official hand would cause her untold suffering. Furthermore he preferred to carry out his mystification of the French agents without any interference; it was an infinitely delicate operation and in his view it had to be performed by a single, well-practised hand. 'I shall not open myself today,' he concluded. 'On the other hand, I shall be interested to hear what he has to say about Graham's André Lesueur.'

In the event he was not required to open himself, nor did he hear about Lesueur, for Wray walked off, deep in talk with the Admiral's secretary, with no more than another bow and a significant look as though to say 'You see how I am taken up – my time is not my own.'

During these morning hours Jack Aubrey was in the dock-yard, conferring with the shipwrights far down in the bowels of his dear *Surprise*. The shipwrights and those who controlled them were profoundly corrupt, but they did allow that there was a world of difference between government money and private money, and that a captain's personal outlay called for real value in return; furthermore they were capable of expert craftsmanship, and Jack was thoroughly satisfied with her fine new Dalmatian oak diagonal hanging-knees and the stringers abaft the mainchains, where the frigate had been cruelly mauled. He also believed the ship-wrights when they told him that apart from saints' days they had just over a full week's work to do. They were tolerably vague about the number of saints' days, however, and as Jack climbed the temporary ladders to the ravaged deck, brushing wood-shavings off his coat and breeches, they sent for the calendar, telling off the holidays one after another and disagreeing furiously about whether St Aniceto and St Cucufat amounted to twelve hours or only an afternoon for carpenters as well as caulkers. Jack wrote it all down. He knew the Admiral of old: Sir Francis might not have been the first officer in the Navy to require his people to do everything at the double, but he was certainly one of the most forceful and persistent; he hated sloth on the quarter-deck as much as anywhere else, and when he called for a decision, a report, or a statement of a ship's condition he liked to have it very briskly. Sometimes of course these brisk decisions, reports or statements did not wear quite so well as more deliberate, pondered versions; but, as he said, 'If you stand considering which leg to put into your breeches first, you are likely to lose your tide; and in the meanwhile your breech is bare.' He maintained that speed was the essence of attack; and in his own actions this had certainly proved true.

'Mr Ward,' said Jack to his clerk, who was waiting on the quarterdeck with the ship's open list under his arm, 'be so good as to draw up a statement of condition showing that *Surprise* should be ready for sea in thirteen days, her guns in, her water completed and her shrouds rattled down, and let me have it as soon as the muster is over.'

They walked over the brow to the black huts where the Surprises lived. Captain Aubrey was expected and all his officers were present to receive him; poor lost Thomas Pullings was also there, standing somewhat apart so as not to appear to be encroaching upon the territory of William Mowett, his successor. Four more commanders had been made in the Mediterranean fleet alone: they too had been turned loose upon the Maltese beach, and if any vacancy occurred – an improbable state of affairs – it was likely that one of them would be given it, all four having considerable interest. He now wore a plain round jacket rather than his gold-laced splendour, and an old, sea-worn hat; but most of the other officers were also in working clothes – all, indeed, except for Mr Gill the master and Mr Adams the purser, who both had assignations in Valletta – because as soon as the inspection was over the whole ship's company was marching off to shoot for Mr Pullings' prize, a weekly iced cake in the form of a target that was much valued by the men and that gave the Commander a tenuous remaining connection with the ship. Marching off by boat, that is to say, for as nothing would induce them to keep in step or stand up straight their officers were unwilling to parade them through streets filled with redcoats, and they were to be taken as far as possible by sea. They were now standing in free and easy attitudes holding their muskets more or less as they saw fit: and when, his formal tour being over, Jack said to Mowett, 'Mr Mowett, we will muster by the open list, if you please,' and Mowett said to the bosun, 'All hands to muster,' and the bosun sprung his call, uttering the sequence of howls and short sharp notes designed to bring people from the farthest depths of the orlop and forepeak, the seamen piled their weapons in heaps that would have made any soldier blush and assembled in a straggling group on the bald dusty stretch of ground that purported to be the larboard side of the quarterdeck. The clerk called their names, and one by one they crossed over, just abaft an imaginary mainmast, to the starboard, touching their foreheads to their captain as they did so and calling out 'Here, sir.'

They were a sadly diminished band. Although some of course were in hospital, naval prison or military guardhouse, many, far too many had been drafted away. Yet for all that, Jack had fought with extraordinary fury for his older shipmates and his best seamen, sometimes going so far as substitution, misrepresentation and downright falsehood when he was absolutely forced to give up a certain number, and now, as they crossed over, there was scarcely one he had not known for years. Some indeed had served in his very first command, the fourteen-gun brig *Sophie*; and among the rest there were hardly any boys, no landsmen and no ordinary seamen. They were all able, and many of them might have been rated quartermaster in a flagship: at least as far as skill was concerned. They looked at him with mild affection as they went by, and he looked at them with profound disgust. Never, never had he seen such a squalid crew: crapulous, down-at-heel, frowsty. Mowett and Rowan and the master's mates laboured heroically keeping them busy through much of the day, but it would have been inhuman to deny them all liberty, and worse than inhuman – contrary to custom. And if this liberty were to go on much longer . . . Davis had not answered his name, twice repeated.

'Has Davis run?' asked Jack eagerly. Davis was his Old Man of the Sea, a dark, powerful, dangerous fellow who insisted upon volunteering or being transferred into any ship Captain Aubrey commanded; and nothing, nothing, would induce him to desert.

'I am afraid not, sir,' said Mowett. 'He only took some Scotch soldiers' kilts away from them, and they have laid him up in their guard-room.'

Much the same kind of fate accounted for the temporary absence of three more Surprises. Far graver was the real difference between this muster and the last, no less than eleven men having been taken to hospital, four with Malta fever, four with the great pox, two with limbs broken in drunken falls, and one pierced with a Maltese knife, while a twelfth was in prison, waiting trial for a rape. There were no desertions, however, although several merchant vessels had been in and out: the Surprises were mostly steady men-of-war's men, and they belonged to a happy ship.

'Well, at least I have all the figures,' said Jack, sighing and shaking his head.

It was just as well that he had got them then, for he had

scarcely finished his notes and uttered the wish that the frigate might have a chaplain – 'Someone to reclaim them – the fear of Hell-fire might do better than the cat – anything to stop this wasting away' – when a midshipman arrived, at the double, requiring his presence aboard the Commander-in-Chief.

Thanking Heaven that he had put on a good uniform for the muster, Jack said, 'Captain Pullings, would you be so very kind as to take my place? I was just going to see our people at the hospital. Mr Mowett, carry on. Bonden, my gig. Youngster' – to the flagship's midshipman, who had come across in a dghaisa – 'come along with me. It will save you fourpence.'

As the gig sped across the Grand Harbour Jack said, 'I thought the Admiral was ashore.'

'So he is, sir,' said the boy in his high clear treble, 'but he said he would be aboard long before I found you, and longer still before you put on your breeches.' The gig's crew grinned, and bow-oar uttered a strangled hoot. 'But I did not even go to the lady's house,' the boy went on in perfect innocence, 'because one of our bargemen said he had seen you putting off at Nix Mangiare steps for the dockyard, and I found you first go!'

Going up the *Caledonia*'s side, Jack noticed with satisfaction that the gathering of officers on the quarter-deck was far more impressive than was called for by the arrival of a mere post-captain: clearly the Admiral had not yet returned. Indeed, the *Caledonia*'s bell had time to be struck twice while Jack was talking to her commander before the Admiral's barge was seen to shove off and come racing out, pulling double-banked as though for a wager. The whole quarterdeck stiffened: the bosun's mates wetted their calls, the Marines straightened their stocks, the sideboys put on their white gloves. The Admiral came aboard in style: hats flew off, and Marines presented arms with a ringing unanimous stamp and clash, while their officer's sword cut a gleaming curve in the sunlight and the bosun's calls wailed over all. Sir Francis touched his own hat, glanced about the quarterdeck, caught sight of Jack's bright yellow hair and called out, 'Aubrey! Now that is what I call brisk. Good: very good. I had not looked for you this hour and more. Come along with me.' He led the way to the great cabin, waved Jack to an elbow-chair, settled behind a broad, paper-lined desk and said, 'First I must tell you that *Worcester* is condemned. She should never have been attempted to be repaired: it was a damned job to firk money out of Government. The new surveyors I have brought with me say that without she is completely rebuilt she can never take her place in the line of battle, and she ain't worth it; we have already spent far, far too much on her. So since we are in need of one, I have ordered her to be converted into a sheer-hulk.'

Jack had been expecting this; and since he had the *Surprise* for the present and the firmly-promised *Blackwater* for the future he was not much concerned, particularly as the *Worcester* was one of the few ships he had known that he never could love or even esteem. He bowed, saying, 'Yes, sir.'

The Admiral looked at him with approval, and said, 'How is *Surprise* coming along?'

'Pretty well, sir. I went over her this morning, and barring mishaps she should be ready for sea in thirteen days. But, sir, unless I am given a very large draft of men I shall not have hands enough to work her. We have been bled white.'

'You have enough to work a moderate ship?'

'Oh yes, sir: enough to work and fight any sloop in the list.'

'And I dare say most of them are seamen? I dare say you kept the hands that had served with you in other missions?' said the Admiral, taking the list Jack brought from his pocket. 'Yes,' he said, cocking it to the light and holding it at arm's length, 'scarcely a man that is not rated able. Now that is just what I want.' He searched among the folders on his desk, opened one, and said with his rare smile, 'I believe I may be able to put you in the way of a plum. You deserve one, after turning the French out of Marga.' He looked through the papers for some minutes, while Jack gazed out of the stern-windows at the vast sunlit Grand Harbour with the *Thunderer*, 74, wearing red at the mizzen, gliding towards St Elmo under topsails before the west-north-west breeze, bearing Rear-Admiral Harte away to the blockading squadron and its everlasting watch on the French fleet in Toulon. 'Plum?' he thought. 'How I should love a plum. But there are precious few left in the Mediterranean: can he be topping it the ironical comic?'

'Yes,' said the Admiral, 'turning the French out of Marga was a capital stroke. Now' – taking a chart from the folder and speaking in quite another tone, in the rapid, urgent, emphatic way that came naturally to him when any naval undertaking was in hand – 'bring your chair over here and look at this. Have you ever been in the Red Sea?'

'Only as far as Perim, sir.'

'Well, now, here is the island of Mubara. Its ruler has some galleys and an armed brig or two; he is obnoxious to the Sublime Porte and to the East India Company, and it was thought he could be quietly deposed by a small force arriving unexpectedly, the Company providing an eighteen-gun ship-rigged sloop and the Turks a suitable body of troops and a spare ruler. The sloop is there, lying at Suez with a small crew of lascars and conducting herself as a merchantman, and the Turks are ready with their soldiers. It was thought that Lord Lowestoffe would go out, travelling overland with a party of seamen, and carry out the operation some time next month. But Lowestoffe is sick, and in any case a new situation has arisen. The French want a base for the frigates they have and plan to have in the Indian Ocean and although Mubara is rather far to the north it is a great deal better than nothing. They offered the ruler – his name is Tallal, and he has always been a friend of theirs – gunners and engineers to fortify his harbour, together with a present of gewgaws. But Tallal was not interested in gewgaws: hard cash was what he wanted, and a very great deal of it. Indeed, his demands have increased at every interview. I say, his demands have increased at every interview.'

'Pray why is that, sir?'

'Because now there is a scheme for Mehemet Ali to conquer Arabia right down to the Persian Gulf, declare himself independent, and join with the French in bundling us out of India; and since Mehemet Ali has no navy in the Red Sea, Mubara has become very valuable indeed; all the more so as the French want it in order to keep a check on their ally. Furthermore, Tallal has relations all along the coast, and the present has grown into a sum that is to bring them over to the French side too. Well, now, they have come to an agreement at last and Tallal has sent one of his galleys down to Kassawa to take the Frenchmen aboard and to load the treasure. How much I do not know: some reports put it as high as five thousand purses, some at only half as much, but they all agree it is the silver that Decaen sent away from the Mauritius just before the island was taken, in a brig loaded to the gunwales. But you know all about that, of course.'

Of course he did: apart from the last purely formal stages, when his admiral assumed command, Jack it was who had taken the Mauritius, at the head of a small squadron. 'Yes, sir,' he said. 'I heard about that wretched brig. I even saw her, hull down to the north, but could not chase: I much regretted it.'

'I dare say you did. Well, now, that was at the beginning of their Ramadan: when it is over the galley will return. Do you wish to hear about their Ramadan, Aubrey?'

'If you please, sir.'

'It is a kind of Lent, but far more thorough-paced. They are not allowed to eat or drink or have to do with women from sunrise to sunset, and it lasts from one new moon to the next. Some say travellers are excused, but these people, these Mubaraites, are uncommon pious and they say that is all stuff – everyone must fast or be damned. So since no one can be expected to row a galley some hundreds of miles up the Red Sea – at this time of year the prevailing winds are all northerly, and it is a matter of pulling all the way, galleys being so unweatherly – hundreds of miles, I say, without a drop of water under that infernal sun, nor yet a bite to eat, they mean to sit in Kassawa until Ramadan is over. Now I do not like galleys – frail ricketty affairs that cannot stand a sea and too crank to bear much sail unless the wind is right aft: dangerous, too, if two or three of them come up on you in a dead calm and hammer you for a while and then board you on both sides with several hundred men – do not like galleys, but all officers with local knowledge and all our other informants agree that in those waters they are as regular as the post, pulling their twelve hours and then snugging down for the night. So at least we know where to find them. A ship cruising off the southern channel to Mubara, keeping well clear of these shoals and small islands here, you see, could hardly fail to intercept the galley with the treasure aboard on about the fifteenth day of the moon. She would then proceed to Mubara with the Turks for them to carry out the deposition, which is none of our business.'

'It would call for rapid, well-coordinated movement, sir,' said Jack in reply to the Admiral's expectant pause.

'Speed is the essence of attack,' said the Admiral. 'It also calls for a man who is not slack in stays and who is used to dealing with Turks and Albanians – Mehemet Ali is an Albanian, you know, and so are many of his soldiers and associates. That is why I thought of you. What do you say?'

'I should be very happy to go, sir; and I am much obliged to you for your good opinion.'

'I thought you would be: and in any case you are certainly the best man, being so well with the Porte: your chelengk should give you far greater authority in those parts. You will sail with all your people in the *Dromedary* transport this evening, then, and you will proceed to the eastern extremity of the Nile delta, going ashore at a little out-of-the-way place called Tina on the Pelusian mouth, so as not to offend Egyptian sensibilities – they have never cordially liked us since that wretched business at Alexandria in the year seven – and travel overland to Suez with a Turkish escort. I wish I could send Mr Pocock, my oriental counsellor, with you, but I cannot; however, you will have a dragoman, a most exceptionally learned and able dragoman, an Armenian by the name of Hairabedian, particularly recommended by Mr Wray; and after dinner Mr Pocock will give you an outline of the political situation in those parts: I dare say you would like Dr Maturin to attend?'

'If you please, sir.'

The Admiral looked at Jack for a moment, and then said, 'It was strongly urged that you should take another surgeon – that Maturin should be left here for consultation of one kind or another – but on mature consideration I overruled that. In an enterprise of this kind you want all the political intelligence you can get, and though no doubt Mr Wray's high opinion of Hairabedian is quite justified, it must not be forgotten that the poor fellow is only a foreigner, after all. Now I shall not load your mind with the details of the plan you are to carry out; you will find them, together with a number of recommendations, in the orders that will be writing while we have dinner. They would have been wrote before, but that we only had the news this morning. I wish it were dinner time already: I had no breakfast. If it were not that guests are coming I should have it put on the table this minute; but at least we can have something to drink. Pray touch the bell.'

The Admiral's rapid flow of words, his interlocking parentheses that did not always come out, and his strong, emphatic way of speaking left Jack Aubrey not indeed exhausted but perhaps a little old and certainly very willing to drink up a glass of Plymouth gin. As it went down, and as the Admiral was silently occupied with his own tankard of pale ale, Jack tried to dismiss his hurry of spirits, so as to look objectively at the scheme and at the plum it might contain. His excitement, his beating heart, and his longing for it to succeed must not blind him to the fact that everything would depend on the wind: a few days of calm or of unfavourable breezes anywhere along the hundreds of miles up the Mediterranean or down the Red Sea would bring it all to nothing. And then there were Turks to deal with as well as a completely unknown ship. The plan was somewhat visionary; it would call for consistent good luck in all its stages; yet it was not an impossible stroke by any means. One thing was certain: there was not a minute to be lost. 'With your permission, sir,' he said, putting down his glass, 'I will write a note to my first lieutenant, desiring him to have all hands ready to go aboard at a moment's notice. They are at small-arms exercise, behind Sliema, at present.'

'All of 'em?'

'Every man jack, sir, including the cook and my only two youngsters. I flatter myself our musketry is the finest on the station. We have shot against the Sixty-Third without disgrace; and I believe we could take on any ship of the line. Every single man is there.'

'Well, at least you will not have to scour all the prisons and guard-houses and brothels and wine-shops and low drinking-booths in this God-damned town – Sodom and Gomorrah – discipline goes by the board,' said the Admiral. 'But I wish you may not have turned them into a parcel of soldiers. If there is one thing I dislike more than another it is a fellow dressed up like a ramrod in a red coat with pow-dered hair and pipe-clay gaiters doing his exercise like a God-damned machine.' He was growing a little snappish from hunger: he looked at his watch and asked Jack to touch the bell again.

But the Admiral fed was more amiable than the Admiral fasting. He had several other guests, a Monsignore, a travel-ling English peer, three soldiers, his secretary, and three sailors, one of whom was the midshipman, or to be more exact the volunteer of the first class, who had come to fetch Jack and who turned out to be George Harvey, the Admiral's grand-nephew. Sir Francis was a good host: he gave his guests excellent food and a great deal of wine, and he never bored or puzzled the landsmen with the doings of ships either in peace or war; indeed, the meal might almost not have been a naval dinner at all, but for its noble surround-ings, the gentle rhythm of the living deck underfoot, the particular manner of drinking the King's health, and one small aspect of the proceedings.

It was clear to Jack that the Admiral was very fond of his grand-nephew and that he wished the boy to go the way he should, especially in the service line: this was very well, and Jack was entirely in favour of George's being guided in the right direction – he did a good deal of guiding youngsters himself, when he had time – but he did feel that the Admiral (who had no children of his own) exaggerated a little, and it did make him uneasy to find that he was being held up as a model. He did not mind the Admiral's saying 'that nodding rather than bowing when taking wine with a man was a vile habit among the young people of today' and then shortly afterwards directing a meaning glance, a glance that would have pierced a nine-inch plank, at the boy, who raised his glass, caught Jack's eye, and with a blush said, 'The honour of a glass of wine with you, sir,' bowing until his nose touched the tablecloth. But he did not much care for being commended as an example of briskness; and he positively disliked it when Sir Francis observed that some officers had taken to putting RN on their visiting-cards, a pert and flippant thing to do, meaning nothing – that Captain Aubrey, however, did not put RN on his card, and that when Captain Aubrey wrote a letter to a fellow-officer he did not add a couple of foolish initials to the direction but the words 'of His Majesty's navy'. Captain Aubrey also wore his hat athwartships in the good old way, not fore and aft. These were only a few remarks in a general flood of conversation – the English traveller, who was very rich, and the prelate, who was very well with the King of the Two Sicilies, were not at all oppressed by a sense of rank – but they were enough to cause Jack's neighbours, post-captains of about his own seniority, a good deal of quiet pleasure.

Captain Aubrey was therefore by no means sorry when dinner was over and he was led to a small cabin where he found Mr Pocock and Stephen, already deep in the tortuous politics of the eastern end of the Mediterranean. They went through the main heads again for his benefit, and Mr Pocock observed, 'In the present delicate state of affairs, with Mehemet Ali doing all he can to win Osman Pasha's confidence, there will be no difficulty about your journey overland; indeed, the official at Tina has shown great good will in assembling a competent number of pack animals, such as camels and asses; and of course your Turkish decoration, your chelengk, will make you seem a person of real importance. A person of even greater importance, that is to say. Yet even so it would be as well to keep out of Ibrahim's way, a froward, turbulent fellow, impatient of control; and of course any encounter with the roving Bedouin is to be avoided – not that they are likely to attack so large and well-armed a party as yours: for I presume your men will march with their weapons well in evidence.' He then returned to the rise of Mehemet Ali and the fall of the beys, unfortunately backed by the English government; but he had scarcely slaughtered the last Mameluke before Sir Francis himself came in. 'Here are your orders, Captain Aubrey,' he said. 'They are short and to the point: I hate verbiage. Now I do not wish to hurry you away, but the last of the *Dromedary*'s remaining stores will be on the wharf in half an hour, far earlier than was expected. Your first lieutenant – what is his name?'

'Mowett, sir. William Mowett, a very capable, active officer.'

'Aye, Mowett. He set all *Surprise*'s people on work, rigging an extra pair of sheets and clearing the fore-hold. So if you choose to make any tender farewells on shore, now is the time.'

'Thank you, sir,' said Jack, 'but I believe I shall leave my farewells for my return and pull across directly: there is not a moment to lose.'

'Quite right, Aubrey, quite right,' said the Admiral. 'And what is more, speed is the essence of attack. Goodbye to you, then, and I hope to see you again within a month or so, trailing clouds of glory and perhaps something more substantial too. Doctor, your humble servant.'

Once more the gig sped across the Grand Harbour, and as it sped Stephen observed, 'I had a very pleasant encounter this morning, on leaving the palace. Do you remember Mr Martin, the Reverend Mr Martin?'

'The one-eyed parson? That is to say, the clergyman who preached so well on the subject of quails in *Worcester*? Of course I do. A chaplain any first-rate would be proud of: and a great naturalist too, as I recall.'

'Just so. He met me as I was turning into the Strada Reale and carried me to Rizzio's, where we had an excellent dinner – octopodes and squids in all their interesting variety. His ship has been among the Greek islands, and being particularly interested in cephalopods he learnt to dive with the sponge-fishers of Lesina; but although he anointed his person with the best olive-oil, and put oil-saturated wool in his ears, and held a large piece of sponge, also soaked with oil, in his mouth, and clung to a heavy stone to carry him down, and although there were cephalopods in plenty, he found he could not stay on the sea-bed for more than forty-three seconds, which gave him pitifully little time to observe their ways or win their confidence, even if he could have seen them clearly which he could not, by reason of the circumambient water; and even then blood would gush from his ears, nose and mouth, while sometimes he would be hauled up insensible, so as to be obliged to be recovered with spirits of camphor. You may imagine, then, how interested he was, when I told him about my bell.'

'I am sure he was. I should like to see it again myself, some day.'

'So you shall. The bell is aboard the good *Dromedary* once more, and Mr Martin is there too, contemplating it. I had taken him out to show him its finer points after dinner; and it was there that your message found me.'

'What in God's name is that machine doing aboard the *Dromedary?* asked Jack.

'Sure I could not burden Captain Dundas with it; and I was not going to leave my valuable bell among those thieves at the dockyard. The master of the *Dromedary* was all complaisance: he was used to the bell, he said, and it was welcome aboard. And I must confess that if we should have any leisure . . .'

'Leisure!' cried Jack. 'If we are to be south of Ras Hameda by the full of next moon or before, there will be precious little leisure. Leisure, forsooth. Stretch out, there,' he called to the gig's crew. 'Pull hearty.'

The *Dromedary* had warped across to the dockyard; she was tied up alongside the wharf; and there was no sign, no sign at all of leisure, upon her decks or between them. Sailors carrying their bags, beds and hammocks ran across the brows like ants and vanished down the fore-hatchway, while up the after-hatchway ran others, those charged with cleaning out the holds, carrying huge bales of filth – bilge-soaked straw, light, bulky packing, and broken sproggins – which they threw overboard, together with improbable amounts of dust and spoilt flour. At the same time water was coming aboard, and barrels and beef, pork and wine and bags of biscuits and bales of slops, with Mr Adams, his steward and Jack-in-the-dust, the steward's assistant, skipping about them in a fine frenzy; while the crew of the transport, the Dromedaries proper, were extraordinarily busy about their own affairs, and the whole fore part of the ship rang with the hammering of the carpenter and his crew. The diving-bell stood like some archaic idol at the main-hatch, but there was no Mr Martin by it; Stephen walked right round the bell as well as he could for the hurrying crowd, and on his second circuit he came face to face with Edward Calamy, a young gentleman belonging to the *Surprise*. Mr Calamy was technically a youngster, and in fact he had only been at sea a matter of months, coming aboard the *Worcester* at Plymouth, a pale, nervous little boy; but no one would have thought so from his present hard-bitten, commanding demeanour and his profusion of nautical terms. For some time past he had assumed a kindly, protective attitude towards Dr Maturin, and now he called out, 'There you are, sir. I was looking for you. I have nabbed you a little cabin on the larboard side of the cuddy. Come along out of the way. Watch your step on those roban-staves. Mr

Martin is down there; I took him; and so is all your dunnage.'

All Stephen's dunnage did not amount to a great deal, his habits being of the simplest; but it did include a hortus siccus, with specimens of the more remarkable Maltese plants, and the volume of the Philosophical Transactions in which Dr Halley described his experiences at the bottom of the sea. Mr Martin and he were deep in these, sheltered from the din, sheltered from the hurrying, urgent world, when the *Dromedary* cast off her moorings, loosed her fore-topsail, and moved out into the harbour, while Captain Pullings, standing desolate on the quay, waved good-bye to those few friends who were not too busy to notice him; nor had they nearly exhausted the subject of sponges before the *Dromedary*, now under all plain sail, rounded Point Ricasoli and stood away east-south-east with a fine top-gallant breeze; still less that of corals.

'I have of course seen coral in the Indian Ocean and the Great South Sea, vast quantities of it,' said Stephen. 'But mine was only a most superficial view, limited in space and time; snatched away and hurried on I was, and often, often have I regretted my lost opportunities. For a contemplative mind, there can be few greater felicities than walking on a coral reef, with nondescript birds above, nondescript fishes below, and an unimaginable wealth of sea-slugs, plumed worms, molluscs, cephalopods in the nearby depths.'

'I am sure there cannot be a much more blessed state this side of Paradise,' said Martin, clasping his hands. 'But you will have plenty of coral again in the Red Sea, will you not?'

'What makes you say that, my dear sir?'

'Is not the Red Sea your destination? Do I mistake? Many people in Valletta spoke of a confidential expedition to those parts, and when the young gentleman brought me down here out of the press he seemed to take it for granted that Captain Aubrey had been entrusted with the command, just as I took it for granted that you had brought your bell to dive upon the reefs at your leisure. But I beg your pardon if I have been indiscreet.'

'Not at all, at all. To dive in the Red Sea would indeed be the rarest joy, above all at my leisure; but that alas is a word that offends the naval ear; and hardly ever, except when we were virtually cast down on Desolation Island, that blessed plot, have I been allowed to do anything at my own pace, at my ease. There is a restless itch to be busy, a tedious obsessive hurry: waste not a minute, they cry, as though the only right employment for time were rushing forwards, no matter where, so it be farther on.'

'Very true. There is also a passionate and perhaps even a superstitious preoccupation with cleanliness. The very first thing I heard on setting foot aboard a man-of-war was the cry "Sweepers!" and I suppose I must have heard it twenty times a day every day since then, although with the perpetual swabbing and scrubbing there is really nothing for a single broom to do, let alone a dozen. But now, sir, I fear I must take my leave: they say you are to sail by the evening, and already the light is growing dim.'

'Perhaps we might take a turn on deck,' said Stephen. 'There seems to be far less noise and hurry, and I am sure Captain Aubrey would be happy to see you again.'

They made their way along the unfamiliar passages to the companion-way; yet even before they reached the deck Stephen felt uneasy in his mind. The ship was leaning over more than she had a right to do tied up against a quay; and the cry of 'Cast loose your guns' did not suit with any kind of preparation for sailing that he knew. But this uneasiness was nothing to the blank consternation that came over both of them when they slowly rose above the coamings and found nothing but pure blue evening sea around them on every hand, the ship bowling along at six and a half knots, and the sun preparing to set in glory right astern, while all along the deck on either side the seamen were wholly taken up with naval activities, as though the land no longer existed. Captain Aubrey had borrowed the *Dromedary*'s six-pounders and by way of recalling the Surprises to some sense of decency, order, and regularity he was putting them through the great-gun exercise, blazing away in dumb-show at a furious rate. 'House your guns,' he said at last. 'A very pitiful exhibition, Mr Mowett. Two minutes and five seconds with little seventeen-hundredweight cannon is a very pitiful exhibition.' He turned, and his grim expression instantly lightened as he caught sight of Stephen and Martin. They were still both standing transfixed on the penultimate step of the ladder, which cut them off at the knee, and they were both staring away to leeward with their mouths open, looking like a pair of moonstruck landsmen. 'And, poor fellows, I am afraid they are little better,' he thought. 'Mr Martin, sir,' he said, stepping towards them, 'how happy I am to see you again. How do you do?'

'Heavens, sir,' said Martin, weakly shaking his hand and still gazing about the horizon as though land, or a miracle, might appear. 'It seems as though I have been carried away – as though I did not leave the ship in time.'

'No great harm. I dare say we shall see a Valletta fishing-boat that will carry you back, unless you choose to bear us company for a while. We are bound for the Pelusian mouth of the Nile.' A very shocking battle between the *Dromedary*'s carpenter and Hollar, bosun of the *Surprise* (both irascible men), broke out at this moment, and Captain Aubrey was obliged to break off. But he invited the chaplain to supper, and at this meal Martin said, 'Sir, perhaps you were not speaking seriously when you suggested that I should accompany you; but if you were, allow me to say that I should be very happy to do so. I have a month's leave from my ship, and Captain Bennet was good enough to say that he would have no objection whatsoever were I to prolong it by another month, or two, or even more.' Jack knew that Bennet had accepted a parson only under pressure from the former Commander-in-Chief: it was not that Harry Bennet had anticlerical notions, but he dearly loved female company, and as his ship was often on detached service he often indulged in it. Yet his respect for the cloth was such that he felt he could not ship a miss and a parson at the same time, and this he found a very grievous restraint. 'I should of course pay my battels, and I could perhaps help Dr

Maturin, since he has no assistant at the moment: I am not unacquainted with anatomy.'

'With all my heart,' said Jack. 'But I must warn you that we do not mean to linger at Tina. We are to march across a desert filled with serpents of various malignity, as the Doctor puts it . . .'

'I was only quoting Goldsmith,' said Stephen sleepily: the emotions of yesterday and his short night were overpowering him now, and he murmured, 'Sopor, coma, lethargy, carus.'

'. . . as far as the Red Sea, where we must carry out a mission that is sure to be strenuous and very hot and uncomfortable, and that may well be dangerous too.' As he spoke he saw a glow of delight spread over Martin's face in spite of obvious efforts to maintain a grave and serious countenance. 'Furthermore,' said Jack, 'I must tell you that the service is not designed for those that wish to gather beetles and henbane on some far coral strand and that grow snappish and petulant when desired to mind their duty. That murmur and look dogged,' he said a little louder; but seeing that Stephen would not respond he ended, 'Apart from that I should be very happy to have your company. And so I am sure would all your shipmates in the *Worcester*: we have not forgotten how you laboured in preparing the oratorio – perhaps some evening we may have a chorus or two; there are several of your old pupils aboard.'

Mr Martin said that the serpents, the exertion, heat, discomfort and danger were a small price to pay for beholding a coral reef, even though it might not be lingered on; that he should certainly do his duty without murmuring; and that he was very happy to be among his old shipmates again.

'Now that I come to think of it,' said Jack, 'I was regretting the absence of a chaplain only this morning. The people are grown horribly dissipated, and it occurred to me that . . .' He had been about to say 'that a thundering Hell-fire sermon might terrify them into good behaviour,' but on recollection it did not seem to him quite the thing to dictate his course to a parson and he went on, 'that it would be as well to rig church, so that they might hear some suitable words. Against vice and dissipation, I mean. What now, Killick?'

'Which Mr Mowett asks may he disturb you, sir,' said Killick; and since he liked to be the first with any news going he added, 'Don't know where to stow the foreign gent.'

'Beg him to come in: place a chair and fetch another glass.'

The foreign gent was the dragoman; and Mowett, sitting down and drinking a glass of port, asked whether he was to sling his hammock before the mast or aft? And where was he to mess?

'Where dragomans or dragomen mess in general I do not know,' said Jack. 'But the Commander-in-Chief spoke of this one as uncommon clever – particularly recommended by Mr Secretary Wray – so I think he must eat in the gun-room. I saw him for a moment when he came aboard, and although he is said to be so learned he looked a reasonably cheerful soul. I do not think you will regret it, and in any case I hope, I very much hope it will not be for much longer than a week. And it will not be, if only this blessed wind holds – Nelson's wind. Lord, I remember when we were after the French fleet in ninety-eight, and how we ran from the straits of Messina to Alexandria in seven days . . .' Those long urgent summer days shone clear in his mind, the blue white-flecked sea and fifteen men-of-war racing eastwards on that blessed wind, studdingsails aloft and alow on either side, royals and skysails, and Rear-Admiral Nelson pacing the *Vanguard*'s deck from before sunrise until after sunset: all that, and the fury of the battle by night, with the darkness perpetually torn and lit by gunfire, and in the midst of it all the unbelievably vast explosion as *L'Orient* blew up, leaving nothing but silence and blackness for several minutes after. He described the search for the French, and had carried the fleet from Alexandria back to Sicily and from Syracuse to Alexandria again – '. . . and there we found them at last, moored in Aboukir Bay' – when the *Dromedary* gave a modest heave and pitched Stephen, fast asleep, from his chair. Jack made a nimble spring, creditable in a man of his weight but not quite nimble enough to prevent Stephen from striking his forehead on the edge of the table and splitting the skin a handsbreadth across: a reasonably close imitation of Nelson's wound at the Nile, and almost as bloody.

'All this confusion and calling out,' said Stephen angrily. 'One would think you had never seen blood before, which is absurd in a band of hired assassins. Mome, capon, malthorse, lobcock' – this to Killick – 'hold the basin straight. Mr Mowett, in the top left-hand drawer of my medicinechest you will find some curved needles with gut already to them; pray be so good as to bring me a pair, together with a phial of styptic in the midmost rack, and a handful of lint. My neckcloth will serve for a bandage: it is already in need of washing.'

'Should you not lie down?' said Jack. 'The loss of blood . . .'

'Nonsense. It is merely superficial, I tell you: mere hide, no more. Now, Mr Martin, I will thank you to apply the styptic and to place twelve neat sutures while I hold the lips of the wound.'

'I do not know how you can bear to do it,' said Jack, looking away as the needle went deliberately in and through.

'I am accustomed to stuffing birds,' said Martin, working steadily on. 'And to sewing them up . . . much more delicate skin than this, very often . . . except in the case of old male swans . . . there: I flatter myself that is a tolerably fine seam.'

'The Chaplain says you are all right now, sir,' said Killick in a loud, officious voice, close to Stephen's ear. 'Sir, I am obliged to you,' said Stephen to Martin. 'And now I believe I shall retire. I had but a short night of it. Gentlemen, your servant. Mr Mowett, I beg you will leave my arm alone. I am neither drunk nor decrepit.'

He had but a short night of it again, since just before dawn an unknown very passionate voice not six inches from the cuddy scuttle cried, 'Don't you know how to seize a cuckold's neck, you God-damned lubber? Where's the bleeding seizing?' with such force as to banish sleep. His forehead hurt, but not very much, and he lay there swinging with the long motion of the ship, watching the grey light grow and musing upon cuckoldry, cuckoldom, and the almost universal mirth excited by that state. When he was in Malta one of the few letters he received from England – the Mediterranean fleet had been extraordinarily unlucky in the matter of post these last two months – had told him that he was a cuckold: that his wife was deceiving him with a gentleman attached to the Swedish embassy. He did not believe it. The same bag had brought him a hurried, blotted, but most affectionate scrawl from Diana, and although he did not suppose that any ordinarily moral considerations would stop her from doing whatever she had a mind to do, he did know that she was a gentlemanly being and that a highly personal aesthetic sense would prevent her writing him such a note at a time when she was adorning his forehead with horns: he was persuaded that she would not disgrace him unprovoked. On the other hand she lived an active social life in London; she had many rich and fashionable friends; and since she had never given a damn for public opinion he had no doubt that she laid herself open to unkind or envious tattle.

Her cousin Sophie, Jack Aubrey's wife, was completely different. She was not a prude, and she cared no more for Mrs Grundy than Diana; and yet no one but a maniac would ever write to tell Jack that he was a cuckold, although on a basis of reciprocity he deserved a whole hall-full of antlers. He pondered upon this: was it a question of sexual appetite, or rather of potentiality, dimly yet accurately perceived by others? He pondered upon sexual appetite in elegant females as opposed to the freer products of nature; and he was pondering still when the cabin door quietly opened and Jack looked in. 'God and Mary be with you, Jack,' he said. 'I was just thinking about you. Pray what is a cuckold's neck, by sea?'

'Why, if you wish to make a rope fast to a spar, you cross its two parts the one over t'other and clap a seizing on 'em, and that is your cuckold's neck. But tell me, how do you do?'

'Very well, I thank you.'

'Perhaps you will take a little weak tea, and a lightly boiled egg?'

'I will not,' said Stephen in a strong, determined voice. 'I will take a large pot of strong coffee, like a Christian, and some kippered herrings.'

Jack considered for a moment and then said with a stern look, 'What the devil did you mean by saying, I was thinking about you – what is a cuckold's neck?'

'Someone hallooed the words outside my window: I wanted to know what they meant, so I asked you, as a nautical authority. I desire you will not top it the Othello, brother, for shame: suff on you. If any man so far forgot himself as to make a licentious suggestion to Sophie, she would not understand him for a week, and then she would instantly lay him dead with your double-barrelled fowling-piece.'

'It is kind to call me a nautical authority,' said Jack, smiling at the idea of Sophie slowly coming to understand the hypothetical rake, and her polite attention changing to icy rage. 'And you may call me a nautical diplomat too, if you choose. I had a most satisfactory interview with the master of the *Dromedary* last night. It is a very, very delicate matter, telling a man how to conduct his ship or suggesting improvements, you know; and Mr Allen is in no way my subordinate. Besides, the masters of merchant ships often have a grudge against the Navy for pressing their men, and they resent the airs some officers give themselves. If I had offended him, he might, out of mere contrariness, have reduced sail to courses alone. But, do you see, he came below to ask what was afoot just after you had turned in – he had been told that you had attacked us in a drunken frenzy and that we had beaten you almost to death – and he stayed to drink a glass while I finished telling Mowett and the parson how the squadron cracked on like smoke and oakum, sailing over this very same tract of water before the battle of the Nile.'

'I believe I remember your mentioning the Nile,' said Stephen.

'I am sure you do,' said Jack kindly. 'Well, now, he proved a most capital fellow, once it appeared that we did not mean to take him up short or snib him aboard his own ship; and when Mowett and the parson were gone I put it to him frankly – brought it out without any guile or premeditation. I did not criticize his handling of the *Dromedary* in any way, he was to understand – he knew her humours and her possibilities better than any man – but I should be happy to offer him a couple of score of hands, and if with a much stronger crew he saw fit to spread more canvas, and if in consequence anything should carry away, why then I should be perfectly happy to indemnify his owners, straight away and out of hand. He said he asked nothing better – had seen me fretting, but could not put himself forward for fear of being brought up with a round turn – yet I must not expect too much of the old hooker even if she was manned like Jacob's ladder or the Tower of Babel, because not only was her bottom foul but she had not a mast, no, nor a yard that was not more woolding and fishes than wood, and all her rigging was twice-laid stuff; though indeed she had the lines of a swan – the sweetest lines he had ever seen – and with a proper crew she could show a fine turn of speed with the wind before the beam. So we shook hands on it, and when you go on deck you will see a very different state of affairs.'

To a seaman's eye it was no doubt a very different state of affairs, the *Dromedary* having set her weather stud-dingsails, her spritsail and her spritsail topsail, but Stephen was more immediately struck by a row of scarlet patches on the deck. The *Dromedary* had not yet rigged any awnings and the brilliant sunlight gave the red an extraordinarily vivid life, a pleasure to behold. He contemplated the scene, slowly adjusting his nightcap so that it should not press on his stitches, and presently he understood what was happening. The crew of the *Surprise* were being mustered with arms and bags; the order 'on end clothes' had been given and each man's possessions were now in a heap in front of him, a meagre heap, but in almost every case one topped by a beautifully laundered, pressed and folded pair of white duck trousers, a watchet-blue jacket with brass buttons, and an embroidered waistcoat, usually scarlet, for the frigate had recently touched at Santa Maura, famous for cloth of that colour. These garments, the hands' shore-going rig, were carefully spread abroad in an attempt at concealing the absence of a proper supply of everyday clothes beneath – a perfectly hopeless attempt even with a newly-joined youngster, let alone a post-captain who had spent most of his life at sea, but one that a sort of imbecile cunning had suggested to almost every man on deck. Jack angrily poked about among the unsaleable rags concealed beneath the finery and dictated the list of clothes required to the officer of the division. It was worse than he had expected: the arms were in excellent order, for in the hope of deprecating wrath the men had furbished their muskets, bayonets, pouches, pistols, cutlasses to a state of more than military brilliance, but the clothes were in a very shocking state. 'Come, Plaice,' he said to an elderly forecastleman, 'surely you must have something in the way of a spare shirt? You had several, embroidered down the front, when last we mustered bags. What has happened to them?'

Plaice hung his grizzled head and said he could not tell, he was sure: perhaps it was them rats, he suggested, without much conviction. 'Two shirts and two duck frocks for Plaice, as well as the stockings and petticoat-trousers,' said Jack to Rowan, who wrote it down; and they passed on to the next shiftless soul, who in a drunken frolic had contrived to leave himself with only one shoe as his whole sea-stock. 'Mr Calamy,' said Captain Aubrey to the young gentleman attached to this division, 'tell me what constitutes a well-regulated seaman's kit in high latitudes – a sober, responsible seaman in a King's ship, I mean, not a fly-by-night piss-in-the-corner privateersman that cannot hold his liquor.'

'Two blue jackets, sir, one pea jacket, two pair of blue trousers, two pair of shoes, six shirts, four pairs of stockings, two Guernsey frocks, two hats, two black Barcelona handkerchiefs, a comforter, several pair of flannel . . .' he blushed and in a low voice said, 'drawers. And two waistcoats; as well as one bed, one pillow, two blankets and two hammocks, sir, if you please.'

'And in warm climates?'

'Four duck frocks, sir, four pair of duck trousers, a straw hat, and a canvas one for squalls.'

'And any man that falls much short of this by his own vicious waste and negligence or vile debauchery deserves to be on the defaulters' list – deserves to be brought to the gangway, seized up to a grating and given a round dozen for every item he does not possess: is not that so?'

'Yes, sir,' very faintly.

'This man is in your division; he is one of your boat's crew; yet knowing all this you have seen him bring himself down to one solitary shoe. Have you no sense of responsibility for your men, Mr Calamy? You are a disgrace to the service. Your grog is stopped until further notice. This is very bad.'

It was indeed worse than Jack had expected, acquainted though he was with squalor, naval squalor; but he and Mr Adams had provided for something near total destitution and all that morning the purser's steward served out slops, while all that afternoon those Surprises who made no part of the *Dromedary*'s watch on duty sat in little groups on deck, unpicking the Navy Board's contractor's slops, carefully refitting, recutting and resewing them again, to avoid the intolerable reproach of 'looking like a pusser's shirt on a handspike'.

Jack, rambling about the upper rigging with Mr Allen and discussing various ways of increasing the ship's pace when the breeze should haul forward, looked down on a deck that resembled a tailor's sweat-shop with shreds of cloth everywhere and ends of thread and earnest forms sitting cross-legged, bowed over their work, right arm rising, needle flashing rhythmically. He looked down with guarded satisfaction, for not only were the hands recovering from their debauchery, but even with the wind right aft, by no means the *Dromedary*'s or any other square-rigged vessel's favourite point, she was throwing a modest bow-wave and running at five knots four fathoms, enough to accomplish the voyage in a week with an unchanging breeze.

The wind was in the same quarter the next day, and the morning after that; and most of the Surprises were still busy with needle and thread. Their working clothes were now in order, and they were moving on to the fine work: it was known that church was to be rigged on Sunday – Mr Martin was already leading some of the better voices through the Old Hundredth in the empty fore-hold and the deck vibrated like the soundbox of some vast instrument – and it was thought that the Dromedaries would attend dressed fancy. The Surprises had no intention of having their eyes wiped by a parcel of merchantmen, and since on the one hand shore-going rig would be ostentatious and inappropriate while on the other there was no time for really delicate embroidery, they were putting ribbon in their seams.

Yet some had taken time off to polish the Doctor's bell, and now the massive plates of lead that covered its lower sides gleamed as brightly as sand and brickdust could ever induce lead to gleam, while the brass top of course outfaced the sun. This they had done by way of expressing their sympathy, for Stephen, walking about with a bloody night-cap, was a pitiful sight; and as they were all perfectly convinced that he had been dead drunk when he received his wound, they had even more than their usual kindness for him.

But today no nightcap was to be seen: it had been represented to Dr Maturin on all sides that since the *Surprise*'s captain and officers had invited the master of the *Dromedary* and his first mate to dinner, a wig must be worn, however great the agony: it might be pushed back after the cloth was drawn, they said, and it might even be taken off altogether if they should chance to sing towards the end of the meal; but in the early stages it was as necessary as a pair of breeches. In a wig, therefore, Stephen walked forward to his temporary sickbay, examined and confirmed two new cases of syphilis, abused them for presenting far too late as usual – would lose their teeth and noses and even lives if they did not follow his instructions to the letter – their wits they had lost already – stopped their grog, put them on number two low diet, started them on a course of salivation, and told them that the cost of their physic should be stopped out of their pay. He then looked at a Dromedary, distracted with toothache, decided that the tooth must come out, and sent for the drummer and two of the man's messmates to hold his head.

'Which we ain't got no drummer, sir,' said his loblolly boy. 'All the jollies was left at Malta.'

'Very true,' said Stephen. 'But a drum I must have.' He was not very good at drawing teeth and he liked his patient to be deafened, amazed, stupefied by a thundering in his ears. 'Has this ship never a drum for a fog?'

'No, sir,' said the Dromedary's messmates. 'We uses conchs and a musket.'

'Well,' said Stephen, 'that might answer too. Let it be so. My compliments to the gentleman in charge of the watch and may I have conchs and a musket. No. Stay. The galley must surely have cauldrons and kettles that could be beat.'

But few messages are ever perfectly understood, few are delivered unimproved upon, and the tooth came out – came out at bloody last, piece by piece – to the howling of conchs, the fire of two muskets, and the metallic thunder of several copper pots.

'I beg pardon for being late,' said Stephen, as he slipped into his seat, for Jack and his officers and their guests were already at table – 'I was delayed in the sickbay.'

'It sounded as though you were having a battle there,' said Jack.

'No. It was only a tooth, a troublesome tooth: sure I have delivered many a child with less pains to all concerned.' The remark was generally considered to be in very poor taste, and indeed Stephen would never have made it had he not been so hurried: at ordinary times he perfectly recollected the odd delicacy of sailors where gynaecological matters were concerned. Now he relapsed into silence, and having eaten enough soup to take off the keen edge of his appetite he looked about the table. Jack sat at its head, with the captain of the *Dromedary* on his right and Mr Smith, her first mate, on his left; then next to Mr Allen came Mowett, with Rowan opposite him, while Stephen, Mowett's neighbour, faced Martin. Mr Gill, the master of the *Surprise*, sat to the right of Stephen, with Hairabedian the dragoman over against him, while the two master's mates, Honey and Maitland, were on either side of Mr Adams, who, as vice-president of the mess, sat at the foot of the table.

In the presence of their captain these two young men were dead weights at the present utterly sober stage of the meal, and the melancholy Gill would be perfectly mute at all stages, having no conversation whatsoever. Martin and Hairabedian, unburdened by the weight of naval convention, were already talking away in the middle of the table, but at the head Jack would have had to go through the usual hard labour of flogging things along until the dinner got under way if it had not been for the fact that just before his arrival his two lieutenants had very nearly come to blows over the meaning of the word dromedary. They were both good seamen and amiable companions, but they were both given to writing verse, Mowett being devoted to the heroic couplet while Rowan preferred a Pindaric freedom, and each thought the other's not only incorrect but devoid of grammar, sense, meaning, and poetic inspiration. At two bells in the afternoon watch this rivalry had spilled over on to the name of the transport: why, it was difficult to make out, since dromedary could not conceivably be made to rhyme with anything – and both were still so heated that although Captain Aubrey was at this time quietly engaged with his Valletta mutton Rowan called across the table, 'Come, Doctor, as a natural philosopher you will certainly confirm that the dromedary is the hairy animal with two bunches that moves slow.'

'Nonsense,' said Mowett. 'The Doctor knows perfectly well that the dromedary has one bunch and moves quick. Why else would it be called the ship of the desert?'

Stephen darted a look at Martin, whose face was studiously blank, and replied, 'I should not like to commit myself, but I believe the word is used somewhat loosely, according to the taste and fancy of the speaker, much as sailors say sloop for a vessel with one mast or two, or even three. And you are to consider, that as there are swift-sailing sloops and slow, so there may be brisk and sluggish dromedaries; yet I am inclined to suppose, if only from the example of this excellent ship of Captain Allen's, that the ideal dromedary is a creature that moves fast, giving one a smooth and agreeable ride, however many bunches it may have.'

'Some say drumedary,' observed the purser; and there Jack cut the topic short, as being perhaps distasteful to their guests. But the word had sunk into Mr Allen's mind, and after a while, peering round Mowett, he said to Stephen, 'Sir, I thank you kindly for your attention to poor Polwhele's tooth; but pray why did you need a drum to draw it?'

'Oh,' said Stephen, smiling, 'it is an old mountebank's trick to be sure; but it has a real value. The toothdrawer's man, his Jack-Pudding or Merry-Andrew, beats the drum at the fair not only to drown the sufferer's screams, which might deter other customers, but also to induce a partial, temporary insensibility, which gives his master time to work. It is empirical, but it is sound practice. Again and again I have noticed that when the ship is in action and men are brought below, they are often scarcely aware of their wounds. Indeed, I have taken off mangled limbs, hearing scarcely a groan; and many a sad gash have I probed, with the patient talking in a normal voice. This I attribute to the din of battle, the excitement, and the extreme activity.'

'I am sure you are in the right of it, Doctor,' cried Mr Allen. 'Only last year we had a set-to with a privateer in the chops of the Channel, a St Malo lugger that brought up the breeze, sailing three miles to our two. She gave us a couple of broadsides and boarded us in the smoke; and not to spin a long yarn of it, we persuaded them to go back into their boat – the *Victor* of St Malo she was – as quick as ever they come out of her, and she sheered off. But what I mean is, when it was all over and I was sitting down to a cup of tea with Mr Smith here,' nodding at his mate, who nodded solemnly back, as though on oath, 'I felt something queer in my shoulder, and taking off my coat, there was a hole in the cloth, and a hole in me too, and a pistol-ball lodged so deep it had almost gone through. I had felt the blow, mark you, but thought it was only a falling block, and paid no attention.'

Yes, cried others, and much the same had happened to them or their friends; and after a decent pause in which Captain Aubrey gave an account of a ball that had entered his side when he was a master's mate, that had been indistinguishable from a pike-thrust received at almost the same moment, and that had wandered about his person until he was a commander, when the Doctor extracted it from high up between his shoulders, several more anecdotes came out at once, giving the dinner a pleasant convivial if somewhat ogreish sound.

From then on talk and laughter did not cease, and Stephen, who had lately been at some pains to play a social part, sank back into his more usual silence, musing on Mrs Fielding until the cloth was drawn. Then, while they were eating figs and green almonds he saw Rowan lean forward and call down the table to the dragoman, 'Did I hear you say you had met Lord Byron?'

Yes, said Mr Hairabedian, he had had the honour of dining in his company twice, together with several of the Armenian merchants of Constantinople; and once he had passed a towel as his lordship emerged 'shivering and somewhat blue, gentlemen' from the Hellespont. Stephen looked curiously at his little round merry face to see whether the words were true: many, many people had he met in Valletta who had known Byron, the women repelling his advances and the men taking him down a peg or two. Hairabedian was probably telling the truth, he decided. He had not had much contact with him, but the interpreter was clearly an intelligent man; he had told Martin a good deal about the monophysite Armenian and Coptic churches, showing a nice appreciation of the difference between homoiousian and homoousian, and he had gained the good opinion of the gunroom, not indeed by talking much, although his English was nearly perfect, but rather by reason of his jolly twinkling eye, his most infectious high-pitched laugh, his habit of listening attentively, and his admiration for the Royal Navy.

At this point Mowett was called away, much against his will, and while Rowan and Martin and even the purser and master's mates eagerly questioned Hairabedian Mr Allen leant over towards Stephen and said, 'Who is this Byron they are always talking about?'

'He is a poet, sir,' said Stephen, 'one that writes excellent doggerel with flashes of brilliant poetry in it; but whether the poetry would flash quite so bright were it not for the contrast I cannot tell: I have not read much of him.'

'I like a good poem,' said Mr Allen.

Jack coughed; the talk died away; and filling his glass from one of the fresh decanters he said, 'Mr Vice, the King.'

'Gentlemen,' said Mr Adams, 'the King.'

After this they drank to the *Dromedary*, to the *Surprise*, and to wives and sweethearts, and Jack said to Mr Allen, 'If you like a poem, sir, you have come to the right shop. Both my lieutenants are capital poets. Rowan, tip the captain your piece about Sir Michael Seymour's action, the first one. Start in the middle, so as not to be too long.'

'Well, sir,' said Rowan, beaming upon Mr Allen, 'it was the one with the *Thetis*, you know.' And without the least change in his conversational tone he went on:

'I do declare
Such a hard engagement has not been known for many a year.
At seven in the evening the battle it begun,
And lasted many hours before it was done.
Great numbers there was wounded, a many too was slain,
While the blood from off the decks did change the watery main.
Three hours and twenty minutes we held this dreadful fray,
We lashed her fast unto us, she could not get away;
Many times they tried to board us, but we drove them back so
*   fast –*
Although they were so numerous, we made them yield at last.
Then down she hauled her colours, no longer could she fight;

Our British tars they gave three cheers all at this noble sight.
We took possession of her without any more delay,
And sent her into Plymouth Sound then, my boys, straightway.
Great store of artillery, ammunition too likewise,
One thousand barrels of flour to our tars become a prize.
She was bound out to Martinico, the truth I do declare,
But in the night we met her and stopped her career.'

Mowett came back during the last lines, and seeing his
look of fairly well disguised disappointment Jack said to Mr
Allen, 'My first lieutenant's poems are equally appreciated,
sir, but they are in the modern taste, which perhaps you
may dislike.'

'No, sir, not at all, ha, ha, ha,' said Allen, now strikingly
red in the face and very apt to laugh. 'I like it of all things.'

'Then perhaps you would give us the piece about the
dying dolphin, Mr Mowett,' said Jack.

'Well, sir, if you insist,' said Mowett eagerly; and having
explained that this was part of a poem about people sailing
in the Archipelago he began in a hollow boom:

'The sailors now, to give the ship relief,
Reduce the topsails by a single reef;
Each lofty yard with slackened cordage reels,
Rattle the creaking blocks and ringing wheels,
Down the tall masts the topsails sink amain,
And soon reduced, assume their post again.
And now, approaching near the lofty stern,
A shoal of sportive dolphins they discern.
From burnished scales they beamed refulgent rays,
Till all the glowing ocean seemed to blaze,
Soon to the sport of death the crew repair,
Dart the long lance, or spread the baited snare.
One in redoubling mazes wheels along,
And glides, unhappy! near the triple prong . . .'

Stephen's mind wandered back to Laura Fielding and his
perhaps untimely, unnecessary, foolish, unprofitable, sancti-
monious chastity; and he was brought back to the present

only by the applause that greeted the end of Mowett's recitation. Above the general noise rose Mr Allen's strong seagoing voice now free from the genteel restraint of some decanters back: he said that although the *Dromedary* could not return the compliment in kind, having no gentlemen of equal talent aboard, she could at least reply with a song, good will supplying what it might lack in harmony. '*Ladies of Spain*, William,' he said to his mate, beat three times on the table, and together they sang:

> '*Farewell and adieu to you fine Spanish ladies,*
> *Farewell and adieu all you ladies of Spain,*
> *For we've received orders to sail for old England*
> *And perhaps we shall never more see you again.*'

Almost all the hands knew the song well, and they joined in the chorus with splendid conviction:

> '*We'll rant and we'll roar like true British sailors,*
> *We'll range and we'll roam over all the salt seas,*
> *Until we strike soundings in the Channel of old*
>   *England –*
> *From Ushant to Scilly 'tis thirty-five leagues.*'

Then the captain and his mate again:

> '*We hove our ship to when the wind was sou'west, boys,*
> *We hove our ship to for to strike soundings clear,*
> *Then we filled our maintopsail and bore right away, boys,*
> *And right up the Channel our course we did steer.*'

Far below, in the midshipmen's berth, the excluded youngsters began the next verse before the gunroom, and their pure voices sang:

> '*The first land we made is known as the Dodman,*
> *Next Rame Head near Plymouth, Start, Portland and*
>   *Wight . . .*'

But Stephen's most valuable recollection of the dinner was Hairabedian's delighted face, his twinkling eyes, and his counter-tenor soaring above the thunder, declaring that he too, like a true British sailor, should roam over all the salt seas.

Chapter Five

The *Dromedary* was running before the wind, so directly before the wind that there was scarcely a breath of air on deck nor a whisper in the rigging: a silent ship, apart from the run of water down her side and the creak of her masts and yards as she pitched on the gentle following swell. Silent, in spite of the tight-packed crowd of men on her quarter-deck, for the *Dromedary* had rigged church.

She was quite used to doing so, since she often carried soldiers from one place to another, and soldiers were more often provided with chaplains than sailors; her carpenter had turned the capstan just abaft the mainmast into a perfectly acceptable desk, and her sailmaker had turned a spare piece of number eight canvas into a surplice that would have graced a bishop. Mr Martin had taken it off in preparation for his sermon, and in the attentive, respectful silence he was now looking at a little paper of notes. Jack, sitting in an elbow-chair beside Mr Allen, saw that he meant to give them something of his own rather than read from Dean Donne or Archbishop Tillotson according to his usual modest custom, and that the prospect made him anxious.

'My text is from Ecclesiastes, the twelfth chapter, the eighth verse: Vanity of vanities, saith the preacher, all is vanity,' the chaplain began, and in the pause that followed his auditors looked at him with pleased expectation. The wind was fair; the ship had been sailing at a steady five to six knots ever since they left Malta, with a few fine points of eight and nine, and Jack, whose dead reckoning and observations agreed closely with Allen's, confidently expected that they should make their landfall that forenoon: he had quite ceased urging the ship on by a continual effort of will and an unreasonable contraction of his stomach muscles, and now, as he disposed himself to listen to Mr Martin, he was aware of a fine bubbling excitement in the background of his mind, very much like that of his much younger days. The men too were in a happy mood: they were dressed quite as fancy as the Dromedaries; Sunday pork and duff were not much above an hour away, to say nothing of their grog; and it was pretty general knowledge that the Red Sea might hold some kind of a plum.

'When I repaired aboard the *Worcester* at the beginning of my naval ministry,' went on Mr Martin, 'the very first words I heard were "Sweepers, sweepers there".' The congregation smiled and nodded: nothing could be more true to life in a self-respecting man-of-war, particularly with Mr Pullings as her first lieutenant. 'And the next morning I was awaked by the sound of holystones and swabs as the people cleaned the deck, while in the afternoon they painted a large part of the vessel's side.' He went on in this way for some time: his hearers were pleased when his description was technically accurate; they were pleased when he stumbled slightly; and they were still more pleased when he spoke of his visit to their own ship, 'the *Joyful Surprise*, as she is called in the service, a frigate that was pointed out to me as the most beautiful in the Mediterranean, and the best sailer, though small'.

Since he was a Papist Stephen Maturin took no part in these proceedings; but as he had lingered a little too long in the mizzentop, watching a possible Caspian tern through Captain Aubrey's telescope until the service had actually begun, he necessarily heard all that was sung and said. During the hymns and psalms, which a certain rivalry between Surprises and Dromedaries rendered more vehement than musical, his attention wandered, returning to his anonymous letter and his thoughts of Diana – of her particular sort of faithfulness – of her extremely spirited resentment of any slight – and it occurred to him that she was not unlike a falcon he had known when he was a boy in his godfather's house in Spain, a haggard, a wild-caught peregrine of extraordinary dash and courage, death to herons, ducks and even geese, very gentle with those she liked but wholly irreconcilable and indeed dangerous if she was offended. Once the young Stephen had fed a goshawk before the falcon, and she had never come to him again, only staring implacably with that great fierce dark eye. 'I shall never offend Diana, however,' he observed. 'Amen,' sang the congregation and it was shortly after that Mr Martin began to preach. Stephen was unacquainted with Anglican pulpit oratory, and he listened with considerable interest. 'What is his drift?' he wondered, as the chaplain ran through the many, many operations of cleaning and maintenance aboard a man-of-war.

'Yet what is the end of all this polishing and scouring and painting at last?' asked Mr Martin. 'The shipbreaker's yard, that is the end. The ship is sold out of the service, and perhaps she spends some years as a merchantman; but then, unless she founder or burn, she comes to the fatal yard, a mere hulk. Even the most beautiful ship, even the *Joyful Surprise*, ends as firewood and old iron.' Stephen glanced at the *Surprise*'s standing officers, her bosun, gunner and carpenter, men who had been with her for years and years, outlasting captains, lieutenants and surgeons: the carpenter, a peaceful man by temperament and occupation, was merely puzzled, but Mr Hollar and Mr Borrell were staring at the parson with narrowed eyes, pursed lips and a look of intense suspicious and dawning hostility. From the mizzentop he could not see Jack Aubrey's face, but from his unusually straight and rigid back he supposed it had a tolerably grim expression; and many of the older hands were certainly far from pleased.

As though aware of the strong feelings around him Mr Martin passed rapidly on, inviting his hearers to consider a man in his voyage through life – his care of his person, washing, clothing and feeding it – care of his health – sometimes very great care, with exercise, riding, abstinence, seabathing, flannel waistcoats, cold baths, blooding and sweating, physic and diet – yet all to no end – to inevitable defeat at last – to final defeat and perhaps drivelling imbecility, by way of decrepitude – if not to an early death then to old age and loss of health, loss of friends, loss of all comforts, when body and mind were least able to stand it – the unbearable separation of husband and wife – and all ineluctable, the necessary common lot – no surprise in this world, ultimate defeat and death being the only certainties – no surprise, above all no joyful surprise.

'On deck, there,' called the lookout on the foretop-gallantsail yard. 'Land fine on the starboard bow.'

This hail and the total change of atmosphere it brought about cut Mr Martin's flow entirely. He did his best to make it clear that although the earthly life of a man might be compared with that of a ship, a man had an immortal part which a ship had not, and that the perpetual cleansing and maintenance of that immortal part would indeed lead to a joyful surprise, whereas neglect, even in the form of thoughtless insobriety and incontinence, must end in everlasting death. But he had already lost the sympathy of some of his hearers and the attention of many more; he was not a gifted speaker in any case and being thrown out diminished his confidence and his powers still farther; discouraged, he resumed his surplice and brought the service to its traditional end.

A few moments after the last amen Mr Allen led the way to the maintop. 'There, sir,' he said with modest triumph, passing the telescope to Jack. 'The mound on the right is Tina fort, and the mound on the left is old Pelusium: quite a tolerable landfall, though I say it myself.'

'As pretty a landfall as ever I saw,' said Jack. 'I congratulate you, sir.' He studied the low, distant shore-line for a while and then said, 'Do you make out an odd kind of cloud a little north-west of the fort?'

'That would be the waterfowl over the Pelusiac mouth,' said Allen. 'It is only a vile great slough now, and they breed there by wholesale – cranes and water-crows and such. They keep up a sad gabble by night, if you lay over there with a south-west wind, and foul your deck some inches deep.'

'The Doctor will be pleased to hear of them, though,' said

Jack. 'He loves a curious bird,' and a little later, when he was drinking a glass of madeira below, he said, 'I have a joyful surprise for you, Stephen. Mr Allen tells me there are countless waterfowl over the silted-up Pelusian mouth.'

'My dear,' said Stephen, 'I am perfectly aware of it. This extremity of the delta is famous throughout the Christian world as the haunt of the purple gallinule, to say nothing of a thousand other wonders of creation: and I am perfectly aware that you will hurry me away from it at once, without the least remorse, as you have so often done before. Indeed, I wonder at your being so unfeeling as to mention the place at all.'

'Not really without remorse,' said Jack, filling Stephen's glass again. 'But the fact of the matter is, there is not a moment to lose, if you understand me. We have had the most amazing luck hitherto, with this blessed breeze day after day – such a passage as you would hardly dare pray for – and now there is a real possibility of our being off Mubara well before the full of the moon; so it would be the world's pity to spoil our chances for the sake of a purple gallinule. But if we bring it off – I say *if* we bring it off, Stephen,' said Jack, clapping his hand to the wooden table-leg, 'then you and Martin shall have your bellyful of galli-nules, red, white and blue: aye, and of double-headed eagles, too, both in the Red Sea and here when we re-embark, that I promise you.' He paused, whistling gently.

'Tell me, Stephen,' he went on at last, 'do you happen to know what is meant by a purse?'

'I take it to signify a small pouch or bag used for carrying money on the person. I have seen several examples in my time; and have even possessed one myself.'

'I should have said, what do Turks mean by it?'

'Five thousand piastres.'

'Lord above,' said Jack. He was not a particularly greedy man, nor in the least degree avaricious, but even in his youth, well before he fell in love with the higher mathematics, he had been pretty quick at working out prize-money, like most sailors; and now his mind, long used to astronomical and navigational calculation, worked out a captain's share of the sterling equivalent of five thousand purses in a matter of seconds, presenting him with a shining sum that would not only deal with his horribly entangled affairs at home but go a long way to restoring his fortune – a fortune that he had won by a combination of excellent seamanship, hard fighting, and uncommon good luck, and that he had lost or at least gravely imperilled by being too trustful on shore, by supposing that landsmen were more straightforward and candid than was in fact the case, and by signing legal documents without reading them on being assured that 'they were mere formalities'. 'Well,' he said, 'that is very gratifying news, upon my word: very gratifying indeed.' He filled their glasses again and said, 'I have not spoken of this caper before, because it was all so very hypothetical, so very much up in the air. It still is, of course. But tell me, Stephen, what do you think of the likelihood of success?'

'In this particular matter my opinion is worth almost nothing,' said Stephen. 'But as a general principle I should say that any expedition which has been talked about as much as this is unlikely to take the enemy by surprise. It was a common topic in Malta, and there is not a man aboard who does not know where we are bound. On the other hand there is this completely new aspect – the agreement with the French and the coming of the galley with French engineers, gunners and treasure. Of course, I have no knowledge whatsoever of the source of the intelligence or its value; but Mr Pocock was perfectly convinced of its soundness, and Mr Pocock is no fool.'

'I am so glad you think so,' said Jack. 'That was exactly my impression.' He smiled, and in his mind's eye, bright and clear, he saw the Mubara galley pulling steadily northwards, heavily ballasted and swimming rather deep. 'There are still joyful surprises in this world, whatever Mr Martin may say,' he observed. 'I have known dozens of 'em. You heard his sermon, I believe?'

'I was on the mizzentop.'

'I could wish he had not talked about the ship like that.'

'Sure, he did it out of compliment to you – a thank-offering.'

'Oh, certainly: do not think me ungrateful. I am sure he meant it very kindly, and am much obliged to him for his politeness. But the hands are out of temper, and Mowett is furious. He says he will never be able to get them to priddy the deck with a whole heart again, nor take pains with the paintwork, now that it has been preached down as a vanity, and as something leading to the knacker's yard.'

'If he had not been interrupted, I am sure he would have made a better fist of it – I am sure he would have made his figurative language clear to the meanest understanding: but even so, unless one is a second Bossuet, perhaps it is a mistake to use tropes and parallels in this eminently unpoetic age.'

'Not so hellfire unpoetical as all that, brother,' said Jack. 'Rowan came out with as fine a thing as ever I heard only this very morning, just before we rigged church. He and the second mate were looking at the six-pounders and he said, "Oh ye mortal engines, whose rude throats/Th'immortal Jove's dread clamours counterfeit."'

'Capital, capital. I doubt if Shakespeare could have done much better,' said Stephen, nodding gravely. Of late he had noticed a very vicious tendency in these two young men, a tendency to indulge in bare-faced theft, each confident that the other's reading scarcely went beyond Robinson's *Elements of Navigation*.

'Wittles is up,' said Killick, appearing in the doorway together with the homely reek of boiled cabbage.

'And now I come to think of it,' went on Jack, emptying his glass, 'perhaps you may be mistaken about tropes and parallels too. I caught the allusion directly, and I said to Allen, "He means the thunder, I believe." "Yes," says Allen, "I smoked it at once." Smoked it at once,' repeated Jack, smiling pleasantly as the possibility of a brilliant play on the words *cannon* and *smoke* hovered in his mind. Yet even as he turned the matter over it was eclipsed by an even better thing. 'But perhaps Rowan *is* a second Bossuet,' he said. His deep, fruity, intensely amused laugh filled the cabin, filled the after part of the *Dromedary* and echoed forward; he went scarlet in the face, and redder still. Killick and Stephen stood looking at him, grinning in spite of themselves, until his breath was gone; and reduced to a wheeze he wiped his eyes and stood up, still murmuring 'A second Bossuet. Oh Lord . . .'

During the course of dinner the smell of cabbage and boiled mutton changed abruptly to that of rotting mud, for the transport, standing in, had crossed the invisible frontier where the westerly breeze reached her not from the open sea but from the Nile delta and the great Pelusian marsh itself. Mr Martin had been rather silent hitherto, in spite of having been invited to drink wine with Captain Aubrey, Mr Adams, Mr Rowan, Dr Maturin and even, most surprisingly, with the melancholy and extremely abstemious Mr Gill; but now his face lightened. He darted a look of intelligence at Stephen, and as soon as he decently could he left the table.

Stephen had some doses to put up for those invalids who would have to be left behind, but when this was done and the physic and powders entrusted to the *Dromedary*'s first mate, a discreet middle-aged Scotchman, he too hurried on deck. The shore was much closer than he had expected, a long flat shore with a shallow beach of a rufous ochre that made the sea an even more surprising blue: dunes behind it, and beyond the dunes a mound with a fort on top and something in the nature of a village on its flanks: some two miles away on the left hand another mound, and through the shimmering heat there seemed to be ruins scattered over it. A very few palms dotted here and there. Otherwise nothing but an infinity of sand, pale sand, the Desert of Sin.

Mr Allen had taken everything in but the foretopsail and the ship was gliding in with little more than steerage-way upon her, anchor ready to be dropped and a leadsman in the channels calling the depths in steady sequence. 'By the deep twenty; by the deep eighteen; by the mark seventeen . . .' Almost every soul aboard was on deck, gazing earnestly at the shore: and gazing, as was usual upon such delicate occasions, in profound silence. It was with some surprise, therefore, that Stephen heard a cheerful hooting from over the side, and when he reached the rail it was with far greater surprise that he saw Hairabedian gambolling in the sea. He had understood that the dragoman often bathed in the Bosphorus, and he had heard him lament that the ship was never becalmed so that he might make a dip; but he had supposed that if the Armenian ever really went out of his depth it was only for a few galvanic, convulsive strokes like his own, certainly nothing like this boisterous amphibian sporting among the billows. Hairabedian easily kept pace with the ship, sometimes flinging his short thick body half out of the water and sometimes diving under her and merging the other side, spouting water like a Triton. But his hallooing and bubbling vexed Mr Allen, who did not always hear his leadsman's cry: seeing this, Jack leant over the rail and called out, 'Mr Hairabedian, pray come aboard at once.'

Mr Hairabedian did so and stood there in a pair of black calico drawers tied at the knee and waist with white tapes which gave him a somewhat whimsical appearance: water dripped from his squat, shaggy, barrel-shaped person and from the fringe of black hair round his bald pate, but he had caught the air of disapproval and his broad frog-like grin of delight was gone, replaced by a look of profound submission. His embarrassment did not last, however: Mr Allen gave the word to let go, the anchor splashed down, the cable ran out, the ship swung head to wind, and the gunner began his eleven-gun salute, this number having been agreed to be given and received long since.

But the gunfire seemed to stun the Turks; or perhaps it had never roused them from their torpor. In any event there was no reply. During the long waiting silence Jack swelled with indignation. For himself he would put up with a good deal of offhand treatment or downright incivility, but he found the least slight to the Royal Navy perfectly intolerable: and this was not the least of slights by any means – the returning of salutes was a very serious matter indeed. Staring at the fort through his telescope he saw that what he had thought to be a village was in fact no more than a collection of tents with a number of asses and camels among them, together with a few depressed, unmilitary figures sitting in the shade – the whole thing was like some dismal, somnolent fair. In the fort itself there was no movement of any kind. 'Mr Hairabedian,' he said, 'jump into your clothes directly. Mr Mowett, go ashore and desire Mr Hairabedian to ask them what they are about – what they are thinking of. Bonden, my gig as quick as you like.'

Hairabedian plunged below, reappeared some moments later in a loose white garment and an embroidered skullcap, and was handed down into the gig by two powerful seamen, as monumentally displeased as their captain. The gig pulled for the shore at racing speed and ran well up the beach with its impetus; but before Mowett and Hairabedian had gone far into the dunes a gun began to utter weakly in the fort and a small party was seen coming down the path to meet them.

Jack did not wish to appear concerned, so passing his telescope to Calamy he began pacing the starboard side of the quarterdeck, his hands behind his back. Dr Maturin, however, had no such scruples; he was not there to uphold King George's dignity nor anyone else's, and he took the telescope from the reefer, training it on the group ashore. They had now reached the boat, and Hairabedian and three or four of the others were arguing in an oriental manner, waving their arms; but before Stephen could make out the nature of their disagreement (if disagreement it was) Martin drew his attention to a very high-flying bird away up in the pure bowl of the sky, planing against the wind on snowy wings, an almost certain spoonbill, and they watched it until the boat returned, bringing with it an Egyptian official, a civilian, worried, pale and drawn.

Jack took them below and called for coffee. 'Oh, sir, if you please,' said Hairebedian in a low discreet tone, 'the Effendi may not eat or drink until the sun has set. It is Ramadan.'

'In that case we must not tempt him, nor torment him by drinking it ourselves,' said Jack. 'Killick. Killick, there. Scrub the coffee. Well, now, Mr Hairabedian, what is afoot on shore? Is this gentleman come to invite us to land, or must I blow the fort about his ears?' Hairabedian looked alarmed, but then realizing that this was only Captain Aubrey's wit he gave a dutiful simper: the trouble was that the *Dromedary* had arrived too soon. She had not been expected until after the fast, and although the civilians had collected the pack animals – it was they that gave the hillside the appearance of a fair – the military officers were by no means ready. In these last days of Ramadan many Moslems retired to pray: Murad Bey was in the mosque at Katia, an hour or two away, and his second-in-command had accompanied a holy man to his retreat along the coast, taking the key of the magazine with them, which accounted for the delay in answering the *Dromedary*'s salute – the only remaining officer, an odabashi, had been obliged to use what was in the men's powder-horns.

'Is this gentleman the odabashi?' asked Jack.

'Oh no, sir. He is a learned man, an effendi, who writes poetical Arabic letters and speaks Greek. The odabashi is only a brutal soldier, a janissary of about the rank of a boatswain: he dare not leave his post to come aboard without orders, for Murad is a testy, an irascible, and would have him flayed and stuffed and sent to headquarters. But Abbas Effendi – bowing towards the Egyptian – 'the administrative official, is of quite a different kind: he has come to pay his respects, to assure you that everything in the civilian line – camels, tents, food – has been prepared, and to say that should you find anything wanting he would be happy to supply it. He also wishes to state that the day after tomorrow a large number of boats will be brought from the Menzala to carry your men and their equipment ashore.'

Jack smiled. 'Pray make all proper acknowledgments and tell the Effendi that I am very much obliged to him for his exertions: but he need not trouble with the boats – we have plenty of our own, and in any case by the day after tomorrow

I hope to be half way to Suez. Please to ask him whether he can tell us anything about the route to Suez.'

'He says he has travelled upon it several times, sir. A little way south of Tel Farama, the mound over there, it crosses the caravan track to Syria, by a well called Bir ed Dueidar. Then it becomes the pilgrims' road down to the Red Sea, where they take ship for Jeddah. There are other wells, and if they are dry there are the Balah lakes and Timsah. It is as flat as a table nearly all the way, and firm, unless there have been bad sand-storms that sometimes make moving dunes: but mostly firm.'

'Yes. That tallies with all I have heard: I am delighted to have it confirmed. By the way, I presume the odabashi has sent to tell Murad that we are here?'

'I am afraid not, sir: he says that the Bey must not be disturbed in his devotions on any account, and that he may come back to the fort tomorrow night, or the night after, and that anyway it would be best to wait until after the fast. Nothing is ever done during the fast.'

'I see. Then pray desire the Effendi to go on shore at once and to procure horses for you and me and a guide. We will follow him as soon as I have given the necessary directions.'

The Egyptian having been seen over the side, paler, more worried and anxious still, obviously faint from want of food, Jack summoned his officers. He told them to stand by for a landing in divisions, 'a landing vi et armis, gentlemen,' he said: and feeling rather pleased with this he repeated 'Vi et armis', looking for some slight response. He saw nothing but pleased expectancy and total incomprehension on the cheerful, attentive faces before him. They were happy to see him in such high spirits, but what really mattered at this point was clear, specific instructions: with an imperceptible inward sigh Captain Aubrey gave them. As soon as he threw out the signal, probably within half an hour, the men were to go ashore with their weapons and bags; they were to proceed in strict marching order to the encampment pre-pared for them, and there they were to await his directions; there was to be no straggling, and they were not to turn in, since if all went well Captain Aubrey hoped to march a short stage that night. Each watch must be provided with its due allowance of rum and tobacco for four days, so that if they had to be poisoned at least they would be poisoned like Christians: the kegs must be rigorously guarded, a petty-officer sitting on each all the time. And although native bread would be served out, the men were to carry biscuit for the same period; this would do away with any complaints from delicate stomachs. He raised his voice, directing it into the neighbouring cabin, where he knew that his steward was listening intently at the bulkhead and called, 'Killick. Killick, there. Lay out a frilled shirt, my number one coat, blue pantaloons, and Hessian boots: I am not going to ruin my white breeches, riding about all over Asia, etiquette or no. And my best scraper, with the chelengk shipped. D'ye hear me, there?'

Killick heard: and since he had grasped that the skipper was going to call on the Turkish commanding officer, for once he put out the finery with no tedious whining or proposing second-best: indeed, he went so far as to lay out Jack's Nile medal of his own mere notion, together with his hundred-guinea sword.

'Dear me,' thought Stephen as Captain Aubrey came on deck, buckling this same sword, 'he has added a cubit to his stature.' It was quite true: the prospect of decisive action seemed to make Jack grow in height and breadth; and it certainly gave him a different expression, more detached, remote, and self-contained. He was a big man in any case – one perfectly capable of carrying off a diamond spray in his hat without the least difficulty – and with this increase in moral size he became a more imposing figure by far, even to those who knew him intimately well as a mild, amiable, not always very wise companion.

He had a word with Mr Allen and then, just as he and Hairabedian were about to drop down into the waiting gig, he caught sight of Stephen and Martin. His closed, determined face broke into a smile and he called out, 'Doctor, I am going ashore. Do you choose to come too?' And seeing

Stephen glance at his neighbour he called, 'We can make room for Mr Martin as well, by sitting close.'

'To think that in five or ten minutes I shall tread the African shore,' said Martin as the boat pulled in. 'I had never hoped for so much.'

'I am grieved to disappoint you,' said Jack, 'but I am afraid that what you see ahead of you is the continent of Asia. Africa is somewhat to the right.'

'Asia!' cried Martin. 'So much the better.' He laughed aloud; and he was laughing still when the boat ground up on the Asian sand.

The sinister Davis at bow-oar skipped out with the gang-plank so that the Captain's gleaming boots should not be splashed, and he even carried good-nature so far as to give Stephen and Martin a rough, hairy hand as they came blundering forward in their hopelessly lubberly fashion.

A little way from the edge of the sea the sand gave way to a hard, ridged, strong-smelling mud, and the mud to the dunes. As they reached the dunes they lost the breeze entirely: heat rose from the ground and enveloped them, and with the heat came swarms of fat black fearless hairy flies that settled on them, crawling on their faces, up their sleeves and down their collars.

At the turn of the path they were met by a squat broad man with long dangling arms, a janissary who saluted in the Turkish manner and then stood staring at Jack and his chelengk with open consternation on his huge, greenish-yellow face, perhaps the ugliest in the Muslim world. 'This is the odabashi,' said Hairabedian. 'I see,' said Jack, returning the salute; but the man appeared to have nothing to say, and as it was to be hoped that both flies and heat might diminish on the castle hill, Jack walked steadily on. He had not gone five yards before the odabashi was there again, his uncouth person agitated with a variety of bows, his harsh voice filled with deference and anxiety. 'He begs you will pass by the main gate, so that he may turn out the guard and the trumpeters,' said Hairabedian. 'He begs you will step in and sit in the shade.' 'Thank him, but say I am pressed for time and cannot go a step out of my way,' said Jack. 'God damn these flies.'

The wretched odabashi was obviously torn between his fear of angering a person so highly decorated as Captain Aubrey and his dread of Murad Bey: he was barely coherent in his anguish, but one thing showed clear through all his broken observations and excuses – he was not going to take the responsibility of sending to his commanding officer. The Bey had given stringent orders that he was not to be disturbed, said the odabashi, and the first duty of a soldier was obedience.

'Damn the fellow,' said Jack, walking even faster through the flies. 'Tell him to go and moralize elsewhere.'

They were climbing now, climbing the hill of hardened mud upon which the castle stood, and once they had left the lee of the dunes the flies grew less; the heat, on the other hand, was greater still. 'You are going a very disagreeable colour,' said Stephen. 'Should not you throw off that thick coat, and loosen your neckcloth? Heavy, corpulent subjects are liable to be carried off in a twinkling, if not by a frank, straightforward apoplexy, then at least by a cerebral congestion.'

'I shall be all right as soon as I am in the saddle, moving briskly,' said Jack, who was very unwilling to disturb the perfect set of his cravat. 'There he is, the worthy Effendi, God bless him.'

They were approaching the encampment on the hillside to the east of the fort, which was already throwing a fine blue shadow down the slope, and Abbas could be seen, with a number of horses and their grooms, on the hither side of the pack animals and the tents. He sent a boy running down to meet them, a beautiful boy as slim and graceful as a gazelle, who salaamed with a winning smile, said he was to be their guide to Katia, and led them through the lines of tents and huts made of tamarisk branches and camels lying neatly, as composed as cats, looking proud.

'Camels! Camels!' cried Martin. 'And these, no doubt, are the tabernacles of Scripture.' His one eye was shining, and in spite of the flies and the oppressive heat – far worse for those fresh from the sea – his face expressed pure happiness, a striking contrast to the fasting apathetic camel-drivers, who lay in the shade, looking little more than half alive. The horses, on the other hand, were full of spirit: three charming Arabs, two of them bays and quite small, the third a mare of nearly sixteen hands, and all three standing on their toes as it were in pleasurable expectation. The mare was a remarkable golden colour and she was one of the most beautiful creatures Jack had ever seen, with a small high-bred head and huge lustrous eyes. His heart went out to her at once and she for her part was very willing to make his acquaintance, bringing her fine-cut little ears to bear and taking a most intelligent interest when he asked her how she did.

'Mr Hairabedian,' he said, stroking her neck, 'pray tell the Effendi that I admire his taste extremely – most grateful – prodigious handsome mare – and then go on and tell him of the arrangements we have made for the landing of the men. They will wait here until I come back: I hope to return shortly after sunset and by that time therefore the tents should be struck, lanterns provided, beasts watered and all hands fed, so that we may get under way without the loss of a minute.'

Hairabedian conveyed all this: Abbas looked pleased, or at least less anxious, and said that the Captain's directions should be carried out to the letter.

'Capital,' said Jack. 'Dr Maturin, be so good as to throw out the signal to the ship, by waving your handkerchief.' He was just about to mount when the odabashi plunged forward and seized the stirrup to help him up; and as he did so he said something that sounded extraordinarily like 'Beg parm, me Lord.'

'Thankee, odabashi,' said Jack. 'You are an honest fellow, no doubt, though uncommon stupid. What now?' – this to Stephen, who had laid a hand upon his bridle.

'I take it there would be no objection to our going a little way towards the delta, perhaps on a camel, just to set our feet in Africa, and even to see a little of the African flora?'

'None in the world,' said Jack. 'Gather posies by the score, so long as you take care not to be devoured by lions or crocodiles, and, which is even more important, so long as you are back here in time. Should you like Hairabedian to arrange it with the Effendi?'

'Not at all, not at all. We can manage very well in Greek. Good day, now, and God bless you.'

Jack turned his horse's head, following the boy, and they rode cautiously down the slope, bearing left-handed round the castle; as they reached the level ground on the farther side a group of black tents came into sight, with camels and tethered horses, a Bedouin encampment, and the mare, raising her head high, uttered a fine ringing whinny. A gross figure in a dirty nightshirt and a long grey beard came out of one of his tents and waved: she whinnied again, looking steadfastly in his direction.

'The boy says that is Mahommed ibn Rashid, the great enormous fat man of the Beni Khoda, the heaviest man in the northern wilderness. The horse is his. It was thought most suitable for you,' said Hairabedian.

'Well,' said Jack, 'there is nothing like candour. Come, my dear,' he went on, addressing the mare, who showed a distinct inclination to join the tents, 'it is only an hour or so to Katia: just carry me there, and then you shall go back to your master.'

He had no sort of doubt that she understood him perfectly well: she twitched her little ears once or twice, then brought them to bear right-forward, gave a curious little skip, changing foot, and set out at a swinging pace. They left the ruins of Pelusium and its mound on their right; and now there was nothing but flat hard sand, more reddish than dun and sprinkled with small flat stones, before them and on either hand; and now the mare really got into her stride, a very long, smooth, powerful trot, so light and even that she might have been carrying a child, and a meagre child at that, rather than a massive post-captain in something near full-dress uniform with a world of gold lace on it. But this was nothing to her gallop. The boy had pushed his horse ahead; she could not bear it, and Jack felt her grow tense. He gave her her head and she instantly changed pace, with an immensely powerful drive from behind. In a few moments she was far beyond the little bay, going fast and free out over the dead-flat plain, faster than Jack had ever known, yet still with this same effortless even perfection, high-sprung and aerial – a kind of flying, for indeed they only touched the ground at long intervals. Now the welcome wind streamed in his face, pierced his thick coat, and filled his heart with joy; never had he so delighted in being on a horse's back; never had he felt such a good rider; and never in fact had he ridden so well.

But it could not last: very gently he reined in, saying, 'Come, my dear, this ain't sober, responsible conduct. We have a long way to go.' She whinnied again, and to his astonishment he found that she was scarcely breathing faster than before.

When the others came up (Hairabedian labouring heavily) he asked her name. 'Yamina,' said the boy.

'If we bring this caper off,' thought Jack, 'and if money can tempt the great enormous fat man of the wilderness, I shall take her home and keep her as a pet. She would teach all the children to ride, one after another; and she would even reconcile Sophie with horses.'

They rode on at a sober, responsible pace, and his thoughts moved forward to his meeting with Murad. He knew, from his experience in the Ionian, that there was often a wide difference between the interests of the Sublime Porte and those of local Turkish commanders, a wide difference between what the one ordered and the other performed. He turned over various lines of approach in his mind, but dismissed them all. 'If he is a straightforward candid Turk we shall agree directly: if he is a devious brute, I shall have to find out the nature of his deviousness. And if I cannot deal with it, I shall make the passage on my own, even though that would be a damned bad beginning.'

Now that this somewhat remote and hypothetical scheme

had more nearly become a possibility, he longed for its success with his whole being. The treasure that the galley was said to be bringing up to Mubara entered into the line of count of course: but it was not the whole reason for his eagerness, nor anything like it. For some time now he had been dissatisfied with himself and although as a result of his being sent into the Ionian the French had been turned out of Marga he knew very well how much had depended on luck and on the excellent conduct of his Turkish and Albanian allies. He had also sunk the *Torgud*. But that was more in the nature of a massacre than an evenly-fought battle, and mere slaughter could not cure that deep dissatisfaction. It seemed to him that his reputation in the service (and with himself as one who watched Jack Aubrey's doings from a certain distance and with an almost perfect knowledge of his motives) was based on two or three fortunate actions, sea-fights that he could look back upon with real pleasure, small though they were; but they belonged to the past; they had all happened long ago; and now there were several men who stood far higher in the esteem of those whose opinion he valued. Young Hoste, for example, had done wonders in the Adriatic, and Hoste was junior to him on the post-captain's list. It was as though he were running a race: a race in which he had done fairly well for a while, after a slow start, but one in which he could not hold his lead and was being overtaken, perhaps from lack of that particularly nameless quality that brought some men success when it just eluded others, though they might take equal pains. He could not put his finger on the fault with any certainty, and there were days when he could say with real conviction that the whole thing was mere fatality, the other side of the good luck that had attended him in his twenties and early thirties, the restoration of the average. But there were other days when he felt that his profound uneasiness was an undeniable proof of the fault's existence, and that although he himself might not be able to name it, it was clear enough to others, particularly those in power: at all events they had given many of the good appointments to other men, not to him.

'Sir,' said Hairabedian. 'Here is Katia.'

Jack looked up. He had been riding so easy, with such a perfect rhythm under him, that he had sunk deep in his reflection, and he was surprised to see a small town quite close, with groves of date-palms to the left, apparently springing directly from the sand, and the turquoise-blue dome of a mosque to the right, and white-walled, flat-roofed houses in between. Their path had already joined the caravan route to Syria, a broad track running as straight as a stretched cord eastwards, and far ahead a string of laden camels striding away towards Palestine.

As they rode into the town they passed a great heap of rubbish just by the wells, and a mixed flock of vultures rose from it. 'What are those birds?' asked Jack.

'The boy says the black and white ones are Pharaoh's hens,' said Hairabedian, 'and the large dark kinds are all called the Sons of Filth.'

'I hope the Doctor sees them,' said Jack. 'He loves a singular bird, whatever its parentage. God help us, what an oven,' he added to himself, for now that they had slowed to a walk the air was still, and the heat reverberated from the shimmering walls of the town, while the declining sun, low in the west but still ferociously strong, beat full on his back.

Katia was small, but it possessed an unusually fine coffee-house: the boy led them through the narrow, empty, sleeping streets to its inner courtyard and called for grooms in a shrill authoritative voice. Jack was glad to see that the horses were well known here: indeed, Yamina was treated with what he would have thought an extravagant degree of respect if he had not ridden her.

They walked into a large dim high-ceilinged room with a fountain in the middle; a broad padded bench ran round three sides, under latticed, unglazed windows, shaded with green fronds outside; and on this bench, cross-legged, sat two or three small groups of men, silently smoking hookahs or conversing in low voices. The talk stopped dead at their coming in, but in scarcely a second it carried on, still in the same low tone. There was a delicious coolness in the air, and as the boy led them to a secluded corner Jack said to himself, 'If I sit here without moving, perhaps in time the sweat will stop running down my back.'

'The child is going to tell the Bey that you are here,' said Hairabedian. 'He says that he is the only person who could disturb him at such a time without danger: he also observes that as we are only Christians we may call for food and drink, if we choose.'

Jack checked the words that came naturally to his mind and coolly replied that he preferred to wait. It would not only be uncivil to these bearded gentlemen to eat and drink when they could not, but it might quite reasonably vex the Bey to come in and find him swallowing the pints of sherbet that he longed for. He sat there listening to the fountain, and the coolness flowed into him; as the daylight faded his mind dwelt with pleasure on that glorious horse, and it was not until he saw the boy come running back that he felt a stab of anxiety. The boy had evidently been eating: he swallowed hastily, brushed crumbs from round his mouth, and cried, 'He comes!'

He came indeed, a small trim figure with a cropped white beard and moustache, a close-wrapped turban and a plain uniform, the only glory being his jade-hilted yataghan and his fine red boots. He came straight across to Jack and shook his hand in the European manner, and Jack saw with great pleasure that he might have been own brother to Sciahan, his former ally, a candid, straightforward Turk.

'The Bey welcomes you and asks, are you here already?' said Hairabedian.

A soldierly question of this kind made Jack feel quite at home: he said that he was; that he thanked the Bey for his welcome; and that he was very happy to see him.

'The Bey asks, will you take some refreshment?'

'Tell the Bey that I shall be happy to drink sherbet whenever he sees fit to do so himself.'

'The Bey says he was at Acre with Lord Smith when Buonaparte was defeated: he recognized your uniform directly. He desires you will walk into the kiosk and smoke tobacco with him.'

Around the bubbling water-pipe in a small green privacy the interview went on in the direct, uncomplicated way that Jack had longed for. Murad urged Captain Aubrey to wait until the new moon and the end of Ramadan, since the escort, being janissaries and strict observers, could hardly march long stages fasting in the heat of the day; and it would only be a little while until Sheker Bairam, the feast at the end of the fast, when the Captain and the Bey could eat together all day long. But when Jack very earnestly represented to him that there was not a minute to be lost, that delay must have the most unfortunate effects on the whole expedition, and that his plan was to march by night, he smiled and said, 'You young men are always impatient to be doing. Well, I will ride back with you this evening and give orders for your escort. I will give you my odabashi: he is stupid, but he is as brave as a bear and obedient to command and he beats his men into equal obedience; and I believe he has notions of the Low Dutch. He will pick three or four men, if they can be found, who are not afraid of spirits or the night-demon – the desert is full of them, you know. But I am an old man, and I have been fasting all day; I need some sustenance before the ride. You will not mind waiting until the sun has set?'

Jack said that he should be very happy to wait, and in the meantime he begged Murad to tell him about the siege of Acre. 'I am acquainted with Sir Sidney Smith,' he observed, 'and I had some friends in the *Tigre* and *Theseus*, but I never heard an account from the Turkish point of view.'

He heard one now; and Murad was giving him a very lively description of the last desperate assault, with the French colours actually flying from one of the outer towers, furious fighting in the breach, and Jezzar Pasha sitting in his chair behind it, handing out ammunition and rewarding those who brought him Frenchmen's heads, when a general noise throughout the coffee-house and the town itself showed that the long, long day of abstinence was at a lawful end and that men might eat and drink again.

It was quite dark when they rode out of the courtyard, their horses' hoofs muffled in the sanded alleys, and the darkness was made even deeper by the lanterns that accompanied them to the gate; but once they were well out on the caravan route, with eyes used to the night, the whole desert was bathed in gentle starlight. Venus had set, Mars was too small and too low in the east to shine with any effect, and there were no other planets in the sky; yet the fixed stars alone, hanging like lamps in the pure sky, were so strong that Jack could see all general forms and even the white of Murad's beard moving as he spoke.

He was still speaking of the siege of Acre, and what he said was extremely interesting; but Jack wished that he would keep his tale for later. In the first place the Bey rode slowly when he was talking; in the second Hairabedian had to post himself between them to pass the words on, turned from Turkish to English, and being a nervous rider, unaccustomed to the darkness, he made progress slower still by perpetually jagging his horse's mouth; in the third Yamina was eager to be home, so that Jack had to keep holding her in, and she was beginning to dislike him; and in the fourth he was himself very much in want of food. The Bey, in the Spartan janissary fashion, had eaten no more than a mess of curds and whey; he had indeed offered some to Jack, but with the reserve that there would be a roast sheep at the fort which Captain Aubrey must share and that perhaps it might be a pity to spoil his appetite. Captain Aubrey had acquiesced, confining himself to sherbet: now he regretted it bitterly.

On the way to Katia the desert had seemed perfectly sterile; now it was, if not full of life, then at least tolerably well inhabited. Three or four times small dark creatures ran or bounded across their path so close that Yamina skipped and danced in a wide half-circle, and once something very like a fat serpent two yards long made her stand up on her hind legs and give a bound that very nearly unseated him. Then, when the mound of Pelusium stood out against the starlit sky fine on the starboard bow, a pack of jackals set up a prodigious din not far from the track, screaming and yelling so as to drown Murad's voice, and in a momentary pause came the even more disagreeable noise of a hyaena, whose howl ended in a long mad quavering laugh, enormously loud in the warm still air.

'Are those your spirits or night-demons?' asked Jack.

'No, no, those are only jackals and a hyaena,' said the Bey. 'I noticed a dead ass over there not long ago, and no doubt that is what they are quarrelling over. No: for real fiends you must go to that mound. In the ruined tower there sleeps a jinn, about the size of this boy here: it has long upright ears and terrible orange eyes – we often see it. And a troop of ghouls live in one of the old cisterns.'

'I am not at all superstitious,' said Jack, 'but I like to learn about spirits. Have you other fiends or perhaps I should say genii in the neighbourhood?'

'Fiends? Oh yes, yes,' said the Bey impatiently, 'the desert is full of fiends of one kind or another, assuming various shapes: it is common knowledge. If you want to know about fiends you must ask our hakim; he is a learned man and he knows every jinn between here and Aleppo.'

Once they had passed Pelusium and had begun to turn about the hill of Tina they saw the fires of the Bedouins, then those of the naval encampment and the lit windows and gateway of the fort itself. And as they climbed the path – Jack holding Yamina hard to stop her going home at a run – the wafting air brought them the smell of roasting sheep.

A few minutes later they walked into the great hall, and Jack's dazzled eyes beheld the whole body of janissaries seated round their regimental cauldron, officers and all in the democratic Turkish way, with Stephen and Martin on either side of the hakim, the regimental wise man and physician. All hands rose and bowed and in a moment the circle was formed again, with the Bey in his due place and Jack beside him. Apart from ceremonial words as the newcomers washed their hands there was not much conversation, the fasting men being very deeply concerned with their mutton: they ate the first sheep entirely, together with a mountain of saffron-yellow rice, and the second was little more than a bare rib-cage by the time men began to lean back from the pot, to talk, and to move about. Beautiful great brass coffee-pots made their appearance; and after a certain amount of change among the officers Jack found Stephen and Martin at his side. He asked them whether they had had a pleasant afternoon, and whether they had seen the birds and animals they had hoped for. They thanked him and said that it had been very pleasant indeed, apart from a few untoward incidents, such as the frowardness of one of the camels, which bit Mr Martin and then ran away. It was not a very serious wound, but it gave Mr Martin some uneasiness, as the camel's bite was generally held to convey syphilis; the hakim, however, had dressed it with an ointment derived from the skink. Then the other camel, though not vicious, had declined to kneel, so that they could not mount but were obliged to lead it home over the desert, sometimes running lest they should be late. 'Yet at least you did see some birds?' asked Jack. 'There were any number near Katia.' Both gentlemen seemed rather reserved; but at last Martin described their reaching a dense reed-bed, their slow progress through the glutinous mud, the air being thick, thick with feasting mosquitoes, their rising hopes as they heard movements and cries before them, and their eventually reaching an open pool, where they found one common moor-hen and two honest British coots, while on the branch of a nearby willow there was a bird that they managed to identify, though their faces were so swollen with mosquito-bites that their eyes could hardly open, as a hen chaffinch. 'It was perhaps a little arduous at times,' said Martin, 'particularly on our return, when we stumbled in the camel-thorn, but how eminently worth while our pains, since we have seen old Nilus' flood!'

'Furthermore,' said Stephen, 'I have every reason to believe that the eagle-owl is present. Not only have I seen his rejections, but Abbas Effendi imitated his voice unmistakably, a deep, strong Uhu, uhu, calculated to strike terror into mammals as large as a gazelle, and birds the size of a bustard.'

'Well, that is a mercy, I am sure,' said Jack. 'Mr Hairabedian, I believe that at this stage we may tell the Bey that I should like to see Mr Mowett and the Egyptian official, so that if their report is satisfactory we may take our leave as soon as it is civil.'

The Bey said that he was acquainted with Captain Aubrey's impatience, and that he would not detain him if it appeared that the column was ready to move off. 'And,' he added, 'since the odabashi will lead the escort, he had better go and pay his compliments to the corresponding officer.' He contorted his face sideways, and with an English intonation and a knowing look he said, 'Boatswine.' Then he rapped on the ritual cauldron, and there was an instant silence. Everything was now perfectly regimental. 'Odabashi,' he said, and the odabashi stood up. 'Odabashi, you and five men will escort the Captain, beloved of the Sultan, to Suez, marching by night just as he bids you. Choose them directly and go with the dragoman, who will lead you to the officer of the same rank as yourself.'

The odabashi put his hand to his forehead and bowed. In a hoarse voice he named five men and followed Hairabedian out of the castle.

Mr Hollar the boatswain, Mr Borrell the gunner, and Mr Lamb the carpenter were drinking tea in the warrant-officers' tent when the dragoman brought them their visitor. He explained his status and function, saying, 'I presume he will mess with you.' He then said that he must hurry on and find the first lieutenant and Abbas, because the Captain wished to know how things stood.

'They stand pretty well,' said the bosun, 'all stretched along and the anchor apeak. Every fifth camel has a lantern shipped abaft its load, ready to be lit, and all the saucy ones have been muzzled. There is only this and the gunroom tent to be struck, and in five minutes we are under way. As for

Mr Mowett, you will find him beyond the big fire where the starboard watch are sitting.'

'Thank you,' said Hairabedian. 'I must run.' He vanished into the darkness, leaving the odabashi standing there.

'Have a cup of tea,' said the bosun in a very loud voice; and then louder still, 'Tea. Cha.'

The odabashi made no reply but an awkward writhe of his body and stood looking at the ground, his arms dangling low on either side.

'Well, this is a hairy bugger, and no mistake,' said the bosun, surveying him. 'Such a ugly cove I never seen: more like a hape than what you might call a human.'

'Hape!' cried the odabashi, stung out of his shyness. 'You can put that where the monkey put the nuts. You're no oil-painting yourself, neither.'

The dead silence that followed this was broken at last by the bosun, who asked, 'Did the odabashi speak English?'

'Not a fucking word,' said the odabashi.

'No offence intended, mate,' said the bosun, holding out his hand.

'And none taken,' said the odabashi, shaking it.

'Sit down on this bag,' said the gunner.

'Why didn't you tell the Captain?' asked the carpenter. 'He would have been right pleased.'

The odabashi scratched himself, muttering something about being too bashful. 'I did speak up once,' he added, 'but he did not mind me.'

'So you speak English,' said the bosun, who had been staring heavily for some time, turning the matter over in his mind. 'How does that come about, if I may make so bold?'

'Which I am a janissary,' said the odabashi.

'I'm sure you are, mate,' said the carpenter. 'And very much to your credit, too.'

'You know how janissaries are recruited, in course?'

They looked at one another with perfectly blank faces, and all slowly shook their heads.

'Nowadays it is not so strict,' said the odabashi, 'and all

sorts of odds and sods get in, but when I was a little chap it was all by what we call the devshurmeh. It still is, but not so much, if you understand me. The tournaji-bashi goes round all the provinces where there are Christians, mostly Albania and Bosnia, the others being what you might call scum, and in each place he takes up a certain number of Christian boys, sometimes more, sometimes less, whatever their parents may say. And these boys are fetched away to a special barracks where their pricks are trimmed pardon me the expression and they are learnt to be Mussulmans and good soldiers. And when they have served their time as ajami, as we say, they are turned over to an orta of janissaries.'

'So I suppose a good many janissaries talk foreign,' observed the carpenter.

'No,' said the odabashi. 'They are took so young and so far off they forget their language and their religion and their people. It was different with me. My mum was in the same town. She was from the Tower Hamlets in London, and went cook-maid with a Turkey-merchant's family to Smyrna, where she took up with my dad, a cake-maker from Argyrocastro, which made trouble with the family. He took her back to Argyrocastro, but then he died and the cousins put her out of the shop, that being the law, so she had to sell her cakes from a stall. Then the tournaji-bashi came round, and the cousins' lawyer gave his clerk a present to take me, which he did – took me right away to Widin, leaving her alone.'

'And she a widow-woman,' said the carpenter, shaking his head.

'It was cruel hard,' said the bosun.

'I hate a lawyer,' said the gunner.

'But I had not been a prentice-soldier in Widin six months before there was Mum with her stall of cakes outside the barracks: so we saw one another every Friday, and often other times; and it was the same in Belgrade and Constantinople when I was out of my time. Wherever the orta went. And so I never forgot my English.'

'Perhaps that was why they sent you here,' suggested the bosun.

'If it was, I wish I had cut my tongue out,' said the odabashi.

'Don't you like it here?'

'I hate it here. Present company excepted.'

'Why so, mate?'

'I always been in cities, and I hate the country. And the desert is ten times far worse than the country.'

'Lions and tigers, maybe?'

'Worse, mate.'

'Serpents?'

The odabashi shook his head, and leaning towards them he whispered, 'Jinns and ghouls.'

'What are jinns?' asked the bosun, somewhat shocked.

'Fairies,' said the odabashi, after a moment's consideration.

'You don't believe in fairies, do you?'

'What, not when I seen a fucking great fairy in the old tower over there? This high' – holding his hand a yard from the ground – 'with long ears and orange eyes? In the night it goes Uhu, uhu, and every time some poor unfortunate bugger cops it somewhere or other. No worse omen in this mortal world. I've heard it almost every night the last week and more.' He paused, and then said, 'I didn't ought to have said fairies. Spirits is more like. Unholy ghosts.'

'Oh,' said the bosun, who might scorn fairies, but who, like most sailors and certainly all his shipmates in the *Surprise*, most heartily believed in ghosts and spirits.

'And what are ghouls?' asked the gunner in a low, almost furtive voice, dreading to hear yet drawing his bag closer.

'Ho, they are far, far worse,' said the odabashi. 'They often take the shape of young females, but the insides of their mouths are green, like their eyes. You see them walking about in graveyards sometimes, and after dark they dig up the fresh corpses and eat them. Ay, and not always so fresh, either. But they take all sorts of shapes, like the jinns, and you meet them both at every turn in this bloody desert we got to walk across. The only thing to do is to say transiens per medium illorum ibat very quick without a mistake or you're . . .'

At this time of night throughout the fast the castle cooks flung the bony remains of their feast over the outer wall; and now the jackals were ready waiting. But once again they fell foul of the hyaena and four more of her kind, and the odabashi's words were cut off by a sudden Bedlam of screaming, howling and terrible laughter not twenty yards away. The *Surprise*'s warrant-officers leapt to their feet, grasping one another; and as they stood there aghast a heavy body landed on the pole above them. A moment later its enormous voice filled the tent: Uhu, uhu, uhu.

A frozen silence inside the tent and a startled silence outside followed the last Uhu, and in this silence they heard a still larger voice cry, 'Strike that tent up forward there. D'ye hear me there? Where's the bosun? Pass the word for the bosun. Mr Mowett, the first party may light its lanterns and stand by to move off.'

Chapter Six

'Dearest Sophie,' wrote Captain Aubrey to his wife,

'I take advantage of the kindness of Major Hooper, of the Madras establishment, to send you these few hurried lines: he is on his way home, travelling over-land – last from the Persian gulf across the desert on an amazingly fine white thoroughbred camel that carried him a hundred miles a day – and so far he has only spent forty-nine days on his journey: he means to go on by way of Cairo.

'We came here in pretty good order, marching by night and resting under tents and awnings during the heat of the day, and we crossed the isthmus sooner than I or the head camel-driver had thought possible, having made four stages in three in spite of a late start the first night. This was not because of any extraordinary zeal on the part of the men (although they are a very decent ship's company, as you know) but because a mighty stupid English-speaking Turk in command of our escort had filled their heads with tales of ghosts and genii, and the poor silly fellows hurried forward all night long at a sort of shuffling trot, all crammed together, each dreading to be left any distance behind, and all want-ing to be very near Byrne of the foretop, a man with a lucky snuffbox, warranted to preserve the owner from evil spirits and the falling-sickness. And unhappily there was always something to keep them

in a high pitch of superstitious dread. We camped
by wells; there were always bushes and stretches of
camel-thorn nearby, and in them there was always
some creature to howl or scream like a soul in torment at dawn or dusk or both. Then as if that were
not enough there were the mirages by day, scores of
them; I remember one that happened when we
moved off early, well before sunset, from Bir el Gada.
No great way from us, so clear and sharp you would
have sworn they were real, there appeared shining
water and green palm-trees, with girls walking under
them, carrying pots and talking. "Oh, oh," cried my
pack of idiots, "it's ghouls – we are lost." And there
was that great savage brute Davis (a cannibal, to my
certain knowledge) clinging to the bosun with his
eyes tight shut and the bosun clinging to a camel-
girth and both of them calling out to little Calamy,
begging him to tell them when it was all over. A
most pitiful set of poltroons; and I should have been
ashamed of their being seen, but that the Turks were
just as bad.

'And I must say that Stephen was not always quite
as discreet as he might have been. When Parson
Martin tried to dismiss ghouls and the like as weak
superstition he set him down with the Witch of
Endor and the Gadarene swine and evil spirits by
the dozen out of Holy Writ – cited all sorts of classical
ghosts, appealed to the unvarying tradition of all
nations and ages, and gave us a circumstantial
account of a Pyrenean werewolf of his acquaintance
that absolutely terrified the younger mids. He and
Martin hardly had any sleep at all (unless they dozed
on their camels by night when we were on the march)
for while the rest of us lay under our awnings they
hurried about the bushes finding all sorts of plants
and creatures; but I think he might not have brought
in so many serpents – he must know how uneasy
they make seamen feel – and he certainly should

never have brought the monstrous bat, three foot across. It flew from the table and clapped on to poor Killick's chest, and I thought he would faint away from mere terror, believing it to be an unclean spirit, as well he might.

'He did faint away the next afternoon – you would have felt for him – from a mixture of heat-stroke and vexation. A pair of camels ran mad (they often do when they come in season, I am told) and they had a frightful set-to on and over my tent, roaring and bubbling and scattering my belongings far and wide. All hands clapped on to their legs and tails and hauled them apart in time, but by then my best hat had been most cruelly used. I was sorry for it, because it had my Turkish decoration by way of cockade: I had meant the diamonds as a present for you, and in the meantime I hoped they would give me greater weight with the Turks. But the chelengk had been trod deep into the sand, and although Killick, helped by many others, turned over tons of desert until the sun set and as I say he fainted clean away, we had to march on without it, poor Killick slung over a camel.

'Reverting to Stephen: you know his sparing way of life, of course – one new coat every ten years, threadbare breeches, odd stockings, nothing spent except on books and philosophical instruments – well, he perfectly astonished me by flashing out an extraordinary quantity of gold at Tina and buying himself a positive herd of camels (like Job) to transport this precious diving-bell I have told you about: it takes to pieces, but each piece needs a stout beast to carry it. The Egyptian who assembled the pack-animals for our journey had not reckoned on a diving-bell, but fortunately there was a Bedouin encampment, with camels for sale, near at hand. And oh Sophie, in that same encampment there was such a mare . . .'

Reaching the end of his description he paused for a while, smiling, and then went on,

'So we arrived here in excellent time, and with only one casualty – the dragoman most unhappily pulled on his boot when there was a scorpion in it, and now he is laid up with a leg like a bolster. I am heartily sorry for it, he being a most capable, obliging man, speaking all the languages of the Levant and excellent English too – might have built the Tower of Babel singlehanded. We arrived, but alas, once again our friends were not ready for us. The Company's ship was here, looking very much the bluff-bowed, broad-beamed merchantman, with nearly all her guns out of sight below and a lascar crew, the only European being one of the Company's Mocha pilots; and there was a fine northerly breeze to carry her down the gulf. But where were the Turks who were to go aboard her?

'I called at the Egyptian governor's house, but he was away, and it appeared that the lieutenant-governor, a new man, the product of some recent upheaval, was not acquainted with the scheme: he seemed anxious only to be paid some absurd sum by way of harbour-dues and watering-fees for the *Niobe*, and customs on her fictitious cargo. Pressed by Hairabedian, who was brought on a stretcher, he did admit that there was a Turkish detachment in the neighbourhood – they had moved some way off – he was not quite sure where – they might come back after the end of Ramadan – however, he would send to tell them we were here. But it was clear he did not love the Turks; and it would have been strange if the Turks could possibly have loved him, even if they had tried with all their might. He was pretty off-hand with me – how I regretted my chelengk! – but Hairabedian said that at this point, in view of the very delicate relations between Turkey and Egypt, it would not do to fall out with him. He did not send to the Turks, of course, and with Hairabedian laid up I was hamstrung; and all the time there was this perfect wind a-blowing, infernally hot but in the right direction, and all the time the precious hours fled by, the moon smaller every time she rose. It was only by a stroke of luck that I found my soldiers in the end: our escort had spent some time in the town, waiting for the end of the fast before going back to Tina and spending the gratuity I had given them in high living after dark; and before leaving their odabashi came to say goodbye to our warrant-officers. He told them that in consequence of a disagreement between the Egyptian governor and the Turkish commanding officer the Turks had withdrawn to the Wells of Moses, and that according to the bazaar rumour the Egyptian contemplated setting the Beni Ataba, a marauding Bedouin tribe, on them: and although that was probably nonsense, the Egyptians were certainly not to be trusted. I sent at once to the Wells of Moses, but by now it was Bairam, the end of the fast, and the Turkish officer's only reply was to invite me to their feast, swearing that he should not stir till we had shared a camel-calf – one or two or three days more, said he, made no great odds. Most unhappily the Egyptian had also asked me, and Hairabedian said he would be mortally offended if I did not go, and in my best uniform too. So I went to both.'

For a moment he thought of telling her about the Egyptian's feast, the interminable Arab music, the enormous heat as he sat there hour after hour, smiling as pleasantly as he could, and about the fat ladies who danced, or at least writhed and quivered for so long, ogling as they did so; about the ride to Moses' Wells, the Turkish welcome with kettledrums, trumpets and salvoes of musketry, and the glutinous, viscid texture of camel-calf seethed with almonds, honey and very large quantities of coriander, and the effect of a temperature of a hundred and twenty degrees in the shade on a body crammed with two successive feasts. But instead of doing so he spoke of the difficulty of communicating with Midhat Bimbashi, the Turkish commanding officer.

'Since the dragoman was in too bad a way to be moved, poor fellow, Stephen very kindly came along, to do what he could with Greek and the lingua franca and a little of the kind of Arabic they speak in Morocco. This answered tolerably well for ordinary dinner-time remarks like *Capital soup, sir*, or *Allow me to offer you another of these sheep's eyes*, but towards the end of the meal, when everyone withdrew except for the two senior officers and the splendid Arab gentleman we are to put on the throne of Mubara, and when I very much wanted to make the Bimbashi aware of the extreme importance of dispatch, our jargon failed us miserably. It had become clear that neither the Turk nor the Egyptian had any notion of the galley that was to put off from Kassawa that very day or perhaps the next carrying the Frenchmen and their treasure north (which was odd, I may say in passing, because before he became so very ill Hairabedian told me that an Arabian merchant in Suez had confirmed the loading of the galley down there in Kassawa with a large number of cases, small, but strongly guarded and heavier than lead), so it was obviously essential that we should make him understand the present situation. But every time we did so both the officers roared with laughter. Turks don't laugh easy, as you know, and these, though young and active, had been as grave as judges hitherto. But when he said *hurry*, they could not contain; they burst out and fairly hooted, rolling from side to side and beating their thighs; and when they could speak they would wipe their eyes and say *tomorrow* or *next week*. Even Hassan, the stately Arab, joined in at last, whinnying like a horse.

'Then the hookah was brought in and there we sat smoking, the Turks chuckling to themselves from time to time, the Arab smiling, and Stephen and I sadly out of countenance. At last Stephen had another try, turning the phrase about, and blowing to show that we must take advantage of the favourable wind – that everything depended on the wind. But it was no good. At the first hint of that unhappy word the Turks exploded, and one sent such a blast of air down his hookah-tube that the water spurted up, putting out the tobacco. "Ah, zut alors," says Stephen; the Arab turns to him – "You speak French, Monsieur?" says he, and straight away they fall to it, talking about twenty to the dozen: for it seems that Hassan, like his cousin the present Sheikh, was taken up by the Frenchmen when he was young.

'Man and boy I have seen some pretty sudden changes of expression, but none quite as instantaneous and thoroughgoing as the Bimbashi's shift from twinkling, full-fed merriment to the most intense and concentrated seriousness when the Arab translated the piece about the French treasure. At first he could not credit the amount, though Stephen had very wisely plumped for the lower estimate of two thousand five hundred purses, and he turned to me. "Yes," I said tracing the sum with half-melted Turkish delight on the floor (our figures are much the same, you know) "and perhaps this", writing five thousand.

'"Oh, indeed?" says he, clapping his hands, and in another minute the whole place was as busy as an overturned beehive, with men running in every direction, petty-officers bawling, drums beating and trumpets sounding. By dawn they were all aboard, every last man-jack of them: and the breeze was blowing steadily in our teeth.

'It had changed overnight and it has stayed there

ever since, blowing hard; and if you look at the map you will see that to run SSE down the long narrow Gulf of Suez we absolutely have to have a leading wind. From time to time the Bimbashi tears his hair and flogs his men; from time to time the damp heat and the frustration make me feel that my little body is aweary of this great world; and from time to time the men (who are all perfectly aware of what we are about and who are all pirates at heart) get at me through the midshipmen or the officers or Killick or Bonden to let me know that they would be very happy to kedge the barky out if I should see fit, and be d——d to sunstroke and apoplexy. While such a wind is blowing I cannot conscientiously do so in this shallow unsheltered harbour, with its dog-leg channels, its sharp coral rocks and its poor holding-ground, but I may try if it lessens; though Heaven knows a man can scarcely walk the length of the ship without breaking into a muck-sweat, let alone engage in the very laborious task of warping a ship. Even the lascars can hardly bear it. In the meantime we do what we can by way of preparation – setting the guns in place, and so on – otherwise we sit gnashing our teeth. Mowett and Rowan are apt to quarrel: I am sorry to have to say so, but I am afraid there is no room for two nightingales in one bush. The only contented men are Stephen and Mr Martin. They spend hours bubbling away down there in their bell, sending up worms and little bright-coloured fishes and pieces of coral, and even eating their meals in it; or else they wander all day on the reefs, peering at the creatures in the shallow water and the birds – they tell me they have seen ospreys by the score. Stephen never has minded the heat, however excessive; but how Mr Martin supports it, even with his green umbrella, I cannot say. He is grown as thin as a crane, if you can imagine a crane that perpetually smiles. Forgive me, Sophie; here is Major Hooper,

urgent to be on his way. With my dear love to you
and the children, your most affectionate husband,

Jno Aubrey.'

When he had seen the Major off Jack returned, gasping, to
his cabin, where air without the least refreshment came tearing through the open scuttles. Far away, against a line of
tall, bowing palms on the western shore, he saw Stephen
and Martin carrying a fair-sized turtle between them. A boat
came alongside: still another Arab visitor for Mr Hairabedian. Through the skylight overhead he heard Mowett say,
'I love to linger near the leafless wood, Where cold and shrill
the blasts of winter blow,' and for some reason this brought
a picture of last night's moon before his eye – no longer the
sickle of Bairam, but an odiously thick slice of melon in the
sky, a fat moon that must shine on the galley well advanced
in her voyage to Mubara. 'And yet we did not lose a minute,
coming across the isthmus: I really cannot blame myself for
that,' he reflected. But perhaps he should have handled the
Egyptian more tactfully, or have found some cleverer,
quicker way of getting into touch with the Turks in spite of
him; he turned the possibilities over in his mind, but sleep
came welling up through the accusations, softening them a
little. 'The best-led mice gang oft astray,' said one side of
his mind, and before the other had quite formulated the
answer, 'Yes, but unlucky leaders are not the men to be
entrusted with a delicate, ill-prepared mission,' he dropped
off: though indeed the notion lingered deep, ready to come
to life again.

He had acquired the ability to go fast asleep at any time
early in his naval career and although years had passed since
he kept a watch he still possessed it; he could still sleep
on, however great the din and the discomfort, and it still
needed some significant nautical disturbance to rouse
him. A coir cable being dragged across the deck with shrill
Indian cries was not enough, nor was the sound of his own
enormous snoring (for his head had fallen back and his
mouth had opened), nor was the smell of Turkish cooking

that came eddying aft as evening fell. What woke him, and woke him completely, was a change in the wind: it had quite suddenly shifted two points; it was slackening and coming in gusts.

He went on deck, on to the unusually crowded little quarterdeck: his officers at once led the Turks and the Arab to the lee rail, uncomprehending, but meek aboard a ship. The windward side was cleared in a moment, and he stood there looking at the evening sky, the broken clouds high over Africa and the haze on the Arabian shore. The weather was on the change, he was sure; and that too was certainly the opinion of a number of the *Surprise*'s forecastle hands, elderly men with an immense experience of the sea; they were as sensitive as cats to these alterations and they now lined the gangway, directing meaning glances at him.

'Mr McElwee,' he said, turning to the Company's pilot, 'what do you and the serang make of it?'

'Well, sir,' said Mr McElwee, 'I have not often been north of Jeddah or Yanbo, as I said, nor has the serang, but we both think it looks mighty like dropping for the night, with maybe an Egyptian coming on tomorrow.'

Jack nodded. The Egyptian wind, though by no means as favourable a breeze as could be wished in so narrow a channel as the Gulf of Suez, with its strong currents and its coral reefs, would at least be abaft the beam; and if the *Niobe* was as weatherly as she was said to be, and skilfully handled, it might carry her down into the relatively open sea. 'Well,' he said, 'I believe we may lay out a kedge, so that if this damned breeze has slackened enough by the height of flood, she may be warped out beyond the harbour mouth, not to lose a minute of the Egyptian, if ever it comes on to blow.'

'Doctor,' he said, as Stephen and Martin came aboard, having handed up box after box of coral and shells, and as the hawser crept out from the *Niobe*'s bows, carried by the long-boat through the crowd of Arab dhows and djerms, 'we are half-promised an Egyptian wind.'

'Would that be the same as the dread simoon?'

'I dare say,' said Jack. 'I have heard it is most uncommon

hot, even for these parts. But the great point is that it is westerly, and even a little north of westerly; and so long as it comes abaft the beam, it may blow as hot as it pleases.'

'As hot as it pleases,' he said again, when they were drinking tea in the cabin. 'It really cannot be much hotter, or nothing but crocodiles would survive. Have you ever known a heat like this, Stephen?'

'I have not,' said Stephen.

'Nelson once said he did not need a greatcoat – love for his country kept him warm. I wonder whether it would have kept him cool, had he been here? I'm sure it has no effect on me: I drip like Purvis's distilling machine.'

'Perhaps you do not love your country quite enough.'

'Who could, with the income-tax at two shillings in the pound, and captains docked an eighth of their prize-money?'

The first wafts of the Egyptian wind came a little after dawn. The *Niobe* was lying at single anchor well outside the harbour, having warped clear of all shipping in the night: the breeze had dropped to a dead calm during the middle watch, and even with all scuttles and hatches open it was stiflingly hot below; yet these first Egyptian wafts were hotter still.

Jack had taken a couple of cat-naps, but he was on deck at first light and he saw the wind move across the troubled, tide-rippled water with a great lifting of his heart, a feeling of liberation, of hope renewed. With so many and such willing hands the capstan fairly spun round, plucking the anchor up with scarcely a pause; and soon after the *Niobe* had got under way, casting as prettily as could be wished in spite of the cross tide, he found that although she could not compare with the *Surprise* in breeding and instant response nor in speed, she was a stiff, serviceable little ship, not much inclined to sag to leeward, at least when sailing large; and this was a great satisfaction to him. Yet there was something strange about the breeze: not only its extraordinary heat, like the breath out of an oven, nor its uneasy, unsettled gusting, but something else that he could not define. The young sun blazed clear in the pure eastern sky, terribly strong already, but over there in the west there was a lowering murk, and all along the horizon, rising some ten degrees, an orange-tawny bar, too thick for cloud.

'I do not know what to make of it,' he said to himself. As he turned to go below for his first breakfast, the first wonderfully reviving cup of coffee – the genuine Mocha, straight from that interesting port – that he had already smelt, he caught the eyes of his four young gentlemen fixed thoughtfully upon him. 'Of course,' he reflected, 'they expect me to know what to make of it. A captain is omniscient.'

Stephen walked in, holding a small bottle. 'Good day to you, now,' he said. 'Do you know the temperature of the sea? It is eighty-four degrees by Fahrenheit's thermometer. The salinity I have not yet calculated, but suppose it to be extraordinarily high.'

'I am sure it is. This is an extraordinary place altogether. The glass has not dropped very much, yet ... I tell you what, Stephen, I should take it kindly if you would ask Hassan what he thinks of the bar in the western sky. Since he spends much of his time roaming about the Arabian desert on a camel he must take notice of the local weather. But there is no hurry; let us finish our pot first.'

It was as well that there was no hurry, because the pot was huge and Stephen unusually prosy, on the subject of scorpions. A large number had been found below and the Surprises were hurrying about killing them. '. . . most illiberal – your scorpion never wantonly attacked – stung only if provoked – might cause a certain amount of discomfort, even coma, but was rarely lethal – it might almost be said never, except in the case of those whose hearts were out of order, and they were probably condemned in any case.'

'What about poor Hairabedian?' asked Jack.

'He will be running about tomorrow, rather better for his rest,' said Stephen, and at this moment a squall struck the *Niobe*, laying her over almost on her beam ends. The coffee shot to leeward, though they ludicrously preserved their empty cups; and as the ship righted Jack recovered his feet, making his way through the tumble of chairs, table, papers and instruments. The moment he passed the cabin door he was enveloped in a tawny cloud of sand – sand flying, sand underfoot, sand grating between his teeth – through which he dimly saw a fine scene of confusion. Sailcloth was threshing wildly, the wheel, spinning round, had broken the helmsman's arm and flung him against the rail, the booms and the boats were all abroad, and a ghostly maintopmast staysail, blown almost out of its bolt-rope, streamed away to leeward. The situation was critical, though the present damage was not very grave; the breechings of the guns had held – had even one of the nine-pounders plunged through the other side in that monstrous lee-lurch the ship might have foundered directly – the sheets had instantly been started, preserving the masts, and two quartermasters were already at the wheel. What was much more serious was the crowd of horrified Turks: some were running about the forecastle and the waist in the swirling dust and sand, still more were swarming up the main and fore hatchways. Many of those on deck clung to the running rigging, blocking the seamen's efforts; and if more joined them it would be impossible to work the ship: another squall must lay her down, perhaps for good, certainly with great loss of life – the landsmen would be washed overboard by the score.

Mowett, Rowan and the master were there – Gill half naked. 'Drive them below,' cried Jack, running forward with his arms spread and going 'Hoosh, hoosh,' as though he were herding geese. The Turks were furious fighters by land, but now they were at a loss, out of their element; many were sea-sick and all were terrified, disarmed. The total competence and authority of the four officers advancing so easily over the heaving deck daunted them. They stumbled and blundered to the hatchways and climbed or fell in heaps below. Hardly had Jack given the order 'Lay the hatches' which would keep them there, than he felt the vacuum in his ears that came a split second before the second squall.

The blast laid the ship over, nor did she fully recover, for now the Egyptian had set in, blowing irregularly but hard and without a pause. As Jack made his way aft, his eyes almost closed against the sand, he had time to wonder whether people could breathe in such hot, thick air, and to thank his stars that he had not sent up topgallantmasts.

He could also have thanked them for a strong crew of able seamen and an entirely professional set of officers – Mowett and Rowan might be given to verse in the gunroom, but they were all hard tough driving prose on deck in an emergency. Yet even if he had had time he would probably not have done so, since he took seamanship for granted in those who belonged to the Navy, abhorring its absence as extremely discreditable if not downright wicked and praising only its highest flights: however, the question did not arise, because for almost all the twenty hours that followed he was wholly absorbed in preserving his ship and directing her course.

The first long, long stretch was taken up with reducing sail, dealing with such problems as securing the spars and the remaining boats, sending up preventer stays and braces and rolling tackles, providing the guns with double-frapped preventer-breechings, making good the damage aloft, and perpetually looking out for squalls, as far as that was possible in a twilight of sand flying through a haze of very finely-divided yellow dust, a haze so thick that the sun at noon showed like a red orange hanging there as it might have hung over London in November, a November with a temperature of a hundred and twenty-five in the shade.

Then at some point in the forenoon, when the sprung foretopmast had been fished and the Egyptian had settled into a steadier, less gusty stride, the balance changed: it was now less a question of survival than one of wringing every possible mile from the wind, of 'spoiling the Egyptian' as Jack said to himself, a wild glee having succeeded the intense gravity of those first hours, when a false move might have meant loss with all hands. There were few things that moved him more than driving a ship to the limit of her possibilities in a very strong blow, and now his great concern was finding just how much sail the *Niobe* could carry and where it should be set: the answer obviously varied with the force of the wind and the scend of the sea, and that variation itself was by no means simple, because of the strong and continually changing tidal streams in the gulf and its strange shifting currents.

But it was not only his delight in driving her that made him send the *Niobe* racing along in this headlong course, with her bow-wave tearing away white in the murk to larboard and coming in steadily like a storm of salt rain over the starboard forecastle. Very early he had found that the faster the ship moved through the water the less leeway she made; and in a narrow, reef-lined gulf with no harbours, no sheltered bays, not a yard of leeway could he afford. And since there was no lying-to with the Arabian coast so near, he must necessarily crack on and pelt down the middle of the channel, or rather to the windward of the middle, as near as he could judge; unless of course he preferred to wear ship, run back to the dubious protection of Suez harbour, and abandon the expedition. For once the French engineers had reached Mubara they would certainly put the fortress into such a state of defence that no Company's nine-pounder sloop and a handful of Turks could attempt it – he had to get there first or not at all.

Running south was a perilous undertaking, but rather less so now that there was a heavy sea running, making the reefs more evident; and he was splendidly seconded, with the Mocha pilot conning the ship from the foreyard and calling his observations down to Davis, the man with the strongest voice in the crew, who stood half drowned on the forecastle and roared them aft, and with all the Surprises perfectly used to his ways, understanding him at the first word and as seamanlike as men could well be. Yet even so there were moments when it seemed that they were lost. The first when the ship hit a heavy, half-sunk palm-tree, her cutwater striking it in the middle with a shock that almost stopped her in full career: three backstays parted, but her masts held firm and the trunk passed under her keel, missing her rudder by inches. The second came during a particularly long and blinding flurry of sand. The *Niobe* gave a shudder; there was a grating sound below, loud over the voice of the wind, and in the turn of the rising sea to larboard Jack caught the gleam of a great length of her copper ripped off.

By noon it was less perilous. They were still running at a breakneck pace under close-reefed topsails and courses, but the invisible land of Egypt over to starboard was now low parched stony hill rather than pure desert; it had rather less sand to offer, and the visibility improved. Life on deck became more nearly normal: no noon observation was possible, to be sure, and the galley fires could not yet be lit for the hands' dinner, but the regular succession of bells, of relieving the wheel and heaving the log had resumed, and Jack observed with great pleasure that the last heave showed twelve knots and two fathoms, which, considering her sober, matronly form, was probably very near to the greatest speed at which the *Niobe* could be urged through the water without serious damage, though he might possibly add a fathom or so with a mizzentopmast stormstaysail.

He was reflecting upon this when he noticed Killick at his elbow, holding a sandwich and a bottle of wine and water with a tube through its cork. 'Thankee, Killick,' he said, suddenly aware of being famished in spite of the impossible heat and the peck of sand in his gullet, and thirsty in spite of being soaked with spray, spindrift, and sometimes green water, coming warm and solid over the side. As he ate and drank he listened vaguely to Killick's bellowed yet still whining complaint '. . . never get the bleeding sand out . . . got in all your uniforms . . . in all the chests and lockers . . . in all the bleeding cracks . . . sand in my ear 'ole . . .' and as soon as he had swallowed the last of the wine he said, 'Mr Mowett, we must relieve the pilot and Davis: they are hoarse as crows. Let the hands be piped to dinner by watches. They will have to put up with soft tommy and whatever the purser can find, but they may all have their grog, even the defaulters. I am going below to see how the Turks are coming along.'

The Turks were coming along surprisingly well. Stephen and Martin were with them, and they too sat cross-legged on the floor in the sensible eastern way, wedged against the side of the ship and padded with all that was available in the way of cushions. They were all very quiet, sitting there as placidly as a band of domestic cats round a fire, staring at nothing in particular and saying little more. They smiled at him gently and some made slight welcoming motions with their hands: Jack's first impression was that they were all dead drunk, but then he recollected that the Turks and Arab were Mussulmans, that he had never seen Stephen affected by wine, and that Martin would rarely take a second glass.

'We are chewing khat,' said Stephen, holding up a green twig. 'It is said to have a tranquillizing, sedative effect, not unlike that of the coca leaf of the Peruvians.' There was some quiet conversation behind him and he went on, 'The Bimbashi hopes that you are not unduly fatigued, and that you are pleased with the progress of the voyage.'

'Pray tell him that I have never felt better, and that the voyage goes along reasonably well. If this wind holds till the day after tomorrow, we should make up the distance lost and have a fair chance of being south of Mubara in time to intercept the galley.'

'The Bimbashi says, if it is written that we shall take the galley and become immeasurably rich, then we shall take her; if it is not so written we shall not. There is nothing that can be done to alter fate, and he begs you will not trouble yourself or take unnecessary pains: what is written is written.'

'If you can think of a civil way of asking him why in that case he brought his men aboard so quickly, tumbling over one another in their haste, pray do so. If not, just tell him it is also written that Heaven helps those that help themselves, and desire him to stash it: you may also add that while a tone of lofty wisdom may be proper in a philosopher addressing a groundling, it is perhaps less so when a bimba-shi is speaking to a post-captain.'

When these words, suitably modified, had passed through Stephen into French and through Hassan into Arabic, the Bimbashi said with a placid smile that he was quite content with a soldier's simple allowance, and that he rather despised wealth than otherwise.

'Well, my friend,' said Jack, 'I hope this wind does hold a couple of days, if only to give you a chance of showing your contempt in practice.'

It held indeed that afternoon, a great deal more so than was comfortable; and in spite of the slight lessening at sun-set, Jack supped on chicken and sand washed down with sand and three-water grog reasonably confident that the Egyptian would blow all night. McElwee, Gill and the ser-ang were of the same opinion, and although they had not been able to make any observation through the clouds of flying grit their dead-reckonings all agreed in setting the *Niobe* a little south of Ras Minah, with a fine broad stretch of unencumbered channel before her.

He stayed on deck until the graveyard watch – the hottest graveyard he had ever known – listening to the roar of the wind and the strong deep voice of the ship as she ran, and watching the extraordinary phosphorescence of the long curve of the sea, rising high at her bows, dipping to her copper amidships, and then rising again by her mizzenchains, to break in a tumbled blazing furrow aft, a line that stretched quite far out into the darkness now, for although there was still a good deal of sand sweeping across the deck the smaller fog-like dust had stopped. From time to time his eyes closed as he stood there swaying to the heave, and in those moments the ship ran through a dream as well as a storm of sand: but she ran fairly easy – they had furled the courses while both watches were on deck and under this reduced sail she scarcely laboured at all; the backstays were no longer iron-stiff, and her larboard cathead rarely touched the sea.

'Sharp look-out before, there,' he called, a little after four bells.

The answer came back over the wind 'Aye-aye, sir,' and he knew from the voice that it was young Taplow of the maintop, a thoroughly reliable hand. 'Mr Rowan,' he said, 'I am turning in. Let me be called as soon as the islands are sighted.'

As he moved across the deck the gale thrust him from behind, almost as strong as it had ever been, and almost as hot and unbreathable as the noonday blast. Yet when he struggled up from the extreme depths of leaden sleep, Calamy shaking his cot and shouting 'Islands in sight, sir. Islands ahead, if you please,' he was not surprised to find that the ship was scarcely heeling a strake and that no air came racing through the open skylight. The unsleeping part of his mind (though very small it must have been) had told him that the wind was dropping. It had chosen an odd way of getting through the barrier of immense weariness – a dream in which he was riding a horse, a very fine horse to begin with but one that progressively dwindled and shrank until he became more and more uneasy and at last most painfully ashamed, because his feet were touching the ground on either side and people in the crowded street looked at him with indignation. Yet although the message about the wind was coded, its meaning must have been pretty clear to him for some time, because now he was quite resigned to the present state of things.

He made his blear-eyed way on deck, and there in fact were the islands right ahead and on either bow, clear in the newly-risen sun: they formed a little archipelago guarding the end of the gulf, an intricate navigation; but beyond them lay the Red Sea in all its comfortable breadth. Although the air was still hazy it was not to compare with yesterday and beyond the left-hand island he could see the cape that marked the limit of the gulf and then the coast beyond it, trending away eastwards far out of sight, running a good fifty miles and more, as he knew from the chart. There was no lee-shore to be dreaded now; Mr McElwee had taken particular notice of the fairway between the two easternmost islands; the *Niobe* had made up a most astonishing amount of her distance; and apart from the breeze everything was perfect. But the breeze was the whole essence of the matter, and the breeze was dying, dying. He looked around, gathering his wits: the starboard watch were washing the deck, sending great quantities of water aft from the head-pump to get rid of the masses of caked mud that had come aboard in the form of dust and that had lodged in every corner that was not directly swept by the sea, and from the scuppers shot thick jets of sand-coloured water to join the turbid yellow sea. Usually he never interfered with operations of this kind nor disturbed the watch below, but now he said, 'All hands to make sail. Up topgallantmasts.'

The *Niobe* spread her wings, the water began to sing down her side again as she leant to the thrust of the not inconsiderable remaining wind, and with the tide helping she ran quite fast through the islands and into the open sea, a pretty sight with her topgallants and studdingsails aloft and alow.

A prettier sight still as the sun crept to the zenith, for by now she was wearing almost everything she possessed – royals, skysails, skyscrapers, and some strange light lofty staysails – and in addition to these she had spread awnings fore and aft against the intolerable heat.

Stephen was busy in the sick-bay much of the morning, since a blow of such sudden severity always meant ugly strains and bruises among the seamen and often broken bones; and this time he also had the poor tumbled Turks to patch. When he had finished with them he went to Hairabedian's cabin. He was not surprised to find it empty: the dragoman had almost completely recovered, and he complained most piteously of the confinement and the heat. Stephen therefore carried on to the quarterdeck, where, if he had looked up through the gap between this awning and the next, he would have seen the pretty sight reduced to a mockery, the carefully spread, exactly braced sails all hanging limp, with no way on the ship at all, while the hands who had laboured so violently and in such danger only the day before could now be seen furtively scratching the backstays to call up a breeze, and whistling gently.

'Good morning, Doctor,' said Jack. 'How are your patients?'

'Good morning to you, sir. They are as comfortable as can be expected, the creatures; but one has escaped me. Have you seen Mr Hairabedian at all?'

'Yes. He went running along the starboard gangway just now, skipping like a lad. There he is, just abaft the cathead. No, the cathead, the thing that juts out. Do you wish to speak to him?'

'Not I, now that I see him so well; though indeed he seems the only happy soul in this mournful ship. See how cheerfully he talks to William Plaice; see how sullenly Plaice turns away, grieving for the want of wind, no doubt.'

'Perhaps he does. Perhaps not all of us possess the Bimbashi's philosophy; and there may be some Surprises who would rather be rich than poor – who fret at the notion of the galley escaping us, pulling steadily north, breeze or no breeze, while we sit here broiling in idleness. If the squall had left us boats enough, I am sure they would be out ahead at this moment towing the ship, if they had their own way.'

'I was speaking to Hassan about the winds in these parts. He says that the Egyptian is often followed by a calm, and that the usual northerly breeze sets in again.'

'Does he, indeed? Honest fellow. I had certainly understood that that was the case, but I am heartily glad to hear it confirmed from such a source.' The other inhabitants of the quarterdeck, apart from the men at the helm and the con who were necessarily fixed, had all moved over to the larboard side, where they put up a creditable appearance of not listening. But the *Niobe* was a little ship and in this quietness, with nothing but the gentle lap of the still water against her side, they were obliged to hear whether they wanted to or not. The 'usual northerly breeze' meant the possibility of wealth, and a general grin spread among them; in an access of cupidity Williamson sprang into the mizzen shrouds, saying to Calamy, 'Race you to the truck.'

'Did he mention the length of the calm?' asked Jack, wiping the sweat from his face.

'He spoke of two or three days,' said Stephen, and the grins faded. 'But he observed that it was all in God's hands.'

'What the devil is he about?' said Jack, as he saw the dragoman take off his shirt and stand on the rail. 'Mr Hairabedian,' he called. But it was too late: although Hairabedian heard he was already in midair. He dived into the warm, opaque sea with scarcely a splash and swam aft along the side under the surface, reappearing by the mainchains, looking up at the quarterdeck and laughing. Abruptly his cheerful face jerked upwards – his chest and shoulders shot clear of the water. A long dark form could be seen below him and while his face still looked up, his wide-open mouth uttering an enormous cry, he was shaken from side to side with inconceivable ferocity and he vanished in a great boil of water. Once again his head rose up, still recognizable, and the stump of an arm: but now at least five sharks were striving furiously in the bloody sea and a few moments later there was nothing but the red cloud and the fishes questing eagerly in it for more, while others came racing in, their fins sharp on the surface.

The shocked silence went on and on until at last the quartermaster at the con gave a meaning cough: the sand in the half-hour glass was running out.

'Shall I carry on, sir?' asked the master in a low voice.

'Aye, do, Mr Gill,' said Jack. 'Mr Calamy, my sextant, if you please.'

The ceremony of the noon-observation went mechanically through its ritual words and motions, at the end of which Jack, in a harsh official voice said, 'Make it twelve.' A few moments later eight bells was struck and Rowan cried, 'Pipe to dinner.'

The bosun piped, the men ran to their places, the cooks of each mess assembled in the galley, where (though it seemed unbelievable) their lumps of pork had been simmering for a great while, together with their dried peas, this being Thursday. The movements were quite automatic, having been repeated so often, but they did not bring appetite; few men ate much, and that little almost in silence. The atmosphere changed a little with the coming of the grog, but even so there was no cheering, no calling out of old jokes, no banging of plates.

Later in the afternoon Mowett came to Captain Aubrey and said, 'Sir, the men wish me to say that they would be glad of permission to use the shark hooks and tackle: they had a respect and esteem for Mr Hairabedian, and could wish to serve a few of them out.'

'Not with the poor man still in their bellies, for God's sake?' cried Jack, and it was clear from the faces of the listening hands that they quite took the point, and agreed. 'No,' he went on, 'but at quarters this evening we shall exercise the small-arms, and they may each fire half a dozen rounds at 'em, if they please.'

The sun crept down the sky, and a little after quarters it set in a blaze of glory over Egypt, the whole sky vivid crimson from pole to pole, while the *Niobe* slowly turned in the current, east, east-north-east, and so to north-west by north, where she had come from, and the brighter stars began to show. Jack, having fixed his discouraging latitude with a twilight observation, and having drunk coffee with the Turks, retired to gasp in his cabin.

'God help us, Stephen,' he said, throwing a towel over his nakedness as Stephen came in, 'we might be in a hammam, a bagnio, a Turkish flaming bath. I must have lost a couple of stone.'

'You could spare as much again,' said Stephen. 'And since you are of a very full habit, you would certainly benefit from blood-letting. I will draw off sixteen or twenty ounces directly: you will feel more comfortable, and there will be a little less danger of siriasis or apoplexy,' he said, putting down the box he was carrying and drawing a lancet from his pocket. 'This is rather blunt' – trying it on the locker – 'but I dare say we shall get it into the vein in time. I must sharpen the whole set tomorrow; for if this calm continue, I think of bleeding the whole ship's company.'

'No,' said Jack. 'It may sound girlish, but I really do not want to see blood again today, my own or anyone else's.

I cannot get Hairabedian out of my mind. I regret him extremely.'

'I wish he could have been saved,' said Stephen, cautiously. He hesitated, turning the box in his hand. 'I attended to his papers and belongings, as you desired me to do,' he said after a pause. 'I did not find his family's direction in any of the letters I could read – they were mostly Arabic – but I did find this.' He passed the box, took out its false bottom, and passed the chelengk.

'Oh what a damned thing,' cried Jack. 'I am so sorry. Poor fellow.' He tossed it into a drawer, stood up and put on his shirt and trousers. 'Let us take a turn on deck,' he said. 'In five minutes we should see that God-damned moon rise up, a great deal nearer the half than I could wish.'

The God-damned moon was nearer still the following night, yet still the *Niobe* sweltered there in the gently heaving calm, turning in the current but advancing not at all. The Bimbashi's khat ran out, and with it his philosophy; he had two of his men beaten in the Turkish manner, beaten with rods, and with such severity that one was carried off insensible, while the other staggered away with blood running not only from his lacerated back but from his mouth. The beating was very savage even by naval standards, yet the watching Turks seemed unmoved and the victims uttered nothing but a few involuntary grunts. This raised them in the Surprises' opinion; and there were some who thought it not unlikely that it was their bloody, well-borne punishment that earned the ship her relief, the small breeze that sprang up almost as soon as the deck had been cleaned.

But if that was so, then at least a dozen Turks should have suffered to produce a wind strong enough to carry the *Niobe* south in time to intercept the galley: for this breeze remained small, desperately small, little more than a light air. It did allow them to breathe, and it did just fill what sails could be set with advantage; but as it kept obstinately dead aft these were comparatively few – spritsail, foresail and lower studdingsails, and foretopsailyard scandalized, main topsail and all she could wear above, but nothing below and nothing on her mizzenmast at all – and even with the hoses in the tops wetting all the canvas they could reach and buckets whipped aloft to be flung over the higher sails, the *Niobe* rarely moved at more than three knots.

By now the moon was long past the first quarter and Jack Aubrey felt the bitterness of slow defeat rise in his heart: the heat grew if anything more oppressive, and the marked unfriendly reserve of Hassan and the Turkish officers made the position even more unpleasant, if possible. From the very first they had cried out against the reduction of sail, but as he explained to them through Stephen that spreading more canvas did not always mean moving with greater speed and that in this instance sails set aft must necessarily becalm those farther forward, he now supposed that their wry looks must have another cause, probably his remarks about the soldiers' filthiness. It never occurred to him that they thought he was playing false until Stephen came to him one unspeakably harassing tedious evening and said, 'I have promised to execute a commission, and I will be as concise as possible, boiling three hours of delicate hint, surmise, theoretical case and half-avowal into one coarse minute: Hassan suspects that the Egyptians have offered you a great reward not to capture the galley. Everyone knows, says he, that your dragoman saw messengers from Mehemet Ali; and everyone knows, says the Bimbashi, that the more sails there are the more wind they will catch: it stands to reason. Now Hassan's proposition is that you should accept a great sum from him and bilk the Egyptian. There: I have done.'

'Thank you, Stephen,' said Jack. 'I suppose it is no good explaining the elements of seamanship all over again?'

'None whatsoever, my dear.'

'Then I suppose I shall have to put up with their mumpishness,' said Jack. But here he was mistaken. The wind, such as it was, backed north-west during the night, breathing in over the *Niobe*'s quarter, and when Hassan and the Turks came on deck the next morning they found as many sails set as could possibly be desired. They exchanged discreet but exceedingly knowing glances, and presently Hassan came up to Captain Aubrey and addressed some complimentary remarks him to in French, a language with which Jack had at least a nodding acquaintance, while the Bimbashi made some Turkish observation in a low, conciliating voice. Jack however wished to give their suppositions no countenance whatsoever; he only bowed, and then climbed to the maintop, from which he viewed the great expanse of misty, heat-quivering blue, staring south with intense longing through the gaps in the cloud of sail. Having gazed his full, with a heavy and desponding heart, he called Rowan and told him quite sharply that he liked to walk his quarterdeck in peace, that in the service it was usual for the officer of the watch to protect his captain from the vapid good days and how d'ye dos of passengers who did not understand naval customs, and that the foretopsail yard was by no means as square as it ought to be.

A cloud of sail indeed, and tended with the most religious care; but even so they were still nearly two degrees north of Mubara when the moon reached the full, and by the time they actually raised the island she was a seventeen-day-old object, disagreeably gibbous, late in rising.

It was on a Thursday afternoon that Mubara appeared at last, clear in the light of the setting sun and standing out sharply against the far background of mountains in Arabia. Jack at once hauled his wind to pass unseen and very carefully shaped his course for the passage between the smaller islands and reefs to the south. They were now in a region of trustworthy charts, and with the help of two excellent seamarks he and McElwee set the *Niobe* half way down the channel, dropping anchor in thirty-five fathom water.

There was still a possibility that the galley might not have passed. It was a very slight possibility, since the usual northerly winds had either not blown at all or had breathed so faintly that they would not have held her back; yet still a certain more or less theoretical hope subsisted, particularly in those bosoms that most desired it, and well before dawn Captain Aubrey, all his officers except the surgeon and the chaplain, and most of the watch below were on deck.

It was a misty end to the night, and a slightly fresher west-north-west breeze blew a scud of warm vapours and exhalations over the waning moon; but she still shed a general, diffused light, and the larger stars showed through as orange blurs.

The *Niobe* swung to her anchor, the leeward tide running with a continuous gentle ripple; if the people spoke at all it was in an undertone. The eastern sky grew perceptibly lighter. Jack had been looking at Canopus, an indistinct glow in the south, and thinking about his son: would a boy brought up by his mother, with only sisters to play with, grow up a milksop? He had known smaller boys than George go to sea. Perhaps the clever thing to do was to take him for a four seasons' voyage and then put him to school for a year or two before returning to the Navy, so that he should not be as illiterate as most sea-officers, including his father. Some friend would certainly keep George's name on his ship's books, so the schooling would not mean the loss of any time before he could pass for lieutenant. Two bells. At the sound he glanced forward; and when he looked back again the star was gone.

The head-pump started wheezing, and in this uncomfortable hour when the peace of night was dead and the true life of day had not yet returned the starboard watch began cleaning ship. The tide of water and sand had reached the waist and the holystones were grinding away on the forecastle when the rim of the sun showed red on the horizon. Calamy, sitting on the capstan with his trousers rolled up to keep them from the wet, suddenly leapt down and splashed over the deck to Mowett, who cried, 'Forward there, belay,' and strode across to Jack. 'Sir,' he said, plucking off his hat, 'Calamy thinks he hears something.'

'Silence fore and aft,' called Jack. All hands froze where they stood, as in a children's game, often in ludicrous attitudes, a holystone or a swab upraised, and an expression of the most intense listening on their faces; and from far over to leeward all hands heard a remote chant *Ayo-huh hah, ayo-huh hah* that came in snatches against the breeze.

'Stand by to slip,' said Jack. 'Pass the word for Mr Hassan and the serang.'

But Hassan and the serang were already there, and both, as he turned to them, nodded emphatically, making the motion of pulling an oar: it was indeed the galley-rowers' song.

Where it came from they could not tell, though all but the hands preparing to slip the cable were listening with extreme attention: somewhere in the dimness to leeward was all they could make out. The sun rose and rose, grew blinding, heaved its whole disc clear of the horizon; but still the drifting white scud veiled the surface of the sea. Jack leant far out over the rail, trying to pierce the mist; his mouth was open and he could hear his own heart beating, a hoarse panting sound, quite loud. Two voices from aloft. One screeched, 'There she lays!' from the fore jackcrosstrees: the other, in the maintop, hailed, 'On deck there. Galley just abaft the starboard beam.'

'Mr Mowett,' said Jack, 'slip the cable with a really good buoy to it, and let us make sail handsomely. Topsails and courses quite leisurely, as though we were a Company's ship making for Mubara in the ordinary course of events, having lain to in the night to get our bearings. Not many men are to go aloft – the watch below to go below, and most of the others to keep out of the way. We will not pipe up hammocks.'

He went below for his telescope and another glance at the chart he knew so well, and when he returned the cable was already gliding out of the hawse-hole as the *Niobe* swung from the wind under her backed foretopsail. Her main and mizzen topsails were being hoisted in a deliberate, stolid fashion, and a few hands were standing ready to lay out on the lower yards.

'Where away?' asked Jack.

'Two points on the starboard bow, sir,' said Mowett.

In these few moments the sun had burnt off the vapours of the night and there she was, a good deal farther off and farther ahead than he had expected from the sound, but as

plain as heart could desire. She was right over on the far
side of the channel, on the very edge of the white-fringed
coral reef that ran five or six miles north-west to the islet
of Hatiba, which marked the entrance of the long, narrow
Mubara bay, with the town at the bottom of it. She was
heading for the island, pulling close to the wind, and in spite
of all their care in avoiding the appearance of haste, of chase,
of hostility, it looked as though she was alarmed: the rowers
had stopped singing and they were pulling pretty hard.

Two questions instantly arose: could the *Niobe* weather
the islet Hatiba, and if not could she cut the galley off before
that point? Neither answer was clear. Each depended not
only on their relative speeds and sailing qualities but on the
varying forces of the breeze, the current, and the changing
tide: in any case it would be a near-run thing. McElwee and
the serang were familiar with the ship; they knew how she
sailed on a bowline; but their faces were full of doubt.

Jack stepped over to the wheel. 'Full. Keep her full,
Thompson,' he said to the helmsman, and then, as the way
increased on the ship with the last sails set and drawing,
'Luff and touch her.' She came up, nearer and nearer the
wind, and when the weather-leeches began to shiver in spite
of the taut bowlines, he took the spokes, let her pay off until
he felt her happy, said, 'Dyce and no higher; very well dyce,'
and walked back to the rail. He must make up his mind
quickly, and while he was doing so this course would
compromise neither of the possible solutions.

He stared at her. A long, low vessel, dead black like a
Venetian gondola, much the same black as the southern side
of Mubara beyond the reef, a totally sterile uninhabited
desolation of craggy volcanic rock: perhaps a hundred and
twenty feet from stem to stern: she had the curious forward-
raked masts of the Red Sea galley, with a green swallow-
tailed pennant streaming from the main, and two long
curved lateen yards, their sails tight-furled. Each mast had
a kind of basket-top or crow's-nest abaft the head, and in
each there was a figure turned towards the *Niobe*, one with
a telescope. Just how frightened was she? They were pulling

hard, to be sure, but by the arched cabin right aft, which presumably sheltered the French officers, he saw no European faces, only a person in baggy crimson trousers who walked up and down, fanning himself. And how fast was she going? It was difficult to tell, but probably not much above five knots.

'So that is a galley,' said Martin, with great satisfaction: he and Stephen were standing at the fife-rails, sharing an indifferent spy-glass. 'And if I do not mistake, it has five and twenty oars of a side. That makes it the exact equivalent of the classical penteconter: Thucydides must have seen just such a boat. What joy!'

'So he must, too. Will you look at the oars now, how they beat? They are like the wings of a great low-flying, strong-flying bird, a vast celestial swan.'

Martin laughed with pleasure. 'It is Pindar, I believe, who makes the same comparison,' he said. 'But I see no chains: the men seem free to move about.'

'Hassan tells me that the Mubara galleys have never employed slaves; and that is another parallel with the penteconter.'

'Yes, indeed. Shall we catch her, do you suppose?'

'Why, as to that,' said Stephen, 'my opinion is not worth a straw. I will only observe that your Thucydides speaks of a galley that went from the Piraeus to Lesbos between one noon and the next or rather less, which is some ten miles in every hour, a most terrible pace.'

'But, my dear sir, Thucydides' boat was a trireme, if you recollect, with three banks of oars, which must surely have propelled it three times as fast.'

'Is that right? Perhaps we shall catch her, then. But if we do not, and I must say that little small island seems awkwardly placed for sailing round, then I make no doubt Captain Aubrey will pursue her right into the harbour of Mubara itself. The only trouble is, that if they get there first, having been obviously chased, even attacked, the effect of surprise will be lost entirely, and they may oppose our landing with force, perhaps with extreme violence.'

'Doctor,' called Captain Aubrey, breaking off his calculations, 'pray desire Mr Hassan to keep himself and all the Turks out of sight.'

Two possible solutions: he could make a direct dash, hoping to intercept the galley before Hatiba. The inshore breeze was likely to freshen as the land grew even hotter, and it might well back a point or two; while the turning tide would counteract the eastward-setting current in less than an hour. But would that be soon enough? The galley could probably go faster if she chose. How much faster? He had seen one row at ten knots for a short burst. And if the *Niobe*, sagging to leeward, failed to weather the tip of the reef, the galley would run clean away from her, rounding the point and then setting those immense lateen sails with the wind right aft to race down the bay and give the alarm in Mubara, perfectly certain that she had been chased. On the other hand he could stand out to sea for a while, calming the galley's present apprehensions and opening the narrow entrance so that later in the day (or even by night) he could sail placidly in under topsails, with a nonchalant air, perhaps with French colours. Yet that meant loss of time, and he had not needed the Admiral to tell him that speed was the essence of attack. He glared at the remote islet with the utmost intensity, measuring the angle, estimating the ship's leeway and adding the thrust of the current and the effect of the coming slack water. Already the heat was making him sweat and the island quiver, and in an exasperated aside he said to himself, 'Lord, the comfort of being under orders, the comfort of being told exactly what to do.' Then raising his voice, 'Topgallants. Lay aloft, lay aloft.'

As the upperyardmen raced up the ratlines he watched the galley with the greatest care, and when the sails flashed out aboard the *Niobe* he saw the man in crimson trousers drop his fan, snatch up a long round-headed pole and start beating time with it, shouting at the rowers as he did so. The oars cut up more white water and the galley's speed increased almost instantly, far sooner than the *Niobe*'s.

'There is no doubt but they are thoroughly frightened of

us,' said Jack, and he made up his mind to stake everything on the direct dash: if the galley was already aware of his motions there was no point in standing out to sea.

Having given orders to make all possible sail he said to Stephen, 'Perhaps we should let poor Hassan come on deck, now there is no call for any disguise. You may tell him that it will all be decided in thirty minutes or so: and if the Turks were to stand along the weather-rail their weight would make the ship a trifle stiffer.'

Royals and flying kites caused the *Niobe* to heel another strake, but they did not propel her at much above six knots at first. The galley drew away; for a good five minutes she drew away, but then her lead steadied, and so they ran, straining to the utmost, over the mild gently rippling sea, at just the same distance from one another. The half-hour glass turned; the bell was struck. The fierce predatory faces lining the *Niobe*'s rail did not change in all this while, nor did any man say a word; but when she began to gain on the chase all the faces lightened, even at the first few barely perceptible yards, and they uttered a general howl.

'The rowers are beginning to tire,' said Jack, brushing the sweat from his eyes – the sun was full on him as he leant out over the hurrying sea – 'And I don't wonder at it.'

Another cable's length of gain, and now the tide was on the change. The *Niobe*, right out in the fairway, profited much more than the chase and she began to overhaul her fast. The tension mounted higher still. By now it was almost certain that the ship could not weather the island, could not get round without tacking – a fatal loss of time – yet on the other hand the likelihood of her cutting the galley off before Hatiba was growing every minute.

But now there appeared a danger that Jack had not foreseen: far on the galley's starboard bow there was a gap in the white line of surf, a narrow passage through the reef into the lagoon beyond, one that the galley, with her shallow draught, could take and that the *Niobe* could not.

Yet their courses had been converging from the start and now the galley was well within reach of the nine-pounders.

'Pass the word for the gunner,' he said, and when the gunner came, 'Mr Borrell, I dare say you have the bow-chasers cleared away?'

'Why, yes, sir,' said Mr Borrell reproachfully. 'This last glass and more.'

'Then put me a ball across her bows, Mr Borrell. But not too close, hey? Hey? Don't you touch her, whatever you do; those flimsy one-and-a-half inch plank affairs sink for a nothing. And all our eggs are in one basket.'

Mr Borrell had no intention of sinking five thousand purses, and his shockingly successful shot brought his heart into his mouth. The ball pitched six feet ahead of the galley, sending a great fountain of water over her deck. It did not induce her to bring to, but it did give her something else to think about. She instantly backed water with a great flurry of oars, jigged, and then made for Hatiba again, while the opening in the reef slid fast astern.

They raced on, now the one gaining, now the other; but the general advantage lay with the *Niobe*. The distance between them dwindled to point-blank range and less, and if the galley had not obviously been convinced that no one would fire into her she must have struck her colours long since to avoid destruction: but a vessel with a cargo too precious to sink could run all risks except that of being boarded.

There was nothing Jack Aubrey loved more than a chase at sea; yet for some little time now his blazing delight had dwindled – the old story of the shrinking horse again. A carping voice in the back of his mind asked why all this alarm at the sight of a Company's ship on her lawful occasions? Why was the inlet passed so easily? And although Crimson Breeches was perpetually running up and down the gangway between the rowers, thumping his staff and haranguing them, surely the galley's real speed did not correspond to the threshing labour of the oars? Something was not quite right. He had deceived too many enemies at sea to be easily misled himself; and when they were within musket-shot and a subdued cheering had already started on the forecastle his uneasiness was confirmed and wholly justified by the sight of an inconspicuous line running from the galley's stern into her strangely troubled wake. 'Mr Williamson, Mr Calamy,' he called, and the midshipmen came running, their faces all aglow. 'Do you know what a lame duck does?'

'No, sir,' they said, beaming.

'It attempts to pull wool over your eyes. Lapwings do much the same when you are near their nest. Do you see that line from the galley's stern?'

'Yes, sir,' they said, having stared awhile.

'It is fast to a drag-sail under water, so that they can seem to be pulling like fury and yet let us catch up. There, you can see the grommet in her wake. They mean to lead us into a knacker's yard. That is why I am going to sink her. Mr Mowett: starboard guns.'

The moment the gunports opened Crimson Breeches ran aft and cut the line: the galley leapt forward with a bow-wave that reached half way down her side. Hassan came hurrying across the deck, his white robes flying and a look of extreme urgency and concern on his usually impassive face. Stephen said, 'He urges you not to fire on the galley. It has treasure aboard.'

Jack said, 'Tell him we are here to take Mubara, not to make money. We are not privateers. We cannot catch the galley this side of the island – look at her speed now – and once she gets round she gives the alarm. Mr Mowett, Turkish colours. Mr Borrell, a ball low under her counter, if you please.'

The galley turned ninety degrees to starboard in her own length: she now presented nothing but her stern and her flashing banks of oars as she pulled away at racing speed for the reef, and it was at this stern that the gunner presented his piece. He was firing from a steady platform at a steady mark: in professional conscience he could not miss, and if he did the whole starboard broadside would do his work for him. With death in his heart he pulled the laniard, arched his body over the violently recoiling gun and stared through the smoke as the gun-crew clapped on to the train-tackle and swabbed the hissing barrel.

'Well done, Mr Borrell,' called Jack. From the quarter-deck he had seen the ball go home, sending the frail wood flying at the waterline; so had most of the ship's company, and they uttered a low grunting sound, not of triumph nor of joy, but of sober appreciation. For a single stroke of her oars, still perfectly timed, the galley carried on: then the rhythm broke; the oars were all ahoo, abandoned, criss-crossed, entangled, and in his glass Jack could see all hands busy at their boats. They had barely cut the last gripes and lashings before the galley slid away from under them, leaving them and the boats afloat on the smooth sea. At the same moment an unsuspected battery on the island over against Hatiba, on the far side of the entrance to Mubara bay, opened fire on the *Niobe*; but it was more an expression of anger than anything else, since the ship was a quarter of a mile beyond the extreme range of its guns.

'Bring her to. Reduce sail,' said Jack, automatically careful of his spars; and as the way came off the ship he stood there with his hands behind his back, considering the trap he had escaped and the fortune he had lost, while at the same time he watched the crowded boats paddle away across the reef and into the shallow water of the lagoon. Was he more glad or more sorry? Did he rejoice or did he grieve? In this hurry of spirits he could hardly tell: he only observed, 'And yet to the very end I never saw the Frenchmen. No doubt they were dressed as Arabs.'

'Sir,' said Mowett, 'the galley's pennant can still be seen. Should you wish us to take it?'

'Certainly,' said Jack. 'Lower away a boat.' His eye followed the galley's path, and there, well this side of the reef, he saw the truck and the last two feet of her mainmast with the green swallowtail rippling out on the surface. 'No, stay,' he said, 'let us bear up and run over to it. And let us, for God's sake, get some awnings over our heads. Our brains will boil, else.'

The water was extraordinarily clear. When they had

dropped the small bower they could see not only the galley lying on an even keel down there upon a coral plateau fifty yards wide but the encrusted anchor of some ancient wreck far deeper and their own cable running away and away. The hands hung over the rail, gazing down with dumb longing.

At dinner Jack said, 'While Hassan and the Turks argue about whether to land in some other part of the island or not, I have decided to lie here: it would be foolish to stand off and on all day, wearing ship in this hellfire heat. But I rather wish I had chosen somewhere else. The sight of five thousand purses no more than ten fathom under our keel makes me almost regret my virtue.'

'To what particular virtue do you refer, brother?' asked Stephen, his only guest, since Mr Martin had begged to be excused – could not swallow a morsel in this heat, but should be very happy to join them for tea or coffee.

'God help us,' cried Jack. 'Did you really not appreciate the heroism of my conduct?'

'I did not.'

'I deliberately threw away a fortune, sinking that galley.'

'But you could not catch it, my dear; you said so yourself.'

'Not on this leg, no. But with a quick tack to round the island I could have chased her right down the bay, and it would have been strange if they could have kept us from the treasure, sooner or later, whether we took Mubara or not.'

'But the batteries were primed, they were ready and waiting: you would have been blasted from the water.'

'Exactly so. But I did not know that at the time. I gave the order with the purest virtue, so that the expedition's success should not be compromised and so that the French and their ally should quite certainly be deprived of their money. I am amazed at my own magnanimity.'

'Parson asks can he come in now,' said Killick in a sharper and more disagreeable tone than usual. He looked at the back of Captain Aubrey's head with a very sour expression and made a disrespectful gesture, muttering the word magnanimity under his breath.

'Come in, my dear sir, come in,' said Jack, rising to greet

Mr Martin. 'I was just saying to the Doctor that this was a tolerably whimsical situation, with a crew of paupers floating over a fortune, knowing it to be there, seeing its coffer as you might say, and yet unable to reach it. Killick, bear a hand with that coffee, d'ye hear me now?'

'Very whimsical indeed, sir,' said Martin.

Killick brought the coffee-pot, setting it down with a sniff; and after a short silence Stephen said, 'I am an urinator.'

'Really, Stephen,' exclaimed Jack, who had a great respect for the cloth. 'Recollect yourself.'

'It is well known that I am an urinator,' said Stephen, looking at him firmly, 'and in recent hours I have felt a great moral pressure on me to dive.' It was quite true: no one had openly suggested anything of the kind, and after Hairabedian's fate no one could decently even hint at it, but he had observed many low-voiced conferences, and he had intercepted many glances directed at his diving-bell, now stowed upon the booms – glances as eloquent as those of a dog. 'So with your permission I propose descending as soon as John Cooper shall have reassembled the bell. My plan is to attach hooks to the openings in the galley's deck, which being hauled upon will break up the floor-boards, revealing all that lies below. But I need a companion, a mate, to help me with the necessary manoeuvres.'

'I too am an urinator,' said Martin, 'and I am thoroughly accustomed to the bell. I should be happy to go with Dr Maturin.'

'No, no, gentlemen,' cried Jack. 'You are very good – infinitely generous – but you must not think of such a thing for a moment. Consider the danger; consider poor Hairabedian's end.'

'We do not intend going out of the bell,' said Stephen.

'But may not the sharks come into it?'

'I doubt that: and even if they were to do so, sure we should induce them to go out again, with an iron prong, or maybe with a horse-pistol.'

'That's right,' said Killick, and to cover the remark he let fall a dish, retiring with the pieces.

On going below to attend the Captain's dinner Stephen had left a dismal deck, full of tired, deeply disappointed men, gasping-hot, apt to quarrel with one another and with the Turks; he returned to find sunny faces, affectionate looks, a holiday atmosphere, laughter fore and aft, his bell beautifully put together, ready to be swung clear of the rail and lowered; its glass had been newly polished and a series of beckets within held six loaded pistols and two boarding-pikes, while a variety of hooks, tackles, lines and ropes lay neatly coiled upon the bench. But the laughter stopped and the mood changed entirely when what had been in prospect became immediate reality. 'Should you not wait until the evening, sir?' asked Bonden as Stephen prepared to get into the bell, and it was clear from their serious, concerned faces that he was speaking for a good many of the crew.

'Nonsense,' said Stephen. 'Remember, now, at two fathoms we pause and renew the air.'

'Perhaps we should try with a couple of midshipmen first,' said the purser.

'Mr Martin, pray take your seat in the usual place,' said Stephen. 'James Ogle' – this to the man in charge of the pair of barrels – 'mind you do not let us want for air.'

There was no fear of that. The cranks whipped round as though for James Ogle's own salvation, and the bell had not sunk its first gentle two fathoms before the fresh air was there, ready to be let in. Everything that anxious care on board could do was done, and twenty picked hands with muskets lined the side; but there was little that could be done apart from tending the tackles, and there was not a man aboard who did not feel sick with apprehension when a huge fish, thirty-five to forty feet long, glided between them and the bell, far too deep for any musket. It turned above the glass, darkening the day. 'That must be the big carcharodon,' said Stephen, looking up. 'Let us see what he will make of this.' He reached for the cock and let out a furious bubbling stream of used air. In a single swift move-ment the shark turned its vast bulk and was seen no more.

'I wish he had stayed a little longer,' said Martin, reaching down for the hose from the next barrel. 'Poggius says he is excessively rare.' He raised the tube and the compressed air hissed into the descending bell, driving the few inches of water that had entered it down to the rim. 'I believe this is the clearest day we have ever had.'

'I am sure you are right. I never have made an ascent in an air balloon, alas, but I imagine it to give this same immaterial floating even dreamlike sensation. There is a small Chlamys heterodontus.'

A few minutes later the bell settled on the galley's deck, neatly placed abaft the rowers' benches and just over the after hatchway, whose grating had floated off.

Time passed: interminable for those above, quite short for those below.

'What can they be at?' cried Jack at last. 'What can they be at?' There was no signal from the bell, no sign of life apart from the streams of air that made the surface boil and froth from time to time. 'How I wish I had never let them go.'

'Perhaps,' said Martin, after their tenth attempt at connecting line, hook and tackle, 'perhaps we might send up a message desiring them to lower down a stout hook already tied to its necessary ropes and pulleys.'

'I am very unwilling that they should suppose I am not the complete seaman,' said Stephen. 'Let us try just once again.'

'There are two young tiger-sharks peering through the glass,' observed Martin.

'No doubt, no doubt,' said Stephen testily. 'I do beg you will pay attention, and pass the rope through this loop, while I hold it open.'

Through the loop or not, the assembly would not hold, and the shameful message, written with an iron stylus on a small sheet of lead, was obliged to be sent up.

A perfectly simple, perfectly foolproof hook came down. Working it from the *Niobe*'s deck called for much more labour, but the hands who tailed on to the fall cared nothing for that, although the temperature was now a humid hundred and twenty-eight degrees under the awnings, and presently great stretches of the galley's deck came floating to the surface. It was so thin and light, apart from the beams fore and aft of the masts, that a grapnel could pull it apart; and the beams themselves yielded to the first heave of the *Niobe*'s kedge. The entire hull lay open, and although by now the water was so troubled that nothing could be clearly made out from the ship, the bell sent up a message 'We see small rectangular chests, or large boxes, apparently sealed. If you will move us a yard to the left we can reach the nearest, which we shall attach to a rope.'

'I should never have believed that so small a bulk could be so heavy,' said Martin as they lifted it across to the middle of the bell, where there was most light. 'Do you see that the French seals, with the Gallic cock, are red, while the Arabic are green?'

'So they are, joy. Now if you will tilt it up, I will pass the rope around twice.'

'No, no. We must do it up at both ends, like a parcel. I do wish the Navy had ordinary string: this thick rope is so plaguey stiff and hard to tie. Do you think this bow will answer?'

'Admirably well,' said Stephen. 'Let us slide it out under the rim again, and give the signal.'

'Bell signals *heave away*, sir, if you please,' said Bonden.

'Carry on, then,' said Jack, 'but handsomely, handsomely.'

At this time the bell was emitting no bubbles. The chest could be seen, at first dimly, then quite clear, rising slowly through the water; and the grinning hands perceived its weight.

'Oh my God the knot's slipping,' cried Mowett. 'Bear a hand, bear a hand, bear a . . . Hell and death.'

On reaching the surface the chest glided through its bonds and plunged free, directly over the bell. 'If it hits the glass they are dished,' thought Jack, following its course with appalled anxiety while at the same time he roared, 'Stand by the bell tackle-fall – jump to it.'

The plummeting chest missed the glass by inches, striking the bell an echoing blow and landing by its rim. 'The next time we must cross the knot the other way,' said Martin.

'I cannot stand this any longer,' said Jack. 'I shall go down and make them fast myself. Mr Hollar, give me some spun-yarn and marline. Raise the bell.'

The bell came up; it swung dripping inboard, and Stephen and Martin stepped out, cheered by one and all. 'I am afraid we did not tie it quite tight enough,' said Stephen.

'Not at all. You did splendidly, Doctor. Mr Martin, I congratulate you with all my heart. But perhaps this time I will take your place. Every man to his trade, you know, and the cook to the foresheet.'

A gale of laughter followed this, and his shipmates thumped the cook on the back: they were in such tearing spirits they could scarcely contain themselves. Captain Aubrey, on the other hand, had to overcome a very real repugnance as he mounted the bell and sat on the bench; his look of flushed triumphant happiness faded to sobriety and it was all he could do to keep it to that; he hated being confined – he would not have gone into a coal-mine for anything in the world – and during their passage down he was obliged to repress a very strong irrational urge to escape whatever the cost. However, their pause in midwater, the business of renewing the air and letting out the old, kept him occupied; and when he was standing on the galley's floor he felt somewhat better – at least in full control.

'We have returned to our old place exactly,' said Stephen. 'Here is the very one we dropped. Let us pull it in.'

'Are they all like this?' asked Jack, looking at the stout chest with its deeply recessed ends.

'As far as I can see they are all exactly the same. Look under the rim – there is a whole range of them running forward.'

'Then it is great nonsense using a line. Iron cask-slings would deal with them in no time. Let us go up and fetch a pair. We will put this on the bench and carry it with us.'

Once again the bell rose up and swung inboard: once again the people cheered, and louder than before. Bonden and Davis, two strong men, carried the heavy little chest to the middle of the quarterdeck.

'Make a lane, there,' cried the bosun, pushing at the intensely expectant, happy, tight-packed crowd of Surprises, Turks and Lascars. The carpenter came through the lane, bearing his tools. He knelt to the chest, drew three nails, and levered back the lid.

The expectant, happy faces, even more crowded now, looked taken aback, puzzled. The more literate slowly read *Merde à celui qui le lit* painted in white upon a dull grey block of metal.

'What does this mean, Doctor?' asked Jack.

'Roughly *whoever reads this is a fool*.'

'It's a fucking pig of lead,' cried Davis, catching up the block with frightful force and dancing as he stood, holding it high over his head, his mouth white with spittle and his face black with rage.

'Give me t'other end,' said Jack kindly, patting him on the shoulder, 'and we'll toss it overboard.'

'Sir,' said Rowan hesitantly, 'should we like to buy some fish?'

'I can imagine nothing that would give me more pleasure, Mr Rowan,' said Jack. 'Pray, why do you ask?'

'There is a boat alongside, sir, and the man is holding up something like a skate with red spots; but he has been here quite a while, and I am afraid he will shove off if we don't attend to him.'

'Buy all he has and bring him aboard,' said Jack. 'Doctor, be so good as to question him about the situation on the island with Mr Hassan. That will enable the Turks to decide about their landing, and it will tell us how we stand.'

He walked into his cabin, and it was there that Stephen found him in the torrid late afternoon. 'Listen, Jack,' he said, 'the position is clear. The French have been here for a month and four days; they have repaired the fortifications and they have set up batteries wherever they are needed.

There is no possibility of landing. For the last week they have been sending this galley down the south channel in the night and bringing it up again in the day. The fishermen were firmly persuaded that it had great quantities of silver aboard, and I imagine the original cases were kept aboard to keep the notion alive, so that if we met any casual dhow or felucca we should still hear of treasure and be lured in.'

'We have been done brown,' said Jack. 'What flats we must look.'

'Perhaps one should look for such a result when an expedition has been so much talked of as this was,' said Stephen. 'But even so I am surprised at the precision of their intelligence.'

Chapter Seven

During the *Niobe*'s return to Suez the usual northerly breezes blew with scarcely a pause; she had to beat up all the way, often tacking two or three times in a watch, and the cry of 'All hands about ship' was even more frequent than that for sweepers, seeing that it came by night as well as by day. And by now her bottom was very foul, especially where her copper had been ripped off: this not only caused her to miss stays more often than was agreeable but it also made her dreadfully slow, a point of some importance in a crowded ship that had relied on getting rid of her Turks at Mubara and on completing her water there. The people were put on short allowance, and the scuttle-butt, which ordinarily stood on deck for anyone to drink from, was now deprived of its dipper: those who wished to drink had to suck the water up through a dismounted musket-barrel; and so that no man should do so wantonly the barrel was kept in the maintop, since only great thirst would make the climb worth while in such overwhelming heat. This was felt to be unjust by the Turks, who said that neither their fathers nor their mothers were apes, and that climbing did not come naturally to them, whatever might be the case with others: the seamen retorted that as the Turks did not work, and as they fouled the heads so horrid, they had no right to be thirsty; but the argument carried no conviction and there might have been serious trouble if the *Niobe* had not put into Kosseir, where water was to be had in abundance, although the wells were awkwardly placed for the boats and the ship had to lie far offshore.

It would in any case have taken a considerable time to fill

all the casks and get them aboard, but now it took longer than usual. In the ordinary course of events the air over the Red Sea was so extremely humid that the sun did not burn but only boiled those exposed to its rays and the hands went about stripped to the waist, most of them still quite pale after weeks of it. But on a Friday – still another Friday – the breeze came right off the land, the air grew parching dry, biscuit, charts and books became crisp again from one watch to the other, and the seamen burnt brick-red or purple. An order to the effect that no hands who were not already black, brown, or yellow were any longer to be indulged in the liberty of going shirtless came too late, and although Stephen lavished sweet-oil on their tender backs the burns were so deep that it had little effect. Watering was therefore painful as well as slow; and while it was running its tedious course the Bimbashi, who had never forgiven Jack for having been misled, very carefully and at great length showed him the scene of another of the Royal Navy's failures – the little five-gun fort defending Kosseir roads, which had been bombarded by two thirty-two-gun frigates, *Daedalus* and *Fox*, for two days and a night, when it was in the hands of the French. They fired six thousand rounds, said the Bimbashi, writing it down so that there should be no mistake, six thousand rounds, but they failed to take the fort and their attack was repelled with the loss of a gun and of course a great many casualties.

'Pray tell the Bimbashi how deeply I am obliged to him for his information,' said Jack to Stephen, 'and how highly I value it as an example of his politeness.' This necessarily had to pass through Hassan, a man of delicate breeding who had been uneasy throughout the Bimbashi's account and who now looked uneasier still.

Yet Hassan's farewell was as cold as the Bimbashi's when they took leave of Jack in Suez, the Turk to take his men to Ma'an and the Arab to return to his wilderness.

'That was an odd way to say good-bye,' said Jack, looking after him with a certain regret and some slight shade of indignation. 'I always did the civil thing by him; we always got along perfectly well, I cannot imagine what made him so chuff.'

'Can you not?' said Stephen. 'Surely it is that he expected you to come down on him for the seven hundred and fifty purses he promised you to bilk the Egyptian. As he saw it you had fulfilled your part of the bargain while he was unable to produce a single purse at the moment of parting, let alone several hundred: he felt that you must scorn him, which is enough to make any man stiff and proud.'

'I never agreed to his monstrous proposal for a moment – gave it no countenance whatsoever.'

'Of course you did not, but he thought you did, which is what matters. He is not at all a bad horse, however: I spent much of the forenoon with him, while you were breaming the ship, together with a French-speaking Coptic physician he had known since his childhood, a gentleman who will act for us if we have any further dealings with the Egyptian governor, a gentleman, moreover, with wide connections among the Greek and Armenian merchants of these parts, and an insatiable appetite for information. Will I call for another pot of this admirable sherbet, the only cool thing in creation, perhaps, and tell you what I learnt?'

'If you please.'

They were sitting in the loggia over the gatehouse of the caravanserai in which Stephen had left his personal troop of camels and which was now given up to Captain Aubrey's party. Most of the Surprises were to be seen under the shaded arcades that surrounded its central square, reposing after their morning's labour and contemplating the camels, which lay in the full sun, not far from their future burdens, the dismantled bell and the many, many boxes of coral, shells and natural wonders collected by Stephen and Martin. Some had adopted members of the tribe of half-wild dogs that roamed the streets of Suez, and Davis was bargaining with the leader of a female Syrian bear for her cub. They all had a pleasant, drowsy, peaceable air, but at the far end there stood pyramids of muskets, piled in the naval manner; and it was perhaps these weapons as much as Jack's chelengk that made the Egyptian governor so much more obliging than he had been before. All his own troops had been drawn off for Mehemet Ali's campaign, and although he still mentioned harbour-dues he did not dwell on the matter, just as his customs-officers did not insist when told that the boxes contained not merchandise but personal property and could not be opened.

The sherbet came, frosted with the cold, and having drunk a voluptuous pint Stephen said, 'Well, now, it appears that our intelligence was right about the galley's cargo but mistaken about its time of departure. The Frenchmen were perfectly aware of our general intentions and even I suspect of our specific motions and they hired a crew of Abyssinian Christians, who rowed it up during Ramadan. But after the Abyssinians had gone home they kept the vessel going up and down that repulsive channel, and they spread the rumour that more treasure was being moved from one of the southern islands: this so that the tale might reach us. It was hoped that we should take the galley in chase, fully convinced of its value, and that it should lead us into a particularly narrow inlet beyond the batteries, where its crew was to abandon it and we, having rushed aboard, were to be captured or destroyed.'

'That is why they had so many boats,' said Jack. 'I wondered at the time.' He gasped for a while, fanning himself, and then said, 'Killick caught one of the governor's people trying to open one of the boxes with seals that Mr Martin begged for his echinoderms. I believe the governor suspects we may have boarded the right galley after all. He was very pressing to be invited aboard. I wonder what the Turks told him.'

'They told him the simple truth. But it is now quite certain that Mehemet Ali is playing a double game with the Sultan, and naturally the Egyptians expect the Turks to do the same by them. Some people here think we took the French treasure or at least some of it; some think we took long-sunk treasure from the depths; some think we took pearls in those waters where they are known to exist but where no man dares dive; and some think we failed; though I believe every reasoning two-legged creature in the town is convinced that the bell was taken for the purpose of material gain. Where the governor belongs in this array of opinion I know not; but Hassan warned me not to trust him. Apart from anything else, since an open breach between Mehemet Ali and the Sublime Porte is very probable, he need not fear Turkish resentment if he treats us ill. I shall tell Martin to take particular care of his echinoderms.'

'I will not say a fig for the governor,' said Jack, 'nor that since he has no troops he has no teeth, because that might be unlucky; but in any case we shall be shot of him tomorrow. And I must say this for him: he has been mighty civil, gathering a good train of camels for us. If I understood him aright they will be here at dawn. Then three or four days later, if we take it easier this time, marching in the morning and evening and resting at midday and night, and if all goes well, we shall be shot of this horrible country too. We shall be aboard that blessed *Dromedary*, sailing down the Mediterranean like Christians; and all I shall have to do will be to write my official letter. God help us, Stephen, I had rather be flogged round the fleet.'

Jack Aubrey had always disliked writing official letters, even those in which he had a victory to announce: the prospect of writing one which must speak of total failure in every respect, without the least alleviating feature or favourable circumstance – no chance prize taken, no valuable ally acquired – depressed him extremely.

His depression lifted with the appearance of a visitor, however, the Coptic physician, Dr Simaika, come to call on Stephen and to talk about European politics, ophthalmia, and Lady Hester Stanhope; he had brought a basket of fresh khat, and as they chewed it, to find whether in fact it made the heat seem less, he branched off to Egyptian adultery, fornication and paederasty – Sodom itself was only a few days' march east-north-east, behind the Wells of Moses – in their less tragic aspects, and he was so droll, so intensely amused, that although Jack did not follow a great deal of what he said and often had to have the point explained, he spent a very pleasant evening, laughing much of the time. Suez seemed a much less revolting place; the changing breeze wafted the stench out to sea; the heat was certainly more bearable; and when the governor's secretary came to say that on second thoughts it might be better if Captain Aubrey were not to start tomorrow after all he received him with a fine equanimity. Fortunately Dr Simaika was still there and the position was soon clarified: as the governor had been disappointed of even the half-platoon of guards he had been promised, he thought it advisable to send to Tina, so that a body of Turks might return with the messenger, thus providing Captain Aubrey with an escort across the desert. It would only take ten days or so, and during that time the governor would have the pleasure of Captain Aubrey's much-valued company.

'God forbid,' said Jack. 'Please to tell him that we know the way perfectly well, that we have no need of an escort, since the men will march with their weapons, and that although nothing would give me deeper satisfaction than sitting with his Excellency, duty calls me away.'

The secretary asked whether in that case Captain Aubrey would assume full responsibility, and hold the governor blameless if for example one of his men were bitten by a camel, or if thieves picked his pocket at one of the wells?

'Oh yes,' said Jack. 'On my own head be it – best compliments to his Excellency, and should be happy to keep to our former agreement – camels at dawn.'

'Shall we ever see them, I wonder?' said Jack, when the secretary had gone.

'Perhaps you may,' said Dr Simaika with a very significant look; but before its significance could become explicit the purser came to ask for instructions about victualling and Mowett for Captain Aubrey's views on liberty – liberty in the technical sense – while at the same time a fight broke out in the square below, a fight between Davis and the bear, which resented his familiarity in chucking it under the chin.

The Copt bowed and departed. Stephen hurried down to

repair the bear, and Jack, having dealt with the question of provisions, said that there was to be no liberty – there was a possibility of their getting under way in the morning, and he did not choose to spend all day combing the brothels of Suez for stragglers. The one great gate into the caravanserai was to be locked, and Wardle and Pomfret, two misogynistic, puritanical, ill-favoured old quartermasters, the grizzled fathers of seventeen children between them, and perfectly reliable when sober, were to guard it. 'For my part,' he added, 'I must go down and see the last of the *Niobe*; she sails on the first of the ebb. But I shall turn in very early, in case the camels appear.'

The camels appeared, noisy, smelly, grumbling; and as the great gateway opened they strode through in the first grey light; and dodging among their legs, bent low to pass unseen and led by Wardle and Pomfret, came a discreditable number of Surprises who had crept out by night, now pale, hollow-eyed and weary. However, there was nobody missing, and after a brief inspection Mowett could report 'All present and sober, sir, if you please,' without more falsehood than could be borne, since the few hands who were still drunk by naval standards did not fall until after the inspection; and they were quietly slung on to camels' backs among the tents and seamen's bags.

While the few stores that remained from the voyage – a little biscuit, a little tobacco, a quarter keg of rum, and a few barrel hoops that Mr Adams had saved (he was accountable for every one of them) – the seamen's bags, the officers' chests and Stephen's belongings were being loaded, Killick stripped Jack of all his finery, packed it into his sea-chest and lashed the chest, triple-locked and covered with sailcloth, on to a particularly docile, reliable she-camel led by a black man with an honest face, allowing his captain no more than a pair of old nankeen pantaloons, a linen shirt, a broad-brimmed sailor's hat, made of straw, a pair of common ship's pistols, and the shabby sword he used for boarding – these to be hung on the chest when they were out of the town.

Yet plain though he was, Captain Aubrey marched in

state, coming first, with Mowett on his right, a midshipman on his left, and his coxswain immediately behind him; then came the Surprises with their officers, forecastlemen in front, then foretopmen, maintopmen and afterguard, and then the baggage-train. They left Suez in quite good style, escorted by a cloud of excited yellow curs and little boys, for although those seamen who started in step soon fell out of it they did at least keep in recognizable groups until they were well out into the desert.

But presently there came a long stretch of heavy going, sand so soft that unless a man had feet like a camel he sank to the ankles; furthermore the whole party had been long enough at sea to grow quite unused to walking, and by the time Jack gave the order to halt for breakfast the column was a long straggling line.

'I see that there are some camels with nothing on their backs but drunken sailors and a few tents,' said Martin. 'Army officers generally ride, even in the foot regiments.'

'So they do in the Navy, sometimes,' said Stephen, 'and an eminently comic spectacle it is, on occasion. But there is a tedious and I fear increasingly powerful sentiment that when something exceptionally arduous and disagreeable is to be done, like walking over a hot, shadowless desert, then all hands must share alike, ton for ton and man for man. It seems to me foolish, inconsistent, ostentatious, useless, illogical. I have often represented to Captain Aubrey that no one expects him to join in cleaning the filth from the ship's heads, nor in many other vile offices, and that it is therefore mere froth and showing away, spiritual pride, nay downright sin, voluntarily to strut about the wilderness like this.'

'And yet – forgive me, Maturin – you are doing so yourself, with camels of your own at hand.'

'That is only moral cowardice. My courage will increase as my ankles swell and my feet grow more blistered, and presently I shall silently mount my beast.'

'We rode, you and I, on the march down.'

'That was because they marched at night, while it was

known that we spent the day botanizing. We were also unperceived.'

'How we botanized! Do you think we shall reach Bir Hafsa tomorrow?'

'Which is Bir Hafsa?'

'The resting-place where there was such a fine stretch of centaurea for the camels and where we found the curious euphorbia among the dunes.'

'And the spiny lizards, the crested desert-lark, the anomalous wheatear. Perhaps we may: I hope so, indeed.'

Yet at one time it seemed scarcely possible. The party did not get along well at all: those men who had spent the night in song and dance were horribly jaded, and once the sun had climbed a little way the heat was very great; but there was another factor that had not come into play when they marched down to Suez in the darkness – by day the vast expanse of desert, perfectly level in every direction, offered no shelter for those who wished to relieve themselves; and as several of the Surprises, including their captain, were as shamefast and bashful in their actions as they were licentious in their speech, this led to a great loss of time as men hurried off so that distance, often very great distance, should preserve their modesty. So much was this the case that the party advanced no more than a pitiful stage the first day, only reaching a place called Shuwak, a rocky outcrop with some tamarisk and mimosa scrub less than sixteen miles from Suez. But had they gone farther Stephen would never have been able to show Jack his first Egyptian cobra, a magnificent specimen five feet nine inches long that was gliding about the small ruined caravanserai with its head raised and its hood expanded, a most impressive sight. Nor would he and Martin have been able to take a camel over to the shores of the Little Bitter Lake, where in the last rays of light they saw the pied kingfisher and the houbara bustard.

But by the next day most people had recovered; they were now on firm stony sand with a certain amount of low vegetation, and they went along at a fine rate. It was the same easy going after the long midday halt, and the sun was still a handsbreadth over the horizon when Bir Hafsa came in sight far ahead – another ruined building by the side of the track and three palms by the well, in a region of fixed dunes.

'I think we might as well pitch camp by the well,' said Jack. 'Going on another hour would be neither here nor there, and we might as well sup in comfort.'

'You will not object if Martin and I go ahead on our camel?' asked Stephen.

'Never in life,' said Jack, 'and I should be most uncommon obliged if you would clear the ground of the more disgusting reptiles while you are there.'

The camel in question, a comparatively good-natured animal with a long swift stride, soon outpaced the column even with its double load, and set them down in the centaureas near the palms with half an hour of sunlight to spare. They had seen two very curious wheatears, black with white polls, and they were climbing a dune to the east of the camping-place to see more when Martin said, 'Look. How extremely picturesque.' He pointed westwards, and there on a corresponding dune, black against a brilliant orange sky, Stephen saw a dromedary and its rider. He shaded his eyes against the glare, and down on the level desert he saw more camels, a great many more; and not only camels but horses too. He looked to the south, and there was the column marching in or rather straggling in over a furlong of ground, with the baggage-train fast catching up as the camels smelt the thorny pasture. 'I think we should hurry down,' he said.

Jack was pointing out the places for the tents when Stephen interrupted him. 'I beg your pardon, sir, but there is a large force of camels a short mile to the west: when I last saw them from up there their riders were changing to horses, which I understand is the Bedouin mode of attack.'

'Thankee, Doctor,' said Jack. 'Mr Hollar, pipe to quarters.' And raising his voice enormously, 'Afterguard, afterguard there. Double up, double up, double up.'

The afterguard doubled up, falling into their place on the fourth side of the square formed by the forecastlemen, the foretopmen and maintopmen. 'Mr Rowan,' said Jack, 'take some hands and make the camel-drivers take shelter in that enclosure with all their beasts. Killick, my sword and pistols.'

The square was not military in its neatness, and when Jack said 'Fix bayonets' there was no simultaneous flash, click and stamp; but the sharp blades were there, the muskets were there, and the men were thoroughly used to using them. The square was small, but it was formidable: and as Jack stood there in the middle of it he thanked God that he had not tried to increase the rate of march by having the weapons loaded on to the pack animals. He was not so pleased when he looked at the slow-moving animals themselves, however; his own chest was on one of the foremost beasts and Killick was already coming back, but although Rowan and his men had most of the camels in the enclosure they were still having to beat the stragglers along and he was just about to call out when he saw horsemen appear on the top of Stephen's dune. He hailed, 'Rowan, Honey. Rejoin at once,' and they came running, their shadows long on the sand.

More horsemen gathered, and then with a concerted shriek they raced breakneck down the hill upon Rowan and Honey, easily catching them and cutting them off, enveloping them but avoiding them by inches as they stood there: after a moment they were past, riding furiously up the opposite slope, where they reined in so hard that their horses stopped dead. Here they poised for a long moment, all armed, either with swords or very long guns.

Jack had seen many a fantasia on the Barbary coast – Arabs galloping full tilt at their chief and his guests, firing in the air and turning at the last moment – and as Rowan and Honey came gasping into the square he said, 'Perhaps it is only their fun. No man is to fire unless I give the word.' He repeated this with emphasis and there was a general grunt of agreement, though old Pomfret muttered, 'Funny fun.' The men looked grave, displeased, but perfectly competent and sure of themselves. Both Calamy and Williamson were nervous, naturally enough, since they had seen almost no action on shore, and Calamy kept fiddling with the lock of his pistol.

High on the dune a red-cloaked man threw up his gun, fired it into the air and launched his horse down the slope, followed by all the others, firing and crying, 'Illa-illa-illa.'

'It is a fantasia,' said Jack, and aloud, 'Do not fire.'

The troop raced towards them, split in two and swept round the square, a bewildering whirl and counter-whirl of flying robes, swords flashing in the sunset, guns going off, the unceasing 'Illa-illa-illa', and a great cloud of dust.

The sun set: the opaque dust glowed golden. The ring of galloping horsemen came closer, shouting over the thunder of hooves. Calamy dropped his pistol, which flashed in the pan: Killick sprang from his place as though he had been wounded, crying, 'No, you don't, you black bastard,' and somebody shouted, 'They're off!'

They were indeed. The last wild round spun away, racing in a straight line westwards, and now it was seen that the camels too were fleeing in the same direction, flogged to their uttermost stretch by their drivers. For a few moments they could just be made out in the brief twilight; then they vanished among the dunes. All the camels but two: one of which had broken its leading-rope and was now placidly grazing, while the other lay on the ground, its forelegs still clamped together by Killick; he was half buried in the sand and dazed by a variety of blows; he had been trampled upon, struck and kicked, but he was not much the worse. 'I served the bugger out,' he said, looking at his bloody fist.

Silence fell: the darkness gathered fast. It was over and no one had been killed or even seriously hurt. But on the other hand they had lost everything except Captain Aubrey's uniforms and decorations, some papers and instruments, and two large tents, which were carried by the other beast.

'The best thing we can do,' said Jack, 'is for every man to drink as much as he can hold, and then for us to steer for Tina, marching by night again. No one needs food in this heat, and if they do we can eat the camels. Gather some branches and make a fire by the well.'

The dry tamarisk flared up and by its light they saw not what Jack had dreaded, a dry bottom with a long-dead camel in it, but a reasonable body of water. They had no bucket, but Anderson the sailmaker soon whipped one up, using the canvas that covered Jack's sea-chest and the hussif that lay within, and they dipped and filled, dipped and filled until no man could drink again and even the camels turned away.

'Come, we shall do very well,' said Jack. 'Shall we not, Doctor?'

'I believe we may,' said Stephen, 'particularly those among us who breathe through their noses, to prevent the dispersion of the moist humours, who hold a small pebble in their mouths, and who refrain from pissing and idle chat; the others may fall by the wayside.'

A deep strong voice from the dunes came almost immediately after these words: Uhu, uhu. It certainly checked all idle chat, but after a pause there was a good deal of low, earnest talking and presently the bosun approached Mowett. Then Mowett came to Jack and said, 'Sir, the men are wondering whether the chaplain might ask a blessing on our march.'

'Certainly,' said Jack. 'A bidding-prayer in times like these is a damned sight – a great deal better, more decent I mean, than most of your Te Deums. Mr Martin, sir, would it be in order to hold a short service?'

'Yes, it would,' said Martin. He paused for a few moments, recollecting; and then in a plain, unaffected manner he recited part of the litany and then desired them to join him in the sixtieth psalm.

The singing died away over the starlit desert: the terrors of the night receded. Jack said, 'Now I am quite sure that we shall do very well – that we shall reach Tina and the Turks in fine trim.'

They reached Tina – the hill and its fort had been in sight for half a torrid day as they laboured over the last stretch, accompanied by vultures – but they did not reach it in fine trim. The camels were uneaten only because they were needed to carry those whose strength had failed them, either from thirst and hunger or the extreme heat or the dysentery they had caught in Suez, and the poor beasts were so loaded that they could hardly keep up even with the creeping pace of the column, if indeed the mute parched wizened band could be called a column and not a dying mob. Nor did they reach the Turks. Very early on Jack's spyglass had shown him that no colours flew over the fort; and when at last they came near enough they could all see that the great gate was shut, that there was no movement whatsoever within, and that the Bedouin encampment was gone, leaving an impression of everlasting sterility. Whether the Turks had retired to the Syrian border because of a breach between Egypt and Turkey or whether they were gone on some military expedition there was no telling; nor did Jack greatly care. All his anxiety was concentrated on the *Dromedary*. Was she still there, or had she given them up after so long? Had some storm or some crisis between Turks and Egyptians driven her off? Sunk her?

The low mud hills and the sand-dunes along the coast hid the nearer part of the bay, and the farther part, where they had left the ship, was as empty as the desert. The prospect of her not being there, so that they would be left on that fly-blown strand under the murderous sun, was very horrible and he had to force himself to be calm as he began the last climb. Even so it was at a scrambling run that he reached the crest. He stood there for a moment, savouring the immense relief that flooded into him, for there she lay, moored head and stern quite close inshore, and her people were scattered all about the bay in boats, fishing over the side.

He turned, and the sight of his happy face brought the others up at the double, though before a stumbling walk was all that most of them could manage: but they had not a hail between them. All they could do was to utter some hoarse croaking sounds that did not carry a hundred yards, and when they waved the boats took no notice for a great while and then only waved back in the calmest, most provoking manner.

'Fire a volley,' said Jack, for although some men had dropped their muskets in the last intolerable miles others still had theirs. At the sound of firing the nearest boat made for the ship and for a moment it seemed that the Dromedaries might have taken fright, might have supposed that Turks and Egyptians were attacking them or one another so that it would be better to stand out to sea; but it was only Mr Allen going back for his telescope.

Nothing could more have endeared the Dromedaries to the Surprises than the cups of tea, the huge quantities of wine and water with lemon-juice, and the food they lavished on them; nothing could have endeared the Surprises to the Dromedaries more than the appalling time they had had, their gratitude, and the failure of their mission. They sailed westwards as friendly as very old shipmates, all distinction between man-of-war's men and the merchant service gone by the board; and they had remarkably favourable breezes, almost as favourable as those that had brought them up the Mediterranean and often blessedly cool. Every day Malta came a hundred or a hundred and fifty miles nearer, and every day after the first two or three Captain Aubrey made an attempt at his official letter.

'Listen to this, Stephen, will you?' he said, when they were in longitude 19°45' East. '"Sir, I have the honour to acquaint you that pursuant to your orders of the third ultimo I proceeded to Tina with the party under my command and from thence to Suez with a Turkish escort, where I embarked in HEI Company's sloop *Niobe* and, having eventually taken the Turkish contingent aboard, proceeded in adverse weather to the Mubara channel . . . where I made a complete cock of it." Now the point is, how can I best say that without looking too much of a fool?'

Chapter Eight

Jack Aubrey came aboard the Commander-in-Chief ten minutes after the *Dromedary* picked up her moorings, his official letter in his hand. He was received at once, and the Admiral looked up eagerly from his desk: but the face Sir Francis saw did not wear the look of a man who had recently captured five thousand purses of piastres, and it was without much hope of a favourable reply that he said, 'Well, here you are at last, Aubrey. Sit down. How did the expedition answer?'

'Not at all well, sir, I am afraid.'

'Did you not catch the galley?'

'We caught her, sir. Indeed, we sank her. But she had nothing aboard: they were expecting us.'

'In that case,' said the Admiral, 'I shall finish this report while I have all the facts in my mind. There are some newspapers on that locker, and the latest Navy List: it reached us only yesterday.'

Jack took up the familiar volume; he had not been away long, but already there were important changes. Some admirals had died, and their places, as well as certain vacancies, had been filled, so that everybody on the post-captain's list moved up, the highest to the glory of rear-admiral, blue or yellow as the case might be, and the others to a point somewhat nearer their apotheosis. J. Aubrey was now well past half way: farther past than the number of new admirals accounted for, and looking for the reason he found that several captains senior to him had also died – a sickly season in the Indies, east and west – while two had been killed.

'A pack of lies – mean shuffling excuses – anything to throw the blame elsewhere – infernal scrub,' muttered the

Admiral, tapping the pages of the report into a neat pile and ranging them exactly among many others. 'You have seen the flag promotion, Aubrey? It has indeed removed a number of officers from the command of ships who at no period of their lives were capable of commanding them; but I am sorry to have occasion to observe, that the present state of the upper part of the list of captains is not much better than it stood before. It is impossible for a Commander-in-Chief to accomplish anything if his subordinates are incompetent.'

'No, sir,' said Jack, awkwardly enough; and after a disagreeable pause, 'I have brought you my official letter, sir,' – laying it on the desk – 'and I am concerned to say that it is unlikely to change your opinion.'

'Zounds,' said the Admiral – he was the only serving officer known to Jack who still said zounds – 'it goes on for ever. Two, no three pages, wrote small on both sides. You have no idea of how much I have to read, Aubrey. I am just in from off Toulon, and there was a great mass waiting here. Give me a précis.'

'A what, sir?' cried Jack.

'A succinct abridgment, a summary, an abstract, for God's sake. You remind me of a half-witted midshipman I took aboard the *Ajax* once, in kindness to his father. "Have you no nous?" I asked him. "No, sir," says he. "I did not know it would be wanted aboard ship, but shall certainly purchase some when next ashore."'

'Ha, ha, sir,' said Jack, and he launched into an account of his voyage, ending, 'And so, sir, having made a cock of it, if you will allow me the expression, I came away, my only consolation being that there were no casualties, apart from the dragoman.'

'Clearly our intelligence was at fault,' said the Admiral, 'and we shall have to go into the reasons for that.' A brooding pause. 'It is possible that you might have accomplished something by a direct dash at Mubara, throwing your Turks ashore at dawn and supporting them with a cannonade, rather than hanging about for the galley. Speed is the essence of attack.' Jack's orders had distinctly required him to proceed first to the southern channel: he opened his mouth to say so, but closed it again without a word. 'I do not mean that as any kind of reproof, however. No, no ... The fact is that I have some unpleasant news for you. *Surprise* is to go home, either to be laid up or sold out of the service. No, no,' he said, holding up his hand, 'I know exactly what you are going to say. I should have said it myself at your age and in your position. She is in very good shape, with many years of useful life before her, and for sailing she has not her equal. All that is very true, though in passing I may say that very costly repairs may be needed soon: but what is equally true is that she is very, very old; she was old when we took her from the French at the beginning of the last war, and by modern standards she is very small and very weak, an anachronism.'

'You will allow me to observe, sir, that *Victory* is older still.'

'Only a little: and you know what she has cost in repairs. But that is not the point. The *Victory* can still batter any French first-rate, whereas there is virtually no frigate in the French or American navies that the *Surprise* can fight on anything like equal terms.'

It was quite true. For many years the trend had been to bigger, heavier ships, and the most usual frigate in the Royal Navy was now an eighteen-pounder thirty-eight-gun vessel that gauged well over a thousand tons, almost twice the size of the *Surprise*. Still, in his distress Jack did say, 'The Americans have their *Norfolk*, sir, as well as their *Essex*.'

'Another anachronism – the exception that proves the rule. What would the *Surprise* have to say to their *President* or any of the other forty-four gun frigates with their twenty-four pounders? Nothing at all. She might as well tackle a ship of the line. But do not take it so hard, Aubrey: there are as good fish in the sea as ever came out of it, you know.'

'Oh, I do not mind it, sir,' said Jack. 'Not at all. It was understood, when I brought the *Worcester* out, that this spell in the Mediterranean was to be a mere parenthesis, until the *Blackwater* should be ready.'

'The *Blackwater*?' said Sir Francis, surprised.

'Yes, sir. I had a firm promise of her, for the North American station, as soon as she was ready.'

'From whom?'

'From the First Secretary himself, sir.'

'Ah, indeed,' said the Admiral, looking down. 'I see, I see. However, before you take the *Surprise* home I have some little jobs for her: a run up the Adriatic, to begin with.'

Jack said that he should be very happy, and then, 'But I am afraid you must think me very uncivil, sir, for not having congratulated you on your promotion. I saw your flag had changed to red at the fore as I came over: I give you joy with all my heart.'

'Thank you, Aubrey, thank you kindly; though at my time of life these things are only a matter of course. I hope you will live to hoist yours at the main. You will dine with me? I have some interesting people coming aboard.'

Once again Jack said that he should be very happy: and superficially happy he was, eating hearty and drinking the Admiral's good wine with an elegant woman on either side of him and his old friend Heneage Dundas smiling at him from across the table; but when he was being rowed back across the harbour sorrow for his ship welled up and nearly choked him. He had served in her as a midshipman and he had commanded her in the Indian Ocean, a difficult and temperamental little frigate, but wonderfully responsive, fast and mettlesome for those who knew her ways; she had never failed him in an emergency, and he would never know a more sea-kindly ship, by or large, in light airs or in a strong gale. The idea of her rotting away in some foul creek and then being broken up or sold out of the service to be cut down into a creeping merchantman was more than he could bear. If that galley had been what it seemed, he would have bought her himself, to preserve her from such a fate: he had known ships, particularly enemies' ships, sold for no great sum if they were not wanted for the Navy.

Nor was it likely that he should ever command such a crew again, a crew of hand-picked seamen, every one of whom could hand, reef and steer, and practically every one of whom he knew and liked as a man. He knew exactly where he was with the Surprises and they knew exactly where they were with him and his officers; the Surprises could be allowed liberties unheard-of in a ship with a mixed set of people, including landsmen and thieves as well as a large proportion of sullen, understandably resentful pressed men, a ship's company that needed the perpetual tight discipline usual in the service, the repetitive drilling in reefing, furling, shifting topmasts, hoisting out boats and so on, all adapted to the capacities of the least endowed, the hard driving, and almost inevitably the hard punishment. Jack Aubrey was a taut captain, but he had never shared the zeal for punishing that characterized so many officers; he loathed flogging; he could never with a clear conscience order it for faults he had committed at times himself, and although the traditions of the service being what they were he had in fact ordered many a round dozen in his time he found it a great relief not to have to do so, a great relief not to be righteously indignant and perpetually holier than everyone else in the ship. There had scarcely been a flogging aboard the *Surprise* since he took her over; and if only her people had included a somewhat more amiable, less uncouth captain's steward, a captain's cook with more than two puddings at his command, a couple of officers who could play well enough for Stephen and him to have an occasional quartet, and a stronger midshipmen's berth, he would have said that before Pullings was promoted and before so many of the hands were drafted away, the frigate had had the finest ship's company in the squadron, if not in the entire service.

'I shall not tell them until I am forced to it,' he thought, as the boat turned among the lighters and he saw his ship. She was moored well outside the yard, but he was not at all surprised to see two lumpish scows still attached to her and a party of dockyard mateys busy about her stern.

'Larboard side,' he said to his coxswain. Any ceremony

in receiving him aboard would be ridiculous: he was the only man in the ship at this moment who possessed more than a thin duck shirt and trousers and a battered straw hat.

'Sir,' said Mowett, taking off his with what grace its broken brim allowed, 'I am very sorry to tell you that the villains will not have caulked the quarterdeck abaft the mizzen before Tuesday. Your cabins are open to the . . .'

'No glass in the stern windows, neither,' cried Killick in a shrill fury.

'Killick, pipe down,' said Jack.

'Sir,' said the purser, 'the storekeeper would not let me have hammocks and beds on my personal indent. He made game of my clothes, affected to believe I was in liquor, desired me to tell my story of camels and Arabs to the Marines, and walked off, laughing.'

'Nor in the quarter-galleries,' muttered Killick.

'No slops, either,' said the purser. 'And this to a purser of fifteen years' standing.'

'And the post, sir,' said Mowett. 'There is a sack for us, but it has been sent across to St Isidore's, and they say they are shut today, because of the feast.'

'Closed?' said Jack. 'Be damned to that. Bonden, my gig. Killick, jump across to Searle's, take me a room for the next few days, and lay on dinner tomorrow for *Dromedary*'s officers. Mr Adams, come along with me.'

Then, turning at the gangway, 'Where is the Doctor?'

'He has taken Rogers, Mann and Himmelfahrt to the hospital, sir.'

To the hospital, like a conscientious surgeon, to see his earlier patients, to bring three more, and to talk and even operate with his colleagues; but also, like a conscientious intelligence-agent, to Laura Fielding's house, quite late in the evening.

The outer door was open, but the lantern at the far end was not lit, and as he walked along the dark stone passage he thought, 'What a cut-throat place it is, to be sure: as silent as death.' At the door he groped for the bell-chain, heard the faint answering peal, instantly drowned by Ponto's bellowing, and then Laura's voice asking who was there.

'Stephen Maturin,' he said.

'Mother of God,' she cried, opening the door and letting out a flood of light. 'How happy I am to see you again.' And as he walked in, clearly visible, 'Oh, oh! Have you been shipwrecked?'

'Not at all,' said Stephen, rather nettled, for he had borrowed a pair of purple breeches at the hospital, and he had been shaved. 'Do you find my appearance not quite the thing?'

'Not in the least, dear Doctor. Only you are usually so . . . so point-device, shall I say?'

'By all means.'

'And always in uniform, so I was a little surprised to see your white coat.'

'We call it a banyan,' said Stephen, considering the garment, a loose sailcloth jacket with tapes instead of buttons, run up by Bonden out of what little light canvas the *Dromedary* had to spare. 'Yet perhaps it may look a little desperate on shore: perhaps it may. An ancient gentlewoman, Colonel Fellowes' mother, I believe, gave me this coin as I turned the corner of the street, saying, "Not for drink, my good man. Pas gin. Niente debaucho." But for the moment I have nothing else. A parcel of black thieves on horseback took away my bell may they rot for ever in the deep cinders of Hell and my collections and all my clothes was the way of it. However, like a prudent man I had not taken my other chest with my good uniform, at which I rather rejoice.' By this time they had reached the sitting-room and the little round table upon which Mrs Fielding's supper was laid out: three triangles of cold polenta, a hard-boiled egg, and a jug of lemonade. 'Will you believe it, my dear,' he said, sitting down opposite her and instantly seizing upon one of the triangles, 'that best coat of mine cost eleven guineas. Eleven guineas: a shocking sum indeed.' He was embarrassed – a rare state for him – and he talked somewhat at random: she poured him a glass of lemonade and watched a little wistfully as he reached out for the egg. 'But,' said he, unconsciously withdrawing his hand, 'if I had fetched all this splendour from the hotel where I left it, and put it on, I should never have had time to reach this house with any chance of finding you still up; and I thought it better to compromise your reputation in a banyan, as we agreed, than to leave it intact in a gorgeous coat.'

'It is truly benevolent in you to trouble with me, and to come so soon,' she said, taking his hand and looking at him with great troubled eyes.

'Not at all, my dear,' said Stephen, returning the pressure. 'Tell me now, have these people been pestering you since I went away?'

'Only twice. I had to go to St Simon's the next day, and I told him you had spent the night with me. He was pleased, and said I should have a letter the next time.'

'The same foreigner with the Neapolitan accent – the small pale middle-aged man?'

'Yes; but the one who gave me the letter was an Italian.'

'How is Mr Fielding?'

'Oh, he is not well. He does not say so – only that he had a fall and hurt his hand – but he is not himself. I am afraid he is very ill: sick to his heart. I will show you his letter.'

It was certainly devoid of some quality that the earlier letters had possessed: not elegance, for Mr Fielding had no talent that way, but rather flow, cohesion, natural sequence, and in some obscure way the affection that had showed through: it was a painstaking letter that hobbled along, recounting his fall on the icy steps into the exercise yard and his kind treatment in the prison infirmary, and urging Laura to do everything in her power to show their gratitude to the gentlemen who made this correspondence possible: they were certainly able to influence the government.

It would not do, thought Stephen as he looked at the carefully-formed writing. The tale of the injured hand was just a little too circumstantial and in any case it had been used far too often. His earlier impression became something very near a certainty: Fielding was dead and his forged hand was being used to keep Laura in subjection. The strong likelihood was that the French agent in Malta was Graham's Lesueur, and that Wray had failed to catch him: perhaps it was just as well, since a Lesueur fed false information through Laura would be far more useful than a Lesueur tied to a post in front of a firing-squad. But he would have to be fed fast, before the *Surprise* moved on, for without consulting Sir Joseph or one of his closest colleagues Stephen would not like to entrust the matter to anyone else in Malta: and of course before Fielding's death was known – once that happened Laura's function vanished. Not only would Lesueur disbelieve everything she told him, but since it would be in her power – indeed her interest – to compromise him and his whole organization he would certainly eliminate her. She would vanish with her function.

All this passed through his mind with the utmost rapidity, never even reaching the stage of words, while he looked at the letter. They were much the same reflections that had occurred to him the first time, but now they were informed with a far greater certainty, and, because of his very strong feeling for her, with a far greater sense of urgency. He made much the same comforting reply as he had made before, and their talk drifted away to the technical side of her connection with the intelligence agents. She was less cautious now and she gave him an accurate description of Lesueur and some of his colleagues, and she spoke of one Basilio's criminal levity – he had told her, for example, that it had never been intended that Dr Maturin should go to the Red Sea: another man was to have taken his place. From all she said it became distressingly clear that some at least had committed the common blunder and sometimes mortal sin of underestimating the power of a woman, and that even if Lesueur did not know that she had recognized him it was obvious that she knew so much about his network that he could not possibly tolerate her defection.

'Alas,' said Stephen, after a long pause, and then his face lightened. 'There she is,' he said, nodding at his 'cello, which stood against the wall on the far side of Laura's piano. 'I fairly longed for her on this last voyage.'

'You think of the 'cello as a woman?' she said. 'It has always seemed to me so masculine. Deep-voiced, perhaps unshaved.'

'Man or woman,' he said, 'let you make us some coffee and eat up your supper, which I have half demolished God forgive me unthinking, and then we might play the piece we crucified last time.'

'Man or woman,' he said as he took the instrument out of its brutish wrapping, or sack, 'what a coil there is between them.'

'What did you say?' she called from the kitchen, and it was evident that she was still eating.

'Nothing, nothing, my dear: muttering was all.' He tuned the 'cello, reflecting upon his feelings for her. Very strong desire, of course; but also tenderness, esteem, liking, an amitié amoureuse carried to a higher degree than he had known it before.

He came out in the street in the first light, detected the watcher with intense satisfaction, and made his thoughtful way down to the quay, there to wait until the dghaisas began to ply for hire. It had been arranged that he should take a room at Searle's, that she should come to him in a domino and a faldetta, and that he should provide her with something to set Lesueur in appetite. Just what should it be? He stood on the steps of the landing-place turning the wealth of possibilities over in his mind, staring with wide-open unseeing eyes at the degraded *Worcester*, which, amid the frigid indifference of all who had served in her, had already been turned into a sheer-hulk; and through his musing came the familiar London waterman's cry, 'Up or down, sir?' repeated at intervals. At the third repetition he collected himself, looked at the foot of the steps, and saw the grinning faces of the *Surprise*'s bargemen. 'For the barky, sir?' asked Plaice at bow-oar. 'Captain will be down directly minute. Bonden is just gone up to Searle's: I wonder you did not see him as he passed. But you was in a study, no doubt.'

'Good morning, Doctor,' cried Jack, appearing behind him. 'I did not know you were in the hotel.'

'Good morning, sir,' said Stephen. 'I was not. I slept with a friend.'

'Oh, I see,' said Jack. He was pleased, in that Stephen's frailty gave countenance and justification to his own, but at the same time he was disappointed, more disappointed than pleased, since a frail Stephen necessarily fell short of the very highest standard of virtue. Jack regarded him not so much as a saint as a being removed from temptations: he was never drunk, nor was he given to dangling after women in far foreign ports, still less did he go to brothels with the other officers, and although he was notoriously lucky at cards he very rarely played; so this commonplace fall, negligible in another man or in Jack Aubrey himself, took on a heinous aspect. Not without malice Captain Aubrey said, as the boat crossed the misty, steaming harbour, 'Have you seen your letters? We have had a whole sack of mail at last,' meaning 'Diana has written to you: I saw her hand on the covers: I hope it will make you feel guilty.'

'I have not,' said Stephen, with a provoking composure. But he was not in fact at all indifferent to the arrival of the post, and as soon as he had his letters he hurried down to read them in the privacy of his cabin. Diana had indeed written, and at some length for her, describing an intensely social life: she saw a good deal of Sophie, who had come up to town twice for the children's teeth and had stayed at Half Moon Street each time, and of Jagiello, a young attaché at the Swedish embassy who had been imprisoned in France with Jack and Stephen and who sent his love, and of various other friends, many of them French royalists. She also said she positively longed to see him back again, and hoped he was taking care of himself. Then there were several communications from fellow-naturalists in various countries, bills of course, and a statement from his man of business, showing that he was far richer than he had supposed, which quite pleased him. And there was the usual letter from the anonymous correspondent who wished him to know that

Diana was deceiving him with Captain Jagiello: they had now taken to 'doing it' in St Stephen's church, standing behind the altar. 'Would that be a man's notion, now, or a woman's?' he wondered, but he did not dwell on the question, because the next letter was from Sir Joseph Blaine, the chief of naval intelligence, a colleague and friend of such long standing that he could mingle news of the learned societies to which they both belonged (Sir Joseph was an entomologist) with veiled comments on various plans and on the progress of their particular war. The whole letter was interesting, but the part that Stephen re-read with unusual care was the observation that 'by now his dear Maturin would no doubt have met Mr Wray, our acting Second Secretary'. Just that and no more: no remarks about Wray's task, no request that Stephen should help him, and a slight insistence upon the word *acting*. In a man like Sir Joseph these were significant omissions, and coupled with the fact that Wray had brought no personal message they convinced Stephen that although Sir Joseph no doubt thought Wray capable of dealing with an affair like the leakage of naval information at Valletta he had not seen fit to let him into quite all the secrets of the department: it was natural enough, after all, that a recently-appointed and perhaps temporary official, unless he were a man of the most exceptional ability in that line, should not be treated with a complete lack of reserve in the matter of intelligence, where an otherwise unimportant lack of judgement or of discretion might have such disastrous effects. And since Wray did not enjoy Sir Joseph's fullest confidence – since he had presumably not yet been found to be a man of the most exceptional ability as far as intelligence was concerned – it appeared to Stephen that it would be wise to imitate his chief's reserve, and to deal with the case of Mrs Fielding by himself.

He had barely reached this decision before two messages arrived, the one requiring him to repair aboard the *Caledonia* at fifteen minutes past ten o'clock in the forenoon and the second inviting him to dine at the palace to meet Mr Summerhays, a very wealthy and well-connected botanist, with a civil note from Sir Hildebrand apologizing for the short notice – Mr S was proceeding to Jerusalem tomorrow and would infinitely regret leaving Malta without having heard Dr M on the plants of Sinai.

The first of these messages necessarily came to him through Captain Aubrey, who said or rather bellowed (the dockyard caulkers were hammering away overhead and both watches were busy scraping the deck the caulkers had already dealt with from the mainmast forward), 'A quarter past ten: my word, you will have to bear a hand to be there in time, Stephen, with your decent uniform on shore.'

'Perhaps I shall not go until tomorrow,' said Stephen.

'Nonsense,' said Jack impatiently, and he called for his coxswain and steward. It took some little time to find them, since they too were fetching the clothes that they had left at the dockyard in the chest they shared, and in the interval Stephen said, 'Brother, I am afraid the post brought you sad, sad news; I have rarely seen you look so down.'

'No,' said Jack. 'It was not the post: they are all well at home, and send their dear love. It is something else. I will tell you: you will not repeat it to anyone.' He pointed to a broom in a corner of the echoing cabin and said, 'We are to wear that at the masthead.' But seeing that this conveyed no meaning at all he forced himself to put it into plain words. '*Surprise* is to be laid up or sold out of the service, and we are to take her home.' Stephen saw the tear well in his eye, and for want of any more adequate remark he said, 'It will not affect you professionally?'

'No, since the *Blackwater* will be ready very soon: but I cannot tell you how it wounds . . . Killick,' he said, breaking off as his steward and coxswain arrived, 'the Doctor is to be aboard the flag at ten minutes past ten: you know where his uniforms are stored: he will change in my room at Searle's. Bonden, he will travel in my gig, and he will not forget to pay respect to the quarterdeck, nor his compliments to the Captain of *Caledonia* and the Captain of the Fleet, if they are on deck. You will see that he goes aboard dryfoot.'

Dr Maturin reached not only the *Caledonia*'s quarter-deck

but even her great cabin dryfoot, Bonden having carried him bodily up the accommodation-ladder; and there he found Mr Wray, Mr Pocock, and young Mr Yarrow, the Admiral's secretary. A moment later the Admiral himself hurried in from the quarter-gallery, buttoning his clothes. 'Forgive me, gentlemen,' he said. 'I am afraid I must have eaten something. Dr Maturin, good morning to you. Now the purpose of our meeting is first to find out how our intelligence came to be so mistaken about the Mubara affair, and in the second place to consult about the steps to be taken to prevent the enemy from obtaining information concerning our movements here. Mr Yarrow will begin by reading the relevant passages from Captain Aubrey's letter and then I shall ask you for your comments.'

Pocock was of the opinion that it all arose from the English refusal to back Mehemet Ali in his plan for becoming independent of Constantinople, thus throwing him into the arms of the French: the date of the temporizing English reply – in effect a refusal – coincided almost exactly with what must have been the first conception of this plot, which was obviously designed to win French support and to destroy British influence in the Red Sea, far more than to capture a ship.

Wray agreed, but he said that a scheme of this kind required a man on the spot, a person in French or Egyptian pay to transmit information and to coordinate the movements of the other side; and he was sure that the man in question was Hairabedian. It was most unfortunate that he had been killed; he might have been induced to make the most important revelations. He had brought the strongest recommendation from the resident in Cairo and glowing testimonials from the embassy in Constantinople at the same time as the first news of the French designs on Mubara; but with so urgent a matter there had been no time to verify either the resident's message or the testimonials. No doubt they would prove to be false, for it appeared that in Suez the dragoman had repeatedly passed on encouraging rumours about the galley's being loaded at Kassawa, which he must have invented or have known to be untrue. Dr Maturin would confirm that, he believed.

'Certainly,' said Stephen, 'but whether he was deceiving us or whether he was himself deceived I cannot say. Perhaps his papers will resolve the question.'

'What did he leave in the way of papers?' asked Wray.

'A small box containing some poems in modern Greek and a number of letters,' said Stephen; and partly because he had liked Hairabedian and partly because he was naturally sparing of information he suppressed the words 'and Captain Aubrey's chelengk' and continued, 'I went through them at Captain Aubrey's request, in case there should be any family we should communicate with; but those few that were in Greek gave us no indication, and those that were in Arabic or Turkish I could not read. I am not an oriental scholar at all, alas.'

'Were they not lost in the Bedouin raid?' asked Pocock.

The Admiral darted out of the room with a muttered excuse.

'They were not,' said Stephen. 'They were in the sea-chest that was saved, Captain Aubrey's sea-chest.'

While they waited for the Admiral Pocock spoke about the complexities of the relationship between Turkey and Egypt, and when he came back he said, 'I think you will agree, Sir Francis, that from our last Cairo report it seems certain that Mehemet Ali would never have left the new sheikh in Mubara for more than a month or so, even if he had been installed.'

'Oh, quite so,' said the Admiral wearily. 'Well now, the first question must remain in suspense until Hairabedian's letters are deciphered: let us pass on to the next. Mr Wray?'

Mr Wray very much regretted that at this juncture he was unable to report as much progress as he could have wished. At one moment, thanks to a precise, detailed description given him by Mr Pocock's predecessor, he had thought he was on the point of seizing an important French agent together with his colleagues; but either Professor Graham was mistaken or the man in question was aware that he had been seen – it came to nothing. 'Still, I have laid a couple of clerks by the heels, unimportant fellows who may nevertheless lead us further; and in the course of my investigations into dockyard corruption I have discovered some very curious facts. I scarcely like to say so yet, but in spite of a certain lack of really cordial cooperation on the civil and military sides, I may possibly be on the verge of uncovering the prime source of the trouble; yet since it is not inconceivable that some very highly-placed – astonishingly highly-placed – officials may be concerned, it would be improper to mention any names at this stage.'

'Quite right,' said the Admiral. 'But the matter must be dealt with before I go back to the blockade, if it is at all possible. There is no sort of doubt that information is passing to the French as quick or even quicker than the post. Yarrow, read the account of our last three Adriatic convoys.'

'Yes,' said Wray, when the reading was done, 'I am fully alive to the necessity of dispatch; but as I say, I am hampered by the lack of cooperation from the soldiers and civilians. I am also hampered by the lack of expert colleagues: as you know, sir, the Mediterranean command has always been very poor in the matter of intelligence – far poorer than the French, as far as *organized* intelligence handed down from one Commander-in-Chief to the next is concerned. I obviously cannot open myself entirely to my local subordinates nor wholly rely upon what they say; and as this is the first affair of the kind that I have been called upon to deal with, I am obliged to improvise, and to advance step by step, feeling my way. If any gentleman,' he said, dividing a smile between Stephen and Pocock, 'has any observations to make, I should be happy to hear them.'

'Dr Maturin?' said the Admiral.

'It appears to me, sir,' said Stephen, 'that there is some misapprehension as to my qualifications. In the nature of things I have a certain knowledge of the political situation in Spain and Catalonia, and I have been able to provide your predecessors and the Admiralty with informed comment, together with appreciations of reports sent to them. My competence does not extend farther. And perhaps I may be allowed to observe that this counsel, recommendation or advice has invariably been given on a purely voluntary basis and not in any way as part of my official duties.'

'So I have always understood,' said the Admiral.

'But, however,' Stephen went on after a pause, 'I was at one time intimate with the former Commander-in-Chief's adviser on intelligence, the late Mr Waterhouse, and we often discussed the theory and practice of obtaining information and of denying it to the enemy. He was a man of vast experience, and since the maxims of counter-espionage are rarely committed to paper, perhaps it might be acceptable if I were to summarize his remarks.'

'Pray do, by all means,' said Sir Francis. 'I know that Admiral Thornton thought the world of him.' But Stephen had not spoken five minutes before the Admiral sprang up again and hurried away. This time he did not return. After a long wait his Marine servant came in and spoke to Mr Yarrow, who sent for the flagship's surgeon and declared the meeting at an end.

'I believe we are both to dine at the Governor's,' said Wray to Stephen as they stood upon the *Caledonia*'s quarterdeck. 'May I give you a lift to the shore? But perhaps it would be too early: perhaps you had rather go back to your ship. Sir Hildebrand will not be sitting down for a great while yet.'

'Not at all. I should be very happy to go ashore. The monks of St Simon's sing sext and nones together today, and I long to hear them.'

'Do they, indeed? It would give me great pleasure to come with you, if I may. I have been so taken up with these squalid investigations that I have scarcely been able to go this last fortnight.'

'Squalid investigations,' he said again as they came blinking out of St Simon's into the powerful sun. 'I had meant to tell you about some of the suspicions that have occurred to me – some most surprising people – there is really no one to trust – munera navium saevos inlaqueant duces, you know

– but after that pure bath of music I have not the heart. Shall we step into our arbour, until it is time for dinner?'

'That would be delightful,' said Stephen; and very pleasant he found it, sitting there in the green shade, a small breeze taking the bite out of the fierce heat of the day, and they drinking iced coffee. It was not so much that Wray laid himself out to charm, but a man speaking with disinterested love on a subject he knew well – and Wray had a surprising knowledge of music, ancient and modern – could hardly fail to be an agreeable companion to one with the same tastes. Not all their tastes were the same, however: from behind his green spectacles Stephen watched Wray when the young man of the house, a beautiful youth with caressing ways, brought them their drinks, their cigars, their lights, and then unnecessary lights again, and it occurred to him that the Second Secretary was probably a paederast, or at least one who, like Horace, might burn for either sex. This aroused no virtuous indignation in Stephen; no indignation of any kind. He loved Horace, and, having the usual tolerant Mediterranean attitude, he had loved many another man with the same eclectic inclinations. Yet Wray was not entirely at his ease: as soon as they left music he showed a certain nervous restlessness, calling for more coffee, more cigars before the first were half finished – he was not in form.

'I believe I must abandon you,' said Stephen at last. 'I have to pass by the hotel to put some money in my pocket.'

'Perhaps we should both be moving,' said Wray. 'But as for money, I have plenty on me – five pounds at least.'

'You are very good,' said Stephen. 'But I meant an even greater sum. I am told that they play very high at the palace, and since my man of business states that Croesus is nothing to me, at least as far as this quarter is concerned, I mean to indulge my favourite vice for an hour or so.'

Wray looked at him, but could not make out whether he was speaking in earnest: Stephen Maturin had nothing of the look of a gambler, yet what he said was quite true – from time to time he loved to play, and that to the very uttermost limit of his resources. It was a great weakness, he knew; but he kept it severely in check; and since he had spent a long time in a Spanish prison in the same cell as a wealthy card-sharper (a man not condemned to the garotte for cheating, since he never was discovered, but for rape) it was at least unlikely that he should be grossly imposed upon.

They walked a little way in silence and then Wray said, 'You and Aubrey are at Carlotta's, are you not?'

'At Searle's, to be quite exact.'

'Then I will say farewell, since here I turn to the right, and you carry straight on.'

Their ways parted, but not for long. They were seated fairly near to one another at dinner, and as Stephen's right-hand neighbour, Mr Summerhays, had so weak a head that he drowned in his second glass of claret, while the German officer on his left had no English, French or Latin, he had plenty of time to look about him. Wray got along well with men at this kind of gathering; he was clever and amusing. He might lack weight and substance, and politics might suit his undoubted abilities better than government service, certainly better than intelligence, but there was no doubt that he could make himself agreeable to men as different as the very well-read financial secretary and the brutish provost-marshal.

When dinner was over most of the guests – they were all men, and they included most of the important soldiers and civilians of Valletta – moved into the card-room, and here Stephen, having seen his botanist on his way, joined them. Several grave gentlemen were already set to scientific whist, but most were gathered round the hazard table, where Sir Hildebrand himself held the bank. Stephen watched for a while, and although he had heard of the high stakes these people played for, he was surprised to see the quantity of money that was actually changing hands.

'Will you not call a main?' asked Wray behind him.

'I will not,' said Stephen. 'I promised my godfather never to touch dice again when he rescued me from a sad scrape in my youth, so now I am confined to cards.'

'What do you say to a hand of piquet?'

'With all my heart.'

Maturin, when playing cards, was not the most amiable of mortals. When he was playing seriously he played to win, as though he were conducting an operation against the enemy; and although he scrupulously observed the letter of the rules he always, and in the most civil way, seized upon any advantage that might present itself. He was playing seriously now, as well he might in view of the stakes they had agreed upon, and he had chosen a table near the window, sitting so that the light fell full upon Wray's face and not at all upon his own.

He was not surprised to find that Wray was obviously an inveterate card-player; the pack fairly flowed from his hands as he dealt and he shuffled like a conjuror. Nor was he surprised to find that in spite of all this practice Wray was quite ignorant of the disadvantage of his position, for indeed it was very little known, even among professional gamblers. Although Stephen was a medical man, keenly interested in physiology, he had had no idea of it himself until he was in the gaol of Teruel, when Jaime, his cell-mate, showed him the effect of emotion upon the pupil of the eye. 'It is as good as a mirror behind your opponent's back, showing his hand,' said Jaime; and he explained that the pupil would contract or expand quite involuntarily, quite uncontrollably, according to its owner's perception of the value of his cards and the likelihood of his bringing off a brilliant stroke or the reverse. The more emotional the player and the higher the stakes the greater the effect; but it worked in any circumstances, so long as there was something to win or lose. The only trouble was that you had to have excellent eyes to see the change; you had to have a good deal of practice to interpret it; and your opponent had to be well lit.

Stephen had excellent eyes, and he had had a great deal of practice, having used the method with remarkable effect in his interrogations; and Wray sat with a serene north light full on his face. Furthermore, although Wray had long since learnt to keep his face from showing anything but the urbane complaisance expected in good company, he *was* an emotional man (unusually so today, thought Stephen) and they *were* playing for high stakes. And since almost everything in this game depended on discarding and taking up, his changing fortunes could be read in rapid sequence. Yet even without this Stephen could not have failed to win; luck was with him from the first hand to the last, when he picked up the seven top hearts, discarded three little diamonds, the knave and ten of spades, and took in the three remaining aces, a king and the seven of spades, thus spoiling Wray's splendid point of seven and septième to the king by one pip, repiquing him, and, since Wray misjudged the last card, taking all the tricks and so capoting him into the bargain.

'There is no satisfaction in winning with such outrageous good fortune,' said Stephen.

'I believe I could bear it,' said Wray with a good imitation of a cheerful laugh, as he brought out his pocket-book. 'Perhaps you will give me my revenge some day when you are at leisure.'

Stephen said he should be happy, took leave of the Governor, and walked off, his bosom rustling with crisp new bank-notes. Laura Fielding was to come to him late that evening, and on the way back to the hotel he bought flowers, pastries, some fresh eggs, a cold roast loin of pork, a small spirit-stove, and a mandoline. These he arranged in the sitting-room he had taken for decency's sake, and then called for the hotel's bath to be prepared. Having soaked in hot water for a while, he changed his linen and beautified his person as far as its very meagre possibilities would allow, shaving his face (which he had not done either for the Admiral or the Governor), putting more powder on his wig, brushing his coat, looking in the glass from time to time in the vain hope that some prodigy might transform the reflection; for although he knew intellectually that his relationship with Mrs Fielding must remain perfectly chaste, much of his being longed for it to be otherwise and his breath came short at the idea of seeing her so soon.

Soon, however, was a relative term and it embraced enough space of time for him to rearrange the flowers twice, to drop the cold roast loin of pork, and to become convinced that there had been a misunderstanding about the day, the hour, the place. He was quite morose by the time a waiter knocked on the door and said that there was a lady to see him.

'Show her up,' said Stephen in a dissatisfied tone; but when she was there – when she had thrown back the hood of her tent-like faldetta and taken off her domino – he felt his resentment melt away like frost in the full sun. She was not unaware of its momentary presence, however, nor of the fact that she was disgracefully late, and she did her best to be particularly agreeable, exclaiming at the flowers, the mandoline, the noble array of little cakes. Alas, it was the unkindest thing she could have done; the stifled fires burnt up with a still fiercer flame. After a while he walked into his bedroom, quickly repeated three Aves, and came back with a paper that purported to be the discarded rough draft of a coded message, one that came to an abrupt half because of a fault in the ciphering. 'There,' he said, 'that will convince the man that you are making progress.'

She thanked him. 'Oh, how I hope it does,' she said with a worried face. 'Mother of God, I am so anxious.'

'I am sure it will,' he said in a voice that carried conviction.

She said, 'I rely on you entirely,' and after that neither spoke until some minutes had passed, when Stephen said, 'Should you like a boiled egg?'

'A boiled egg?' she cried.

'Just so. I thought we should have a small collation to see us through the coming hours; and it is common knowledge that lovers eat boiled eggs, to invigorate themselves. We must set the scene, you know.'

'I should love a boiled egg, in any case. I had no time for dinner.'

Laura Fielding was a young woman with a splendid constitution. In spite of her very real, very deep anxiety she ate two eggs; then, appetite coming with eating, she set about the loin of pork; and after a pause she ranged at large among the cakes, a glass of generous marsala in her hand – it was a pleasure to feed her.

And it was a pleasure to listen to her when she took the mandoline. She played it in the Sicilian manner, making it utter an almost continuous whining, nasal music that contrasted charmingly with her husky contralto as she sang a long, long ballad about the Paladin Orlando and his love for Angelica.

Although he had eaten an adequate dinner at the palace, Stephen had thought it was his duty as a host to share their collation, egg for egg, slice for slice; and what with the power of prayer and the effect of surfeit he found the extreme stimulus of desire fade to a perfectly bearable pitch, so that they passed the later hours of their meeting in a calm and amicable manner, though a little greasy, there being no forks. They talked away with scarcely a pause, comfortable, confidential talk, going from one subject to another and eventually reaching memories of childhood and youth; she told him that although she had been far from discreet when she was a girl (her father had a place under the Great Chamberlain, and discretion at the court of the Two Sicilies was absurd), ever since she was married she had been perfectly virtuous. It was therefore all the more wounding that Charles Fielding's solitary fault should be jealousy. He was kind, brave, generous, beautiful, everything the most exacting woman could wish, except that he was as possessive and suspicious as a Spaniard or a Moor. She described some of the unjustifiable scenes he had made, but then, feeling that she had been unfair, disloyal and even wicked, she returned to his merits at far greater length.

Stephen found his merits unutterably tedious, and at last in a pause when she sat looking down and smiling to herself, obviously thinking of merits of another kind, he said, 'Come, my dear, it is time for you to resume your disguise, or there will be nobody about to record your coming and going.'

She put on her mask and her vast hooded cloak, Stephen unlocked the door and they tiptoed along the creaking corridor and down two flights of creaking stairs to Jack's floor; but there the relative silence was broken by a howl of pain, a confused rumbling and thumping, and by cries of 'Avast

– belay, there.' Two slim figures shot across the landing and leapt straight out of an open window: and there was Killick with a candlestick roaring, 'All hands, all hands, all hands. Stop thief!'

He raced past them as doors opened on either side of the corridor, but in the lantern-lit hall they met him again. He had caught nobody, yet he was grinning with malignant triumph. 'There was two of the buggers,' he cried to the gathering assembly: then, catching sight of Stephen's companion, he plucked off his nightcap and said, 'Beg pardon, Miss: two individuals.'

'They went out of the first-floor window,' said Stephen.

'They didn't take it with them, though,' said Killick, and he explained to the company that the thieves had been after Captain Aubrey's chelengk, but that he, Preserved Killick, had been one too many for them, with his fish-hooks and double action rat-trap of extra power. One of the indiwiduals had left a finger in it and both on 'em a mort of blood: a joy to behold.

More people came scurrying from below and above. On seeing Stephen the sea-officers glanced quickly away: out of discretion they did not address him by so much as a nod, but even so Laura shrank farther back into her hood – it was one thing to be marked by French agents, quite another to be recognized by people she lived among, her own and her difficult husband's friends.

'Where is Captain Aubrey?' asked a voice.

'A-wisiting,' said Killick shortly, and he began his explanation again for the benefit of the newcomers. The thieves might have swiped some gold lace and a trifle of money in the till of the chest, which there wasn't much, the Captain having put most of it in his pocket, and maybe a little box or two, but the diamonds were safe. Killick began to vary his account, increasing the number of fingers left behind and the quantity of blood; he grew insufferably prolix; and Stephen, taking Mrs Fielding by the elbow, guided her through the throng and out into the old, waning night.

'You will not forget Saturday evening?' she said when he

left her at her inner door, with Ponto snuffling monstrously on the other side of it. 'And please bring Aubrey too, if he would like to come.'

'He asks nothing better, I am sure. And may I introduce another friend, the chaplain who made the voyage with us, Mr Martin?'

'I shall love any friend of yours,' she said giving him her hand; and so they parted.

'Good morning, my friend,' said Lesueur with his rare smile. 'I thought you would be in time today.'

'What have you to say?' asked Wray angrily.

'All's well,' said Lesueur, 'though the boys were very nearly caught, and one of them lost a finger. Our alarm was quite unnecessary: the box held nothing but private papers. Not the slightest indiscretion: not the slightest trace.'

'Thank God, thank God,' said Wray; but there was still anger mixed with his relief and he went on, 'You might have sent me word. You must have known how anxious I was. I could not rest – I could not concentrate. Apart from anything else it made me lose a large sum of money at cards. A simple note would have saved all this.'

'The less that is put into writing the better,' said Lesueur. 'Litera scripta manet. Look at this.'

'What is it?'

'The rough draft of a coded message. Do you not recognize it?'

'Admiralty B?'

'Yes. But the writer grew confused in the second transposition, threw the draft away – or rather put it between the leaves of a book – and began again. If he had gone on a little longer it would have been of great value: even so, it is useful. Do you know the hand?'

'It is Maturin's.'

From Lesueur's animated expression it looked as though he might develop the subject at some length, but he checked whatever he had been going to say and asked, 'How did he behave at the meeting?'

'He was very discreet – spoke of himself as an occasional and voluntary adviser, no more, and virtually told the Admiral that as such he had no orders to receive from any man. I believe he trusts no one in Malta. But in effect he gave his advice, fathering it on Waterhouse. You would have laughed to hear him speaking of restricted committees, precautions with ciphers, the detection of spies by planting false information and so on.'

'If this advice came from Waterhouse, even in part, it would have been sound. He was a most exemplary, intelligent agent, wholly professional: I was present at his last interrogation. There was not the least hope of getting any sort of hold upon him. As for Maturin, I do have a certain indirect hold for the time being, but I am afraid it cannot last, and the moment it is gone he must be eliminated. The Dey of Mascara will answer the purpose, as you suggested before.'

'Certainly,' said Wray. 'And I remember I said that the Dey might be used to kill two birds with one stone. Now I might go so far as to say three.'

'So much the better,' said Lesueur. 'But in the meanwhile surely you would be well advised not to frequent him so much.'

'Officially I shall probably only see him once more: I have no wish to see a disciple of Waterhouse's looking into my proceedings here, and I do not think he wishes to interfere in any way. And unofficially I shall in all likelihood spend no more than an afternoon with him, to have my revenge for a ridiculous run of bad luck. But you will allow me to say that I do not at all relish this spying, this supervision, this advice on the choice of my companions, or these airs of superiority.'

'Let us not disagree; it must necessarily lead to the destruction of us both,' said Lesueur. 'You shall see Maturin every day of the week if you choose: I only beg you to remember that he is dangerous.'

'Very well,' said Wray, and then rather awkwardly, 'Have you heard from the rue Villars?'

'About paying your card-debts?'

'If you like to put it that way.'

'I am afraid they will not go beyond the initial grant.'

As Wray had predicted, he and Maturin met again aboard the flagship, where it was agreed that Hairabedian was certainly a French agent and that for obvious reasons his friends or colleagues in Valletta had arranged for the stealing of his papers. At the same time the Admiral put forward the suggestion that perhaps Dr Maturin might be seconded to Mr Wray's department to help look for these friends or colleagues; but the suggestion was coldly received by both sides and he did not pursue it. Unofficially they met far more frequently; not indeed every day of the week, but, since luck still ran against him, pretty often. This was not because Stephen's sudden intense desire for gambling was unsatisfied, but rather because his cabin in the *Surprise* was filled with pots of paint, and his peace aboard destroyed by incessant hammering and vehement cries, while his natural companions were all taken up with wholehearted, purely naval activities, and once he had made his morning rounds at the hospital, he felt obliged to give Wray what part of the afternoon he did not spend in the hills or along the shore with Martin. His evening he usually passed with Mrs Fielding, and it was at her house that he most often saw Jack Aubrey.

The dockyard had indeed made a very fine job of the *Surprise*'s inwards; in their tortuous way they had fulfilled their side of the bargain. But the private agreement had not gone beyond certain clearly-defined structural repairs, and the shipwrights had left her more visible parts in a very horrid state: nor did Jack much care for her trim, the rake of her masts, or the look of her rigging. He felt very strongly that if the ship was to die to the Navy she should do so in style, in great style; besides, there was always the possibility that he might take her into action again before the end. All hands therefore turned to and tended her as she had rarely been tended before: they shifted her massive cables end for end, they roused out her lower tier of casks and restowed the hold to bring her a little by the stern, her favourite trim, they painted her inside and out and scraped her decks; Mr Borrell and his crew cosseted the guns and their furniture, the magazines and the shot; while Mr Hollar, his mates and all the young gentlemen sped about aloft like spiders. For once they were not in a tearing hurry, since the Captain of the Fleet had assured Jack that the *Surprise* would not be sent to sea until she had her Marines aboard once more and at least 'a reasonable proportion' of the hands that had been taken from her; yet even so her captain and first lieutenant, who had heard a good many official promises in their time, carried the work forward at a good round pace. In principle Jack disliked much in the way of shining ornament, but he felt that this was a special case, and for once in his life he laid out a considerable sum on gold-leaf for the gingerbread work of her stern and he called in the best inn-sign painter in Valletta to attend to her figurehead, an anonymous lady with a splendid bosom. All this was fine, satisfying, sea-manlike work – as he told the exhausted midshipmen, it gave them a deeper insight into the nature of a man-of-war than months or even years of simple sailing – and he was at last able to do many of the things that he had always intended to do; but it all had a cruelly bitter taste at times, and he was glad to follow his fiddle, carried by a Maltese super-numerary, to Laura Fielding's musical evenings, there to play or to listen to others playing, sometimes very well indeed.

By now he had grown quite used to the notion that Laura and Stephen were lovers; he did not mind it, though he admired them a little less, but he did think it more than usually unfair that Valletta should still suppose that he, Jack Aubrey, was the happy man. People would say 'If you hap-pen to pass by Mrs Fielding's, pray tell her that . . .' or 'Who will be coming on Tuesday evening?' as though their relationship were an established thing. Of course, a great deal was owing to that vile dog Ponto, who had welcomed him with a vast and noisy demonstration of love in the crowded Strada Reale within ten minutes of his setting foot on shore; but it also had to be admitted that Stephen and Laura were extraordinarily discreet. Nobody seeing Stephen at one of her evening parties would ever suppose that he spent the rest of the night there.

Wray certainly did not. Quite early in this period he made scarcely-veiled laughing allusion to 'your friend Aubrey's good fortunes that we hear so much about'. But as the days went by he was less and less inclined to laugh about anything at all. He had not come to the end of his run of bad luck and by now he had lost so much that Stephen could not in decency deny him his continually-repeated revenge, though at present the game bored him sadly. Although Wray had had a great deal of practice he was not a very good player; he could be deceived by a sudden change from stolid defence to risky attack; and his own attempts at deceit, which went little beyond slight hesitations and faint looks of disgust, were tolerably transparent. But above all he held no cards and Stephen had such good ones that the game grew duller still. Furthermore an anxious, unlucky Wray was by no means such an amusing companion as he had been before. As they became better acquainted Stephen found that Wray was more of a rake than he had supposed, that he attached an excessive importance to money, and that he was not over-burdened with principles; a clever man, to be sure, but one with little bottom. Wray did not attempt to correct fortune, however: some question of irregularity at cards had at one time attached to his name, and no man in Wray's position could afford a second accusation.

They usually played at the officers' club or in their green arbour, and it was in this arbour that they met for what had been agreed upon as their final session. For some time Wray had been waiting for a remittance, and being short of cash – Stephen had taken it all – he settled his losses with promissory notes. They played now for the entire debt, Stephen caring little for the issue, so long as he could get away in plenty of time to visit a cave full of bats with Martin and Pullings.

Wray lost again, and even more emphatically than before.

He spent some while over his score and his calculations, and with preparing what he had to say. Looking up with a particularly artificial smile he said that he was very much concerned to have to tell Dr Maturin that because of recent losses in the City his remittance had not come and he was unable to clear accounts with him; he regretted it extremely; but at least he could offer some kind of solution – he would give his note of hand for the whole sum now, and in the course of the next few days he would have a deed of annuity on his wife's estate drawn up, payments at the usual rate being sent to Maturin's banking-house every quarter until Mrs Wray inherited, when the principle would be cleared off without the slightest difficulty: everybody knew the Admiral had come into a noble fortune, entailed as to nine tenths.

'I see,' said Stephen. He was not pleased. They had been playing for ready money, and it was perfectly immoral in Wray to have embarked upon their last game when he could not put cash down if he lost. Stephen had not particularly wanted this sum of money once his gambling fever was over, but having risked his own in perfectly good faith, he had certainly earned it.

Wray was aware of his feelings. 'Is there anything I can do to sugar this pill? I have a certain amount of influence on patronage, as you know.'

'I think you will admit that the pill you propose calls for a world of sugar,' said Stephen. Wray admitted it entirely, and Stephen went on, 'I heard a very ugly rumour at the club this morning: it was said that the *Blackwater*, though long promised to Captain Aubrey, had been given to a Captain Irby. Is this true?'

'Yes,' said Wray, after a moment's hesitation. 'His parliamentary interest required it.'

'In that case,' said Stephen, 'I shall look to you to provide Aubrey with a similar vessel. You know his fighting-record, his just claims, and his desire for a heavy frigate on the North American station.'

'Certainly,' said Wray.

'Secondly I should like a sea-going command for Captain Pullings, and thirdly your general benevolence with regard to the Reverend Mr Martin, and a helping hand if ever he should require a transfer from one ship to another.'

'Very well,' said Wray, noting down the names. 'I shall do what I can. As you know, sloops are in very short supply – there are twice as many commanders as there are ships for them to command – but I shall do what I can. As for the chaplain, there will be no difficulty: he may go wherever he wishes.' He put his notebook back in his pocket and called for more coffee. When it came he said, 'I am very much obliged to you for your forbearance, Maturin, indeed I am. I do not think you will be kept waiting very long, however. My father-in-law is sixty-seven and he is far from well.' Admiral Harte had a dropsical tendency, it appeared, and although the actuaries' table of expectation of life gave him nearly eight years he was unlikely to last half that time. In his agitation Wray spoke with such a want of common hypocrisy that Stephen scarcely knew how to reply. He observed that some physicians were treating dropsy with a new preparation of digitalis, but that for his own part he should be very cautious in exhibiting so potentially danger-ous a drug. The conversation continued on these lines for some little while, and Stephen had the impression that any dose that might diminish the Admiral's expectation of life still further would be heartily welcome; but before Wray could commit himself on that point Pullings and Martin came to take Stephen to the cave.

'That cave, my dear,' he said to Laura as they settled down to a midnight feast in his room, 'that cave is one of the wonders of the universe. I absolutely saw every species of Mediterranean bat, and two that I suspect of being Afri-can; but they were somewhat shy, and retired to a crevice beyond the reach of Pullings' rope. A monstrous fine cave indeed! In the more favoured places there was two foot of their dung upon the floor, with a large number of bones and mummified specimens. I shall carry you there on Friday.'

'Not on Friday you will not,' said Laura, spreading his bread with red mullet roe.

'Do not tell me you are superstitious, for shame!'

'I am, though. I should not spit in a wolf's eye for the world. But it is not that. On Friday you will be far away. Oh, how I shall miss you!'

'Are you prepared to reveal the source of your information?'

'Mrs Colonel Rhodes told me that a party of Marines were going aboard the *Surprise* on Thursday to sail the next day, and her brother, who commands them, is much put out, because he had an engagement on Saturday. And the port-captain's daughter said it was decided that the *Surprise* was to take the Adriatic convoy.'

'Thank you, my dear,' said Stephen. 'I am happy to know it.' And after some reflection he said, 'It would seem natural that our farewell embraces should produce something unusually substantial for your foreign gentleman.' He went into his bedroom, chose carefully among the poisoned gifts he had prepared with such loving pains, and picked out a small dirty-white sheepskin pocketbook with a clasp. 'There, my friend,' he said to himself, 'with the blessing that should confound your knavish tricks for quite a while.'

Chapter Nine

The surgeon's cabin in HMS *Surprise* would have been a dark, cramped triangle, like a slice of cake, if its sharp end had not been cut off, which made it into a dark, cramped quadrilateral. It was so low that a moderately tall man would have struck his head on the deck above if he had stood upright, and it did not possess a single right-angle in its entire construction; but Dr Maturin was rather short, and although he was reasonably fond of right-angles he was fonder still of a place that did not have to be stripped bare every time the ship cleared for action, as the *Surprise* did every evening, a place where his books and specimens could remain undisturbed. As for the want of room, long use and his friend the carpenter's ingenuity in the matter of folding cot and table and of lockers built in unlikely places dealt with that to some degree; and as for the darkness, Stephen had devoted a very small fraction of his preposterous winnings – the winnings he had actually received, in elegant Bank of England notes – to the lining of all free surfaces with sheets of best Venetian looking-glass, which increased the light that filtered down to such an extent that it allowed him to read and write without a candle. He was writing now, and to his wife, his feet wedged against one stanchion and the back of his chair against another, for the frigate was behaving in a very skittish manner as she beat up against a short head-sea: the letter had begun the day before, when the *Surprise*, steering for Santa Maura, where two ships of her convoy were to be left, had been forced away by stress of weather, forced away almost to Ithaca. 'To Ithaca itself, upon my word of honour. But would any amount of pleading on my part or on the part of all the literate members of the ship's company induce that animal to *bear away* for the sacred spot? It would not. Certainly he had heard of Homer, and had indeed looked into Mr Pope's version of his tale; but for aught he could make out, the fellow was no seaman. Admittedly Ulysses had no chronometer, and probably no sextant neither; but with no more than log, lead and lookout an officer-like commander would have found his way home from Troy a d—d sight quicker than that. Hanging about in port and philandering, that was what it amounted to, the vice of navies from the time of Noah to that of Nelson. And as for that tale of all his foremast hands being turned into swine, so that he could not win his anchor or make sail, why, he might tell that to the Marines. Besides, he behaved like a very mere scrub to Queen Dido – though on second thought perhaps that was the other cove, the pious Anchises. But it was all one: they were six of one and half a dozen of the other, neither seamen nor gentlemen, and both of 'em God d—d bores into the bargain. For his part he far preferred what Mowett and Rowan wrote; that was poetry a man could get his teeth into, and it was sound seamanship too; in any case he was here to conduct his convoy into Santa Maura, not to gape at curiosities.'

Then, feeling that he was exposing his friend rather too much (for the animal in question was of course the captain of the *Surprise*) he laid the sheet aside and wrote: 'Jack Aubrey has faults and to spare, the Dear knows: he thinks a sailor's highest aim is to carry his ship from A to B in the shortest possible time, losing not a minute, so that life is a kind of perpetually harassing race, and only yesterday he was doggedly, mechanically stubborn in his refusal to turn a little way aside so that we might view Ithaca. Yet on the other hand (and this is my real point) he is capable of a most surprising degree of magnanimity and self-command when the occasion calls for it: a much higher degree than you might suppose from his impatience over trifles. Of this I had an instance the day after we left Valletta. Among other passengers we are carrying a Major Pollock, and at dinner this gentleman happened to observe that his brother, a lieutenant in the Navy, was amazingly proud of his new ship the *Blackwater*, and that he made no doubt but she should prove a match for any of the heavy Americans. "Are you sure he said the *Blackwater*, sir?" asked Jack, surprised, as well he might be, since as you know he has been promised the vessel ever since its keel was laid down and has wholly relied upon taking it to the North American station as soon as this short spell in the Mediterranean was over. "Quite sure, sir," replies the soldier. "I had a letter from him with the last mail that came in, the very morning I came aboard. It was dated from the *Blackwater* in the Cove of Cork, and he said he hoped to be in Nova Scotia before it reached me, since there was a fine northeaster blowing and Captain Irby was a great one for cracking on." "Then let us drink to his health," says Jack. "The *Blackwater* and all who sail in her." In the evening, when we were alone in the great cabin and I made some allusion to the broken promise, all he said was, "Yes. It is a d—d heavy blow; but whining don't help. Let us get on with our music."'

It was indeed a very heavy blow, and when Jack woke in the morning and the recollection came flooding into his mind, the brilliant day darkened. He had counted upon the *Blackwater* with absolute certainty; he had counted upon continuing employment at sea, a matter of the first importance to him now that his affairs on shore were in such a lamentable state; and not only that, he had relied upon being able to take his officers and his followers with him, and with any luck almost the whole of the *Surprise*'s crew. Now all this was at an end. The whole efficient, smoothly-working organization – all the makings of a happy ship and a deadly fighting-machine – must be dispersed: and in all likelihood he must be thrown on the beach. Furthermore, since Mr Croker, the First Secretary, had used him badly, even dishonourably, he would almost certainly look upon the name of Aubrey with disfavour in the future.

A very heavy blow indeed, but few would have guessed it, watching him tell Major Pollock how the *Surprise* and her allies had turned the French out of Marga when last she was in these waters. The frigate, with the remaining convoy under her lee – a well-behaved convoy, keeping exactly to station in these dangerous waters – had stood well in to the southern side of Cape Stavro, a great headland that jutted far out into the Ionian Sea, and now they were abreast of the walled town nestling at the foot of its tall cliffs and straggling some way up them in rock-hewn terraces. 'There is the citadel, do you see,' he said, pointing over the pale green, white-flecked sea, 'to the right of the green-domed church and above it. And down by the mole there are the two tiers of batteries that guard the entrance to the harbour.'

The soldier gave Marga a long, knowing look through the telescope. 'I should have thought it was perfectly impregnable from the sea,' he said at last. 'Those flanking batteries alone would surely sink a fleet.'

'That was my impression,' said Jack. 'So we set about it another way. If you follow the line of the wall behind the citadel you will see a square tower, about a quarter of the way up the cliff.'

'I have it.'

'And behind that a round masonry affair, like a prodigious great field-drain.'

'Yes.'

'That is their aqueduct – they have no water of their own – and it comes from springs above Kutali, some two or three miles away on the other side of the cape. On the brow of the cliff you can just make out something of the road or rather path that covers the water-channel before it plunges down the pipe. That is where we placed our guns.'

'Is the other side of the cape as steep-to as this?'

'More so, if anything.'

'Then it must have been a most enormous undertaking, getting a gun up there. You made a road, I presume?'

'No, a ropeway. We winched them up by two stages to the path of the aqueduct, and once they were there we could trundle them along without too much difficulty, particularly as we had six hundred Albanians and a great number of Turks to tally on to the tow-ropes. When we had a reasonable battery up there we fired a few sighting shots into the harbour and sent down to tell the French commanding officer that if he did not surrender directly we should be under the painful necessity of destroying the town.'

'Did you offer them any terms?'

'No. And I particularly desired that no counter-proposals or conditions should be put forward, our superiority being so great that they could not possibly be entertained.'

'To be sure, a plunging fire from such a height would have been perfectly murderous; and he could have made no reply.'

'He could not scale the cliffs to come at us, either. There is only one shepherds' path, like the one in Gibraltar that leads up from Catalan Bay, and my Turkish ally, Sciahan Bey, had sharpshooters covering every turn of it. But even so I was surprised when the surrender came back straight away.'

'I wonder he did not make at least some show of resistance, or wait until a few houses had been knocked down. It is the usual thing, after all.'

'It would perhaps have been a little more decent, and it would certainly have looked better at his court-martial; but then we learnt that his wife was having a baby and the doctors were very anxious for her – gunfire and falling houses not at all the thing – so he preferred not to make a mere noisy demonstration that must come to the same thing in the end.'

'No doubt it was quite a reasonable decision,' said Major Pollock, in a dissatisfied tone.

'Lord,' said Jack Aubrey, casting his mind back, 'I have never seen anyone so disappointed as my Albanians. They had sweated like galley-slaves getting the guns up, for when we had hoisted them to the top of the ropeway they still had to travel along the covering of the aqueduct, and that called for hundreds of four-inch planks from the shipyards perpetually shifted to spread the weight, as well as strong teams for pulling; they had carried round-shot like heroes, and any amount of powder, and they had covered themselves with weapons of one kind or another, and now they were going to have to take everything back again, without a single shot fired in anger. They very nearly set about the Turks, so as not to be done out of a fight altogether, and my Pope – they have any number of popes in these parts, you know – and the Bey had to lay about them, roaring like bulls in a basin. However, it all ended happy. We packed the Frenchmen off to Zante, bag and baggage, and then the Margiotes gave us a feast that lasted from noon till dawn the next day, Christians in one piazza, Mussulmans in the next, with plenty of kind words passing between, and songs and dances whenever we could eat no more for the time being.' He remembered the arcade between the piazzas, the swaying line of tall Albanians in white kilts, their arms linked at shoulder-height and their feet moving in perfect rhythm, the flare of torches in the warm night, the strong singing and its insistent beat, the taste of resiny wine.

'Do you mean to put in there now, sir?' asked Major Pollock.

'Oh no,' said Jack. 'We are bound for Kutali, on the far side of the cape. And if only that infernal slug' – glancing at the *Tortoise* store-ship, the heaviest sailer in the convoy – 'don't miss stays again, we shall round the point on this tack, and so run in before nightfall; and then you will be able to see the other end of the story. Mr Mowett, I believe we may throw out the signal, and prepare to go about ourselves; but give the poor *Tortoise* plenty of time. We may be old and fat ourselves one day.'

The *Tortoise*, given ample warning, came round nobly, cheered by one and all, and the convoy steered steadily for the far point of Cape Stavros, weathering it with half a mile to spare at about the time that Captain Aubrey was finishing his solitary dinner. Until his finances grew so very uncertain Jack had kept a table in the traditional way, nearly always inviting two or three officers and a midshipman; and even now he still entertained a good deal – apart from anything else he felt that it was part of his duty to make sure that in the squalor of the midshipmen's berth his young gentlemen did not forget how to eat like human beings – but he did so more often at breakfast, which called for less preparation on all hands. Yet since learning of their ship's fate he had felt a reluctance to ask anyone: they were so cheerful, all except the melancholy Gill, and he felt so false, concealing the knowledge that would make their days almost as dark as his own.

He was eating his dinner not in the dining-cabin but right aft, sitting with his face to the great stern-window, so that on the far side of the glass and a biscuit-toss below the frigate's wake streamed away and away from him, dead white in the troubled green, so white that the gulls, poising and swooping over it, looked quite dingy. This was a sight that never failed to move him: the noble curve of shining panes, wholly unlike any landborne window, and then the sea in some one of its infinity of aspects; and the whole in silence, entirely to himself. If he spent the rest of his life on half-pay in a debtors' prison he would still have had this, he reflected, eating the last of the Cephalonian cheese; and it was something over and above any reward he could possibly have contracted for.

In the lowest starboard pane appeared the tip of Cape Stavros, a grey limestone cliff seven hundred feet high with the remains of an archaic temple on it, one column standing yet. Slowly the cape invaded pane after pane, rising and falling with the swell: a file of Dalmatian pelicans flew across, vanishing to larboard: and just at the moment Jack would have raised his voice he heard Rowan's cry 'Hands about ship,' and immediately afterwards the sharp cutting notes and prolonged howl of the bosun's call. But this was followed by no rush of feet, indeed by no sound at all, since the Surprises had been expecting the manoeuvre these last five minutes. They had put their barky about thousands of times, often in pitch darkness with an ugly sea running, and it was hardly to be expected that they should now rush flat-footed up and down like a parcel of grass-combing landsmen. Indeed, the subsequent orders were little more than a matter of form: 'Off tack and sheets,' called Rowan, and Jack felt the beginning of the swing; then 'Mainsail haul.' The pelicans and the cape moved steadily back across the window: the *Surprise* was head to wind, and they were certainly getting the main-tack down and the sheet hauled in. 'Let go and haul,' cried Rowan in a perfunctory voice, and the impetus of the turn increased, the Chian wine in Jack's glass took on a centrifugal lean, quite independent of the lift of the sea, until the ship steadied on her new course, and Rowan's voice could be heard again crying, 'Davis, do for God's sake leave the damned thing alone,' since every time the *Surprise* came about and braced her yards sharp up, Davis would give her foretopsail bowline an extra swig-off for what he considered smartness; and being a horribly powerful man with poor coordination he would sometimes pluck the bridle bodily out of the cringles.

'Killick,' called Jack, 'is there any more of the Santa Maura cake left?'

'No, there ain't,' said Killick from within. His mouth was obviously full, but this did not disguise his ill-natured triumph. When the Captain ate in the great cabin, his steward had to carry the dishes several yards farther in either direction, which angered him. 'Sir,' he added, swallowing.

'Well, never mind,' said Jack. 'Bring the coffee.' Then after some minutes, 'Bear a bob, man.'

'Which I'm coming, ain't I?' cried Killick, bringing in the tray, bent as though he were labouring over a very great distance, a limitless desert.

'Is the hubble-bubble ready, in case the Turkish officers come aboard?' asked Jack, pouring himself a cup.

'Ready, aye ready, sir,' said Killick, who had been smoking it, off and on, most of the morning with Lewis, the Captain's cook. 'But I thought it my duty to run it in, like, and the tobacco is rather low. Shall I take some more?'

Jack nodded. 'And what about the cushions?'

'Never you fret, sir. I stripped the gunroom's cots, and Sails is at work on 'em. Cushions is ready, and so is the conversation peppermints.' These were to be had in Malta; they were extraordinarily popular in the eastern Mediterranean, and many an awkward pause had they filled in Greek, Balkan, Turkish and Levantine ports.

'That is a comfort. Well, now in five minutes' time I should like to see Mr Honey and Mr Maitland.'

These were the senior members of his meagre midshipmen's berth; they had been rated master's mates for some considerable time now and they were quite capable of taking a watch – pleasant, seamanlike young fellows, neither of them a phoenix but both good average officers in the making. But the making, that was the trouble. To be made a young man had first to pass for lieutenant, and then somebody or something had to induce the Admiralty to give him a lieutenant's commission and appoint him to a ship, for without that he might remain a passed midshipman for the rest of his naval life. Jack had known many a 'young gentleman' of forty and more. He was unlikely to be able to do much about the second stage, but nothing whatsoever could be done until they passed the first, and he could at least help them through that.

'Come in,' he said, swinging round. 'Come in and sit down.'

Neither was aware of any really heinous crime, but neither meant to tempt fate by rash confidence, and they sat meekly, with cautious, respectful expressions. 'I have been looking at the muster,' went on Jack, 'and I find that both of you are pretty well out of your servitude.'

'Yes, sir,' said Maitland. 'I have served my full six years, all of it genuine sea-time, sir; and Honey only lacks two weeks.'

'Just so,' said Jack. 'And it seems to me that you might be well advised to try to pass for lieutenant as soon as we get back to Malta. Two of the sitting captains will be friends of mine, and although I do not mean that they will show you any improper favour, at least they will not savage you, which is a great thing if you are anxious: and most people are anxious when they are examined. I know I was. If you wait until you are in London you will find it a far more awe-inspiring affair. In my day it was the only place: you had to go to the Navy Office to pass, even if it meant waiting for years and years, until you could get back from Sumatra or the Coromandel coast.' Once again he saw the stony magnificence of Somerset House on that first Wednesday in the month, the vast round hall with thirty or forty long-legged gawky youths clutching their certificates, each with a troupe of relatives, sometimes very imposing and nearly always hostile towards the other candidates: the porter calling their names two by two: the climbing of the stairs, one being admitted while the other waited by the white circular railing, straining his ears to hear the questions: the tears on the face of the boy who came out as he went in. 'Whereas here, do you see, it is more of a family affair.'

'Yes, sir,' they said.

'I am not afraid of their failing you in seamanship,' he went on. 'No. It is navigation that may lay you both by the lee. Now these,' he said, picking up the young gentlemen's workings, the papers that both oldsters and youngsters were required to hand to the Marine sentry at the cabin door every day as soon as they had fixed the ship's noon position, 'these are all very well, and it so happens that they are reasonably accurate. But they are worked out by rule of thumb, and I am afraid that if you were asked any fine points of theory – and examining captains are doing so more and more nowadays – you would be all to seek. Honey, suppose you know the ship's leeway and her rate of sailing by the log, how do you find the angle of correction to lay off the course she has made good?'

Honey looked aghast, and said he believed he could find it out, sir, if he were allowed paper and time. Maitland thought he might do the same: the rule was in Norie.

'I dare say you could,' said Jack. 'But the whole point is that if you come up against a Tartar you are not allowed to look into Norie, nor are you given time or paper. You have to sing out straight away that as the ship's rate is to the sine of the angle of leeway, so the leeway is to the sine of the angle of correction. Now I do not suppose that we shall have a great deal to do this run, so if you like to come here in the afternoons we will try to polish your navigation in its finer points.'

When they had gone he noted down some particularly knotty points to do with oblique and right ascension – points that had arisen when he was talking to Sextant Dudley, a scientific captain who despised mere seamen and who might easily appear on the examining board together with Jack's closer friends – and then he went on deck. The *Surprise* was already half way down Kutali bay, wafting along to the windward of her convoy like a superlatively elegant swan with a band of common and in some cases rather dirty goslings. All her passengers were gazing at the scene, and although he knew it so well Jack caught some of his first astonishment in their admiration: the vast sweep of the bay, filled with small craft and trabaccoloes, the prodigious shore-line of mountains plunging straight into deep water, the close-packed fortified town rising from the harbour at an angle of forty-five degrees and shining in the sun – pink roofs, white walls, light grey ramparts, green copper domes – and beyond it higher mountains still, their sides sometimes bare, sometimes dark with forest, and their peaks tangled in the thin vaporous white clouds.

'Now, sir,' he said to Major Pollock, 'now you can see where we began. At the corner of the mole over there we set up an extraordinarily massive double holdfast and ran a line straight up over the lower ramparts, over the middle town, and so to the citadel itself. We bowsed it as taut as a fiddle-string, and with props clapped on just before and just after the passage of the most delicate places, the guns ran up as sweetly as kiss your hand. That was the first stage. The second I cannot show you very clearly from here because of the dead ground behind the castle crag, but there where it rises again, on the swelling green below those light-coloured bluffs, do you see, you can make out the line of the buried aqueduct, following the contour. Though now I come to think about it, perhaps first of all I should give you some notion of the political side. It was tolerably complex.'

'I beg your pardon, sir,' said Mowett, 'but I believe the Bey has put off.'

'Damme, so soon?' said Jack, taking his telescope. 'You are quite right, though: and there is that dear Pope with him. Begin the salute. These were my allies in this affair,' he said to Pollock as the gunner came hurrying aft with his salamander, 'and I believe I shall have to break off for a while, particularly as I see half a dozen other boats getting ready to follow them.'

The *Surprise*'s salute had not finished before the Turks began blazing away from a battery a little to the south of the lower town; they had done very well out of the French artillery in Marga, both in guns and ammunition, and in their cheerful Turkish way they sent the occasional round-shot skipping across the water among the fishing-boats. Within minutes the Christians in the citadel, who had done rather better, joined in with their twelve-pounders. Heavy smoke drifted across Kutali from below and from above: the mountains sent the echoes to and fro across the bay; and in the intervals the sharper crack of muskets, pistols and fowling-pieces could be heard. The *Surprise* was a most uncommonly popular ship among the Kutaliotes, she having preserved them from two rapacious tyrannical beys and having provided them with the means of preserving what in fact amounted to their independence. She had not done so out of disinterested benevolence: it arose from her campaign against the French: but the result was much the same and so was the good will.

The virtual rulers of the little state came beaming up the side to the full ceremonial welcome of bosun's calls, Marines presenting arms, bareheaded officers in their best coats, the ruffle of the drum; and Sciahan Bey, a short, broad-shouldered, scarred and grizzled Turkish warrior, skipped over to Jack with his arms spread wide and kissed him on both cheeks, immediately followed by Father Andros, which so pleased the Surprises that they uttered a discreet but universal cheer.

'Where is the Pullings?' asked Father Andros in Italian, looking about.

For a moment Jack could not recall the Italian for being made a commander so he made a dart at the Greek. 'Promotides,' he said, pointing upwards. But seeing that they looked shocked and grieved and that the priest crossed himself in the Orthodox manner, he tapped his epaulettes, crying, 'No, no. Him capitano – pas morto – elevato in grado,' and raising his voice, 'Dr Maturin. Pass the word for the Doctor.'

In the pause the priest called down into the boat for a petrified little girl who stood in the bows, not daring to sit, starched, frizzled and powdered almost out of humanity, carrying a bunch of roses as large as herself. It was something of a task getting her aboard, since she passionately resisted any motion at parting her from the flowers or any that might ruffle her stiff crimson dress; but it was accomplished at last and with her eyes fixed on Father Andros she went through her address to Jack, reluctantly yielding her bouquet at the end. While this was going on the *Surprise* had come to an anchor, and the clewing up of the maintopsail revealed Dr Maturin at the crosstrees, an extraordinarily elevated post for him. Much of the afternoon he had spent sitting in the broad, comfortable platform of the maintop in the hope of seeing a spotted eagle, one of the great prizes of this coast, and his patience had been rewarded with no less than two, playing together and flying so low that he could almost look into their eyes; but the topsail kept shutting out his view, and with the combined energy of frustration and delight he swarmed slowly up to this bold eminence, his gaze constantly turned towards the sky. There in the crosstrees he had indeed had a glorious sight of the birds; but they had vanished long ago, circling up and up into the sky until at last they were lost among the wispy clouds; and since then he had been horribly puzzled to get down again. The more he contemplated the void below the more impossible it seemed that he should ever have reached these vile crosstrees and the more convulsively he grasped the heel of the topgallantmast and any rope that offered. He was aware that if he instantly and with a firm manly resolution let himself dangle, perhaps with eyes closed, then his questing feet would most probably find a hold; but this awareness did him little practical good – it led to no decisive action, only to endless reflections about the imbecility of human will and the true nature of vertigo.

Jack, following his lieutenant's significant look at the close of the ceremony with the flowers, seized the position at once. He kissed the little girl, passed the bouquet to his coxswain, and said, 'Bonden, lay aloft: make these fast to the maintruck, and on your way down show the Doctor the most convenient way of reaching the deck. My compliments, and should be glad to see him in the cabin.'

By the time Stephen reached the deck it was covered with smiling, gift-bearing Kutaliotes of one kind and another – Catholic, Orthodox, Muslim, Jew, Armenian, Copt – and more were coming in little boats. And by the time he reached the cabin it was deep in the fragrant smoke of Cephalonian tobacco; the hookah was bubbling away in the middle, and Captain Aubrey, Father Andros and Sciahan Bey were sitting about it on cushions, or to be more exact on all the *Surprise*'s pillows hastily covered with signal flags, drinking coffee out of Wedgwood cups. They welcomed him cordially, even affectionately, and gave him an amber mouthpiece to smoke with. 'We have fallen wonderfully lucky,' said Jack. 'If I do not mistake, the Bey's people have found a monstrous fine bear, and we are going to hunt him tomorrow.'

'He was a monstrous fine bear indeed, my dear,' wrote Captain Aubrey in a letter dated *Surprise*, off Trieste, 'and if only we had been a little braver, you should have had his skin. He stood at bay, with his back to a rock, rearing up seven or eight feet tall – eyes flashing, red mouth foaming, hair on end – looking very like Admiral Duncan, and we could have shot him through and through. But no, no, cried Stephen – a bear is a gentleman, and must be dispatched with a spear. Very true, we said, and begged him to show us how. Not at all, said he: he was concerned only with seeing that the bear was not abused: the honour of killing him obviously belonged to a man of war, not to one of peace. This we could scarcely deny, but the question was, which man of war? I thought the Bey should certainly have the precedence, being of higher rank; he said that was great nonsense – common good manners required him to give way to a stranger. While we were arguing the toss the bear dropped down on all fours and walked quietly into a little bushy dell beside the rock, a most devilishly awkward place to tackle him in. Finally some meddling fellow suggested that both Sciahan and I should set about him together. We could not very well refuse, but I assure you we took our time about creeping in among those infernal bushes, crouching and grasping our spears and glaring into the deep shadows and expecting the brute to charge any second – he was as massive as a cart-horse, though lower on his pins. The only dogs left alive by this time were the cautious ones that kept well behind us, and we had them taken up, in case their silly din prevented us from hearing the bear. And so we minced along, listening with all our ears; and I have never been so frightened in all my life. Then there was Stephen screeching out 'Gone away' and hallooing and waving his hat, and there was the bear a quarter of a mile off, going straight up the mountainside like a vast great hare. There we were obliged to leave him, I am afraid, since I had to get back to the ship; but Lord, sweetheart, how that day with even a very indifferent pack of hounds did lift my heart! So did a trifle of action the next night, when we were becalmed off Corfu, and the very enterprising Frenchman in command of the island, a General Donzelot, sent out a number of boats, trying to snap up one or two of the convoy. They did not succeed, and no one was seriously hurt, but we had a lively night of it, and in her agitation one of the merchantmen fell foul of us when a breeze got up, carrying away our jibboom; so we are quite glad to have reached the comparative peace of these waters, where there are plenty of our friends to protect us: three frigates and at least four sloops or brigs. We have only just arrived and I have not seen them all yet: Hervey, the senior naval officer, is looking into Venice until tomorrow. But Babbington is here in the *Dryad*, and he sent to ask me to dinner even before we had dropped our anchor. So is young Hoste. He has done wonders – a very active officer – and I wish I could like him better, yet there is something of Sidney Smith about him, something a trifle self-congratulatory and theatrical; and then he does burn a shocking number of small prizes, which does him no good and the French no harm, but which does ruin the poor unfortunate men that own and sail them. This is strictly between ourselves, my dear, not to be repeated to anyone. Henry Cotton is here too, in the *Nymphe*. He was on shore when we arrived, but his surgeon came over – you remember him, I am sure, Mr Thomas, the talkative gentleman that called on Stephen when he was staying with us – to beg that Dr Maturin would lend a hand in some particularly delicate operation; and he told me that there is now an overland post by way of Vienna that is fairly sure to get through, at least for the moment. The position in these parts is very confused: the local French commanders are able, energetic, resourceful men and sometimes I feel that our allies – but perhaps I had better leave that subject alone. Indeed, sweetheart, I must leave my letter alone too, for I have just heard Harry Cotton's barge come alongside, his hoarse old coxswain wheezing out "*Nymphe, Nymphe*", like an asthmatic grampus.'

Aboard the *Nymphe* herself, Dr Maturin leant over his patient's yellow, glistening, horror-filled face and said, 'There: it is all over now. With the blessing you will do very well.' And to the man's messmates, almost as wan and horrified as their friend, 'You may untie him now; you may *cast him off.*'

'Thankee, sir,' said the patient in a whisper, as Stephen took the piece of padded leather from between his back teeth, 'thankee very kindly for your pains.'

'I have read your description of the operation, of course,' said the surgeon of the *Cerberus*, 'but I had not expected such dispatch. It might have been an act of presti – presti – legerdemain.'

'I admire your courage, sir,' said the surgeon of the *Redwing*.

'Come, gentlemen,' said Mr Thomas, 'I think we have all earned a little refreshment.'

They all walked off into the empty gunroom, where Mr Thomas treated them to a bottle of Tokay. 'My next case,' he said, after they had gossiped for a while about Malta and the Toulon blockade, 'is a perfectly common-place wandering ball, a pistol ball received some years ago and now causing a certain amount of pain as the result of recent physical exertion. It is lodged just at the external edge of the levator anguli scapulae, and it presents no particular interest to the philosophical surgeon, but for the fact that it is lodged in a most romantic frame.'

'Indeed?' said Stephen, seeing that some remark was called for and that neither of the others felt inclined to make it.

'Yes, sir,' said Thomas with great satisfaction. 'Perhaps you will allow me to begin at the beginning?' This seemed a reasonable request, but his friends, who knew Mr Thomas, who had heard it all before, and who had seen Dr Maturin perform his suprapubic cystotomy, drank up their Tokay and took their leave; and even Maturin gave only the faintest smirk of assent.

'Well, now, some time ago we were off Pola, steering south-west with a light breeze at north or thereabouts, very early in the morning or perhaps I should say late at night – before the idlers had been called, in any case; and in passing I may observe that it is tolerably whimsical to speak of them as idlers, more whimsical if anything than calling the master, purser and surgeon noncombatants. I am sure that when I was surgeon's mate in the old *Andromeda*, or assistant-surgeon as we say nowadays, and indeed it is far more proper, *mate* having a certain colloquial, familiar connotation by no means suitable for a member of a learned profession – I am sure I went away in cutting-out expeditions or in sweeps along the coast in the yawl – twice I had command of the yawl! – or in the barge more often than the great majority of line-of-battleship mids. But as I was saying or at all events intended to say, this hour between night and day is the very best time, so long as there is no great wind, for believe me, anything more than a topgallantsail breeze will infallibly put them down, the very best time for catching those fish they call scombri in these parts which I take to be close kin to our mackerel, though they eat far more delicate; and there I was with my wand over the taffrail, fishing along the side of the wake with a piece of bacon-rind cut in the shape of a sand-eel – some say they can be caught in greater numbers with red flannel, but I swear by my bacon-rind. Mark you,' he said, raising one finger, 'it must be well soaked. But once it has spent four and twenty hours in the steep-tub, once it is really pliable, there is nothing to touch your lithe white unctuous rind for enticing the big fellows. So there I was with the lieutenant of Marines beside me, in full expectation of catching the gunroom's breakfast – simple broiling on a piping hot well-oiled gridiron is best, I assure you: elaborate sauces and Persian apparatus take away their true flavour – but, however, before I had had so much as a single bite Norton cried out "Hold" or perhaps "Hush" – something to that effect. Norton, I should have said, was the Marine: William Norton, of a Westmorland family, related to the Collingwoods. "Listen," he says, "Ain't that musketry?"'

Musketry it was, and after an exact account of what the officer of the watch said – his initial scepticism and growing conviction – and how the *Nymphe* was put about, Mr Thomas very slowly brought the sun up over the eastern horizon to reveal a houario that had evidently just captured the small skiff it was now taking in tow. The frigate at once gave chase, and with all the more zeal because the increasing light showed French uniforms aboard the houario. But pretty soon it appeared that the chase, which could sail closer to the wind than the square-rigged *Nymphe*, would weather Cape Promontore whereas the frigate would not – in short, that the houario would escape. Here Mr Thomas branched off on to considerations to do with sailing – the fore-and-aft rig as opposed to the square – various combinations that might with advantage be tried – the true force of windmills, how measured by a friend of his – and Stephen's attention wandered until he heard the words 'But to cut a long story short, down came her foresail when she was within a cable's length of the point – she flew up into the wind directly, of course – and there was a fellow bounding about the deck like a Jack-in-a-box, knocking people down right and left. The very last moments I did not see, because the captain called out to me, with that unnecessary, illiberal vehemence so many sailors affect, desiring me to take my tackle out of the way – parenthetically I may say that I gave him such a dose, such a comfortable dose, the next day, when he was to take physic: I did not *scruple* to add two scruples of col-ocynth to his black draught, ha, ha, ha! Colocynth for ever, and the strong watery gripes. Are you not amused, my dear sir?'

'Very much amused, colleague.'

'But I was on deck again by the time we were lying to and our boat was coming back from the captured houario, and there he was, laughing all over his face and waving to his friends as they stood there lining the rail and cheering.'

'To whom do you refer, colleague?'

'Why, to the Jack-in-a-box, of course. He was laughing all over his face because he had escaped from the French, and he was waving to his friends on the quarter-deck because he had served in this very ship before he was captured. He had once been third lieutenant of the *Nymphe* and there were still many people aboard who had been shipmates with him. That was what was so romantic, don't you see? He escaped from the French, rowed out to sea in a little boat hoping to find the English frigate he had heard was cruising off the cape, was taken by an enemy patrol when he could actually see our topsails against the sky, and then when he was saved at the last moment he found that his rescuer was his very own ship, or had been. I should have said it was he who cut the houario's halliard, bringing down her foresail with a run. Rescued by his very own ship! If that ain't romantic, I don't know what romance is.'

'Sure, Bevis of Hampton is nothing to him. And this is the gentleman we are to operate upon? I am glad of it. I have always found that a man in high spirits heals quicker than another; and although this wandering ball does not sound the gravest of interventions, it is as well to have all the chances on our side.'

'Yes, to be sure,' said Thomas doubtfully. 'And perhaps I should have operated earlier, when he was so cheerful; but these last days he has been very low – a deep surly melancholy – like to hang himself – because some busy fool acquainted with Valletta gossip like the rest of us saw fit to tell him he was a . . .' Thomas paused and gave Stephen a meaning look. 'To tell him his wife had not been quite discreet. *You* will know what I mean; and with whom. But I hope this little blood-letting may bring resignation with it: after all, the same misfortune has befallen many another man, and most survive it.'

Thomas's meaning eluded Stephen, a fact that left him perfectly indifferent. He said, 'Have you prepared him at all?'

'Yes: three drachms of mandragora on an empty stomach.'

'Mandragora,' began Stephen with some contempt, but a Marine servant coming in cut him short.

'Mr Fielding's compliments,' said the Marine, 'and why ben't he to be cut? Says, he has been waiting in the sickbay this last glass and more.'

'Tell him we shall be there directly,' said Mr Thomas. 'What have you against mandragora, colleague?'

'Nothing at all,' said Stephen. 'Is it Mr *Charles* Fielding that you have been speaking of? Lieutenant Charles Fielding, of the Navy?'

'Why, yes. I said so, do you not recall? Charles Fielding, the husband of the lady with the dog that is so fond of Captain Aubrey. So you had not smoked it? You had not gathered my meaning? How droll. But hush, not a word.'

They walked into the sick-bay and there, standing in the strong light from the grating overhead and looking out of the scuttle was a tall dark heavy man who might have stepped straight from the picture in Laura's bedroom: he was even wearing the same striped pantaloons. Mr Thomas made the usual introductions and Fielding replied with a civil 'How do you do, sir' and a bow, but it was clear that he paid no real attention. It was clear too that either Mr Thomas's mandragora or his own rum had had a considerable effect; his voice was thick and his words somewhat confused. Stephen had never known any man come cheerfully to the surgeon's table, chest or chair; even the bravest recoiled from the deliberate incision suffered in cold blood, and most sailors added what they could to the official dose. Yet Mr Fielding had not run to extremes, as did many patients who had the means; he was completely master of himself, and when he had taken off his shirt he submitted to having his arms tied – 'For was you to make a sudden involuntary start, we might plunge a knife into an artery, or sever an important nerve' – with a good grace, and sat there looking set and dogged, his jaw clenched tight.

The ball was deeper than Thomas had supposed and although while they worked on his back Fielding uttered no more than a grunt or two, by the time it was out he was breathing deep and sweating profusely. When they had sewn him up and released his arms Thomas looked into his face and said, 'You must stay here quietly for a while. I will send the loblolly-boy to sit with you.'

'I should be happy to sit with Mr Fielding,' said Stephen. 'When he is recovered I should very much like to hear of his escape from the French.'

Coffee, hot and strong, recovered Mr Fielding fairly soon. After the second cup he reached over to his coat, took a slice of cold plum-duff from the pocket and devoured it out of hand. 'I beg your pardon,' he said, 'but I have been so hungry these last months that I have to keep a bite about me.' Then raising his voice for the loblolly-boy he told him to bring the case-bottle from his cabin. The loblolly-boy was an aged, authoritarian creature, of great medical standing on the lower deck, and since spirits were forbidden in the sick-bay he hesitated, looking at Stephen; but Fielding's dark face instantly took on a still darker, extremely dangerous expression and his voice the ring of a hard-horse driving lieutenant, the kind whose blow might follow an order in a split second – he was clearly a man of very strong passions. The case-bottle appeared, and having offered it to Stephen, Fielding swallowed first one stiff tot and then another. 'That must be all for the present,' said Stephen, taking it away. 'We cannot afford any further loss of blood. You are very much reduced. Yours was a long and very trying journey, I have no doubt.'

'As a straightforward ride it would not have amounted to any very great distance,' said Fielding. 'I dare say a courier might do it in less than a week. But as we travelled, hiding by day and creeping along by night, generally through by lanes or over wild country and often losing our way, it took well over two months. Seventy-six days, to be exact.' He spoke without much interest and broke off as though he were not going to continue. They sat in silence for some minutes, the frigate rocking gently and the reflection of the sunlit sea shimmering on the deck-head. Two and a half months, thought Stephen: that almost exactly coincided with the first of the letters that had made Laura so uneasy, the first of the forged letters. 'But as for the hardships,' said Fielding at length, 'yes, it was a trying journey. Rarely anything to eat but what we could poach or steal, and not even that in the high mountains. And then the wet and the cold . . . Wilson died when we had a two-days' snowstorm in the Trentino, and Corby's foot was so frostbitten that he could only hobble after that. I was lucky, I suppose.'

'If it is not disagreeable to you, I should very much like to hear even the shortest account of your escape,' said Stephen.

'Very well,' said Fielding. He had been in the penal fort-ress of Bitche, he said, a place reserved for unruly prisoners-of-war or those who had tried to escape from Verdun, and most of the time he had been in solitary confinement, because during his attempt he had killed a gendarme. But a fire in part of the castle and the subsequent repairs had brought him into the same cell as Wilson and Corby, and since this was a time of considerable disorganization – the commander of the fortress had just been replaced – they decided to try again. In their earlier attempts they had all three separately tried to reach the Channel or the North Sea ports, and now they meant to go the other way, eastwards for Austria and so to the Adriatic. It had to be done quickly, while the workmen and their materials were still in the castle, and Corby, who was the most senior, a natural leader and a man fluent in German, abandoned the usual caution and told many of the other officers that the three of them were going to escape. Some were very helpful indeed, providing sketch-maps, a pocket spy-glass, a fairly accurate compass, a little money, and above all pieces of cloth or line to add to their own. While the other prisoners created a disturbance in the inner bailey late one dark and threatening evening the three went over the outer wall, and once they were clear their friends pulled the rope up and hid it. They had a whole night's start and they made for the Rhine as fast as they could go, aiming for the bridge of boats that carried the road over to Rastatt. They did not reach it until nearly noon, far later than they had hoped; but there they had an extraordinary stroke of luck. While they lay in a little wood, watching the bridge-end to see how the sentries behaved, they saw a religious procession pass along the lane below them, a procession formed of separate groups several hundred strong, carrying green branches and singing. The banners in front began to cross the bridge, and the sailors, cutting themselves some greenery, slipped down the bank into the lane and joined the throng, singing as well as they could and looking fervent. Few people took any notice of them – it was a gathering of several villages – and if anyone spoke Corby answered while the others sang. They crossed the bridge with still another troop chanting behind them, and Corby went on into the town, where he bought pumpernickel and dried beef. At this time they looked quite respectable, with their good blue coats stripped of all distinguishing marks; but coming back Corby was questioned, fortunately by a very simple, easily-impressed, easily-deluded young conscript, from whom he learnt that three English officers were being pursued. They therefore kept strictly hidden in the woods for the next week or so, never moving until it was dark; and by the end of that time, what with foul weather, hard lying, and slipping and falling in the mud of a hundred streams, they looked like thoroughly suspicious vagrants. They had a razor, and they kept fairly clean; but it was no good – all dogs barked at them, and if by chance they passed any countrymen Corby's greeting would meet with a startled, uneasy stare. They dared not approach any village. And so the long, slow march south and east went on, far slower than they had expected; and they lived on what they could find – raw turnips from the fields, potatoes, green corn, a very little game – week after week, until they became very feeble, particularly as they had rain almost all the time. They were sometimes hunted, once or twice by gamekeepers but nearly always because they had raided farmyards or because patrols had heard of their presence, and Fielding spoke of their perpetual fear, the fierce, hunted expressions that soon became habitual, almost fixed, and their savage hatred not only for their pursuers but for anyone who might possibly betray them: once they were very near killing a couple of children who stumbled on their hiding-place. He said that this hatred overflowed into their relations with one another, making their disagreements very dangerous and, if possible, increasing the utter joylessness of the last weeks of their journey; and he spoke with feeling that Stephen would never have expected from his lowering, apparently insensitive face.

'I wonder you could stand it,' he observed, when Fielding reached the point where they found that they had lost their way, and that after two days of toiling over bare mountain with no food at all they looked down into a valley and saw not the Austrian post they had expected but the tricolour flying in French-occupied Italy: a narrow treeless valley with a fort on a rise in the middle and no village, no isolated farms, no herdsmen's summer chalets, and no possibility of retreat.

'As far as I was concerned,' said Fielding, 'I was buoyed up by – by a particular sentiment, and I should have walked twice as far, if my feet had held out. I believe the same applied to the others, and when I think of all the hardships they bore in vain, upon my honour, I see no justice in the world. It is not to be believed that both their wives were whores.'

'What happened to Mr Corby?'

'He was killed – murdered. We were chased by a cavalry patrol only three days before the end, when we were on the sea-coast, in sight of ships. He could not run, and the troopers fairly hacked him to pieces, though he was unarmed. I got into a marsh, into deep reeds and water up to here.' He paused, and then in a flat voice he said, 'I was the only one left. I brought them no luck. Except from the professional point of view perhaps it would have been better if I had stayed in Bitche; and even from that point of view . . . in any event, I shall not hurry back to Malta for a ship.' At this point Fielding was talking almost wholly for himself, yet even so Stephen felt that some response was necessary. He said, 'I had the honour of being introduced to Mrs Fielding, and she was so very kind as to invite me to her musical evenings.'

'Oh yes,' said Fielding. 'She is a great musician. Perhaps that was the trouble. I cannot make out God save the King on a penny whistle.'

Captain Aubrey and Captain Cotton of the *Nymphe* had been midshipmen together, and not even midshipmen but youngsters, entered on the old *Resolution*'s books as captain's servants – squeakers, of no use to man or beast. They had used little ceremony at the age of twelve, nor had they grown much more formal with one another as they rose in rank; and now Jack, having led his friend below, was surprised to see a constrained, furtive, awkward, hangdog expression on his face. 'Why, Harry,' he said, 'what ails thee? Art sick? Art vexed?'

'Oh no,' said Captain Cotton with an artificial simper. 'Not at all.'

'What is it then? You look as if you have been found out keeping a false muster, or comforting the King's enemies.'

'Well, to tell the truth, Jack – to tell you the honest truth, the fact of the matter is, I have some damned unpleasant news for you. Charles Fielding, that was a prisoner at Verdun and then at Bitche – Charles Fielding, that was at one time third of the *Nymphe* and then second of the *Volage*, has escaped. We picked him up off Cape Promontore some days ago, and he is aboards us at this moment.'

'Escaped, has he?' cried Jack. 'Upon my word, I honour him for it! Escaped from Bitche! Bless me, what a stroke. I am most heartily glad of it. But tell me, what is your bad news?'

'Why,' said Cotton, turning red and looking more embarrassed still, 'I thought – everybody said – it was generally supposed that you and Mrs . . .'

'Oh, because of that damned dog?' said Jack, laughing. 'No, no. There was nothing in it – all nonsense, alas – mere silly Valleta gossip. No, no, on the contrary: I should be very happy to take him back to her. We turn round tomorrow, so let him come across any time before we sail and I will give him the quickest passage to Malta that is to be had. I shall write him a note directly,' he said, turning to his desk.

The answer to his note came over from the *Nymphe* shortly before Stephen walked into the great cabin. 'There you are, Stephen,' said Jack. 'I suppose you know that Laura's husband has escaped, and is aboard the *Nymphe*?'

'I do,' said Stephen.

'Well, here is a damned thing,' said Jack. 'It seems that some God-damned fool has told him I was his wife's lover. Cotton was here just now, and he said so. I instantly denied it, of course, and to make my denial utterly convincing I sent over straight away, offering to carry Fielding to Valletta at once: he could not be there for a month otherwise. I had no time to consult you,' he said, looking anxiously into Stephen's face, 'but in any case it was necessary – it was the least I could do – and it had to be done immediately. I offered him my dining-cabin, which I thought pretty handsome; but here is his answer.'

'You were quite right to do so, I am sure,' said Stephen, taking it. 'And there was no call in the world to be consulting me, my dear; sometimes you misinterpret my actions. No call at all, at all,' he murmured, reading: *Mr Fielding begs to acknowledge Captain Aubrey's letter of today's date, but regrets he is unable to avail himself of the offer it contains: he hopes however that he may meet Captain Aubrey in Malta before any considerable time shall have passed.* 'I regret it extremely,' he said, and although Jack knew him very well he could not tell what he meant or on what grounds he regretted it so. 'I operated on the gentleman this forenoon, and talked with him for some time afterwards,' said Stephen after a while. 'And although by far the best thing would be for him to come back with us, I do not feel that persuasion would serve any useful purpose. Rather the contrary, indeed. But I may take it, may I not, that we must necessarily be the first to reach Valletta with the news of Mr Fielding's escape?'

'Certainly. We shall have that vile tub of Babbington's with us, so we shall probably not set royals or even top-gallants all the way, but even so there is nothing else sailing back from here until the next convoy.'

There was a silence, each far away. Jack had fought the odd duel in his time, but he had disliked them then and he disliked them even more now that it was almost always a matter of pistols, generally more deadly than the sword. They seemed to him foolish and even wicked: he had not the least wish to make Laura a widow, even less to do the same to Sophie.

'Barge alongside, sir, if you please,' said Bonden in his loud sea-voice, startling the silence of the cabin.

'Barge?' said Captain Aubrey, brought up all standing in his meditations.

'Why, yes, your honour,' said Bonden politely. 'Which you are to eat your dinner with Captain Babbington aboard of *Dryad* in five minutes' time.'

Chapter Ten

Few creatures in the sea gave Stephen Maturin more delight than dolphins, and here in the Strait of Otranto he had them by the score. One particular troop had been with the ship ever since he finished with the sick-bay, and he had been watching them all this time, as far forward as he could get, leaning against the warm figurehead and gazing down. The dolphins would come racing up the larboard, the sunlit side, and leap all together before crossing and going down to play in the wake before running up again: sometimes they would scratch themselves against the frigate's side or even her cut-water before turning, but generally they leapt, and he would see their amiable faces clear of the water. The same troop, with two exceptionally fat, profusely spotted dolphins in it, had appeared several times before; he knew most of the individuals, and he was convinced that they were aware of his presence. He hoped that they recognized him and even liked him, and each time they rose he waved.

The dolphins did not have to exert themselves, for in these gentle breezes the *Surprise* was scarcely making five knots as she steered south-south-west under an easy sail, while far to leeward her lumpish consort the *Dryad* laboured along under almost everything she could spread to keep her station. The two were covering as wide an expanse of sea as ever they could because there was a strong possibility of enemy privateers in the southern Adriatic and the northern Ionian (unaccompanied British ships and even small convoys had been sadly mauled), while a French or Venetian man-of-war was by no means out of the question, nor yet a merchant-man, fat and lawful prize. The *Dryad* was as eager as any sloop in the Navy for glory and even indeed for gain, but although she was small and low she was also ponderous and slow on the rise, and she was making very heavy weather of the long swell that beat against her starboard bow, a sure sign of storms in the western Mediterranean. Sometimes her lower sails were becalmed when she was in the trough, and sometimes their filling on the rise would make her butt into the top of the wave, so that green water swept over her forecastle, along her waist and into her captain's cabin. The *Surprise* on the other hand rose to them like a wild swan; and sometimes, when the swell mounted very high and the ship sank very low, Stephen would see his dolphins swimming away up there in the solid transparent uptilted mass of water as though he were looking through the side of some immeasurable tank. He had been at his post since the sun was only half way up the brilliant eastern sky, reclining at his ease, sometimes reflecting, sometimes merely staring, the bowsprit just above his head gently creaking with the pitch of the ship and the pull of the forestaysail, and the warm breeze wafting by him: he had been there at the time of the noon observation and throughout the hullaballoo of piping the hands to dinner and the piercing scream of the fife for grog, and he might have stayed there indefinitely had he not been called away. He had long since made up his mind what to do about the situation brought into being by Fielding's reappearance: although the *Surprise* would be well ahead of the news it would still be best to act quickly. He would have to open himself entirely to the Admiral and Wray, which, though regrettable, was still a small price to pay for pinning all the important French agents in Malta. Laura would make an appointment with her man, and it would be strange if he did not lead them to the rest. But before they were gathered in she would have to be moved to a place of safety, since some unimportant people among the discontented Maltese would probably escape; he had already worked out a formula that would exculpate her in the Admiral's eyes, and he had no very rigid morality to fear on the part of Wray. That decision belonged to the past: for the present he was giving himself up entirely to immediate, intense pleasure in the warm, astonishingly clear air, the brilliant light, the ship's rhythmic bounding through the clean blue-green sea. The sun had now passed the zenith; it had moved two hands-breadths to the west and the staysail was casting a grateful shade upon him by the time Calamy came forward in a clean frilled shirt with his hair brushed smooth and said, 'Why, sir, what's all this? Surely you have not forgot you are entertaining the Captain?'

'And how am I supposed to entertain the Captain, for all love?' asked Stephen. 'Am I to grin at him through a horse-collar, propose riddles and conundrums, cut capers?'

'Come, sir,' said Calamy, 'the gunroom is entertaining the Captain to dinner, and you have only ten minutes to change. There is not a moment to be lost.' And as he led Stephen aft, 'I am coming too. Ain't that fun?'

Fun it was, although at first the Captain was unusually quiet: not glum, but mum. He had a singularly poignant feeling of loss as he sat there at Mowett's right. He missed Pullings extremely, and when he looked at the rows of faces that he knew so well, liked and esteemed – looked with the knowledge that this society would be broken up in the next few weeks – he had a strong sense of his life being upon the turn, between two seasons, as it were, with the certainties of the one no longer valid for the other. He was not a fanciful man, but for some time now he had had an indefinable sense of chaos following order, of impending disaster; and it oppressed his mind.

By way of comfort he observed that the life of the service was one of continual separation, one in which ships' companies continually broke up. They would serve a commission together for better for worse, and then the ship would pay off and they would be separated: to be sure, if the captain were given another command right away he might take several of his officers, his midshipmen and followers; yet very often there was a general parting, and this would be just another of the many he had known, different in degree, since he liked his ship and his shipmates more, but not in kind. He grew more and more nearly persuaded of this as the excellent meal progressed. In their happy ignorance and with splendid weather over their heads his hosts were unusually cheerful; and in Maclean, their new Marine officer, they had gained a wonderful caterer. Good food and good wine insensibly had their effect; and although the conversation was not particularly brilliant it was so good-natured that a man would have had to be far more morose than Jack Aubrey not to be pleased with his entertainment and his company. By the time the cloth was drawn and the table covered with nutshells, few joined more heartily in the chorus when Calamy was called upon to 'tip us *Nelson at Copenhagen*', a song he sang with the fine lack of self-consciousness brought about by three glasses of claret and one of port in a clear treble that contrasted pleasantly with his seniors' deep voices as they chanted:

> *With their thundering and roaring, rattling and roaring*
> *Thundering and roaring bombs.*

Nor had Maclean a more attentive listener when the Marine said, 'I do not mean to put myself in competition with either Mr Mowett or Mr Rowan – I have not the least claim to original genius in the poetry line – but since I have the honour of being caterer to the mess, perhaps I may be allowed to recite a piece composed by a friend of mine, a Scotch gentleman, on currant jelly.'

'Certainly,' cried some, 'by all means.' Others cried, 'Hear him, hear him,' or 'The Jollies for ever.'

'Currant jelly for breakfast, you understand,' said Maclean, and carried straight on:

> *'Long ere the cups were filled, I'd eager rise,*
> *(The love of jelly flaming in my eyes),*
> *A slice of neatest cut, and spoon, would seize,*
> *And, with my usual much-becoming ease,*
> *Would the ambrosia plentifully spread*
> *In genteel mode upon the wheaten . . .'*

He broke off seeing Williamson, the youngster of the watch, run in and stand by the Captain's chair.

'If you please, sir,' said Williamson, '*Dryad* signals that a ship has just cleared Cape St Mary, steering eastward: *Edinburgh*, she believes.'

Edinburgh she was, a massive seventy-four commanded by Heneage Dundas. Their courses slowly converged, and as they lay-to on the heaving sea Jack pulled across to ask him how he did: Heneage did pretty well, but might have done much better, very much better if he had caught the French privateer he had chased under the guns of Taranto that afternoon, a fine twenty-gun ship with sky-blue sides that he had pursued since dawn and that had outrun him at last. But he had a great deal of news apart from that: there had been two shocking blows in the Gulf of Lions, the blockading squadron had been sadly knocked about and blown as far south as Mahon; some ships were still in that port, repairing as fast as they could. The French had not come out in a body, though some were thought to have stole away: there was some doubt about their number and their strength, even about the fact itself. But there was none at all about the flaming row between the Commander-in-Chief and Harte. Its causes were variously reported, but its effect was certain: Harte was going home. Dundas did not know whether he had been superseded, whether he had hauled down his flag with his own hands and jumped upon it as some alleged, whether he had invalided, or whether he was being sent back in disgrace; but Dundas was perfectly sure that England was Harte's destination. 'And long may he stay there,' he said. 'I have never known a worse commander of ships, or men, or himself. But even if he is offered an appointment, which may well happen, because of his connection with Andrew Wray, I do not suppose he will ever serve again at sea, now he is so hellfire rich. My cousin Jelks, who understands these things, tells me he owns half Houndsditch, a clear eight thousand a year.'

During the night the wind, which had been backing and strengthening all the afternoon, settled in the north-west and began to blow quite hard, so that after quarters Jack struck topgallantmasts down on deck. A little before the moon came up he was thinking of taking a second reef in his topsails, not so much because of the strength of the wind as because it was blowing across the swell and working up a cross-sea that made even the *Surprise* complain. It would have been labour lost, however: even before the moon was clear of the horizon the forecastle lookout bawled, 'Sail ho! Sail on the larboard bow. Two points on the larboard bow,' and there she lay, the *Edinburgh*'s French privateer. Jack instantly shook out his first reef and with equal promptness the privateer bore up for the shelter of Taranto and its powerful guns. But the *Dryad* was to windward of her, and in answer to the *Surprise*'s blue lights she spread all the canvas she possessed and cut the Frenchman off from the land. She carried on in this heroic way for some considerable while, the two of them coursing the nimble privateer like a couple of greyhounds; and although eventually she carried away her jibboom and her maintopmast, all going by the board in one spectacular sweep, by this time the Frenchman could no longer turn. He was directly to leeward of the *Surprise*, not much above two miles away, heading south for the distant Barbary coast as hard as ever he could pelt.

Both sides now settled down to a perfectly straight-forward chase, each captain using every last turn of seamanship, every subtle change of trim and helm, to run the faster. The privateer had the slight advantage of being able to choose his point of sailing, which was with the wind three points abaft the beam, whereas the *Surprise* preferred it on her quarter; but the frigate had a crew that could flash sails in and out slightly quicker; and so they tore across the bright moonlit sea at twelve and even thirteen knots, flinging the white water wide, spray flying aft and all hands intensely alive. The privateer started her water over the side; then came her boats from the beams, splash after splash; her bower anchors; and at last her guns. And with the wind easing slightly she began to draw away, gaining a quarter of a mile between two in the morning and three. The *Surprise* checked the gain by pumping out twenty tons of water and lining all available hands along the weather rail to make the ship a trifle stiffer; and then the wind strengthened again, so that the chase could no longer keep her studdingsails abroad – they parted company before she had time to take them in – whereas the frigate could; and the privateer's lead dwindled, dwindled. In the first light of dawn the *Surprise* was within musket-shot, yet the Frenchman kept racing on, hoping against all probability that the frigate might lose a spar. There was a general feeling in the *Surprise* that he was coming it a trifle high; that this was mere obstinacy and showing away; and that he should be brought up with a round turn, or the galley fires could never be lit and breakfast would be late. Jack caught many a meaning look, many a raised eyebrow and questioning head cocked at the bow-chasers, which had been cleared away long ago and whose priming Mr Borrell now ostentatiously renewed. And in reply to some remark Mowett said to him, 'Sir, I am concerned about the decks. This is the day for a complete grinding with bears fore and aft; and if that fellow . . .' Solid water hurtling aft head-high cut him short, but Jack knew very well what he would have said: shading his eyes from the spray and holding firmly to an iron-taut backstay as the frigate bucked the rise, he stared over the torn water at the flying privateer, a fine sight with every possible stitch of urgent canvas set and the foam so thick around her that her hull was in a haze. 'Very well,' he said, 'we will give her a gun.' And raising his voice, 'Mr Borrell, a wide ball to let her know we are in earnest, if you please. Wide, but not too wide.'

'Wide but not too wide it is, sir,' replied the gunner; and after a calculating pause, filled with pleasurable expectation, Long Tom Turk went off with his usual gruff decided bark. A hole appeared in each of the chase's topsails, well out on the starboard side; the foretopsail, already stretched to the very edge of breaking-point, instantly split; the privateer shot up into the wind and struck her colours. The *Surprise*'s cook and his mates hurried to the galley, muttering.

This solitary gun was all that Stephen knew of the chase, and even that, since the ship had not beat to quarters, he put down to some nautical whim, conceivably a salute, and went back to sleep again; so that when at last he came on deck ill-tempered from having overslept – none of the usual holystones to wake him, no shrieks, no yells, no rhythmic wheeze of pumps – he was utterly amazed to find the frigate lying-to with another ship under the lee and boats plying between them. He replied to no good mornings but stood there with narrowed eyes, and after a while he cried, 'That is not the *Dryad*. It has three masts.'

'There is no concealing anything from the Doctor,' said Jack, and turning directly to him he went on, 'Give you joy of our prize: we took her in the night.'

'Breakfast is disgracefully late,' said Stephen.

'Come and drink a cup with me,' said Jack, 'and I will tell you about the chase.'

This he did, and at somewhat tedious length; but together with the coffee civility flowed back into Stephen, who listened with every appearance of attention. Yet when Jack said, 'I have rarely seen such a sailer, going large: she will certainly be bought into the service. Rowan is to carry her in as soon as we have bent a new foretopsail,' he came to life entirely and asked, 'Is there any likelihood of his reaching Malta before us?'

'Oh no,' said Jack. 'None at all, unless we happen to meet an enemy, or chase another possible prize.'

Stephen hesitated, and then in a low voice he said, 'It is of great importance that the news of Fielding's escape should not be known in Valletta before I am there.'

'I see,' said Jack rather coldly. 'Well, I can make sure of that.'

'What about the *Dryad*?'

'I really do not think you need be afraid of her. She lost her maintopmast and jibboom, and with the wind as it is I doubt she can have made much headway. And then again tonight's run was not altogether out of our road by any means: just south-east instead of south-south-west. We are not likely to see her until we have been in port a couple of days at least.'

Stephen looked upon his friend as infallible where ships and the sea were concerned, and although the *Surprise* met with contrary winds, his mind was at ease until they ran in the Grand Harbour late on a dark, oppressive, thundery Sunday afternoon, a harbour unusually poor in men-of-war. With real concern he noticed the absence of the Commander-in-Chief's flagship: and two minutes later, with a shock that cut his breath off short, he saw the *Dryad* lying there at her moorings. She was surrounded with bumboats and dghaisas, and as he watched one of her cutters, filled with liberty-men in shore-going rig, shoved off from the side. The Dryads cheered to see the prize brought in – the prize in which they would share – and the Surprises cheered in reply; and as the *Surprise* wafted by, heading for Thompson's Jetty, where she would discharge her prisoners, a good deal of wit about the sloop's present appearance and the frigate's slow return flew to and fro. Stephen looked anxiously round for Jack, but the signal for the Captain of *Surprise* had been thrown out within minutes of her making her number and he was below shifting his clothes. 'Mr Mowett,' he said through the amiable din, 'pray call out and ask how long they have been here.'

Since Friday night. That gave the whole of Saturday and most of Sunday for the officers at least to go ashore. Without the least apology Stephen hurried into the sleeping-cabin where Jack was pulling on his best white breeches and said, 'Listen. I must go into Valletta at once. Will you take me?'

Jack looked at him hard and said, 'You know the rules of the service: no liberty until the Captain has reported. Is this an exception you can properly ask for?'

'It is, upon my honour.'

'Very well, then. But I must tell you that with such a signal it is very likely we shall be sent off as soon as we have completed our water.'

'Certainly,' said Stephen in an absent voice and he ran down into his cabin for a pistol and to his medicine-chest for a short, heavy surgical knife.

Nix Mangiare steps in the gathering dusk, and Stephen

leapt out of the barge. He hurried as fast as he could through the slowly-moving crowd to the palace, to Wray's quarters in the palace. And here the news that Wray was in Sicily shattered all his plans and notions – destroyed them entirely, so that for the moment he could hardly tell what to do. This was an exceedingly dangerous, delicate situation, and there was no knowing whom he could trust. Wray's words about his suspicions kept recurring: that *navium duces* might refer to anyone in high command. He was making his way against the tide of humanity setting along the Strade Reale towards Floriana when Babbington, Pullings and Martin, all somewhat elevated, barred his way under a golden street-lamp, and told him that rain was on its way – squalls, storms – and that he should stay with them – they would go to Bonelli's and make a night of it, singing till dawn. His cold, reptilian glare shocked them; their jocularity died away; they let him go.

As he turned into her street the long-awaited lightning ripped the sky, instantly followed by a most enormous thunder-clap as though the firmament itself had split and a few moments later by a storm of great hailstones that leapt waist-high. Together with a crowd of other people he took shelter under her outer door: he was almost certain that the watch would not be on, but even so he was glad of the mad running, the jostling, and the darkness, which would have made even the closest watch quite useless. A downpour of rain succeeded the hail, melting the deep white layer and rushing down the gutters in a continual roar. It stopped suddenly, and after a while people moved off, stepping high and gingerly over the puddles; but low clouds were still passing over the moon, lightning still flickered over Senglea, and there was surely more to come.

Stephen walked along the passage. For some reason he was certain that Laura Fielding was not there, and indeed when he came to the door it was shut; nor did his knock set off a bellowing and snorting from within. It was a door with a self-closing lock and Laura had shut herself out so often that she kept a spare key hidden in the gap between two stones: Stephen felt along the wall for it and let himself in.

The court was filled with the smell of thunder-rain, wet earth, and hail-bruised lemon-leaves; and beyond the arches he could hear water still pouring into the cistern. Against the wall on the right hand the paving had been taken up and a passing gleam of moonlight showed him a raised mound, presumably a new flower-bed, though rather high: there were flowers on it, now beaten down by the storm. Otherwise everything was as it had been. High up inside the porch the small lamp still burned before Saint Elmo's niche, untouched by the hail or rain; the house door, as usual, was unlocked; and in Laura's bedroom another lamp, blue this time, glowed between Charles Fielding's portrait and Our Lady of Consolation. The whole place was neat and trim and it felt thoroughly inhabited, as though she had left it only an hour ago: there was a vase of frail rock-roses by the lamp, and not a petal had fallen yet. He sat down with a feeling of relief so great that for a while the release of tension left him quite weak.

He did not strike a light, partly because Laura's tinder-box was notoriously inefficient, and partly because now that his eyes were accustomed to the dim blue glow he could see reasonably well. From where he sat he had no difficulty in making out the portrait, and for a while he considered that formidable, unhappy, passionate man. 'Laura is the only one who can deal with him,' he reflected, as a whole series of flashes made Fielding seem to leap from his frame, to the accompaniment of long, tremendous thunder like the whole Mediterranean fleet saluting. The rain began again and he stood at the sitting-room window, watching it in the inter-mittent play of lightning: the new mound was disintegrating under the downpour, with earth and battered flowers drift-ing towards the door. 'It is very like a grave,' he observed, turning and sitting down at Laura's piano. His hands wan-dered over the keyboard, playing of themselves. Working out the measures to be taken was useless until he saw Laura and learnt how things stood; nevertheless his mind raced through the various possibilities again and again until, during a pause in the rain, he heard the Franciscans' little cracked bell somewhere in the blind tangle of roofs beyond the court ringing for complines.

Mechanically at first and then with real intention he recited the prayer for protection during the darkness of the night; then he began to play a rough version of the first psalm in the Dorian mode. But he did not do it well and in any case the piano was not the instrument for plainchant. He fell silent and sat there a great while, his body quite relaxed. The rain was falling still, sometimes hard, sometimes merely steady, yet by now the cistern was brim-full and it no longer made a noise. The only sound that reached the silent, lonely court was the falling rain; and during a particularly gentle spell an odd metallic grating at the outer door caught his ear: looking from the window he saw light shining under the lintel. The sound again, three times repeated, quite soft, but an uncommon sound and one that he had heard before: someone was picking the lock. Not forcing the door with a bar, but picking the lock.

He waited until it opened – opened carefully, slowly, with none of its usual creak – and before they dowsed their dark lantern he saw two men, one tall, one short. They paused for a moment before running on tiptoe through the rain and across the flooded court, and Stephen moved silently back through the house to the broad window-seat in Laura's bedroom. Undrawn curtains hung on either side; they covered no great area, but in his experience people rarely suspected such a hiding-place.

After a soundless approach they strode into the bedroom, flashing their lights about. 'She is not back yet,' said one in French, with his beam on the unruffled counterpane.

'Go and look in the kitchen,' said the other man.

'No. She is not back yet,' said the first man, returning. 'Though the party should have been over hours ago.'

'The rain is keeping her.'

'Shall we wait?'

The shorter man, who was sitting on the sofa, took the hood completely off his lantern, set it on the low brass table and looked at his watch: he said, 'We cannot afford to miss Andreotti. If she is not back by the time he reaches St James's we shall have to send a couple of reliable men. At about three or four in the morning, when she is bound to be here. She cannot stay at the Commendatore's all night, for heaven's sake.'

With the stronger light Stephen recognized Lesueur from Graham's and Laura's description: a hard man. Then with a most uncommon shock he recognized Lesueur's companion: Boulay, a civilian fairly high in Sir Hildebrand's administrative staff. He abandoned the idea of making sure of Lesueur with his pistol and taking his knife to the other: Boulay was far too valuable to be dispatched out of hand. Unless things turned ugly, he must be preserved.

'Beppo and the Arab?' suggested Boulay.

'No, not Beppo,' said Lesueur impatiently. 'He takes far too much pleasure in it altogether. As I told you, I want it done quick. Clean, no fuss.'

'There is Paolo: very serious and conscientious, and as strong as a bull. He was a butcher's man.'

Lesueur did not reply for some time, and it was clear to Stephen that he hated the whole thing. 'The ideal,' he said at last, 'would have been to find her asleep.' Then for a long interval all three sat still, listening to the rain.

A desultory conversation between Boulay and Lesueur did spring up in time, but Stephen learnt far less from it than he had hoped. A certain Luigi was embezzling much of the money sent to Palermo, and various plans were suggested for confounding him; neither spoke with much concern or conviction, however, and it was clear that nine parts of their attention was fixed on the outer door, waiting for it to open. Yet Stephen did gather that Boulay was a Channel Islander, with relatives at Fécamp; that Lesueur suffered from piles; and that there were two other French organizations represented in Malta, the one cooperative, the other comparatively hostile, neither of much importance. It also became evident that both men had come directly from Città Vecchia in the downpour, which accounted for their having no suspicion of the frigate's return, no notion that he could possibly be present in Valletta.

Valletta, at this juncture, was in the curious position of having a port-admiral's office but no port-admiral. The senior naval officer, to whom Jack Aubrey reported, was an elderly post-captain by the name of Fellowes, a prim, starchy officer who had served much of his time ashore. They hardly knew one another and their meeting was formal. 'It is to be regretted that *Surprise* did not come in two days earlier,' said Fellowes. 'The Commander-in-Chief' – with a reverent inclination of his head – 'delayed his departure until the evening in the hope of seeing her. However, I am charged to give you these orders, to answer any questions that may arise from them to the best of my ability, and to add certain verbal instructions. Perhaps you had better read them straight away.'

'If you please, sir,' said Jack, taking the proffered sheet. *To Captain J. Aubrey, His Majesty's Ship Surprise. By Sir Francis Ives, K. B. Vice-Admiral of the Red, &c. &c.* he read. *Whereas Mr Eliot, His Majesty's Consul at Zambra, has represented to me that his Highness the Dey of Mascara has made the most extravagant, unjust, and inadmissible demands upon the government of Great Britain, intermixed with unfriendly expressions, even to menaces of hostility, if he does not obtain the sums of money he has laid claim to early in the ensuing month:-*

You are hereby required and directed to appear before Zambra and endeavour to have an interview with Mr Consul Eliot, and concert such proper measures to be pursued as the situation may require; whether to have an audience of the Dey, and explain with firmness the unreasonableness of his demands, and the exposure of his trade and marine to annihilation, if he is rash enough to commit the most trifling act of hostility against the persons or property of his Majesty's subjects; to expose the acts and intrigues of the French agents and Jewish merchants who conduct the trade of Mascara and Zambra; or to embark Mr Consul Eliot, his suite and baggage, with any British sub-

jects and their property who may wish to make their retreat.

In your conference with the Dey, it will be absolutely neces-sary to preserve your temper, although he should show the most violent and indecent passion, but not to give way to the absurd positions he may lay down, or to admit that his Majesty's ships have, on any occasion, committed a breach of neutrality; and, finding all remonstrances ineffectual, and that his Highness persists in his exorbitant demands, and carries the threats noti-fied to Mr Consul Eliot into execution, by offering any insult to his Majesty's flag, or other flagrant violations of the treaties subsisting between the two governments, you are to make known to his Highness that from the instant such an act of hostility should be committed by his orders, that war will be declared between Great Britain and Mascara, and that you have my instruction to punish the injustice and temerity of his Highness, by seizing, burning, sinking, or otherwise destroying, all ships bearing the Mascarine flag; and to block up the ports of his Highness, and to cut off all commerce and navigation between them and the ports of other nations; and having fulfilled the object of your mission, you are to lose no time in reporting to me the event thereof at Gibraltar.

'Have you any questions?' asked Fellowes.

'I think not, sir,' said Jack. 'It seems to me quite a straight-forward mission.'

'Then I am to say that on the political side you will seek the advice of Dr Maturin, and that in your passage to Zam-bra you will sail with the *Pollux*, carrying Admiral Harte. It is not contemplated that the Admiral should take any part in the negotiations: apart from other considerations, a ship of the line and a flag-officer would give the Dey and the other local rulers an exaggerated sense of their own impor-tance and lead to undesirable consequences. But a knowledge of his presence in those waters would have a favourable influence. Furthermore, it is probable that some Frenchmen got out of Toulon in the recent blow, and mutual support may possibly be called for.'

'Is Admiral Harte fully aware that *Surprise* alone is to carry out the negotiations?' Their eyes met, each knowing that Harte was notoriously given to interfering and that his recently-inherited wealth had very greatly increased his persuasion that he knew best.

'I believe so,' said Fellowes, and after a significant pause, 'These are notes on the situation in Mascara compiled by Mr Pocock for the information of Dr Maturin. Have you your statement of condition?'

'Yes, sir,' said Jack, taking the notes and passing the summary that showed the present number of hands aboard the *Surprise*, her degree of seaworthiness, and quantities of powder and shot, naval stores and provisions of every kind.

'You are short of water,' observed Fellowes.

'Yes, sir,' said Jack. 'We had to start the upper tier to catch our prize. But if you wish us to get under way directly we can very well complete at Zambra: there is no difficulty about that – water immediately at hand.'

'Perhaps that would be the best solution: *Pollux* is to sail early in the morning. You are acquainted with Zambra, Aubrey?'

'Oh Lord, yes, sir. I was third of the *Eurotas* when she stuck on the Brothers, well inside the bay. It took us a great while to heave her off, and we had to wait for supplies to come from Mahon, so when work was at a stand the master and I surveyed every inch of the northern part and most of the rest. The watering-place is wonderfully convenient, a spring at the foot of a cliff right on the shore, not a biscuit-toss from the boats.'

'Very well. Let us make it so. Now I see you are rather short-handed, too, and at Sir Francis's particular desire I have recovered several of the men who were drafted from *Surprise* during her repair.'

'I am very much obliged to you, sir,' said Jack, to whom this would have been an inestimable blessing if only his ship and his ship's company were not to be broken up in a few weeks' time.

'Not at all. They will come aboard first thing: you are alongside Thompson's Jetty, of course? Heavens,' he said in an unofficial voice as even heavier rain drove furiously against the window, 'how it does come down. You will stay and sup with me and my daughter, Aubrey? It is not a fit night out for man or beast.'

At last, at last, Lesueur said they could wait no longer. 'It will have to be Paolo. I am sorry for it, in a way. You must insist on speed – efficiency, painless efficiency – a lightning-flash.'

The doors closed behind them: Stephen uncocked his pistol and sheathed his knife. A few minutes later, so few that they might almost have met in the street, Laura came home. He heard the door give its usual shriek, saw the lantern shining in the doorway and herself thanking the people who had accompanied her, and there she was, running across the court with a cloak held over her head.

'Laura,' he called.

'Stephen!' she cried, throwing the cloak aside and embracing him. 'Oh how glad I am to see you – is *Surprise* arrived? – I never knew – how did you get in? – why, the key, of course – and have you been sitting in the dark? – come, let us strike a light and have a boiled egg together.'

'Where is Ponto?' he asked when they were in the kitchen.

Instantly her face changed from surprised happiness to pain and grief. 'He died,' she said, and the tears came directly. 'He died suddenly this morning and the charcoal-man helped me bury him in the court.'

'Where was Giovanna?'

'She had to go to Gozo. She was very strange – frightened.'

'Listen, my dear. Your husband has escaped from his prison: he has been out of their hands nearly three months now. That is why those letters were so out of tune – forged, of course, do you see? He is aboard the *Nymphe* off Trieste at this moment.'

'He is not hurt? He is quite well?'

'Quite well.'

'Thank God, thank God, thank God. But why –?'

'Listen,' said Stephen, waving her question aside. 'The *Dryad* came in from the Adriatic before us: they know about his escape. The French agents know that the news will reach you any moment and that then they will have no hold over you. They mean to put it out of your power to give them away. They have already killed your dog and sent your maid to Gozo. They have been here once tonight and they are coming again. Have you any friend with a big house and many servants where you could go at once? Come, my dear, collect yourself. The Commendatore?'

She had sat down, and now she looked at him, scarcely comprehending. 'No,' she said at last. 'He lives with just one old maid-servant. He is poor.' Indeed she had few close friends in Valletta; none at whose door she could knock at this dead hour of the night. And Stephen had no confidential refuge on shore whatsoever.

'Come, my dear,' he said, 'put up a few things for the night and throw a faldetta about you. We must hurry on board.'

As soon as he began making his way along Thompson's Jetty against the wind and the rain, clutching his hat with one hand and his billowing boat-cloak with the other, Captain Aubrey noticed that the *Surprise*'s stern-windows were lit: conceivably Killick was making the most of his absence to scrape or polish in this maniac way, late though it was. The rain redoubled and he fairly ran across the brow, ducked under cover and stood there for a moment gasping and shaking the wet from his hat and his cloak.

The lanterns showed him Mowett, Killick and Bonden, all looking curiously pleased with themselves, and some members of the harbour-watch, also on the grin. 'Is the Doctor aboard?' he asked, and to his intense relief they answered yes. But he was astonished when Mowett added, 'He is in your cabin, sir, with a visitor.'

He was astonished, because in spite of their close friendship Stephen never went into the cabin uninvited, unless he happened to be sailing as a guest, which was not the case at present. He was still more astonished, on opening the great cabin door, to see Mrs Fielding sitting in his elbow-chair.

Her lower person brought a drowned rat to mind, and her wet hair straggled here and there, but her face was perfectly radiant with happiness. Assassination had been so much a part of her Sicilian childhood and youth that she saw it very much more clearly than an Englishwoman might have done, and she had been terrified, utterly terrified, during their last moments in that lonely death-trap of a house and throughout their halting progress across the town, soaked, molested in doorways by drunken soldiers and sailors, always hearing determined steps behind them; and now she was safe, surrounded by two hundred powerful, affectionate men, and though she might not be dry at least she was warm; and now, above all, she had time to realize that she possessed a husband again, one that she loved passionately for all his faults, and one that she had in fact feared dead these last two months. Stephen had told her something of Fielding's sad state of mind: but she knew Charles very well; she had not the least doubt that she could deal with the situation as soon as they met; and at present all that she needed to make her perfectly happy was to see him again. No wonder she glowed so as to rival the lamp.

'Good night, now, Jack,' said Stephen, rising from the Captain's table, where he had been writing. 'You must forgive this intrusion, but as I was bringing Mrs Fielding here she was wetted through and through, and I thought the cabin more suitable than the gunroom. I have taken it upon myself to promise her a passage to Gibraltar in your name.'

Jack looked at his worn, haggard face, picked up the urgent signal in his glance, and with scarcely a pause he said, 'You did very well.' And bowing to Laura, 'We shall be delighted to have you, ma'am.' He raised his voice in a genteel version of his usual hail for Killick and said, 'Shift my dunnage into Mr Pullings' cabin. These will be Mrs Fielding's quarters: break out fresh towels and the scented soap. Bonden will re-hang the cot a foot lower. Carry the baggage into the coach.'

'There ain't no baggage, sir,' murmured Killick behind his shading hand. 'Nothing but a little ditty-bag.'

'Well, then,' said Jack, casting a discreet glance at the small pool that had gathered at Laura's feet, 'warm and lay out a clean flannel nightshirt, worsted stockings and my wool dressing-gown – the *wool* gown, d'ye hear me? – and bear a hand, bear a hand. You must change directly, ma'am,' he said to Laura. 'You will catch your death of cold, else. Do you like toasted cheese?'

'Very much, sir,' said Laura, smiling at him.

'Toasted cheese, then, Killick, and mulled ale: we do not want a guest to die on our hands. Now ma'am,' looking at his watch – 'you must put on dry, warm clothes, however rough; and in ten minutes we shall have the honour of eating toasted cheese with you: then you must go straight to bed, since we sail at dawn, and you will not have much time for sleep before the din awakes you.'

A man-of-war with the captain's cabin ruled out was no place for confidence, many of the partitions being match-board or even sailcloth; yet in Pullings' little den (never filled since his promotion) Jack did say, 'This is all square-rigged, Stephen?'

'As square as Pythagoras, brother; and I am very much obliged to you for the handsome way in which you welcomed our guest.'

'How did you know we were bound for Gibraltar?'

'Since it was known to the port-captain's daughter, it was common knowledge among her female acquaintance throughout the island, Laura included.'

'Sir,' said Killick, hurrying in and addressing Stephen, 'may I set out the gold-bound article for the lady?'

'Do that thing, Killick,' said Stephen. 'Sure, something more than a shaving-glass is called for.' The article in question was an extravagantly ingenious dressing-chest that could also be used as a lectern, a wash-hand-stand, a back-gammon board and many other things. Diana's present to Stephen, ordinarily kept in a waxed sailcloth case, being far too valuable and delicate for ordinary shipboard use.

'Lord, Stephen,' said Jack, suddenly struck by the thought

of his fiery cousin, 'it would be the Devil to pay and no pitch hot explaining this to Diana.'

'Do you think my motives might be suspected?'

'I am mortally sure they would be suspected, even if you were to speak with the tongues of men and of angels too. Think, Stephen: you bring the handsomest woman in Malta aboard in the middle of the graveyard watch – someone who was seen leaving your room at Searle's the night the thieves –'

'If you please, your honour,' said a goggling, excited ship's boy, 'Killick says wittles is up.'

It was not until breakfast the next day that Stephen found how accurately Jack had assessed the ship's opinion. He was in that peculiarly lucid state of mind that comes from having been under very great tension and from having had no sleep – he had spent what was left of the night writing a carefully-considered most secret and confidential statement of the situation to Wray and to Sir Francis, both in the appropriate codes and both sent off together with their duplicates to the port-admiral's office for the most urgent forwarding before the *Surprise* cast off her moorings. He had hesitated long about the Governor; but having seen one of his staff in Laura's house, a man who might easily open the letter, he had thought it better to refrain. Wray was to be back on Wednesday in any event, even if Stephen's dispatch did not travel fast enough to bring him back earlier; and although Laura's disappearance would probably cause a certain amount of anxiety among the French Wray should still be able to make a clean sweep. She was by no means the first young woman to bolt with a lover on the approach of her husband, and the anxiety would not lead to any very drastic measures.

At breakfast then he observed his companions. A certain constraint might be put down to their Captain's presence, unusual at this time of day; but a very real awkwardness persisted after he had left them. Stephen detected embarrassment, a sort of admiration or rather a new kind of respect, and on the part of Gill at any rate some degree of moral disapproval; and drinking his coffee he sighed for deserving none of these things.

After a quick look at his mercifully empty sickbay while the loblolly-boy tolled his bell overhead for those who might feel themselves pale or poorly, and tolled in vain, Stephen retired with a phial of the tincture of laudanum and Pocock's notes on the Dey of Mascara. From these he learnt that the Dey was the ruler of a small but quite powerful state, nominally subject to the Sultan of Turkey but in fact as independent as Algiers or even more so; that although Mascara was the traditional capital, the Dey's principal residence was at Zambra, the port through which all the trade of the country passed; that French agents were active . . . unusually active . . . unusually successful . . . and with this he went to sleep.

Both he and Laura slept throughout the day, through the various dinners served aboard and through all the noise of the wind and the sea and the working of the ship; and this caused a certain amount of ribald comment fore and aft. Stephen slept the longer of the two, but when at last he came on deck he found that he was in time for an evening so perfect that it made all foul weather seem worth while: with a flowing sheet and under an easy sail the *Surprise* was slipping through the sea: and such a sea, smooth, dreamlike, limitless, with an infinity of subtle nacreous colours merging into one another and a vast pure sky overhead. It was one of those days when there was no horizon; it was impossible to tell at what point in the pearly haze the sea met the sky, and this increased the sense of immensity. The breeze was just abaft the beam and it hummed gently in the rigging, while the water slid down the ship's side with a soft lipping sound, the whole making a kind of sea-silence. Yet the feeling of total remoteness and isolation changed when he looked forward, for there, two cables lengths ahead, was the *Pollux*, an old worn-out battered sixty-four-gun ship, one of the last of her class; yet old and battered though she was, she made a noble sight with her towering array of canvas, her exactly-squared yards, her great ensign billowing away to leeward and all the complex marine geometry of curve and straight line lit by the low sun on her starboard bow.

'Sir,' said Calamy at his side, 'Mrs Fielding wishes to show you Venus.'

'Venus, is it?' said Stephen; and to his surprise he observed that not only was Calamy wearing his frilled shirt but that he had also washed his face, a ceremony usually reserved for dinner invitations or for those Sundays when church was rigged. Indeed, as he moved aft to where Mrs Fielding was sitting on Jack's elbow-chair near the taffrail he noticed that most of the officers had their uniform coats on, that all of them were shaved, and that all of them were present.

'Come and see!' she called, waving Jack's smaller telescope. 'It's just to the left of the mainyard. A star in daylight! Did you know she was like a crescent moon only small, oh so small?'

'Little do I know about Venus,' said Stephen, 'except that she is an inferior planet.'

'Oh fie,' cried she, and the purser, the Marine and Jack made a number of gallant and sometimes quite witty remarks. Mowett and Rowan, however, who might have been expected to shine with uncommon brilliance, remained mute, smiling and gazing and chuckling to themselves until the quartermaster at the con called out in a loud official voice to the sentry, 'Turn the glass and strike the bell.'

These words and the brisk double note recalled Mowett to his duty and he said, 'For quarters, sir, do you choose to make a clean sweep fore and aft today?'

Every evening of her life under Captain Aubrey's command the *Surprise* had cleared for action, had cleared in the fullest sense of the term, as if she were really going into battle, with the bulkheads of his cabins vanishing, the great guns in them being run out, and all his belongings hurrying below. But this would necessarily mean disrupting Mrs Fielding's frail economy, and after a moment's consideration Jack said, 'Perhaps for today we may content ourselves with rattling the forward guns in and out; and then if *Pollux* reefs topsails or shifts topgallants we may do the same.'

In fact the *Surprise* never made a single clean sweep fore and aft in the six days of her voyage to Zambra, six days of the sweetest sailing that Jack had ever known. Without the lumbering old *Pollux* she would have accomplished the run in perhaps two days less, and all hands would have regretted it bitterly. These six days, with mild warm prosperous breezes, a gentle sea, and (since their pace was regulated by the *Pollux*) none of that harassing sense of urgency which marred so many naval journeys – these six days might have been taken out of ordinary time, might not have belonged to the common calendar: it was not exactly holiday, for there was plenty to do; but for once the Surprises did have a moment, even a fair number of moments, to lose; though this was not the only factor by any means nor yet the main one.

Some of these moments they devoted to the adornment of their persons. Williamson went beyond Calamy in washing the greater part of his neck as well as his face and hands, a striking gesture, since they possessed only one nine-inch pewter basin between them and almost no fresh water; and they both appeared in clean shirts every day. For that matter the quarterdeck as a whole became a model of correct uniform, like that of the *Victory* when St Vincent had her – loose duck trousers, round jackets and the common broad-brimmed low-crowned straw hats against the sun called benjies gave way either to breeches or at least to blue pantaloons and boots and to good blue coats and regulation scrapers, while the foremast hands often sported the red waistcoats reserved for Sunday and splendid Levantine neckerchiefs. Profane oaths, cursings and execrations (forbidden in any event by the second Article of War) were laid aside or modified, and it was pleasant to hear the bosun cry 'Oh you ... unskilful fellow' when a hand called Faster Doudle, staring aft at Mrs Fielding, dropped a marline-spike from the maintop, very nearly transfixing Mr Hollar's foot. Punishment, in the sense of flogging at the gangway, was also laid aside; and though this was of no great consequence in a ship that so very rarely saw the cat, the general sense of relaxation and indulgence might have done great harm to discipline to the *Surprise* had she not had an exceptional ship's company. She always had been a happy ship; now she was happier still; and it occurred to Stephen that a really handsome, thoroughly good-natured but totally inaccessible young woman, changed at stated intervals, before familiarity could set in, would be a very valuable addition to any man-of-war's establishment.

On most evenings the hands danced and sang on the forecastle until well on in the first watch, while until much later in the night Jack and Stephen played in the cabin or on the quarterdeck or listened with the rest while Mrs Fielding sang, accompanying herself on a mandoline that belonged to Honey.

She was early invited to dine with the gunroom, and when it was understood that she regretted having nothing to wear no less than three gentlemen sent their most respectful compliments and lengths of the famous silky crimson cloth of Santa Maura, which the *Surprise* had recently visited: cloth originally intended for their mothers, sisters, or wives, and from which she made a most becoming dress, Killick and the sailmaker sewing the hems to have it ready in time. She was looked upon with a strong, affectionate admiration, and although it was generally believed that she had run off with the Doctor, what little moral condemnation there was aboard pointed not at her but at him. Even Mr Gill, a melancholy, withdrawn, puritanical man, replied, 'Only three days, alas, if this breeze holds,' when she asked him how long it would take them to reach Cape Raba, the term of the first stage of their journey.

On the last but one of these days, when the ships had little more than steerage-way, Jack was asked to dine aboard the *Pollux*. He regretted it, dinners in his own ship being so very much more enjoyable, but he had virtually no choice, and at ten minutes to the hour he stepped into his barge rigged to the nines, from the silver buckles on his shoes to the chelengk in his hat, his bargemen splendid in watchet blue and snowy duck.

He found both Captain Dawson, whom he scarcely knew, and Admiral Harte, whom he knew only too well, in great form: Dawson was full of remorse for not having invited Aubrey earlier, but his cook had been ill, 'struck down by a treacherous crab he had ate last thing in Valletta. He is recovered now, I am happy to say: we were growing heartily sick of wardroom fare.'

Recovered he had, but he had celebrated the event by getting drunk, and the meal followed a strange chaotic course with very long pauses and then the sudden appearance of five removes all together, and eccentricities such as floating island with an uncooked carrot in it.

'I really must apologize for this dinner,' said Dawson, towards the end.

'You may well say that, sir,' said Harte. 'It was a very bad dinner, and wretchedly put on the table. Three ducks in a dish! Only think of that!'

'This is most capital port,' said Jack. 'I doubt I have ever drunk better.'

'I have,' said Harte. 'My son-in-law, Andrew Wray, bought Lord Colville's cellar, and in one of the bins there was some port that would have this look like something for midshipmen, something from the Keppel's Head. Not that this is not pretty well, pretty well in its way.' Pretty well or not, he drank a good deal of it; and as they sat over their bottle he grew extremely curious about Jack's mission. Jack was vague and evasive and he would have got away with no more than the advice 'to kick the Dey's arse – when dealing with foreigners, and even more so with natives, you must always kick their arse,' if he had not unluckily mentioned his watering-place. Harte made him describe it with great accuracy three times over and said he might stand in to have a look: the knowledge might always come in useful. Jack discouraged the notion with all possible firmness and as soon as he could he stood up to take his leave.

'Before you go, Aubrey,' said Harte, 'I should like to ask

a favour.' He pulled out a small leather purse, evidently prepared beforehand. 'When you go into Zambra, pray redeem a Christian slave or two with this. English seamen for preference, but any poor unfortunate buggers will do. Each time I touch the Barbary coast I usually manage to get a couple of old 'uns, past work; and I set them down at Gibraltar.'

Jack had been acquainted with Harte ever since he was a lieutenant without ever once knowing him to do a handsome thing, and this new aspect of his character added to the dreamlike quality of these last few days. An exquisite gentle dream in spite of its strong sense of 'last time' and even of doom, he reflected, as the barge took him back; but he could find no way of expressing its nature in words. Music would come nearer: he could more nearly define it with a fiddle under his chin, define it at least to his own satisfaction. With the lovely but menacing slow movement of a partita that he sometimes played running through his head he gazed at the *Surprise*. She was as familiar to him as a ship could well be, but because of this train of reflection, or because of some trick of the light, or because it was really so, her nature too had changed; she was a ship in a dream, a ship he hardly knew, and she was sailing along a course long since traced out, as straight and narrow as a razor's edge.

'Pull round her,' he said to Bonden at his side; and viewing her now with a prosaic seaman's eye he observed that she was sailing on a perfectly even keel, whereas she really preferred being slightly by the stern. The twenty-odd tons that he would add to his watering-place would soon see to that.

They raised Cape Raba early in the morning, a dismal morning too, with the barometer falling, the wind backing westerly, low cloud, and the threat of rain. But rain or fine, Mowett, as a zealous first lieutenant, was determined that the *Surprise* should do herself credit in Zambra, and the hands turned to with a perfect deluge of sea-water to remove every possible remaining grain of the hundredweight of sand they had already used for scouring the decks; then they set to drying what they had wetted and to polishing everything they had dulled. Rather before this ceremony had reached its climax the Captain appeared on deck for the second time, glanced about the sea and sky, and said, 'Mr Honey, to *Pollux*, if you please: *permission to part company.*'

Wilkins, the yeoman of the signals, had been expecting this for some time; so had his colleague in the *Pollux*; and the request and the consent flew to and fro with extraordinary speed, together with the civil addition from *Pollux*, *Happy return*.

The *Surprise* stood in for the land and the ship of the line (for that was her official rating, feeble though she was by current standards) went about, to stand off and on according to their agreement, in case the frigate should rejoin before next day. Slowly the shore looming in the dull south grew clearer, and presently Jack called the youngsters, as he usually did on approaching an anchorage new to them. At this time of morning and in this weather there was no likelihood of seeing Mrs Fielding and everyone was in working clothes, most looking cold and wet. Williams was particularly squalid in a woollen Guernsey frock deep in slush, for he had been helping the bosun grease the topmast caps; but he had dutifully brought the azimuth compass, since Captain Aubrey would certainly require them to take the bearings of various sea-marks when he had explained them.

'There, on the larboard bow,' he said, nodding towards a tall dark headland with sheer cliffs falling to the sea, 'that is Cape Raba, and you must give it a wide berth, because of the reef running out half a mile from the point. And right ahead, close on two leagues west-south-west, that is Akroma.' They looked attentively at the distant promontory, which was very like the first, except that it had a fortification high on its seaward end. 'Beyond Cape Akroma there is Jedid Bay, rather open but with a good holding-ground in fifteen-fathom water and an island with rabbits on it that keeps off the westerlies and the north-westerlies – a useful place to run for if it is blowing very hard and you cannot double Akroma. But it is nothing nigh so big nor such a fine anchorage as this nearer bay we are heading for now, Zambra

Bay, between Raba and Akroma.' The breeze had freshened with the rising of the almost invisible sun, and the *Surprise*, no longer held back to old *Pollux*'s pace, was making well over eight knots with the wind two points free: Cape Raba moved rapidly astern and they opened Zambra Bay, a noble body of water, deeper than it was broad, an indented gulf with many spurs and capes, and the whole running roughly south ten or twelve miles into the land. The frigate brought the wind on to her beam and ran faster still for the west shore of the bay. 'You cannot see Zambra yet,' said Jack. 'It is tucked away in the south-east corner. But you can see the Brothers. Run south a couple of miles from Akroma Point until you come to a small headland with a palm-tree on it. A trifle beyond that there are four rocks in a line, each maybe a cable's length apart. Those are the Brothers.'

'I see them, sir,' cried Calamy, and Williamson said, 'They bear just south-west by west.'

'You would see them better if the breeze were strong in the north-east, and if it had had time to work up a hearty sea. There is a reef between them with not much above two fathom water over it, and with a north-east swell it shows white. But ordinarily it looks quite smooth, like this. The Moors of these parts take no account of it, but we were stuck there when I was in *Eurotas*, which drew eighteen foot six abaft. Generally speaking, you would be wise to assume that there is always shoal water between a string of rocks of the same kind. Mr Mowett,' he said, breaking off, 'since we have made such excellent time, we had better complete our water before running down to the port. We do not want to be there too early, and in any event I believe it will rain later in the day, so let us get it over. The watering-place is on the east side, in the inlet beyond those three small islands.' With this he turned to go into his cabin, but then, checking himself when his hand was actually on the lock, he plunged below to the gunroom.

Here he found Stephen looking frowsty and discontented – there was nothing that more thoroughly persuaded Jack of his friend's innocence with regard to Mrs Fielding than

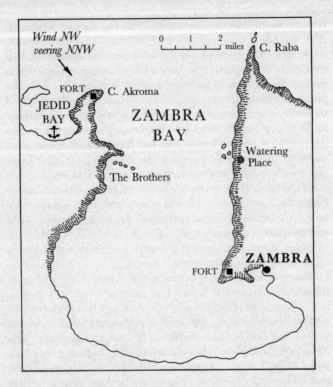

Wind NW
veering NNW

0   1   2 miles

C. Raba

FORT   C. Akroma

JEDID
BAY

ZAMBRA
BAY

The Brothers

Watering
Place

ZAMBRA

FORT

this three days' beard, this vile old wig – and Stephen said to him, 'If the woman does not issue a more Christian invitation in two minutes, I shall drink that' – pointing to the gunroom's coffee, weak, insipid, only just luke-warm. 'She has asked us to take chocolate with her. Chocolate at this time in the morning, dear Mother of God. Suff on her.'

Killick came in, still with a genteel cabin-smirk on his face, and said, 'The lady says certainly there will be coffee if the gentlemen prefer it.'

Certainly the gentlemen preferred it, and they sat drinking cup after cup in their usual exorbitant way until from a change in the ship's motion Jack knew they were close to the shore. He went on deck and guided her in past the green islands to the little cove with its sandy beach, where he dropped no more than a kedge, sheltered as they were. He went ashore with the first boat of empty casks, and for the first time that morning he found himself in touch with that feeling of another and as it were parallel world again, the feeling that had been with him so strongly these last few days. It was the extraordinary familiarity of the watering-place that brought it back. He had not been there for nearly twenty very active years and yet he knew every stone of its ancient worn coping and even the exact scent of freshness and green as he leant over the basin.

But getting twenty tons of water aboard, cask by cask, called for a great deal of immediate attention and energy: and since this was one of the tasks that Jack did not choose to delegate, neither he nor anyone else had much leisure for introspection on a conscious level, particularly as a small rain soon began to drive from the north-west in gusts, making the handling of the slippery, ponderous casks even slower and more difficult.

For some time now the *Pollux* had been edging down towards the opening of the bay, as everybody had already known she would; and at present, impelled by Harte's curiosity and her own notorious sagging to leeward, she was actually within the line between the two capes, backing and filling under the lee of Akroma and exercising her people in the shifting of topgallantmasts. Although she was technically inside the bay, and would have to wear or tack to get out of it, she was still just keeping her promise, since she was well out of sight of Zambra; but her presence irritated the Surprises. 'If Nosey Parker goes on like this, they will have to make two legs of it, wear and wear again, to make their offing,' said Mowett to Rowan; and as he spoke the fortress high on Cape Akroma fired a gun. The sound, borne by the wind, came clearly across the broad expanse of sea, and all hands who were not actively engaged looked up. But nothing happened; and the launch coming alongside with a load of casks immediately afterwards, they very soon looked down again.

Yet it seemed strange to Jack, since the fort flew no colours, and he was still looking at the cape with his telescope when a large ship rounded the point from Jedid Bay. A man-of-war, double-decked, eighty guns, wearing Turkish colours and a commodore's broad pennant: she was closely followed by two frigates, one of thirty-eight or forty guns, the other light, perhaps a twenty-eight. He had just time to observe this and to see that the heavy frigate was passing up along the commodore's larboard side when the Turkish colours came down, the French ran up and the two-decker fired her forward guns into the *Pollux*. The *Pollux* put before the wind – what wind she had under the lee of the cape – but in two minutes the big Frenchman ranged close alongside, almost yardarm to yardarm, and began hammering her with full broadsides, while the heavy frigate passed the commodore's disengaged side and took up a station athwart the *Pollux*'s hawse. Even before she opened her murderous raking fire the *Surprise*, abandoning launch, kedge and hawser, was racing out from her inlet, packing on canvas as she came and at the same time clearing for action.

The *Pollux* was directly to windward, and unless she could come a mile or two down the bay, the *Surprise* would have to tack twice to reach her, once a little short of the Brothers and a second time at the height of the Akroma fort. Nine miles to travel and precious little time to do it in. But the breeze had freshened; the *Surprise* was already running at ten knots; the *Pollux* was now firing at a tremendous rate, and she had thirty-two-pounder carronades on her quarterdeck and forecastle. As far as he could see for the dense smoke streaming from the battle she had all her masts standing yet, and she might well hold out until Jack could come up and either relieve her of the heavy frigate's fire or rake the two-decker's stern. The smaller French frigate seemed neither here nor there; she hovered about, putting in an occasional shot, but she did not appear to do much damage and she did not seem very eager to engage.

'Main topgallant staysail,' he said, and as its sheet was belayed the *Surprise* leant still further over; already her larboard cathead, her larboard chains were deep in a smother of foam; white water raced the whole length of her rail; and yet she was moving faster every minute. 'Hold on, good sticks,' he murmured, and aloud, 'Spindle-jib.'

The deck sloped like the roof of a house and he stood there with his right arm hooked round the aftermost mizzen shroud. Mowett was at his side, and a midshipman for messages; two solid quartermasters, Devlin and Harper, at the wheel and the master behind them, conning the ship; the gun-crews, less the sail-trimmers, at their stations with their officers and midshipmen; the Marines and the small-arms men in their places; and all gazing steadfastly at the close-packed roaring battle, the dark smoke and the perpetual orange flashes.

It was almost time to go about. Jack glanced at the Brothers, half a mile away, and he saw Stephen creeping laboriously up the slope from the companion-way: Dr Maturin's action-station was in the orlop, but he rarely went there until the firing had begun. 'How is Mrs Fielding?' asked Jack, high over the rushing of the water.

'Pretty well, I thank you. Roman virtue. Fortitude.'

'Take care: clap on to Davis. We are going about.' Jack caught Gill's eye and nodded.

'Ready oh!' cried the master, and with a great smooth rush the *Surprise* came about, staying like a cutter in her own length.

Faster and faster still on the larboard tack, and now eddies of the wind brought them the smell of powder-smoke. Jack said, 'They may say what they like about the Admiral, but no one has ever called him a shy cock. Lord, how *Pollux* fights!'

'Sir,' said Mowett, his glass to his eye, 'her foremast is gone.' As he spoke a flaw in the wind swept the smoke aside and there indeed lay the *Pollux* crippled and unable to turn to leeward, but still firing with a splendid regularity. A moment later the heavy frigate, in response to the two-decker's signal, filled and stood south, followed by the other, to intercept the *Surprise*.

'Doctor,' said Jack, 'it is time for you to go below. My best compliments to Mrs Fielding, and I believe she would do best in the hold. Pray show her the way.'

Now that the frigates were clear of the smoke he watched them with extreme attention. The nearer was as he had supposed a thirty-eight-gun ship, beautifully built and fast; but with her thousand tons she was unlikely to be as nimble as the *Surprise*. Her second was, like his own, a twenty-eight-gun frigate; but there the likeness ended – she was broad and bluff-bowed, almost certainly Dutch in origin.

'Half a point a-weather,' he said.

'Half a point a-weather it is, sir.'

When they were within range the leading Frenchman would yaw to give the *Surprise* a broadside and ordinarily the *Surprise* would put her helm hard a-weather to avoid being raked. Yet with this scarcely perceptible half-point in hand he could haul his wind a trifle and not only avoid the broadside but perhaps sweep by before the enemy had time for another. Perhaps. So much depended on what the second ship did. It would be a most perilous business, getting past the two of them. Yet it had to be done. As if they had divined his intention the two frigates altered course, one slightly to starboard, the other slightly to port, to take him between them.

He was exceedingly tense, exceedingly alive; yet some small fragment of his mind remembered Stephen telling him that *à-Dieu-va*, the French for *about ship*, also meant, in ordinary language, *we must chance it and trust to God.* 'That is just about it with us,' he reflected, looking at the distant two-deckers, still battering one another with terrible fury; and as he looked the entire bank of smoke parted, blasted outwards from the centre, and in the middle rose an enormous brilliance, a vast towering jet of flame interspersed with black objects rising, rising, the whole crowned with white smoke. The *Pollux* had blown up; and even before the immeasurable flash had died away the roar of her exploding magazine reached them, shaking the sea and the sails as it came. The French commodore's foremast had also gone by the board, but the explosion and the falling spars and vast baulks of timber had not sunk her.

'Stand by to wear ship,' said Jack. Now that there was no *Pollux* to help he must do what he could to save the *Surprise* and her people; and trying to force his way past those two frigates was not the best fashion of setting about it.

He had not the least doubt that with this overwhelming superiority the French would attack him in Zambra, and it was not to gain the shelter of a neutral port that he ran south-south-east, towards the headland with a fort on it that interposed between him and the town, guarding the entrance to the harbour.

Leaning on the taffrail he trained his glass on the French two-decker. Now and then squalls of rain blurred his view, but he grew more and more certain that she was very badly damaged. What boats she had left were over the side, and they were making a raft or a stage of sorts out of spars; she had already carried out lines fore and aft. As long as he kept out of the range of her remaining thirty-two pounders he probably had little to fear from her. As for the frigates, that was another matter; he could probably deal with either separate, though a well-handled thirty-eight to windward in a confined bay would be hard to escape from. But the two together . . .

He studied them with the most concentrated attention, with a perfectly cold, impartial, expert judgement; and more and more it became evident to him that the heavy frigate, though an elegant ship and a fine sailer, was handled in no more than a conscientious, journeyman fashion – a captain and crew that had spent more time in port than at sea in all weathers. They were not at home in their ship; there was a lack of coordination in her manoeuvres, a slowness, a certain hesitancy, that showed they were not used to working together. It seemed to him that they had no great sense of the sea. But that did not mean that her guns might not be very well served in the usual French style, nor that her broadside weight of metal was not far greater than his own. As for the smaller one, she had a more able commander, but she was slow; quite far astern already by the time the *Surprise* came abreast of the fort. Astern, but to windward: that was the devil of it. The two of them had the weather-gage.

It did not surprise him when the fort opened an ineffectual fire; from the first appearance of the French squadron he had been convinced that the Dey was their ally. But it did give him a most plausible excuse for doing what he had in mind.

He shied away and steered close-hauled for the western shore, once again pushing the *Surprise* as hard as ever she could go. Never had he felt so much one with his ship. In the somewhat lighter wind at the bottom of the bay she could wear a prodigious amount of canvas; he knew exactly how much she could stand and he gave it her; and she behaved like a thoroughbred, drawing well away from the big Frenchman, who had turned almost at the same moment and who was now sailing a parallel course two miles on the *Surprise*'s starboard quarter, firing an occasional shot with her bow-chaser. The western shore came nearer, and several fishing-boats spreading their nets: nearer and nearer at this breakneck pace, and all the time Jack's mind was working out the courses open to him, the strength of the wind, his leeway – a smooth, barely conscious sequence of calculations.

In the quietness Jack called, 'Stand by to go about. And at the word jump to it like lightning.' Another hundred yards: two hundred: and 'Helm a-lee,' he cried.

Once again the frigate came about with a perfect grace and raced northwards up the western coast towards the Brothers and the cape just beyond them. But now the full advantage of the weather-gage appeared: in spite of the *Surprise*'s rapid turn and her greater speed, the Frenchmen had less distance to sail – they were in the position of horses on the inner rail in a race, with the *Surprise* confined to a distant outer rail; and unless she ran herself ashore it seemed that they must either cut her off before the Brothers or, by passing through them, pin her against the cape beyond.

There was dead silence aboard as the Brothers, with their

three channels, swept towards them and the two French ships came pelting in. During this long straight run the heavy frigate had had time to pile on a great deal of canvas and now she was running as fast as the *Surprise* or even faster; and so as not to check their way, neither fired a shot. The heavy frigate was steering for the middle passage, which would bring her to the end of the cape before the *Surprise*: she would be lying there with her broadside presented as the *Surprise* worked along the headland. The twenty-eight-gun ship fetched the *Surprise*'s wake to cut her off if, having passed the first channel, she tried to double back.

The heavy frigate was now rather more than half a mile away just abaft the starboard beam and coming up fast. Jack did not so much reduce sail as reduce speed, discreetly starting sheets and luffing a little too much. The hands were used to his ways, but even so they looked extremely grave as the Frenchman drew first abreast and then ahead while the passage between the first rock and the second came closer still and the wall of the cape beyond loomed up tall and threatening in the rain. In passing the Frenchman gave them a distant broadside but instead of returning it Jack cried, 'Stand by to reduce sail,' and stepped over to the wheel.

The Frenchman raced ahead, flinging a splendid bow-wave, raced on into the middle passage: and struck with unbelievable force, all her masts instantly pitching forwards and to leeward. Her consort at once bore up, running fast to the eastern shore.

'Silence fore and aft,' roared Jack above the cheering. 'Clew up, clew up. Back the maintopsail.' And when enough way had come off he steered her, gently gliding, not through the first passage at all but through a deep cleft between the first Brother and the shore-cliff itself, so narrow that her yardarms scraped on either side. 'Brace up and haul aft,' he said; and the *Surprise*, gathering live way again with the wind on her beam, headed out to the open sea.

As she ran clear of the headland beyond the Brothers a veil of rain swept across the bay from the north-north-west, a thick grey veil that blotted out the shores on either hand and checked the extreme exuberance on deck. Men stopped thumping one another on the back, shaking hands, and crying, 'We served 'un out, the old sod – we foxed 'un – God love us, did you ever see the like?' But even so it was with flushed, shining faces and eager eyes that they looked at their captain when the rain had passed over, leaving blue sky over beyond Cape Akroma.

He was standing firmly planted by the taffrail with his legs wide apart, swinging his telescope from one end of the bay to the other. The first savage blaze of triumph had faded, but his eye still had a fine piratical gleam in it as he turned the possibilities over in his mind. 'Pass the word for the Doctor,' he called after a while; and when the Doctor came, 'Listen, this is the situation,' he said, nodding over the mile and a half of grey heaving sea to where the French two-decker lay motionless, '*Pollux* is sunk – blown up – sunk, of course – but she mauled the Frenchman finely first.' He passed the telescope, and Stephen saw the look of demi-wreck, the midship ports battered in, the foremast gone, the water pouring from her scuppers. 'And the explosion did a vast amount of damage – beams slipped from the clamps, I dare say. She has lines out fore and aft; she is low in the water, very much by the head; and I am convinced she will not move today, whatever we may do.'

Stephen moved his glass about the blackened wreckage covering half a mile of sea. 'Five hundred men in a second's blast, dear Mother of God.'

'Now look back at the Brothers,' said Jack after a short pause. 'That is their heavy frigate dismasted on the reef of the middle passage. She ran on so hard, so far, that she will never come off. It is not even worth our while going over to burn her.'

'Those are her people going ashore in the boats, I collect,' said Stephen.

'Just so. And now' – pointing – 'look right down the bay. That is her poor shabby consort cracking on like smoke and oakum to reach Zambra: a Dutchman, I take it, pressed into the French service, with no notion of shedding her blood for a parcel of foreigners. You have the situation clear in your mind?'

'What are all those boats down there?'

'They are fishermen and the like, coming out to loot anything they can carry from the wreck.'

'And that – that vessel over there with two masts?'

'She is our launch. We left her behind when we slipped: Honey will be joining with the kedge and hawser.'

'In that case I believe everything is clear.'

'Very well. Then be so good as to give me your opinion, your political opinion, on the following plan: we proceed to Zambra without the loss of a minute, engage that miserable Dutch herring-buss and the fort that fired on us, and having taken them send to the Dey stating that unless his government instantly apologizes for the insult to the flag we shall burn all the shipping in the harbour. When that is settled, we can have our interview with Mr Consul Eliot. Do you think this a good scheme?'

'No, sir, I do not. It is clear that the Dey was a party to this carefully-laid trap, and since his fort fired on the *Surprise* he obviously considers that we are already in a state of war. From all I understand he is an unusually bloody-minded, choleric man, and I believe that an attack at this stage, in the present state of excitement, would certainly result in Mr Eliot's death. And with a French two-decker in the bay there is no time for pourparlers, even though she may be obliged to lie at her moorings for a while. I think the plan politically unsound, not only for these reasons but for many more, and beg you will abandon it. In the present circumstances no political counsellor in his right wits could advise you to do anything but sail away with the utmost dispatch and ask for fresh instructions together with a powerful reinforcement.'

'I was afraid you would say that,' said Jack, with a longing glance over the water towards Zambra. 'Yet there is a great deal to be said for making hay while the iron is hot, you know . . . but clearly we must not kill Mr Eliot. And it would be stretching my orders uncommon far to sack the town.'

He took a couple of turns to the mainmast and back, raised his voice in an order to close the launch, and then with his usual cheerfulness he said, 'You are quite right: Gibraltar with the utmost dispatch let it be. And since it has stopped raining, and since we are to have no battle, we must let poor dear Mrs Fielding out of the hold.'

They had moved away from the low-toned privacy of the taffrail, and he spoke in a voice loud and general enough for it not to be indecent, in this particular and most companionable atmosphere of extreme tension relaxed, for Williamson to cry, 'I will fetch her sir,' and for Calamy to call out, 'I know just where she is, sir. Pray let me go.'

She came on deck just as the *Surprise* backed her maintopsail and the launch hooked on alongside. She had been told about the *Pollux*'s fate, and she looked extremely grave: she hoped that Captain Aubrey had not lost any friends in her – for her part she had not known anyone aboard, though her husband, she added with a somewhat doubtful look, had served for a while under poor Admiral Harte. The proper things were said, and indeed they were felt in spite of the predominant mood of victory; but they could hardly be expressed at any length, because of the hoisting-in of the launch, a manoeuvre that called for a great deal of piping and the shouting of orders.

In fact there seemed to Captain Aubrey to be rather more chat than was usual or desirable; and even when the launch was safely inboard and griped on its chocks the chat went on, with the word Hoops continually repeated. By the time he had made Mrs Fielding understand the position of the frigate on the now distant reef he saw Mowett hovering as though to speak, with the purser behind him, looking furious, and behind the purser Honey, looking sulky.

'Mr Mowett?' he said.

'I beg pardon, sir,' said Mowett, 'but Mr Adams wishes to represent, with the utmost respect, that his hoops have not been fetched away.'

'Four bundles of one and ninepennies, and two of half and half,' said the purser, as though on oath. 'Lent to the

cooper for the spare casks and never fetched away by Mr –
never fetched away by Someone.'

Mowett continued: 'He suggests that were we to skirt the
islands, it would not be a moment's work for the jolly-boat
to fetch them.'

'All hoops are the purser's responsibility,' said Mr Adams,
still addressing the universe rather than any particular
person. 'And the Board has checked me something cruel
three times this last quarter.'

'Mr Mowett,' said Jack, 'if those hoops were made of
triple-refined gold they would still remain on shore until we
pass this way again. There is not a moment to lose. Mr Gill,
shape me a course for Gibraltar, if you please, and let us
spread all the canvas she can possibly bear.'

'My hoops . . .' said the purser.

'Your hoops are very well, Mr Adams,' said Jack, 'but
they are not to compare with the chance of catching these
two Frenchmen sitting, if we have any luck with the wind.
Yes, Killick, what is it?'

'The lady's cabin is set to rights, sir, if you please; and I
have made a pot of coffee.'

No one had ever set the cabin to rights in so short a time
for Jack, nor had anyone produced a pot of coffee; but he
did not quarrel with his good fortune, and as the ship, clearing the bay, heeled to the full force of the north-north-
wester, he said, 'I do not like to tempt Fate, but at this pace
and with the breeze veering north so pretty, we may be in
Gibraltar by Tuesday morning – always a lucky day – so I
shall start my official letter this very evening.' If the Admiral
gave him a ship of the line with a captain junior to himself
– the names of half a dozen passed through his mind – the
possible, indeed the probable, taking of the two Frenchmen
would set him on the right road again, the road for employment, a good command, a forty-gun frigate on the North
American station. 'I shall pitch it hot and strong,' he said,
with a very happy smile.

'And I shall write,' said Laura Fielding. 'I shall write at
once to Charles and beg him to come and fetch me. I shall

tell him how kind you have been to me, and he will be so happy to meet you: as soon as we have been together for a little while, he will be so very happy to meet you.'

Stephen said, but to himself alone, 'I too shall write a letter. Not more than eight or perhaps nine men knew the contents of Jack's orders; and if that does not enable Wray to lay his hands upon the prime chief Judas, then there is the very Devil in it.'

P.S.

Ideas,
interviews
& features

THE MEDICAL WORLD OF DR STEPHEN MATURIN

Louis Jolyon West

ABOUT THE BOOK

In 1800 when we first meet Dr Stephen Maturin, there were no fewer than nineteen medical licensing bodies in Great Britain, each with different and often conflicting powers and rights.

> Medical men practised with university degrees, various forms of licenses, sometimes a combination of these, and sometimes with none at all. Medical training varied from classical – university education and the study of Greek and Latin medical texts, on the one hand, to broom-and-apron apprenticeship in an apothecary's shop, on the other – and sometimes involved no recognisable education at all. Quacks, 'empirics', and drug peddlars practised freely with no legal sanctions against them, while a physician in London could be disciplined by his College for preparing and selling a prescription to his patient.[1]

Medical men of Maturin's day were divided into three orders – physicians, surgeons and apothecaries – which took corporate form in the Royal College of Physicians, the Royal College of Surgeons, and the Society of Apothecaries. Each had different duties, privileges, perquisites, and social status. The physicians were at the top of the ladder and Maturin's unusual status as a 'naval surgeon' is noted from the beginning as rare; a physician would not as a rule care to be known as a surgeon, the latter being called 'Mister' rather than 'Doctor'.

The Royal College of Physicians in London

1. M. Jeanne Peterson, *The Medical Profession in Mid-Victorian London* (Berkeley, Calif.: University of California Press, 1978), p. 5.

2

received its charter in 1518 and had a monopoly over the practice of physic in London and oversight of physicians throughout England. Fellows of the College, as opposed to ordinary licence holders, enjoyed certain privileges – they were for instance exempt from jury duty and military service. On the other hand, they were not allowed to engage in trade, practise surgery or compound or sell medicines. These 'pure physicians' were limited to examining patients, diagnosing disease, and prescribing (but not dispensing) medications. A Fellow of the Royal College of Physicians (FRCP) would have to resign if he chose, as Dr Maturin did, to do surgery or to dispense drugs.

The powers of the Royal College of Physicians were confirmed during the reign of Henry VIII by an Act of Parliament which declared that it was 'expedient and necessary to provide that no person . . . be suffered to exercise and practise physic but only those persons that be profound, sad and discreet, groundedly learned, and deeply studied in physic'.[2] This meant a man with a university degree and, if he were to be a Fellow, that degree had to be from either Oxford or Cambridge. Even though medical education at some Scottish and Irish universities was arguably superior, their social status was not. On rare occasions, medical degrees from Dr Maturin's (undergraduate?) Alma Mater – Trinity College Dublin – were 'incorporated' at Oxford or Cambridge, but Stephen Maturin, born on the wrong side of the blanket, was certainly not one of these favoured few from aristocratic families. Nor would he have wanted it. Fellowship in the Royal Society meant far more to him than Fellowship in the Royal College of Physicians ever could. While Maturin's connections to the Royal Society are frequently described by O'Brian, it is clear that he is not a Fellow of the Royal College of Physicians.

Both Jack Aubrey and Stephen Maturin read papers at the meetings of the Royal Society but the latter's involvement was much more profound. For one thing, Dr Maturin and his mentor in naval intelligence, Sir Joseph Blaine, were great admirers of the long-time President of the Royal Society, Sir Joseph Banks. This admiration was probably not only for Banks's extraordinary sponsorship of scientific inquiry worldwide, but for his personal qualities as well. Banks insisted on the freest possible exchange of ideas between British and French scientists (or 'philosophers' as they were then commonly called) during the Napoleonic wars. He nonetheless despised Napoleon, kept him from being made a Fellow of the Royal Society, and even declared his condemnation of 'the cursed name of Napoleon'. In his splendid biography of Banks, O'Brian describes a social encounter between Sir Joseph and Dr Benjamin Brodie, then a 'young, unknown medical man', who eventually succeeded Banks as President of the Royal Society:

2. Alexander M. Carr-Saunders and Paul A. Wilson, *The Professions* (Oxford: Clarendon, 1993), p. 68.

Sir Joseph took much interest in anyone who was in any way engaged in the pursuit of science, and as I suppose partly from Home's recommendation and partly from knowing that I was occupied with him in making dissections in comparative anatomy, was led to show me much kindness and attention, such as it was very agreeable for so young a man to receive from so distinguished a person. He invited me to the meetings which were held in his library on the Sunday evenings which intervened between the meetings of the Royal Society. These meetings were of a very different kind from those larger assemblies which were held three or four times in the season by the Duke of Sussex, the Marquis of Northampton, and Lord Rosse, and they were much more useful. There was no crowding together of noblemen and philosophers, and would-be philosophers, nor any kind of magnificent display. The visitors consisted of those who were already distinguished by their scientific reputation, of younger men who, like myself, were following those greater persons at a humble distance, of a few individuals of high station who, though not working men themselves, were regarded by Sir Joseph as patrons of science, of such foreigners of distinction as during the war were to be found in London, and of very few besides. Everything was conducted in the plainest manner. Tea was handed round to the company, and there were no other refreshments.[3]

Clearly this was a scene in which Stephen Maturin would have felt comfortably at home.

Many real characteristics of Sir Joseph Banks have found their way into the fictional persona of Sir Joseph Blaine. In one of his innumerable bits of whimsy, O'Brian pursues this parallel in Blaine's request to Lord Melville (with respect to the mission of the *Lively*) 'that in compliment to Dr Maturin . . . the temporary commission should be modelled as closely as possible upon that granted to Sir J. Banks of the Royal Society'.[4]

Aubrey learns of Maturin's medical background after their first dinner together. Keen to find a replacement surgeon for the *Sophie* Aubrey declares:

'Had I known you was a surgeon, sir, I do not think I could have resisted the temptation of pressing you.'

'Surgeons are excellent fellows,' said Stephen Maturin with a touch of acerbity. 'And where should we be without them, God forbid . . . But I have not the honour of counting myself among them, sir. I am a physician.'

3. Patrick O'Brian, *Joseph Banks: A Life* (London: Collins Harvill, 1987), pp. 275–283 (pp. 282–283).
4. Patrick O'Brian, *Post Captain* (London: Collins, 1972), p. 391.

'I beg your pardon, oh dear me, what a sad blunder. But even so, Doctor, even so, I think I should have had you run aboard and kept under hutches till we were at sea. My poor Sophie has no surgeon and there is no likelihood of finding her one. Come, sir, cannot I prevail upon you to go to sea?'

Aubrey presses his appeal, citing the opportunity for a 'philosopher' on a man-of-war to see birds, fishes, natural phenomena, meteors, and of course, prize money. At first Maturin demurs:

'But I am in no way qualified to be a naval surgeon. To be sure, I have done a great deal of anatomical dissection, and I am not unacquainted with most of the usual chirurgical operations; but I know nothing of naval hygiene, nothing of the particular maladies of seamen . . .'

'Bless you,' cried Jack, 'never strain at gnats of that kind. Think of what we are usually sent – surgeon's mates, wretched half-grown stunted apprentices that have knocked about an apothecary's shop just long enough for the Navy Office to give them a warrant. They know nothing of surgery, let alone physic; they learn on the poor seamen as they go along, and they hope for an experienced loblolly boy or a beast-leech or a cunning-man or maybe a butcher among the hands – the press brings in all sorts. And when they have picked up a smattering of their trade, off they go into frigates and ships of the line. No, no. We should be delighted to have you – more than delighted. Do, pray, consider of it, if only for a while. I need not say,' he added, with a particularly earnest look, 'how much pleasure it would give me, was we to be shipmates.'

Later, Aubrey gloats to the *Sophie*'s master, Mr Marshall, of their luck in attracting a physician to be the ship's surgeon.

'Think what a famous thing that would be for the ship's company!'

'Indeed it would, sir. They were right upset when Mr Jackson went off to the *Pallas*, and to replace him with a physician would be a great stroke. There's one aboard the flagship and one at Gibraltar, but not another in the whole fleet, not that I know of. They charge a guinea a visit, by land; or so I have heard tell.'

'Even more, Mr Marshall, even more.'[5]

Lucky Jack Aubrey's idol, Admiral Lord Horatio Nelson, was far ahead of his time and his military contemporaries in recognising the need for good medical care in the fleet. This may have been partly due to his own frail health and physical vulnerability: Nelson seems to have contracted most of the diseases known to practitioners of his day and he certainly

5. Patrick O'Brian, *Master and Commander* (London: Collins, 1970), pp. 32–38.

underwent more operations than any other flag officer in the British navy. After being wounded in the eye at Corsica he said:

> We have a thousand sick and the rest are no better than phantoms: I am here a reed among oaks: I have all the diseases that there are, but there is not enough in my frame for them to fasten on.[6]

From 1780 onwards, Nelson corresponded with his medical friend, Dr Benjamin Mosely, and even contributed some material to the 4th edition of Mosely's rather mediocre *Treatise on Tropical Diseases*.[7] Despite their friendship though, Nelson did not always follow Mosely's medical advice himself: Mosely opposed both vaccination and bark whereas Nelson had his own daughter vaccinated and encouraged the use of bark throughout the fleet.

Maturin admits to having had extensive experience with anatomical dissection – including, presumably, dealings with grave-robbers – which proves to have taken him far beyond the expertise of most physicians, or even surgeons, of his day. Before the Anatomy Act was passed by Parliament in 1832, body-snatching had for some 150 years provided medical students with a significant means of obtaining cadavers. Dissection was widely considered a fate worse than death because it deprived the corpse of a grave (from which, presumably, it could rise on Judgement Day).

> There were riots at gallows when surgeons attempted to take the bodies of criminals for dissection, and violent disturbances erupted in graveyards and at anatomy schools when cases of grave-robbery came to light. It was not an easy time to be an anatomist.[8]

Furthermore, Maturin is an experienced accoucheur and possesses considerable practical knowledge of 'the usual chirurgical operations'. He has many opportunities during the course of his naval career for the practical exercise of these skills. In HMS *Sophie*'s early encounter with a corsair, the gunner suffers a depressed cranial fracture. Aubrey is sure the man will die, but Maturin cheerily comments:

> 'I think he is safe until the morning. But as soon as the sun is up I must have off the top of his skull with my little saw. You will see the gunner's brain, my dear sir,' he added with a smile. 'Or at least his dura mater.'[9]

6. Christopher Lloyd and Jack L. S. Coulter, *Medicine and the Navy, 1200–1900*, Vol 3: *1714–1815* (Edinburgh: Livingstone, 1961), p. 139.
7. Benjamin Mosely, *A Treatise on Tropical Diseases, on Military Operations, and on the Climate of the West Indies . . .* 4th edn (London: [n. pub.], 1803).
8. Ruth Richardson, 'Trading assassins and the licensing of anatomy', in *British Medicine in an Age of Reform*, ed. by Roger French and Andrew Wear (London: Routledge, 1991), pp. 74–91.
9. Patrick O'Brian, *Master and Commander*, p. 117.

When the Admiral, Lord Keith, hears of the doctor's successful cran-
iotomy of the gunner, he writes out Maturin's order (a sort of commission
formally appointing him to the fleet) in his own hand – something Aubrey
'never heard of in the service before'. Maturin is intensely moved by the
cheers that go up when the Sophies hear that his post has been made official. Nevertheless, as he reads the document, the physician grumbles:

> 'There is only one thing I do not care for, however,' he said as the order
> was passed reverently round the table, 'and that is this foolish insistence
> upon the word *surgeon*. "Do hereby appoint you *surgeon* . . . take upon you
> the employment of *surgeon* . . . together with such allowance for wages
> and victuals for yourself as is usual for the *surgeon* of the said sloop." It is a
> false description; and a false description is anathema to the philosophic
> mind.'[10]

Surgeons were at that time perceived less as scientists and more as crafts-
men.

Like physicians through the ages Maturin knew the importance of medical mystique. Some of this came naturally through his own achievements:
rousting out a man's brains and setting them right. Other elements of the
mystique came with the deference properly due to a physician's intellec-
tual status and arcane knowledge. The idea that a mastery of Latin and
Greek was a prerequisite to the study of medicine persisted throughout
the nineteenth century. As Maturin puts it when persuading Mr Herapath
to let his polylingual son become a medical student:

> 'His Chinese may be a thousand years old, but you are to consider, that
> Greek and Latin are older still. They are required in a physician, because
> the wisdom of ages has found that they give a nimbleness of mind. They
> supple the mind, sir, they render it pliant and receptive.'[11]

In *The Wine-Dark Sea* a sailor falls on the pointed end of a cut bamboo,
piercing his chest and producing 'the strangest effect on one lung' (a
pneumothorax). Dr Maturin discusses the case at length in Latin with his
assistant, the Rev Mr Nathaniel Martin.

> [This was] to the great satisfaction of the sick-berth, where heads turned
> gravely from one speaker to the other, nodding from time to time, while
> the patient himself looked modestly down and Padeen Colman, Dr
> Maturin's almost monoglot Irish servant and loblolly-boy, wore his Mass-
> going reverential face.[12]

Of course, doctors speaking in Latin did not *always* engender confidence.

10. Ibid., pp. 127–128.
11. Patrick O'Brian, *The Fortune of War* (London: Collins, 1979), p. 170.
12. Patrick O'Brian, *The Wine-Dark Sea* (London: HarperCollins, 1993), p. 10.

As Dr Maturin and a helping surgeon, Mr Cotton, prepare to repair poor Colley's shattered skull, they converse briefly in that ancient tongue.

> 'Whenever they start talking foreign,' observed John Harris, castleman, starboard watch, 'you know they are at a stand, and that all is, as you might say, in a manner of speaking, up.'
>
> 'You ain't seen nothing, John Harris,' said Davis, the old Sophie. 'Our doctor is only tipping the civil to the one-legged cove: just you wait until he starts dashing away with his boring-iron.'[13]

Sure enough the operation is successful: Colley recovers with a handsome silver plate in his cranium, and Maturin's reputation for preternatural skill goes up another notch amongst the sailors.

Nor does Dr Maturin hesitate to open up a skull when disease requires it. The ordinary naval surgeon would never have considered such a manoeuvre in the absence of trauma; but then the ordinary surgeon would not have made the same diagnosis as Maturin in the case of Arthur Grimble in *The Thirteen-Gun Salute,* who suffered from a syphilitic gumma of the brain (a tumorous lesion), and whose skull was opened 'to relieve the pressure on his brain'.

Maturin enjoyed a unique relationship with his maritime companions, not only because he was the ship's surgeon, but because of the special condition of mutual trust that he engendered.

> [He] accepted what seamen told him about ships with the same simplicity as that with which they accepted what he told them about their bodies. 'Take this bolus,' he would say. 'It will rectify the humours amazingly,' and they, holding their noses (for he often used asafoetida) would force the rounded mass down, gasp, and feel better at once.[14]

The sailors expected – and Maturin was resigned to it – that for a medication to be effective it should be significantly unpalatable.

After Aubrey, this time commanding the infamous *Leopard,* hauls the hapless Herapath out of the sea, old hands are confident that the near-drowned swain will survive.

> 'Of course he'll live,' said his messmates. 'Ain't the Doctor pumped him dry, and blown out his gaff with physic?' For it was just as much part of the natural order of things that Dr Maturin should preserve those who came under his hands: he was a physician, not one of your common surgeons – had cured Prince Billy of the marthambles, the larynx, the strong fives – had wormed Admiral Keith and had clapped a stopper

13. Patrick O'Brian, *The Mauritius Command* (London: Collins, 1977), p. 227.
14. Patrick O'Brian, *The Wine-Dark Sea,* p. 7.

over his gout – would not look at you under a guinea, five guineas, ten guineas a head, by land.[15]

This nearly magical confidence in Dr Maturin's medical prowess was also shared by the tough but superstitious Captain Aubrey. On a long voyage in *H.M.S. Surprise*, the *Surprise* is manned in part by sailors (taken from the *Racoon*) who had not been ashore for four years. Aubrey suspects that some of these men – apathetic, puffy-faced, dull-eyed, poorly co-ordinated, glum, lifeless – have scurvy. Maturin confirms it, noting 'weakness, diffused muscular pain, petechia, tender gums, ill breath'. But Aubrey is not nearly as worried as he should be. He is sure that Maturin will be able to 'set them up directly'. Maturin demurs: his lime juice is dubious; the ship lacks green vegetables. But Aubrey is undismayed:

> 'It is a great comfort to me to have you aboard: it is like sailing with a piece of the True Cross.'
> 'Stuff, stuff,' said Stephen peevishly. 'I do wish you would get that weak notion out of your mind. Medicine can do very little; surgery less. I can purge you, bleed you, worm you at a pinch, set your leg or take it off, and that is very nearly all. What could Hippocrates, Galen, Rhazes, what can Blane, what can Trotter do for a carcinoma, a lupus, a sarcoma?' He had often tried to eradicate Jack's simple faith; but Jack had seen him trepan the gunner of the *Sophie*, saw a hole in his skull and expose the brain; and Stephen, looking at Jack's knowing smile, his air of civil reserve, knew that he had not succeeded this time, either. The Sophies, to a man, had *known* that if he chose Dr Maturin could save anyone, so long as the tide had not turned; and Jack was so thoroughly a seaman that he shared nearly all their beliefs . . .[16]

Maturin also shows himself on occasion to be a practical psychiatrist, long before the speciality was even given a name. We see it first in *Master and Commander* in the case of Cheslin, who is stigmatised not only with a harelip but also because the crew have learned that he was a sin-eater. The man is 'dying of inanition'; deeply depressed by his total rejection by his shipmates. Maturin saves him by making him a helper in the ship's infirmary, thereby giving him some sense of self-worth, leading to gradual acceptance by the crew and the chance finally to prove himself heroically in the boarding and capture of the *Cacafuego*.

These skills are further exercised in unravelling the mystery of Clarissa Oakes, and in so doing Maturin comprehends the relationship between sexual abuse in childhood and aberrant behaviour later on.

15. Patrick O'Brian, *Desolation Island* (London: Collins, 1978), p. 123.
16. Patrick O'Brian, *H.M.S. Surprise* (London: Collins, 1973), pp. 100–101.

... for her the sexual act is trivial, of no consequence ... For her, because of the particularity of her bringing-up, kiss and coition are much the same in insignificance; furthermore, she takes not the slightest pleasure in either.[17]

Dr Maturin's perceptiveness about the mental and behavioural side of medicine is remarkably broad for that period, ranging from madness in syphilitic sailors to what might now be called executive stress, or 'burnout'. He discusses one such case with Dr Harrington, Physician of the Fleet:

'Indeed, the effect of the mind on the body is extraordinarily great,' observed Stephen. 'I have noticed it again and again; and we have innumerable authorities, from Hippocrates to Dr Cheyne. I wish we could prescribe happiness.'[18]

Later as Stephen examines Harrington's patient, a chronically overworked Admiral, he finds no diseased organ, 'but rather a general malfunction of the entire being, harassed beyond its power of endurance.' When he tells the Admiral that the cure for his disease would be a naval action against the long-blockaded French fleet, the Admiral cries, 'You are in the right of it, Doctor ... I am sure you are in the right of it.'

Maturin is more introspective than most men, and far more given to speculation about the natural world than the average physician then or now. He is both an astute observer of the human condition and a shrewd clinician when dealing with the mental and emotional needs of his patients. Of course, these are mostly seafaring men, and Maturin finds them to be so totally adapted to the requirements of life aboard ship, and the necessity to live wholly in the present, that they are incapable of adjusting to normal life ashore. He offers a Minorcan colleague, Dr Ramis, the following conjecture:

'Let us take the whole range of disorders that have their origin in the mind, the disordered or the merely idle mind – false pregnancies, many hysterias, palpitations, dyspepsias, eczematous affections, some forms of impotence and many more that will occur to you at once. Now as far as my limited experience goes, these we do not find aboard ship ... Now let us turn our honest tar ashore, where he is compelled to live not in the present but in the future, with reference to futurity – all joys, benefits, prosperities to be hoped for, looked forward to, the subject of anxious thought directed towards next month, next year, nay, the next generation; no slops provided by the purser, no food perpetually served out at standard intervals. And what do we find?'

'Pox, drunkenness, a bestial dissolution of all moral principle, gross

17. Patrick O'Brian, *Clarissa Oakes* (London: HarperCollins, 1992), p. 208.
18. Patrick O'Brian, *Post Captain*, pp. 84–85.

over-eating: the liver ruined in ten days' time.'

'Certainly, certainly: but more than that, we find, not indeed false pregnancies, but everything short of them. Anxiety, hypochondria, displacency, melancholia, costive, delicate stomachs – the ills of the city merchant increased tenfold. I have a particularly interesting subject who was in the most robust health at sea – Hygeia's darling – in spite of every kind of excess and of the most untoward circumstances: a short while on land, with household cares, matrimonial fancies – always in the future, observe – and we have a loss of eleven pounds' weight; a retention of the urine; black, compact, meagre stools; an obstinate eczema.'

Dr Ramis shrewdly observes that Stephen himself (who at the time is suffering from unrequited love, jealousy, and powerful inner conflicts over his duties as a spy) demonstrates some significant signs of stress. He responds to his colleague's discourse on sailors with some personal observations:

'You speak of loss of weight. But I find that you yourself are thin. Nay, cadaverous, if I may speak as one physician to another. You have a very ill breath; your hair, already meagre two years ago, is now extremely sparse; you belch frequently; your eyes are hollow and dim. This is not merely your ill-considered use of tobacco – a noxious substance that should be prohibited by government – and of laudanum. I should very much like to see your excrement.'

'You shall, my dear sir, you shall.'[19]

Maturin tolerates certain types of purely psychological distress rather poorly and he has a distressing tendency to become reliant on drugs such as laudanum (the alcoholic tincture of opium) and cocaine. (Maturin chews the leaf which is admittedly far less dangerous than modern-day use of the purified alkaloid.) He is capable nonetheless of great courage when he encounters life-threatening situations, physical torture, or personal injury. He ministers to his own damaged body with a casual lack of concern. Needless to say others are amazed at Maturin's insouciance in the face of pain: after escaping from Peru through high mountain passes in the Andes, he remarks in a rather offhand way that he was frostbitten.

'Was it very painful, Doctor?' asked Pullings, looking grave.

'Not at all, at all, until the feeling began to return. And even then the whole lesion was less severe than I had expected. At one time I thought to have lost my leg below the knee, but in the event it was no more than a couple of unimportant toes. For you are to consider,' he observed, addressing his words to Reade, 'that your foot bases its impulses and

19. Patrick O'Brian, *Post Captain*, pp. 84–85.

equilibrium on the great toe and the least. The loss of either is a sad state of affairs entirely, but with the two one does very well. The ostrich has but two the whole length of her life, and yet she outruns the wind.'

'Certainly, sir,' said Reade, bowing.

'Yet though the leg was spared, I could not well travel; above all after I had removed the peccant members.'

'How did you do that, sir?' asked Reade, unwilling to hear though eager to be told.

'Why, with a chisel, as soon as we came down to the village. They could not be left to mortify, with gangrene spreading, the grief and the sorrow.'[20]

The old Sophies (now Surprises) are not even astonished when Stephen, wounded while killing Canning in a duel over Diana, designs a special instrument to remove the pistol ball that had lodged in his chest, and then performs the extraction – cold-sober – on himself.

'Christ, Bonden,' said Jack, 'he opened himself slowly, with his own hands, right to the heart. I saw it beating there.'

'Ah, sir, there's surgery for you,' said Bonden, passing the glass. 'It would not surprise any old Sophie, however; such a learned article. You remember the gunner, sir? Never let it put you off your dinner. He will be as right as a trivet, never you fret, sir.'[21]

Maturin could be deadly in duels and combat situations. Nowhere is his potential ruthlessness more poignantly contrasted with both his capacity for detached objectivity and his aesthetic sensibility than in the amazing denouement of his long-running conflict with the traitors Ledward and Wray. When Maturin and van Buren, making certain to leave 'no reconizable remains', finally dissect the corpses of Ledward and Wray – thereby providing van Buren with an 'English spleen at last! . . . the most famous of them all!' – it becomes clear that the two cadavers are very likely of Maturin's own making. This in no way distracts him, however, from a dissection that is an anatomist's delight.

They worked steadily, with a cool, objective concentration: each had a clear understanding of the matter in hand – the relevant organs, those that might be useful for later comparison and those that might be discarded – and words were rarely necessary. Stephen had been present at many such dissections; he had carried out some hundreds himself, comparative anatomy being one of his chief concerns, but never had he seen such skill, such delicacy in removing the finer processes, such dexterity,

20. Patrick O'Brian, *The Wine-Dark Sea*, pp. 224–225.
21. Patrick O'Brian, *H.M.S. Surprise*, p. 297.

boldness and economy of effort in removing superfluous material, such speed; and with this example he worked faster and more neatly than he had ever done before.[22]

Dr Maturin was, however, well aware of the limitations of scientific medicine in his own time. Apart from the bark and steel, lemon juice and linctus (a syrup or paste), opium and alcohol, and a few helpful unguents and herbal draughts, the physician of two hundred years ago had little to call upon except his professional commitment and common sense.

Long before the introduction of chemical anaesthesia in the 1840s, heroic measures were required in Maturin's surgical practice to immobilise the patient under the knife and to minimise his suffering. Alcohol was commonly used, opium preparations were employed on occasion, but the greatest reliance was placed on strong men and ropes to keep the patient from squirming, together with something stout to bite on – 'biting the bullet'. Experienced clinicians have always known however that fear is a large part of pain; modern research has shown that simple distraction can raise the pain threshold by forty per cent. Dr Maturin obviously understood this when he employed the maximum of both distraction and sensory competition when facing an exceptionally unpleasant tooth extraction – the only kind of operation he hated. 'He was not very good at drawing teeth and he liked his patient to be deafened, amazed, stupefied by a thundering in his ears.' Lacking a drum, the good doctor uses what materials are available and 'the tooth came out – came out at bloody last, piece by piece – to the howling of conchs, the fire of two muskets, and the metallic thunder of several copper pots'.[23]

Although appreciative of the dangers of addiction, Maturin does not hesitate to make use of opium when the need arises. When the powerful but inarticulate Padeen saves several shipmates by holding a hot gun, his severely burned hand causes him to weep as he is brought to Maturin.

> The Doctor dealt with the pain, the very severe pain, by an heroic dose of laudanum, the alcoholic tincture of opium, one of his most valued medicines. 'Here,' he said in Latin to his mate, holding up a bottle of the amber liquid, 'you have the nearest approach to a panacea that has ever been found out. I occasionally use it myself, and find it answers admirably in cases of insomnia, morbid anxiety, the pain of wounds, tooth-ache, and head-ache, even hemicrania.' He might well have added heart-ache too, but he went on, 'I have, as you perceive, matched

22. Patrick O'Brian, *The Thirteen-Gun Salute* (London: Collins, 1989), pp. 252–254 (p. 253).
23. Patrick O'Brian, *Treason's Harbour* (London: Collins, 1983), p. 126.

the dose to the weight of the sufferer and the intensity of the suffering. Presently, with the blessing, you will see Padeen's face return to its usual benevolent mansuetude; and a few minutes later you will see him glide insensibly to the verge of an opiate coma. It is the most valuable member of the whole pharmacopoeia.'

'I am sure it is,' said Martin. 'Yet are there not objections to opium-eating? Is not it likely to become habitual?'

'The objections come only from a few unhappy beings, Jansenists for the most part, who also condemn wine, agreeable food, music, and the company of women: they even call out against coffee, for all love! Their objections are valid solely in the case of a few poor souls with feeble will-power, who would just as easily become the victims of intoxicating liquors, and who are practically moral imbeciles, often addicted to other forms of depravity; otherwise it is no more injurious than smoking tobacco.'[24]

Another common practice that Maturin frequently employed was to bleed his patients. Maturin's contemporary, the great American physician, Dr Benjamin Rush, was a strong proponent of venisection in the treatment of many diseases. For all fevers he advocated 'a low diet, heavy purging with calomel and jalap, 10 grains of each, and bleeding to the point of faintness'.[25] Rush and Maturin had many other beliefs in common, such as opposition to slavery and capital punishment.

Not much was curative at that time for the physician or surgeon to apply, beyond the obvious manual skills and a handful of accidentally discovered remedies – which were often misused. The famous 'bark' (the quinine – containing Peruvian or Jesuits Bark from the cinchona tree) was, and still is, a valuable treatment for certain strains of malaria. However, because of its dramatic effect on the tertian malarial fever, it was widely used on fevers of every kind. In fact, long after its specificity was discovered and proved, quinine was incorrectly touted as an antipyretic. Even up to the present day certain well-known bromo-quinine tablets for the common cold contain 'the bromo for the aches and pains, the quinine for the fever'.

If we find the shops and markets of today still peddling useless remedies over the counter for mankind's minor miseries, consider how much more prominent were folk remedies and proprietary nostrums in Maturin's day. This situation is amusingly illustrated in Killick's treatment of Captain Aubrey's wounded eye after the Surprise's battle with the piratical Alastor.

24. Patrick O'Brian, The Letter of Marque (London: Collins, 1988), pp. 55–56.
25. Ralph H. Major, A History of Medicine, 2 vols (Springfield, IL: Thomas, 1954), p. 727.

Unwillingly Killick admitted that they needed no more than the oint-ment; but when he unrolled the bandage covering the captain's eye he cried, 'Now we shall have to have the drops as well as the salve – a horrid sight: like a poached egg, only bloody – and – I tell you what, sir, I shall put a little Gregory into the drops.'

'How do you mean, *Gregory*?'

'Why, everybody knows Gregory's Patent Liquid, sir: it rectifies the humours. And don't these humours want rectifying? Oh, no, not at all. I have never seen anything so ugly. God love us!'

'Did the Doctor mention Gregory's Patent Liquid?'

'Which I put some on Barret Bonden's wound, a horrible great gash: like a butcher's shop. And look at it now. As clean as a whistle. Come on, sir. Never mind the smart; it is all for your own good.'

'A very little, then,' said Jack, who had in fact known of Gregory's liquid together with Harris's Guaranteed Unguent, Carey's Warranted Arrowroot, brimstone and treacle on Friday and other staples of domes-tic medicine, all as much a part of daily life on land as hard-tack and mustering by divisions on Sunday at sea.[26]

When other treatments were not appropriate Maturin made amputa-tion his last resort. Amputations by naval surgeons were commonplace enough, but they were often unnecessary from the strictly medical point of view. Prevention of exsanguination, gangrene, or sepsis (blood-poison-ing) were frequent rationales, but the superior surgeon, then as now, tried to avoid operating whenever he could. After their capture by the Americans in *The Fortune of War* Maturin saves Aubrey's arm by exercising such care. The locale for surgery was also a factor because infection was so frequent and very likely to be transmitted from patient to patient in a hos-pital setting, though the exact mechanisms were not yet understood. In Vienna, Ignaz Philipp Semmelweis published his famous treatise on puer-peral fever in 1860; he went to his grave five years later still unsuccessful in persuading his colleagues to wash their hands after examining an infected patient and before handling the next one. It remained for the more respectable Englishman, Joseph Lister, to publish his discovery of antisep-sis in 1867 and even then many surgeons resisted the idea until clinical results won general acceptance. Hospitals were extremely dangerous places meanwhile, and Maturin tried to avoid them. The American naval surgeon, Mr Butcher, agrees with him.

Besides, although a hospital is far more convenient for operating, surviv-ing is quite another matter: for my part I had rather be at sea. I have known a whole [hospital] ward of amputations die in a week, whereas

26. Patrick O'Brian, *The Wine-Dark Sea*, p. 153.

several of the men who had to be kept aboard for want of room lived on. Some are living yet.[27]

On long, quiet passages the 'medical man's daily fare' comprised mainly scurvy, 'obstinate gleets' (urethral discharges caused by gonorrhea) and 'poxes' (skin eruptions caused by syphilis).

> Stephen could oblige the seamen to avoid scurvy by drinking lemon-juice in their grog, [but] no power on earth could prevent them from hurrying to bawdy-houses as soon as they were ashore.[28]

The treatment for some of these diseases was of course only symptomatic; the best someone with venereal disease in those days could hope for was such nostrums as 'draughts of calomel and guaiacum', which were in themselves harmless, might ease the symptoms a bit and give nature a chance to repair the damage. More strenuous remedies, such as 'the Viennese treatment', posed serious risks of their own, as Dr Maturin's helper, Mr Martin, discovered to his sorrow when he secretly undertook to treat himself for an imaginary case of syphilis with a terrible overdose of bichloride of mercury (corrosive sublimate).

One of Maturin's earliest experiences of disease at sea occurs when the *Sophie* encounters a felucca in distress, with only dead bodies in view. Maturin quickly identifies the signs of bubonic plague amongst the victims and is shocked and infuriated when Aubrey sheers off, thereby preventing him from boarding the unfortunate vessel to treat possible survivors. However, Maturin later turns this experience to advantage when the *Sophie* encounters the deadly *Cacafuego* and is lying at grave peril under her guns. It is the quick-witted doctor who, having learned the naval horror of this dread disease, pleads with the Spaniards for help with fictional plague-stricken shipmates and thus neatly sends them hastily away without a shot being fired.

Beyond the more commonplace complaints of seafaring men was the ever-present danger of plague or typhus. In *Desolation Island* the 'gaol-fever' that kills so many aboard the *Leopard* in a prolonged epidemic that strains Dr Maturin's personal and medical resources to the limit, is undoubtedly typhus. The vessel is alive with rats – fleas transmit the disease to humans – and the symptoms are all there.

> All three patients had broken out in a mulberry-coloured rash, extraordinarily widespread and most ominously dark: there was no possible doubt – this was gaol-fever, and gaol-fever of the most virulent kind. He was certain the moment he saw it, but for conscience' sake he checked the other signs – petechiae, a palpable spleen, brown dry tongue, sordes, raging heat: not one was absent.

27. Patrick O'Brian, *The Reverse of the Medal* (London: Collins, 1986), pp. 46–47.
28. Patrick O'Brian, *The Wine-Dark Sea*, p. 75.

Fumigating the ship with brimstone helps (this is a purely empirical procedure as the role of rats and fleas was not yet understood) but it is too late to halt the epidemic.

> . . . when the disease struck the lower-deck it killed men faster than the plague. They gave up hope, and sometimes it seemed to Stephen that they would almost as soon not take his draughts, but would rather have it over as soon as might be: and soon it was, in many cases – headache, languor, a moderate rise in temperature, and despair at once, even before the rash and the appalling fever, far worse in the stifling heat, and so onwards to what he often believed an unnecessary death.[29]

In Maturin's world, typhus was the most common fever in prisons, prison-ships, military camps, slums, and other miserable settings where rats and humans lived together under desperate conditions. The disease was called by many names, more relating to the circumstances or locale rather than its clinical features which were also similar. Even after scurvy and smallpox were much reduced, typhus remained the scourge of the channel fleet well into the nineteenth century.[30]

It was not only in the Navy that typhus was a scourge. Referring to Sir John Pringle's treatise of 1752, Chaplin tells of:

> an appalling tale of serious disease constantly following in the footsteps of the Army, destroying its efficiency, and producing havoc in its ranks, compared with which losses in battle were trivial . . . Apparently hospital fever was present in every hospital where soldiers were crowded together . . . while in the open camp this disease scarcely ever attacked them.[31]

The situation did not change significantly in the next sixty years. During the British army's ill-fated Walcherin Expedition of 1809, disease (mainly typhus) had 'swept off, or rendered incapable of military service, a fine army of 40,000 men' within a matter of a few weeks.

In Maturin's time, smallpox was another great destroyer of life. He and his colleagues were aware that those who survived the disease were immune, and that variolation (inoculation with pus from a smallpox victim) could produce a mild form of the disease with resulting immunity. During the 1790s Dr Edward Jenner had been advocating the use of a cowpox (vaccinia) inoculation as a preventative of smallpox, but his results were received with scepticism. The Royal Society rejected his report, which he then defiantly published himself in 1798. Even while London doctors were rejecting Jenner's new 'vaccination', it was adopted rapidly in the

29. Patrick O'Brian, *Desolation Island*, pp. 120–126, & 148 (pp. 120 & 124).
30. Lloyd, *Medicine and the Navy*, p. 340.
31. Arnold Chaplin, *Medicine in England During the Reign of George III* (London: the author, 1919), pp. 86–91 (pp. 86, 87 & 91).

United States and Europe. President Thomas Jefferson had several of his family vaccinated; Napoleon ordered all his soldiers vaccinated; the Empress of Russia urged all her subjects to be vaccinated; leading physicians in Germany, Austria and Italy followed suit. Finally in 1802 the British Parliament voted Jenner an award of £10,000 and five years later he was awarded a further £20,000. The long road towards eradication of smallpox had begun.

Elsewhere in the world, however, smallpox was still a deadly plague. It killed innumerable Indians in North and South America, and exterminated many primitive people in the Pacific as Europeans came among them. In *The Nutmeg of Consolation* Dr Maturin and his shipmates salvage two little girls from a South Sea island – the only survivors of smallpox. Captain Aubrey himself is deeply moved by this tragedy as he surveys the ruined native village:

> Again Jack followed them as they went along, talking of the nature of the disease and of how badly it affected nations and communities that had never known it in the past – how mortal it was to Eskimos, for example, and how this particular infection must have been brought by a whaler, its visit proved by the axes. He felt a certain indignation against them, a resentment for his own unshared horror . . . [32]

Although he was an avowed Catholic, Maturin's philosophy sometimes caused him to deviate from the religious teachings of his day. In fact, the Rev Mr Martin, a mere Protestant, is shocked when the doctor declines to revive the miserable, murderous, cuckolded Horner, who has hanged himself and been cut down not quite dead. Maturin poses the question.

> Have you ever brought a determined suicide back to life? Have you seen the despair on his face when he realizes that he has failed – that it is all to do again? It seems to me a strange thing to decide for another. Surely living or dying is a matter between a man and his Maker or Unmaker? [33]

When it comes to abortion, however, the doctor's position is foursquare with the Church, and for that matter with every other respectable physician. While the prohibition against inducing an abortion has been removed from many modern versions of the Hippocratic oath, it was still firmly in place during the nineteenth century. To perform an abortion in most Western countries was a serious crime. When Maturin discovers that his assistant, Higgins, has attempted – and botched – an abortion for Mrs Horner, he rages at him, 'Mr Higgins, Mr Higgins, you will hang for this, if

32. Patrick O'Brian, *The Nutmeg of Consolation* (London: Collins, 1991), p. 208.
33. Patrick O'Brian, *The Far Side of the World* (London: Collins, 1984), p. 226.

I do not save her. You are a rash wicked bungling ignorant murderous fool.' [34]

Maturin's adventures reveal only passing references to his early history (he was, for instance, studying medicine in Paris when the French Revolution of 1789 began) and his developing professional status. As the years go by, we learn in tantalisingly subtle fragments that Dr Maturin's accomplishments in both 'philosophy' and medicine are making him rather famous. Although his presentations at scientific meetings are atrocious, his articles and books earn admiration and respect from those qualified to appreciate them. As a clinician, his reputation for excellence also spreads far beyond the navy: while waiting in Paris to give a lecture on the extinct birds of the Mascarenes – 'he was to address the Institute, and some of the keenest, most distinguished minds in Europe would be there' – he mentally reviews his other recent activities in that great city. 'He had performed three dissections of the calcified palmar aponeurosis with Dupuytren; Corvisart had told him a great deal about his new method of auscultation . . .'[35] We hear no more about these events but only the most highly esteemed foreign colleague could have strolled into Paris and been welcomed by either of these famous doctors. Baron Guillaume Dupuytren was a celebrated French surgeon whose name is attached, not only to Dupuytren's contracture of the hand (which every medical student to this day must learn) but to Dupuytren's amputation, enterotome, fracture, hydrocele, sign and splint. Baron Jean Nicolas Corvisart des Marest, was 'the premiere and outstanding physician of this period'.[36] He defined two important cardiovascular diseases that still bear his name.

It does not apparently bother Maturin that Corvisart was Napoleon's personal physician. What counted was the man's personal qualities. 'Corvisart's fame as a teacher drew brilliant pupils who were attracted by his skill as a diagnostician, by his clarity as a lecturer, and by his frankness, fairness, independence, and generosity as a man.'[37] It was not only Maturin who learned about auscultation of the chest from Corvisart; René Laennec (who studied with both Dupuytren and Corvisart, and was the latter's protégé) invented the modern stethoscope in 1816.

In creating Stephen Maturin, Patrick O'Brian has completely captured the sense of being a doctor in the time of the Napoleonic wars and brought to vivid, bright-coloured life an exciting chapter in the history of medicine. He uses his wide-ranging and authoritative knowledge to stunning effect in writing so convincingly of the era which he has made his own. Though the essence of his books is timeless, the early nineteenth century comes completely alive in the incomparable novels featuring Jack Aubrey and Dr Stephen Maturin.

34. Ibid., p. 179.
35. Patrick O'Brian, *The Surgeon's Mate* (London: Collins, 1980), p. 124.
36. Major, *A History of Medicine*, p. 655.
37. Ibid., p. 659.

JACK AND STEPHEN,
THEIR TRAVELS

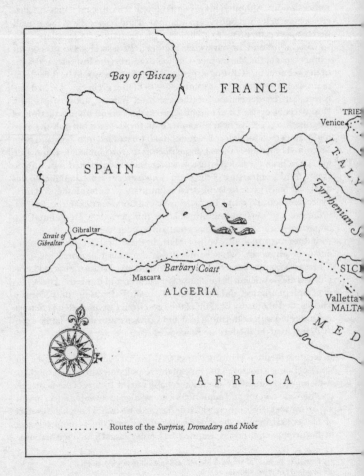

.... Routes of the *Surprise, Dromedary and Niobe*

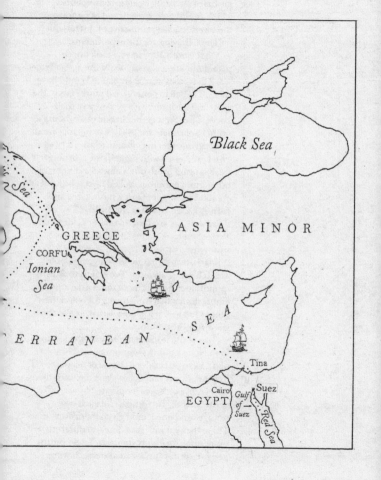

Black Sea

ASIA MINOR

GREECE

CORFU

Ionian
Sea

Sea

MEDITERRANEAN SEA

ERRANEAN SEA

Tina

Cairo

EGYPT

Gulf
of
Suez

Suez

Red Sea

OF THE PREVENTION OF THE SCURVY

I shall conclude the precepts relating to the preservation of seamen with showing the best means of obviating many inconveniences which attend long voyages and of removing the several causes productive of this mischief.

The following are the experiments.

On the 20th May, 1747, I took twelve patients in the scurvy on board the *Salisbury* at sea. Their cases were as similar as I could have them. They all in general had putrid gums, the spots and lassitude, with weakness of their knees. They lay together in one place, being a proper apartment for the sick in the fore-hold; and had one diet in common to all, *viz.*, water gruel sweetened with sugar in the morning; fresh mutton broth often times for dinner; at other times puddings, boiled biscuit with sugar etc.; and for supper barley, raisins, rice and currants, sago and wine, or the like. Two of these were ordered each a quart of cider a day. Two others took twenty five gutts of elixir vitriol three times a day upon an empty stomach, using a gargle strongly acidulated with it for their mouths. Two others took two spoonfuls of vinegar three times a day upon an empty stomach, having their gruels and their other food well acidulated with it, as also the gargle for the mouth.

Two of the worst patients, with the tendons in the ham rigid (a symptom none of the rest had), were put under a course of sea water. Of this they drank half a pint every day and sometimes more or less as it operated by way of gentle physic. Two others had each two oranges and one lemon given them every day. These they eat with greediness at different times upon an empty stomach. They continued but six days under this course, having consumed the quantity that could be spared. The two remaining patients took the bigness of a nutmeg three times a day of an electuary recommended by an hospital surgeon made of garlic, mustard seed, rad. raphan., balsam of Peru and gum myrrh, using for common drink barley water well acidulated with tamarinds, by a decoction of which, with the addition of *cremor tartar*, they were gently purged three or four times during the course.

The consequence was that the most sudden and visible good effects were perceived from the use of the oranges and lemons; one of those who had taken them being at the end of six days fit for duty. The spots were not indeed at that time quite off his body, nor his gums sound; but without any other medicine than a gargarism or elixir of vitriol he became quite healthy before we came into Plymouth, which was on the 16th June. The other was the best recovered of any in his condition, and being now deemed pretty well was appointed nurse to the rest of the sick ...

As I shall have occasion elsewhere to take notice of the effects of other medicines in this disease, I shall here only observe that the result of all my experiments was that oranges and lemons were the most effectual remedies for this distemper at sea. I am apt to think oranges preferable to lemons, though it was principally oranges which so speedily and surprisingly recovered Lord Anson's people at the Island of Tinian, of which that noble, brave and experienced commander was so sensible that before he left the island one man was ordered on shore from each mess to lay in a stock of them for their future security ... Perhaps one history more may suffice to put this out of doubt.

From James Lind's *A Treatise of the Scurvy in Three Parts, 1753*, reproduced by kind permission of Lars Bruzelius.

HAVE YOU READ?
The tenth book in the Aubrey-Maturin series

The Far Side of the World
The dogged transatlantic pursuit of an elusive American quarry intent on destroying British sea interests sees Jack and Stephen beset by obstacles from St Elmo's fire to the shark-infested waters in the South Pacific. With their prize ever tantalisingly on the edge of the horizon, the two friends arrive at last amongst the natural wonders of the Galapagos, where their epic hunt culminates in a mighty battle.

FIND OUT MORE

Peter Weir directed a feature film adaptation of *Master and Commander: The Far Side of the World* (2003) starring Russell Crowe as Jack Aubrey and Paul Bettany as Stephen Maturin (http://www.masterandcommanderthefarsideoftheworld.com). The film combines events from the first, second and tenth books in the Aubrey-Maturin series. The result is a compulsive tale of adventure on the high seas.

Patrick O'Brian

The National Maritime Museum in Greenwich, London (www.nmm.ac.uk), houses the most important holdings in the world on the history of Britain at sea, including maritime art, cartography, manuscripts and official public records, ship models and plans, scientific and navigational instruments, time-keeping and astronomy. The majority of the NMM's small-boat collection is on display at the new National Maritime Museum, Cornwall, at Falmouth (www.nmmc.co.uk).